Kingdom of Ink and Paper

THE BETWIXT AND BETWEEN CHRONICLES: BOOK ONE

Kingdom of Ink and Paper

The Betwixt and Between Chronicles: Book One

Matthew Newman

Sandcrest Publishing

For Ryan, MIG, Cameron, Logan, and Dan
Thank you for giving me my Writer's Eye.

Table of Contents

Prologue

I keep my breathing steady as I walk. It takes everything in me to control my instincts and not sprint. The footsteps are quiet, but something is following me. My ears perk up as I make out subtle squelching against the wet pavement, the raindrops hitting the silhouette of my tracker. As I get closer to my front door, my heartbeat quickens, matching the pace of the thing—human or not—that's trailing me. I shiver despite the humid summer air.

The lights of my apartment building illuminate the area around me, not another soul in sight. And yet, I walk as fast as I can to the door, jamming the lock in place and collapsing to the ground.

I can feel it. Something is coming.

I focus and cast out my thoughts for help. Part of me knows I won't get a response. Something is blocking my communication.

The footsteps finally stop at my door. I hear the light brush of fingertips run across the wood that separates us, and I'm almost filled with a newfound confidence. The hand is human. If it's human, I stand a chance.

A bead of sweat trickles down my face, and I move my hand, silently pressing it off my skin to keep it from hitting the floor. The force outside knocks on the door. I don't make a sound, willing it to leave. I need time to prepare for the fight that is inevitably coming.

I stay still, barely breathing for a few minutes.

The force moves away.

It's time.

I stand and tiptoe to my office, glancing at my notes. I turn, flexing my strong fingers, and in a flash my blade appears in my grip. It feels light and familiar, the same as it has for decades.

I'm ready to fight. I'm tired of running.

Looking at the picture on my desk, my throat tightens. It's almost impossible to swallow back the wretched sadness growing in me. My brother crosses my mind—Tam too. Two more people I won't be able to protect. They don't know what's coming. I hadn't written it down out of fear of it being discovered, and now I'm paying the price.

If I win the upcoming fight, all will be well. If I lose, everything I know will turn to ash. The coming force is strong. Probably stronger than me. My only option is to give up the only thing that has made me who I am for decades, and hope that in doing so, I give the world a chance.

I press my hand to my chest and say goodbye.

To everything.

I let go of my sight, of the world I have made my own, and of everything I know. The sword turns to golden dust, gone for good. My powers rise in my chest and rip from my body becoming a beautiful, fine powder hovering in front of me. A sad smile plays on my lips, and I open the window—the dust dissipates into the Boston sky on its way to someone who will take my place.

Something in my mind slips and Tam is lost to me—I will never speak to him again. I choke back a sob, feeling the full pain of what I've done. I'm normal once again. The exchange is finished, and I watch the last shimmer of dust fade into the atmosphere.

"Tell him I'm sorry," I say, hoping they can hear me. "Be careful. It's coming." It's vague, but it will have to do. I don't have time to explain.

With these words, I entrust the safety of everything I have ever loved to someone I don't even know.

With these words, the stalker is alerted to my presence.

With these words an explosion echoes as my door is blasted to splinters, the sharp wood piercing my skin.

It's here.

I don't even have time to turn …

1
The Body

William Morgan punched his best friend in the face.

"Geez, Will, go ahead and take my eye out while you're at it." Peter massaged his nose with fervor.

"Sorry about that," Will replied, rubbing his eyes as the vision pressed itself onto him in full force, refusing to disappear. "Really weird dream is all." Will stared, mouth open, trying to register what happened. How could a person articulate that they had just seen a man die?

Peter raised an eyebrow, put his headphones back in his ears, and returned to his music. Knowing other students were staring, Will turned his face to the window. He leaned his suddenly burning forehead against the cool glass.

Through specks of dirt and age, Will's face was reflected back at him: a fourteen-year-old soon-to-be high school freshman, medium-length brown hair pushed back into an uneven crew cut, and hazel eyes. At five-foot-eight, Will had always considered himself attractive enough, though the girls who complimented him were restricted to his mom and fifth-grade girlfriend. He was thin, not so much that someone would call him scrawny, though certainly not strong enough that he'd be picked to win a fight.

Will's thoughts were interrupted by the static of the bus intercom. One of the teachers, fresh from college with too much enthusiasm and zest, had an announcement to make.

"Students, we have made it to Cambridge and will be at our first stop in ten minutes. Make sure you gather all your stuff and get ready for some fun!"

Peter groaned and Will sighed. As part of a student-learning initiative, their future high school paid for Will's entire class to go to the Boston area for a set of college tours and some historic sightseeing. Though Will was willing to admit how cool it was, he couldn't help feeling irritated that the end of his summer vacation was going to be spent wandering through universities. And now he had this dream on his mind. It felt so real, like he was standing next to the man who was murdered by some ... What was it? Magic? A person? It was definitely powerful.

The bus stopped and the students were ushered off by the same overly-vivacious teacher. As Will's feet hit the asphalt, a force grabbed him from behind. Still trying to shake off the dream, Will jumped, his heart pumping as if he had just finished a long run.

"Woah, don't hit me again!" Peter exclaimed, a devilish grin playing on his lips.

Will forced a slight smile. Peter could see through his pathetic attempt to cover up how shaken he was.

Peter Roitman was taller than Will by a several inches and wore his short brown hair in an uncombed style. His eyes were a sharp green color, and despite his goofy mannerisms and charismatic nature, it was clear that Peter was always thinking about things more deeply than he let on. His clothing choice was predictable: cargo shorts and a t-shirt with an image of a cartoon character waving comically. It was the same combination he had worn since he was old enough to dress himself.

"So, we're touring Harvard and MIT, even though God knows most of us are too hopeless to ever get in there." Peter gestured broadly at the sprawling campus in front of them. "With that in mind, why don't we spend the day trying to pick up some Ivy League girls?"

"Girls that intelligent are way out of your league," said a voice from behind them.

"Hey Iris," Will said.

Iris McAllister was a few inches shorter than Will; however, what she lacked in height was made up for in feistiness and fashion-focused creativity. Today she was sporting a tank top that accentuated her broad shoulders and toned arms, her curly red hair reflecting the sun like wildfire. She had a blotch of sunscreen on her nose, and maps in one hand. She was certainly prepared for the day ahead.

Iris didn't even *want* to go to the schools they were touring— she was just taking the day in stride for the sake of doing things thoroughly.

She looked at Peter. "Besides, you're way too immature, and don't look anything like a college student. A tall sixth grader, maybe, with that baby face."

"Your doubt only encourages me. Now I won't be able to leave this tour without getting someone's number."

Iris punched Peter's arm, and his eyes gleamed with mischief. Will's vision swam, his discomfort from the dream still lingering.

"You okay, Will?" Iris's stare bore holes into him.

"Yeah," he replied. Hopefully his gruffness would hide the

uncertainty from his voice. "Just had a really weird dream." Will then told them all about it while they followed their chatty teacher at a distance: the man whose face was blurry, the fear he had felt because of the person—or monster?—on the other side of the door, and the man's mysterious words.

"Tell him I'm sorry. Be careful. It's coming," Will muttered, biting his thumb. "Obviously it was just a dream, but it felt so real. More real than any dream I've ever had, that's for sure."

Peter scratched his head. "What's to come seems like some pretty negative stuff. Although!" He grasped Will's shoulder, his toothy grin giving Will conflicting feelings of mirth and frustration. "Maybe you're supposed to solve this guy's murder, and this vision is your only clue. And if you solve it, you'll become a famous detective! No more college tours for William Morgan!" Peter rocked Will, and Will returned his enthusiasm the best he could.

There was no point in worrying about something like this, right?

Several hours later, the class made its way into Boston proper and settled in at a small café where the teachers handed out sandwiches and little bags of chips. Will stared at his turkey club, thoughts drifting back to the dream.

"Will." Peter didn't blink as he gazed at his friend's forehead. "I know Harvard has an acceptance rate of, like, six percent, but you can't let it get you depressed."

Will jolted himself out of his stupor and forced out a laugh. Peter's eyes darkened, and Will shook his head.

"I'm okay, promise. I just think the sandwich isn't sitting well with me. I'm going to go for a walk."

"Do you want company?"

"No, thank you. I just need some air."

Will stood and walked out, giving one of the teachers the excuse that he was going to the coffee shop down the road to get a pick-me-up. She nodded absentmindedly, waving Will off, muttering hurriedly into her cellphone about a shortage of hotel rooms. Once outside, Will was greeted by a perfect Boston afternoon, the smell of summer ripe in the air. The streets awash with sunlight, the shops and stalls beginning to pack up for the day, he found the brisk pace relaxed him. Sweat beaded at his brow as his heart began to pump.

He was brought back to reality when he careened into someone. The impact knocked Will to the ground. He skidded in a way that was guaranteed to leave a bruise.

"Oh… Oh gosh, I'm so sorry," he stuttered in a panic. Will found himself face to face with an unassuming woman. She had sharp eyes that pierced through him like needles. Her wavy raven-black hair matched her dress—so dark it had to be darker than black. A dull silver necklace bounced off of her throat, almost as if it were crawling toward Will. She couldn't have been taller than him, and though she had an athletic build, she looked wiry, like she hadn't eaten properly in weeks. She certainly wasn't strong enough to blow Will to the ground with that level of impact.

"It's fine. Watch where you're going next time." Her voice whipped past him as she rushed on her way.

Will shuddered as a strange cold washed over him, like he had been doused with a bucket of ice water.

"That's not normal," he murmured, staring at her retreating figure.

"Are you okay, bud? That looked like a nasty fall." A man in a suit held his hand toward Will.

With the man's assistance, Will stood and dusted himself off.

"Yeah, I'm fine, thanks. Guess I should watch where I'm going next time."

"Not your fault, kid," the man said. "We all trip on loose cobblestones. You should report that to the police department or something."

Will's gaze narrowed. "I didn't trip. I ran into someone. She's okay though."

"You don't have to be embarrassed. The ground is uneven—people trip all the time." The man gave Will a suspicious look and walked away.

Will was left staring at him, feeling way worse than he had all day. Deciding he must be getting sick, he started his walk back to the class. Maybe he should ask a chaperone if he could check into the hotel early and take a nap.

"Move back! There's nothing to see here."

Will looked around to see a group forming nearby. There was stressed-out policeman calling out to people, though he was having no impact on the gathering crowd. Will snaked his way through the rapidly growing throng of bodies, trying to get a better view of the scene. When he eventually broke through the forest of onlookers, he was greeted by an ambulance, several police cars, and many angry adults talking near the entrance to an apartment building.

"They're coming back out! They must have found a body!"

"I wonder what happened?"

"Move back!" the officer tried again.

Three EMTs pushed a gurney toward the ambulance. There was definitely a body under the white sheet. Will's spine went rigid, his breath catching in his throat. It was his first time seeing a dead person, and even though he couldn't see their face, something about the moment hit Will hard.

Walking alongside the gurney was a man Will vaguely recognized. The man had the familiarity of a B-list celebrity Will had seen on the cover of a tabloid at a supermarket. Will racked his brain. Where had he seen him before?

The man looked to be in his late thirties to early forties, standing at about six feet with jet black hair and a dark, attractive face matched by an intense grimace. He stared at the sheet-covered body with a pained expression, his hand twitching as if he yearned to touch it, though was desperately resisting. He wore a rugged black overcoat, with sharp boots that looked like they'd be better served for running than investigating a crime scene. To top it all off, he had a long sword attached to his hip, the blade swaying back and forth as if it were part of his usual get-up.

No one, besides Will, seemed to notice him.

The man with the sword glanced up from the gurney to the crowd, scanning it. When he made eye-contact with Will, his eyes widened. Will looked away, embarrassed to be caught staring.

"William Morgan."

Will whipped around, expecting to see someone he knew calling for him. He broke out in a cold sweat—there were only strangers in the crowd. When he looked back to the gurney, the man was gone. He watched the doors of the ambulance shut, and he rushed to return to his classmates. As he walked, Will couldn't shake off the entire situation; the dream, the dark-haired lady who knocked him down like a professional athlete, the body on the gurney accompanied by the odd man with a sword, a voice calling him by name ... this had been an abnormal day indeed.

Will caught up with the group and successfully slipped back in amongst the chattering teenagers. Nobody seemed to notice his return. He made eye contact with Peter, who rushed over.

"Dude, you look worse than you did when you left. You okay?"

"I'm fine. I think I just need a nap. The heat must be getting to me."

"Fair enough." Peter didn't look convinced. Nevertheless, he let it go, his eyes darting back to Will from time to time, bright with concern.

The pair traipsed along in silence, looking at the city as the rest of the class talked around them.

"How do you think that guy got away with carrying a sword around those cops? Especially right after a murder?"

Will's neck almost cracked from speed of turning, the movement making him dizzy. His eyes settled on a figure standing a few feet away in the shade of an alley, darkness obscuring her features. Will couldn't see more than a cascade of raven hair falling around her shoulders. He recognized the voice. It was the woman from before.

"You're Will Morgan, right?"

"Who are you?" Will asked, his voice shaking more than he would have liked.

"Dude, Will! Don't mess with me like this. It's not funny," Peter shot at him.

"I wasn't talking to you. I was talking to her."

"Hey Will ... drink this." Peter put a bottle of water under Will's nose, his words oozing caution.

"Really?" Will asked, annoyance creeping into his voice. "That's what you're going to do after that? Offer me water?"

"After what?" Peter had grown still, his voice low.

Will's mouth opened in protest, then shut, eyes narrowing. "That woman. She knew my name!" He didn't even try to hide his annoyance this time. "You don't think that's at least a little bit creepy?"

"Ahaha," Peter laughed, though there was no enthusiasm. "I think you're trying way too hard to pick up girls. You're hallucinating them now. Please, drink some water."

Will could feel his face turning red. Hallucinating? The woman was standing in the alley. At least, he thought she was. He didn't want Peter thinking he was crazy. Or maybe he was crazy? Or maybe it was just something fueled by the shock of having seen a dead body. Will begrudgingly took the liquid.

"As I said ... I need a nap," Will grumbled, not responding to the rest of Peter's protests.

Will ignored Peter the rest of the way to the hotel and went straight to bed.

2

The Package From No One

The next few days passed by uneventfully. The most exciting dream Will had was one featuring his non-existent dog eating his homework. The cliché nature of the dream didn't stop Will from waking up in a mild panic and jumping out of bed to make sure he hadn't missed out on some assignment. Relieved to find he indeed did not have a forty-five-page English paper due on the first day of school, Will was unable to go back to sleep. He went downstairs to grab something to eat. There he found his father, Emery, preparing to leave for work.

Emery Morgan was a tall and wiry man with thin dark hair, and a five-o'clock shadow that never went away. He talked very loudly, and always tried to cover up the fact he was going bald.

"You're up early," Emery commented. "I thought school was the only thing that could get you out of bed before ten?"

"Couldn't sleep." Will fixed himself a bowl of cereal, school on his mind. "Did you know there are 500 kids in my graduating class at Morrison? That's absurd!"

Emery took a bite of his toast. "My high school class was about 700 people. That's pretty normal. You nervous?"

Will chewed his cereal thoughtfully. "Nah. Everyone I know is going to be there. You know what I mean? And there will be a million people I don't know!"

Emery ruffled Will's hair. "I do. Still, you have a week to not worry about it. You doing anything fun today?"

"I might meet up with Peter. See a movie or something. Nothing too exciting." Will shrugged and took another bite.

"Sounds great. Have a good time." Will's father shoved the last bit of toast in his mouth, picked up his briefcase, and made his way to the door. "Have a good day. Summer's almost over!"

A minute or so later he heard his father's car start up and drive away.

Will picked up the newspaper and flipped through the pages. Once he had exhausted his reading material, he became annoyed by the silence in the room. After another hour or so of aimlessly flipping through television channels, Will was grabbed by a wave of restlessness. He needed *something* to get his mind off school. He set his long-empty bowl in the sink and went upstairs to get dressed. Peter was always good for a distraction.

While tying his shoes, Will's pocket buzzed.

Bored. Come over. Iris is coming too.

OMW, he texted back.

Will also texted his mother, letting her know where he was going before running outside. He grabbed his bike and pedaled the few blocks to Peter's house. When he reached Peter's driveway, he was shortly joined by Iris, who hopped off of her bike with gusto.

"Hey Will," she said, pulling off her helmet.

"Yo." Peter waved at the two friends from the open front door.

Will and Iris waved back as Peter ran over to his bike, parked leisurely in the driveway. "I'm feeling the mall," he commented. "Or going into town at least. The stores are open by now. Either of you too tired to go the extra mile?"

Unable to think of anything better to do, Will got back on his bike. Not wanting to be shown up by the two boys, Iris was already pedaling, speeding toward the large metropolitan area.

As the trio biked through the streets of Alexandria, North Carolina, Will was reminded of how much of a college town it really was; there was a reasonably large university in the area, and as a result a lot of the retailers catered to the students. There were soda shops, huge electronics stores, and for the daring, antique bookstores in dilapidated old buildings.

One of Will's favorite stores was called Gustafson and Whiteside, a tiny bookshop in a rickety building on Main Street. It stayed in business because it offered the newest releases; however, Will loved it because it was full of older books. He'd sometimes find signed copies or first editions lurking among the shelves, waiting to be purchased by the occasional student who scoured the depths of the stock.

Will had cleared Gustafson and Whiteside when he had an intense urge to stop. He turned his bike around and screeched to a halt in front of the store.

"Peter!" Iris yelled. "He stopped."

"Figures," Peter called back.

Peter and Iris pedaled back to join Will in front of the large store windows. They understood his obsession with books. Peter and Will had become friends over a favorite book they found at the store years ago: *The Redstone Keep* by Arthur O'Neill. One day at school the two boys saw Iris reading the same novel. The duo became an instant trio.

A bell chimed as the three entered the shop.

"Will! Peter! Iris! How are you today?" Carol, the elderly shop keeper asked.

Will had known Carol since he was ten years old and began biking to school on his own. There had been more than one occasion when his parents would get a call from the school saying Will was absent only to find he had been reading in the store for the entire day, hiding amongst the old volumes and tattered pages.

"Doing great, Carol. How are you?" Will responded.

Iris and Peter greeted her as they walked past the cash register to the *YA Fantasy* section.

"Will, something interesting happened this morning." The shopkeeper beckoned to him. Looking around the room like she expected someone to be eavesdropping, Carol dropped her voice to a whisper. "I came in to work today and found this in the mailbox. The package is addressed to you."

Will took the box and scanned it. Finding only his name on the packaging, he tore the cardboard open.

Inside was a copy of *The Redstone Keep*, the book that had brought him and his friends together. The art on the cover was different from the copy he owned, and the novel and dust jacket were both in pristine condition.

Will's eyes lit up with gratitude and excitement. "This is a first edition! That's awesome! It's older than I am."

Opening the cover, Will took his first look inside.

"It's signed," he breathed out, his voice catching in his throat.

He brought the book to his eyes and held it up against the light at an angle. If he squinted, he could see the slight rise of the ink above the page, showing the signature was genuine, and not just a printed fake. Carol clapped, eyes giddy with excitement, the sound snapping through the quiet shop like a noisemaker.

"That it is!" she exclaimed, smiling ear to ear at Will's shocked expression.

Will hugged Carol and took out his wallet. "How much?" He hoped the $20 he carried with him for emergencies was enough.

"You don't owe me anything, dear. It's a gift. I'm merely the messenger. As I said, it was here when I got to work."

"Where did it come from?" A shiver ran through him as his mind flashed to the dead man and the stranger with the sword.

"I don't know. It was just here. I didn't see anyone and it didn't have a note or anything."

"So you mean there wasn't anything to say who sent it? No return address? Just this box with my name on it?"

She nodded. "Afraid so. It was rather peculiar, in my opinion. I guess you just never know what surprises are in store for you every day. Whoever it's from must know you pretty well."

"Yeah," Will replied. "If you find out who sent it, let me know."

"Of course."

"Hey, Will, you ready to go?" Iris asked, emerging with empty hands, Peter close behind.

"Yeah," Will said.

Waving goodbye to Carol, the trio walked out the door and back to their bikes. As happy as Will was, the strangeness of the situation bothered him more than he cared to let on. The man from his dream nudged at his brain; Will ignored him.

"What did you buy?" Iris asked.

Peter stared at the book in Will's hands. Iris noticed too and clapped her hands to her mouth.

"Oh, Will! That's a first edition," she said. "That's incredible! Did you find it somewhere in the back?"

Will felt like his brain was on autopilot as he stared down at the novel. "No. Carol gave it to me. She said she found it when she got to work, addressed to me. It's even signed!" He looked at his friends. "It's odd. Was it one of you?"

"You think we could afford something like that?" Peter asked, rolling his eyes.

"Do you guys mind if I don't go to the mall? I kind of want to go home and read this."

"Really?" Peter commented, taken aback. "Now? Instead of hanging out with us?"

"Unfortunately, yeah," Will replied, trying to put on a fake grin that masked his uneasiness. "Seeing it makes me want to read it again. Besides. I don't want this bouncing around in my pack and getting damaged."

"Want to meet up for lunch later?" Iris asked, annoyance creeping into her voice; she didn't like it when plans changed suddenly.

"Maybe," Will quipped, his mouth twisting into something he hoped was an apologetic smile. "This is just ... really cool. And I might end up inside reading all day. You know how I am."

"To the mall, my lady." Peter firmly ignored him.

"To the mall!"

"See ya, Will. Have fun reading."

Iris and Peter continued their bike ride. Will turned in the opposite direction. He was lucky to have friends like them.

He sped home with the book wrapped in a sweater inside his backpack. The bike ride had Will feeling nostalgic. He had been given his first copy of *The Redstone Keep* as a birthday present from his parents when he turned ten and tore through the thick novel within three days. It was the first novel in a series called *Byrrus.*

Byrrus was a sprawling city built around a large castle. The people who resided in Byrrus lived in peace and prosperity—the ideal town. The entries in the series all read as individual stories—different tales from different time periods, all focusing on the same castle that always stood strong. The first book in the series, *The Redstone Keep*, focused on an evil tyrant, Daegan, who sought to overtake Byrrus and claim it for his own. As the book progressed, the people came together under the leadership of a warrior named Tam Desmond who defeated the tyrant and saved their home.

Will jumped off his bike and skittered into the house, nearly tripping in the process. He rounded the corner, excited to tell his mother about the events of the morning. Their eyes met and Will stopped. Something was wrong.

It was always very easy for Will to read his mother's emotions, whether it was from the look in her gentle blue eyes, to the way she articulated certain words. Ruth Morgan had a soft face, but the sharpness of her personality was always found in her gaze more than anything else. Today, Ruth looked happy as usual, apart from her cloudy stare.

"How are you, honey?" Her tone was placating.

"Good," he replied, narrowing his eyes and scanning his mother's face.

"How was Peter's?" Ruth had never been a good actor, and the sympathy creeping into her tone proved just as much.

Will's smile dropped, and he walked forward. "What's wrong, Mom?"

"Will," she started, "come sit with me in the living room for a minute."

"What happened? Is it Dad?"

"No, not at all," she said. "Not that serious. Just sad. I was looking through old newspapers as I was cleaning up and found an article I think you need to read."

Will's heart caught in his throat. Somehow, he knew what was coming.

"It's Arthur O'Neill. He passed away while you were in Boston visiting schools. I think he was from Boston too. Give it a read." She gently placed the paper next to Will, mouth curved sympathetically, eyes watering. "I really am sorry. I know you liked him."

"It's okay. Life happens," Will replied, doing his best to mask the panic taking hold of his body.

She frowned but nonetheless retreated to the kitchen. Will took a deep breath and glanced at the article.

Arthur O'Neill, author of the popular Byrrus series, dies of unknown causes.

Popular young-adult fiction author Arthur O'Neill, 60, was found dead yesterday morning in his Boston apartment. The apartment had no signs of a break-in, and O'Neill's body had no visible signs of foul play. A police investigation is underway. Still, investigators are unofficially attributing the death to a heart attack.

"It's always sad to see someone go like this," one officer said. "The man wasn't even that old. We'll know more after the autopsy."

Will put the paper down, staring blankly at the wall in front of him, brain pounding at a mile a minute. He thought back to just a few days ago when he witnessed a body being hauled out of a brownstone. He thought of the mysterious figure with the sword and the woman in the alleyway. He looked at his backpack and thought of the book that had found its way inside, just a few days after its author died.

Putting his hand to his head, Will rested against the arm of the couch. He was physically shaking. Something was going on here. It couldn't have just been a coincidence; the book, the mysterious cloaked figure, the dream, the voice. It felt as if he were in a horror film, in the scene right before the main character met the killer for the first time.

He shook his head. "This is ridiculous," he muttered, looking back at the newspaper and blinking away the tears. The pain tearing through his body was akin to an emotional tragedy. He never met Arthur O'Neill. Sure, he loved the author's books, but it wasn't like the guy was his grandfather or anything.

"Well," Will said to himself, "I suppose the first thing to do is to read this book." *Maybe there's a code or something,* he thought silently. *Maybe it will give me answers.*

He pulled the book from his pack and opened it to the prologue. By the time his eyes reached the third line, the world went blurry. He blinked hard, trying to clear his vision. He fell forward, cracking his head hard on the coffee table as the world around him reduced to darkness.

3

The World of
the Written

Will opened his eyes to a ray of sunshine, and his temple wasn't throbbing like he expected. After all, his last memory was him hitting his head on a coffee table. Even so, he wasn't in pain. In fact, he was extremely content. His hands gripped soft sheets, and the pillow under him felt like a cloud. Will settled deeper into the comfort of the bed.

My bed isn't this comfortable.

He shot up like a bullet, flailing and trying to untangle himself from the satiny blankets. Finally released from the folds of fabric, Will stood on a bare stone floor in a strange room.

"You'd think someone waking up in a nice bed would be a little bit less panicked, right?"

Will spun around, getting tangled in the blankets all over again before tripping and falling over himself. Looking up from the ground, he was met with a spiky haired boy with a rowdy grin standing near a large wooden desk. He was about the same age as Will, maybe a little older, but there was something about him that made him seem ageless. His eyes were a puzzling aqua color that undulated like the ocean, shifting from one shade of blue or green to another.

There were a million things Will should've asked him: *what are your eyes doing? Why are you looking at me like I'm food? Where am I? Where can I get sheets this soft?*

The only thing he could produce from his mouth was, "I'm not panicked."

He untangled himself again and stood. The room was certainly none he had ever seen. The walls were paneled in a light wood, giving them an aged look. The sunlight bounced around the room, coming from several arched windows on the farthest wall. Throughout the room were twin-sized beds holding the same comfortable white sheets Will had just escaped.

This wasn't real. How could this be real? He was obviously in some sort of fever dream.

"You're not dreaming, Will," the boy said.

Will turned to him, finally taking in the rest of the teenager. His clothes looked medieval, a peculiar combination of armor and robe accompanied by a long sword, locked away in a scabbard. Despite the strangeness of the outfit, Will suspected that at some point in time this look had been extremely fashionable.

"Okay," Will scoffed. "I know I can't *not* be dreaming. I'm in some random room that looks like it's from medieval England. I'm from twenty-first century American suburbia. This doesn't exist where I'm from. So, either this is a huge prank, or I'm dreaming. The latter seems more likely."

The boy shook his head, laughing. "Okay. If you're dreaming, then this should wake you up, right?"

Before Will could respond, the boy whipped out his sword, and in a flash, dove the tip of it into the wall directly next to Will's head. Will screamed and scrambled away, tripping over himself and falling into a heap next to the bed, groaning in pain as his knee rammed into something hard. He rubbed his leg and turned back to the boy, who pulled the sword out of the wall and placed it back into its scabbard. He put his hand out toward Will, who took it hesitantly.

"Ignoring the fact that you could have killed me just now," Will started, "that's certainly something that would have woken me up from a dream. Point taken." Will looked around. "If that's the case, then where am I? And who are you?"

The boy's face lit up. "Those questions have complicated answers. I think the easiest thing to do would be for you to look outside."

Hesitantly, Will opened the nearest window, the sun making him blink as his eyes adjusted to the brightness. He covered his mouth in disbelief.

"Welcome to Byrrus Castle, William Morgan."

Directly out the window were the battlements of a large castle, made of light red sandstone, extending in all directions toward large, artistic turrets and towers. Below the castle was the city of Byrrus, a small metropolis that stretched for a mile or two in front of him. Will could see spots of blue where there were ponds and estuaries and fields of green that marked the apple orchards and parks that littered the city. Past the city borders were rolling green hills and forests as far as the eye could see.

There wasn't a cloud in the sky, and the unmarked blue expanse above him was what likely encouraged the distant, gleeful shouts of children in the town below, running around and playing while their parents thoughtfully watched on. Will turned back to the boy.

"This has to be a joke." Will's eyes wandered the room desperately. "That can't be Byrrus. *This* can't be Byrrus. Byrrus is a …"

"A story? Fictional?" the boy responded, raising one eyebrow. "You're correct. *The Redstone Keep* is a book. And you've been transported to its world. Byrrus is a real place."

"How?"

"You're not dreaming. You're a person from the human world, the world where stories are written. And now you're here." He sighed. "In this world, there's a man named Tam. He's the one who is going to explain what's going on. He'll be here in about two minutes, actually."

Will gulped. "So, when you say Tam, do you mean Tam Desmond? The protagonist of *The Redstone Keep?*" He stopped for a moment, nervous the boy wouldn't understand what the word "protagonist" meant, or he'd be offended by it.

"Don't worry, protagonist isn't a dirty word," the boy chortled. "I'm glad you get it. This world is part of a story that's considered fiction in your world. Well, that's half the battle I suppose."

"You say 'this world' like you're not a part of it. Who are you anyways?"

"I've gone by many names. If I'm being honest, I'm not sure which one is the right one." The boy flashed a toothy grin, the youth returning to his face and tone. "You can call me Simon."

"Okay, Simon. Nice name. That still doesn't really answer my question. Who are you?"

Approaching footsteps interrupted their conversation.

"That'll be Tam, I suppose," Simon commented. "I'll be seeing you soon, Will. I'll explain more then." He put a hand to his chin thoughtfully. "By the way, for now, don't mention me to

Tam. Or to anyone, frankly. You're the only person who is able to see me."

"What?" Will turned to look at the door, but as he looked back to Simon for answers, he found the boy had disappeared.

"Creepy," Will whispered.

There was a solid knock on the door before it opened slowly. The man who entered wore a long black coat and armor on his hands and legs as if he were prepared for battle at a moment's notice. A sword hung from his belt, a long hand-and-a-half blade that seemed to radiate power. Faced with a man who embodied every detail of a character from a novel solidified Simon's words.

Somehow, miraculously, Will had been transported to the pages of his favorite book.

Then it struck Will: Tam was the man he saw accompanying Arthur O'Neill's body in Boston. It made sense. If Arthur O'Neill wrote *The Redstone Keep*, and therefore created Tam, it only made sense for Tam to be there when he died. Right?

Tam's face was that of a man in his late thirties, about four inches taller than Will. He had short, black hair, and a goatee curving all the way around his mouth. He looked tired, his eyes sad. Even so, he smiled.

"Will Morgan." Tam extended a hand. "It's a pleasure."

Will shook Tam's hand hesitantly, staring at the warrior in awe.

"So ... um ... what's going on, exactly?"

"Yes." Tam looked around the room. "That's the question of the day, now isn't it? Please, have a seat. Can I get you anything? A drink, perhaps."

"No. I'm okay." Will sat on the closest bed. Tam jumped into an explanation of how Will was actually in the world of Byrrus, the same as Simon had. Will nodded calmly, though the information wasn't any less unbelievable the second time around.

"How many books have you read in your life, Will?"

"I don't really know. Probably a couple hundred or so."

Tam tilted his head forward slightly. "And how many stories do you think have ever been written? Books, movies, plays, or the like? How many?"

"Millions," Will replied, hazarding a guess. "Maybe more."

"Well, they all exist. Not just on paper or on a stage but here."

"They all exist in Byrrus?" Tam's face was unreadable, so Will continued. "*The Redstone Keep* is just a single story. In the long run it means nothing. Sure, it's a good book, but it isn't like it's the best-selling novel of all time. So why, of all novels, is *The Redstone Keep* the chosen one?"

Tam chuckled.

"That was tactless." Will put up his hands in apology. "I just meant, you know, there are way more popular novels, and … um …"

Tam's chuckle evolved into a full-blown howl. "It's okay. I know what you meant." His eyes grew soft. "This, Will," he said, "is Byrrus. This is the world Arthur O'Neill created. This is the fictional castle from your novels. It's all real. You understand this, which is good; however, there is so much more. And no, all the other stories don't exist in Byrrus. They have their own place. Let me show you around. That might help a little."

Tam opened the door and encouraged Will to follow. Will obliged and tailed him through a series of hallways, twisting and turning in every direction. The two eventually made their way to a battlement—a long stretch of pavement on the edge of the castle—that allowed them to see in every direction.

"Byrrus," Tam motioned around him, "is part of a massive universe, parallel to your own. Everything that's ever been published and read by humans, whether it be movie scripts, books, poetry … everything exists in this world. Whenever an author, or artist, or poet, writes a work, completes it, and has it bound, published, and read by an audience," Tam patted his chest dramatically, "it comes to life. It's been called many things over the years by Writers of different generations. Nibiru. Cockaigne. Eden—I'm sure that one was an ego boost for the Characters of the time." Tam snickered at his own joke. "Now we're merely the World of the Written. The Written, for short. It's easier and, frankly, more accurate."

"How is that possible? Is it like an alternate dimension? Is it underground? Are there others, like for dreams or ideas that are written down and not published?"

Tam scratched his head. "Well, I don't know how to explain it. I guess it *is* an alternate universe, in a way. However, it's one most people only fantasize about. Very few people know of its existence." He pointed to the horizon, a never-ending stretch of shining blue sky. "There are only two universes I know of. The first is The Written. The second is The World of the Writers, your world. If there are more, they haven't been revealed to me."

"If there are so many worlds that exist in the Written, why did I come to Byrrus? Why is this world in particular so special? Is it the most important book or something?"

Tam let out a booming laugh and slapped Will lightly on the shoulder. *Tam's hand was solid.* This man couldn't be a hallucination. Sure, Will might have an overly-imaginative mind, but never in his wildest dreams had he felt physically touched by an image. This was one-hundred percent real.

Tam's jovial voice broke Will's train of thought. "You seem to be getting the hang of this quickly! Although, I'm sad to say Byrrus isn't the most important book, as you put it. We're not that important."

"Then where are the other worlds?"

Tam grinned. "Let me show you."

With a dramatic flourish, Tam put his palm out in front of him, as if putting his hand against an invisible wall. An archway appeared, outlining itself in white-gold light. Once the archway was fully formed, Tam beckoned to Will, encouraging him to follow through the brightness.

Will stepped into an empty hallway with white walls and a single wooden door at the other end, about one hundred feet away. Something clicked in Will's brain.

"So this hallway, or whatever it is, connects the different stories? Does it also lead to the Writer's world? Is this how I get home?"

"You got it. This hallway connects to both the other stories as well as the World of the Writers."

"And through that door is another story. Which story is it?"

Tam's grin was now revealing his teeth. "Which one do you want it to be?"

"I choose which story I want to go to, and that door at the end of the hall will open to that world, based on my choice?"

Tam dipped his head formally. "Something along those lines. This hallway is actually part of an even bigger entity, called Betwixt and Between. Think about the Earth. A lot of it is water, right?"

"Yeah. Most of it, actually."

"That's exactly it. Except instead of Earth's continents, think of millions and billions of small islands, all separated by ocean. The ocean is Betwixt and Between, while the islands are the different stories. Therefore, you don't have to go through multiple worlds just to get to a specific one. You can kind of skip around. I guess the best way to put it is that there's no such thing as a connecting flight in the World of the Written. You understand?"

"Kind of," Will said. He paused, blushing and backtracking. "Sorry, no. Not really."

Tam beckoned to the door. Will walked through it, finding himself on a beach; however, instead of the sun shining down on him, there were three multicolored moons—certainly not a feature of Byrrus. He stared in awe, and Tam grasped his shoulder again.

"*Moons of Mars* by Trevor Andres. One of the greatest science fiction novels of all time. Definitely not part of the world I'm from. And I don't think your Earth has three moons." He smirked at Will. "Do you understand now?"

"Yeah, I think so," Will said, still in shock. "So, I can use Betwixt and Between to go to the worlds of every story ever published?"

"Essentially," Tam replied. "Your only limitation is you can't enter worlds whose story you've never read. Or watched, I guess, as it relates to movies or plays." He sighed. "Or if the story has been forgotten, but that's for another day."

Will took a few steps forward, kicking the sand of the beach until he made his way to the water, where he contemplated the waves for a few moments. He could feel Tam's gaze on his back. "Makes sense, but what does this have to do with me? Why is any of this important?"

"You've been given a gift, Will. A gift called the Writer's Eye. Which means you're now a Writer. Writer with a capital W. Writers have the ability to see both worlds and Betwixt and Between, as well as all the Characters in the stories. That's what we're called, by the way—Characters, with a capital C." Tam's voice took a solemn tone, speaking from the back of his throat.

Will turned around, looking Tam in the eyes. "I've been given a gift? How? You mean the book from the book store?" Will noticed the sadness in Tam's eyes and swiftly apologized. Tam waved him off.

"The truth is," Tam said, tone dipping lower than it had all afternoon, "I have no idea. Writers are very rare. Occasionally, there are people born with a gift, a certain *Potential*, if you will. Even then, having *Potential* isn't enough. Most Writers gain their powers from having some sort of triggering event, like being in imminent danger from something in the World of the Written. For better or worse, most of the people in your world are what we call Readers—those who are regular, non-magical, mortal human beings who think the World of the Written is just that: written."

"So how did I get my powers? Nothing happened to me. I haven't been in danger or anything. Someone just gave me a book."

"I think somehow Arthur's powers," he became quiet for a moment, "got transferred to you before he died." He then looked at Will sympathetically. "For whatever reason, Arthur released his powers and you happened to catch them. I think that's why you ended up here. I know it's a lot to take in and I'll be able to explain it to you at a later time. For now, I think you should be getting home. I know coming here today was a bit of a shock."

"You could say that," Will replied, smiling in spite of his confusion. "Is there a way for me to get back here?"

"Yes," Tam said. "However, it's complicated, and we don't have enough time right now. I have a lot to teach you, Will. I can start training you tomorrow night. I just have some personal things to attend to first."

An unpleasant bubbling erupted in the pit of Will's stomach as he remembered the day Arthur had died. "When I was in Boston, there was a woman who knew my name, but other people couldn't seem to see her. I thought she was a hallucination, though now I don't think she was. Could she have been a Character?"

"I can't say I know who that woman is," Tam said slowly. "Just be careful. Now that you can see Characters, you have to be on your guard. I'll explain more tomorrow. Just know you and I are connected. If you're ever in any danger, I'll be there to help you. Then you and I can figure out why we were brought together."

Will let out a nervous sound that he hoped would be taken as agreement.

"Now let's get you home." Tam put his hands in front of him as he did before, summoning a passageway to Betwixt and Between. They walked through, and at the other end of the hallway was a door that looked like the one to Will's house.

"Once you walk through here, you'll be back in your living room, right where you passed out. And, as a side note," Tam's voice was bubbly and light, "you won't have to pass out next time. I'll come get you."

"Thanks, I guess."

Will took one last look at Tam before walking into his living room.

4

The Familiar

The instant Will woke up, his ears picked up the sound of his mother in the next room, doing dishes. He called out to her and she walked in, surprised.

"Hey honey," she commented, a bowl in her hand. "I didn't even hear you come back in."

"I never left." Will tried to keep a straight face. Ruth squinted at him.

"I was here a minute ago and you weren't on the couch. I figured you went upstairs."

Will glanced at her, nonplussed, then looked at the clock. It had been about an hour since he passed out, meaning his body should have been there, comatose. If it hadn't been, did that mean he disappeared completely when he entered the Written?

"Oh, yeah, duh." Will tried to sound casual. "I forgot. It's just been a really off day, you know?"

Ruth's gaze softened and she touched his arm. "Do you want to talk about it? I know you really loved his books."

"I'm fine," Will lied, rubbing his face. "I'm just really drained. I think I might go back to Peter's." Ruth squeezed his hand and left the room, leaving Will with his own thoughts. He absentmindedly fiddled with his phone until a text from Peter appeared, declaring he and Iris had returned home, and Will should join them. Knowing Iris, Will figured there would be school prep going on, so he grabbed his backpack as a preemptive measure. He walked through the front door, running his hands through his hair, thinking about the events of the morning as he got onto his bike.

Sure, it was a cool, crazy idea. Every book character lived in a magical parallel universe, and he, Will Morgan, had the power to see and interact with them. It was incredible, and also incredibly ridiculous. Maybe too ridiculous. What if he was just losing his mind?

Even more terrifying, what if he *wasn't* losing his mind?

And if all of the heroes are alive, Will's breaths got quicker as the thought formed, *then all of the villains are too.* The thought of encountering some of the *Byrrus* series's less-pleasant characters was enough to make him shiver despite the heat.

Along with the World of the Written, there was the entire situation in Boston. That woman was important. She had to be. Why else would he be the only person who saw her? The fact Tam didn't know who she was made Will more nervous.

Will hesitantly touched his hand to his face, trying to feel for some difference, some scar that wasn't there before. He felt nothing. Whatever had changed about him wasn't visible to the eye.

If it turned out he was losing his mind, Will didn't want anyone to know about it. If it turned out he wasn't … well, that was a bridge he'd cross only if necessary. Regardless, he'd know by tomorrow. If Tam returned, and Will was able to be trained in this Writer's Eye, then he'd know it was real.

Peter sat amongst a pile of school supplies, binder in hand, when his friend walked through the front door. Will's skin was paler than usual, his lips a little blue; however, the last thing Peter wanted to do was embarrass Will. Instead, he pretended not to notice. Maybe he would ask him later in private.

"A week, Will! A freaking week!" Peter shouted dramatically, putting his face in his hands. "I barely got to do anything! Between tennis practice and my parents making me do work around the house, I only got two weeks' worth of actual summer vacation!"

"Well, you've got a free day right now. Might as well get organized," Iris quipped.

"Since when are you such a huge nerd?" Will joked, sitting next to them.

"Since the first day you met me. Besides, it's our first day of high school!" she exclaimed. "We need to be prepared! I, or we, need to look good, know what we're doing, and show we're not dorky freshman like the movies say we are!"

She went back to looking at her schedule and a map of the new school, cross-referencing them. Will smirked and leaned back against a chair.

"Those cliché high school movies aren't the real thing. You know that, right? There really isn't any such thing as Freshman Friday. Or rigged homecoming courts. It's just a normal place for normal kids to hate the establishment and wish for their senior year."

"Well, I'd like to make a good impression anyway. Let me see your schedule." She held out her hand expectantly and Will removed the paper from his bag and handed it over, the corners of his mouth twitching. She grabbed Peter's schedule and studied the three side by side.

She muttered to herself before speaking up. "Not much overlap, at least between us and you, Will."

"It must be band screwing it up," Peter said.

Will had been a musician since elementary school. Though Peter and Iris both made fun of him for his nerdy extracurricular when they became friends, they had grown to appreciate it. Will wasn't just committed—he was also extremely talented, though he tried not to admit it.

"So, nothing overlaps?" Will questioned, shoulders drooping.

Iris shrugged. "You and I have biology together first semester," she offered, tracing her finger down the paper. "That's it. Peter and I have English and Geometry together, but you two don't have anything."

Peter groaned again, still lying on the ground.

"What, are two classes with me not enough?" Iris kicked Peter's foot jokingly.

"Not if you talk to me like that all year!"

The three of them laughed, and though Will had a look of joy on his face, Peter could see through it. They made eye contact, and Will flashed his teeth, obviously attempting to eliminate Peter's doubts. Peter shifted his eyes away, though his concern didn't change. Ever since Boston he had been worried about Will. However, Will wouldn't admit what was wrong. If he wanted to talk, he would have said something before now. So, Peter merely went back to shifting paper into one of the large binders sitting next to him.

"So, Will, what do you think the odds of us getting a couple of seniors are?"

"You're disgusting," Iris remarked.

Peter pushed her arm in sarcastic reproach, and Will laughed again.

Iris looked at Will haughtily. "Seriously, if you two ruin this for me, I'll never speak to you again."

"Yeah, okay Ms. I-need-to-be-the-queen-of-Morrison," Will mocked, his eyes betraying mirth. "Since when have you been so concerned about popularity? Everyone loves you!"

Her frown cracked. "That's nice of you, Will."

"So suave," Peter observed, rolling his eyes lazily.

Will leaned back and stared out the large picture window to the front yard. Peter watched him. Will sat up slowly, grabbing for Peter while not taking his eyes off the window.

"Do you see that?" he asked, pointing to the yard. Peter looked out the window and didn't see anything where Will was pointing. He glanced back at Will, doing a double take at his friend's face, now ashen; his arm was quivering, his shoulders tight.

"What is it? You okay?"

Will turned away from the window. "Yeah. I don't know. I guess I saw a bird or something. It's nothing." He smiled and gave Peter and Iris a thumbs up.

Iris made eye contact with Peter, and it was clear she felt uneasy too. She sighed and slammed a stack of freshly stocked binders onto a pile, wiping her hands.

"Well that's it! We're officially ready to be high schoolers! One week to go!"

Peter moaned again and slammed his head against a notebook.

The rest of the day passed in a blur. Eventually, the group went back to their respective homes, with Peter having promised to help his dad with housework, and Iris deciding to go to bed early for the rest of the summer.

Though Will tried to relax, he couldn't help reflecting on what he had seen in Peter's yard: a mysterious figure, cloaked in black, face covered. The figure was definitely there, obvious as day, but his friend couldn't see anything. He hadn't been able to see the figure's face, though given how many mysterious cloaked people he had seen recently, Will could only assume it was the woman from Boston. It made him more desperate to understand the Writer's Eye.

That night and the following day he read his new copy of *The Redstone Keep*, this time searching it for clues about the World of the Written, Arthur O'Neill, *anything*. The fact the book was autographed, was a first edition, and had been the portal into the Written had to mean something. Despite how hard he searched or how many margins he scanned, Will was forced to conclude it was just a plain old novel. Other than the scrawl signature on the title page, there wasn't anything that could be used to solve the mystery of what had been happening.

Maybe Arthur O'Neill sent it to me, he mused. That seemed unlikely. Regardless of how much Will idolized him, Arthur was a bestselling author; there was no way he would have ever heard of Will. Will hadn't even entered the essay contest Arthur hosted a few years ago, out of a combination of laziness and embarrassment.

That night, while sitting on his bed finishing *The Redstone Keep,* Will's father knocked on the door and walked in.

"Hey bud." Emery sat on Will's bed. "How was your day?"

"Fine," Will replied, continuing to flip through the pages of *The Redstone Keep.*

"Ah, *The Redstone Keep*. Nice. How many times have you read that one?" Emery asked, smirking at Will playfully.

Will folded the book onto his chest. "A bunch," he muttered. "I just wanted to read it again before school starts. Who knows when I'll have time to read for pleasure again."

His dad ruffled Will's hair. "Fair enough. Do you need anything for school?"

"Nope. Mom bought everything I needed last weekend and we got it ready at Peter's house. I'm all prepped." Will gestured to his backpack, now stuffed with new school supplies.

"Nice work! Nothing wrong with being prepared. Now, get some sleep. Five days left!"

When Emery shut the door, Will sat up against his wall and looked at the clock—11:00 p.m. Will looked back at *The Redstone Keep* and found he couldn't focus. Tam told him yesterday he would return and teach Will more about the World of the Written. Where was he? Did he get attacked? Did he forget? Or was this proof the entire experience was just some psychotic break from stress?

As the clock ticked closer to midnight, Will jumped out of bed. He had to do something. He wasn't going crazy. It had to be real!

He glanced at his door, praying his parents wouldn't walk in un-announced, and reached out his hands. Will focused all of his energy on imagining Byrrus—the texture of brick, the sound of children playing, and the distant chatter of market-goers. For five minutes, straining as hard as he could, Will focused. Each time he opened his eyes, he was greeted by his bedroom wall.

Will let off a muted sound of frustration and kicked at his back-pack before slumping on his bed. He wanted it to be real. He wanted to have a magical power. Taking a deep breath, he stood up, ready to try again.

Will closed his eyes and thought about Betwixt and Between,

the daunting emptiness that preceded all the stories the world had ever know. The white walls and the long hallway that ended in whatever story he wanted.

He felt a slight shift in the air around him. Will opened his eyes; a white gold passage had appeared before him, a clear archway leading into a long passageway. Will pumped the air with his fist and resisted shouting with excitement.

He plumped up his blankets and pillows, hoping it would look like he was in bed just in case his parents came in to check. Turning his desk lamp off, Will walked into the portal, leaving his bedroom behind.

A long white expanse unfolded before him. A large wooden door stood alone at the end of the hallway, a hopeful beacon that Will had been successful in summoning the portal. Crossing the tunnel, he tugged the door open. He emerged into a dense forest, the portal disappearing behind him.

Crap, he thought to himself. *What if I ended up in* Little Red Riding Hood *or something like that?* Will caught a glimpse of a light through a small gap in the trees, and relief flooded his body. Though he wasn't completely certain, Will was willing to bet the light was from the main lookout tower at the edge of Byrrus.

Will set off with a confidence that wasn't appropriate for the situation. Though he managed to get to the World of the Written without Tam's help, navigating the woods was very difficult. There wasn't a clear path and at one point he sank ankle-deep into a large pool of water. His slippers were caked in mud. He shouldn't have come in pajamas.

He strained his eyes as best he could but still stepped in a few more puddles as he walked. The woods were so dark that Will could barely make out the outlines of the trees. He went for his cellphone so he could have some form of light, and realized he made another great error—he left his phone in his room.

"Seriously, Will. You need to be more prepared," he muttered to himself.

After a few minutes of walking, the moonlight revealed a small clearing and Will took a moment to try and scrape some of the mud from his slippers. Something rustled in the trees to his left.

"Hey!" he shouted into the darkness. "Over here! Traveler in need of assistance!"

The sound stopped for a moment, but then came toward Will, faster than before. Shapes burst from the tree line, carrying torches.

On first glance it was apparent they were at least humanoid. They had distinct faces, bodies, and were standing on two legs. They varied in height, the shortest being only two feet tall and the largest being as tall as Will. Perhaps their most bizarre feature was what they were made of. It was a shadowy substance, a murky gel that seemed to be shifting as they moved. It formed their bodies and gave them an ethereal stature. They weren't denizens of Byrrus. Will didn't know what they were. They definitely didn't belong to this story.

Will took a step back, and one of the creatures let out a beastly shriek, the screech's pitch hurting his ears. The creature ran at Will, two knives appearing in its hands, and Will didn't even have time to put his arms up before the monster thrust the blades at his chest.

A burst of light erupted and a column of white fire shot from the ground, searing the beast where it stood. The other monsters stopped in their tracks. As the fire faded, a figure appeared: Simon.

"What's going on?" Will demanded.

Simon's face was calm and understanding. He pulled his sword from its scabbard. It flashed a gorgeous yet deadly arc over his head. He held it out to Will.

"Take it."

It was an ornate piece with a pommel of red stone, the grip a standard black leather. The hilt was a simple cross-guard, sparkling silver in the light of Simon's presence. A trail of gold curved along the rut and faded out slightly before the tip. It was an impressive weapon.

"Take it, Will," he insisted. "You have to fight. You have to defend yourself."

Will took the sword from him. It felt familiar, as if he had held it before, though Will wasn't sure why. His experience with medieval weaponry was fairly limited.

"Good. Now, you know what to do." Simon's voice had a conclusive ring to it.

The mysterious boy disappeared, and the golden light faded away. The World of the Written had given Will a gift. He twirled the sword around, finding it was balanced in a way that made it seem like it was made for him, though he doubted it would help him in battle—he had never even held a sword. As he reared the weapon back over his head, the monsters began their charge once again, the distraction now gone. Will put his weapon up to block the nearest beast, and as its knives clanged against his blade, something strange happened.

The world slowed.

The monster lunged at him again, except the strike was sluggish, like everything other than Will was moving through a block of gelatin. When the monster pulled its arm back, Will was able to sidestep the strike with ease, thrusting his sword through its inky silhouette.

As soon as the tip of the blade passed through the monster, its body fizzled out like a fire being doused with water.

He turned to see another creature swinging at him with long, razor-sharp claws, and he pulled his sword up, blocking the strike. As its claws hit the blade, the vibrations shot through Will's arm. Pushing the monster away with his sword, he swung the blade through its head. It faded away, as the first one did, and a wave of relief briefly washed over Will.

To your right! Duck, then thrust the sword straight up!

Words crackled to life in his head, as if they were being spoken through an old intercom. Without hesitating, Will threw his body to the ground, arching his sword into the air. He caught a creature in the chest. Feeling himself begin to lose energy, Will swung his weapon at one more being as hard as he could, the blade shooting through its body. It was knocked into the air, like a demonic balloon, before bursting into purple and black-colored dust. With all the shadow creatures gone, Will lowered his sword, the world going back to its normal speed.

A blur of color launched itself in front of him, grabbing Will's shoulders. He instinctively flailed out, his non-sword hand connecting haphazardly with a body.

"Will!" Tam shouted, voice spiking. "What are you doing? Why didn't you wait for me?"

"I thought you weren't coming," Will replied, out of breath. "It was late, so I figured I'd come here. I just overshot Byrrus by a little bit."

"How did you actually get here?"

"I opened a portal." There was no reason to lie—how else would he have gotten to the forest?

Tam shook his head. "That's not possible. You're telling me you just summoned a portal and waltzed into the World of the Written by yourself?"

The disbelief in Tam's voice worried Will. "Yeah. Why? Am I not supposed to do that? I'm sorry if I messed something up."

"No, you're okay. I just didn't think you'd be able to do that so quickly without anyone helping you," Tam mused. "It usually takes time to learn that kind of control. I'm really impressed, frankly."

"Great," Will commented, gripping his sword more firmly.

"And the sword?" Tam asked.

"I just summoned it." Something inside him told him to lie about Simon. "I realized I was in danger, and I thought as hard as I could about a weapon. Then boom—this thing appeared in my hand."

Tam dipped his head in earnest. "That makes sense. Your gaining a weapon is the norm for Writers. The only difference is that you unlocked your Writer's Eye because of Arthur's powers. Usually, the Writer's Eye is gained when someone is in danger directly from the Written. They immediately have the ability to defend themselves. A similar thing happened to Arthur. The first time he ever fought in the World of the Written he summoned a sword, and could fight with it to a certain degree, same as you. The Written made that weapon for you. If the pattern stays true, this sword should be perfectly suited to your body type and combat preferences."

"Huh." Will exhaled to release the tension in his chest, keeping his voice level. "Who knows?"

Truth be told, the weapon *was* perfect for him, even though it originally belonged to Simon. Will instinctively let the sword fall from his hands, it disappearing in a flash of light. Tam nodded with recognition and didn't press further. Will gazed at the spot where the sword faded away, a few sparks of light lingering on the air.

"So, now that we've cleared that up, can you tell me what exactly just happened? What were those things? Why did they attack me?" Will glanced at one of the dying torches, the only remains of a fallen foe.

"Well," Tam started, beckoning for Will to follow him as he began walking toward Byrrus, "in the World of the Written, there are beings that are the embodiment of the negativity within literature. They come from Betwixt and Between, and gain power from the darkness and conflict surrounding all stories. They're called Shades—the creatures you just fought."

"Okay, so they're just this world's version of pests? But if they're made of darkness … does that mean I can't kill them? Or did I?" Will stopped, his mind wandering back to their humanoid shape. "They're not people, right?"

Tam gave him an understanding smile. "I'm glad to see you've got some humanity in you." He put a hand on Will's shoulder. "Shades aren't like people. They don't have souls. They're not like Characters either. If you ran me through with your sword, I would die, same as you. However, Shades—they can't die. They all come from the darkness within literature, and that's where they go when they're defeated, only to be reborn again. They are all part of the same entity. That entity is evil." Tam grimaced. "You can't kill evil."

Will was suddenly very grateful for the light from Tam's torch.

"Okay," Will continued eagerly. "What about main villains? Are they Shades? And what about anti-heroes? Are they like, half-Shade, half-Character?"

Tam chuckled. "The only villains who live as Shades within the

World of the Written are those who don't have names. Named villains take the forms they were written with. Does that make sense?"

"I think so," Will replied. "Shades are the grunts of the World of the Written. Then villains are Characters, but that doesn't make them good. Morality isn't based on if you're a Shade or a Character. Great.

"Now that we've got the villains out of the way, can you tell me what happened in that fight? It felt like time slowed down."

They were now at the edge of the city, the light of the entrance shining down on them. Will could see the focus on Tam's face.

"Okay, Will," he started. "You're clearly intent on learning everything at once so I'm not going to hold back. Absorb as much as you can. Don't worry, I'll clarify anything you don't understand." Tam took a deep breath.

"First of all, the thing that allows you to be in this world—the Writer's Eye—also affords you certain abilities, mostly related to combat. It slows time and gives you more power to counter an enemy's movements. It also allows you to telepathically communicate with certain Characters, such as myself. I'm what's called a Pontifex—every world within the World of the Written has one. Simply put, I'm the first point of contact for every Writer who comes through the world of Byrrus.

"The reason I can read your thoughts is that the energy of every Writer is tied to a specific world. It's your home base, in a way. Your home base is Byrrus, and as a result, I, the Pontifex," he gestured to himself, "am able to communicate with you telepathically, advise you in battle, and teach you how to navigate other worlds and make use of your powers."

"Yours was the voice I heard while I was fighting? And that's because you're Byrrus's Pontifex?"

"Indeed, I was," Tam replied.

"Okay," Will continued, "let me make sure I get this. You're saying Writers who happen to have a strong tie to Byrrus are immediately able to communicate with you? And you're supposed to teach them how to understand their abilities?"

"Essentially, yes," Tam replied. "Are you still with me?"

"I'm okay for now," Will stated, feeling mostly certain.

Tam nodded. "In essence, our communication works like a walkie-talkie. You can talk to me—and I you—at any time, and we'll hear each other. However, I can only read your mind if you want me to, and vice-versa. Privacy is the default of that ability, so I won't be invading your personal thoughts."

"That's good," Will said, relieved.

"Along with being a Pontifex, I also have an ability called Sensorship," Tam continued. "I am able to sense movements and energy, both good and bad. So, when you're in combat—"

"You can tell me what enemies are going to do," Will finished for him.

"Bingo!" Tam cried, maybe a little too enthusiastically. "Look at this kid—he knows Written lore *and* he can summon a portal and weapon on his own."

"That's me," Will replied, embracing Tam's praise. "Now, speaking of this weapon ... can you tell me more about it?" Will summoned the sword and attempted to twirl it before fumbling, the blade clattering to the ground. He blushed and picked it up hurriedly. "What happens if I pull this out in front of a Reader? Does it look like a sword? Or does it just not show up?"

"A Reader won't be able to see your weapon, or anything that originated from the Written," Tam replied. "However, being a Writer, you have the unique ability to impact both the World of the Writers and the World of the Written. If you summon your sword when you're in the World of the Writers, you can use it to fight humans. They just won't be able to see it." Tam gave Will an accusatory look. "There's a lot of power that comes with that sword. Use it wisely. Use it for good."

"Of course," Will sputtered, taken aback. "I'd never use it for the wrong reasons." He paused. "What about Characters? And Shades? How are they able to interact with the World of the Writers?"

Tam looked impressed with Will's questions. "Characters can't interact with the World of the Writers. Readers can't see us, and if we try to touch a Reader or anything in your world, we'll pass through it like ghosts. Shades, on the other hand …" Tam's face got serious. "Because their energy is so negative and chaotic, they're able to interact with the World of the Writers in a much more concrete way than Characters can. Even though they're invisible to Readers, they can still harm them. They can cause explosions, destroy buildings … you name it."

Will was shocked. "That's really dangerous! How come Characters aren't constantly in the World of the Writers, fighting Shades? How come the world isn't always on fire?"

Tam chuckled. "I'm glad you appreciate the potential ramifications. Where Shades can have more impact on the World of the Writers, Characters have more freedom. Shades can't come into the World of the Writers unless they're led there by a Writer. Even Characters who are villains can't bring them in. So, as a result, there have been very few instances of Shades being in a position to hurt Readers."

"That's good to know," Will mused. He was mulling over the information, Tam watching him calculatingly.

"I'm sorry I was late tonight," Tam muttered. "I got caught up in some stuff here. Patrolling. Research. That type of thing. Boring, really."

"It's fine. Just forced me to learn a little bit more about my new powers. Plus, I got to test out my fighting skills. That's good, right?"

"Speaking of which," Tam commented, interrupting Will's train of thought, "did you get hurt? Even a scratch?"

"No. Why?" Tam's tone made Will's stomach feel uneasy.

"Have you considered what happens to your body when you enter the World of the Written?"

Will paused, mouth slightly ajar. "Not really. I know I disappeared from my living room when I came here the first time. I figured my body just comes with me. Is that wrong?"

Tam shrugged non-committedly. "It's half wrong. When you step into Betwixt and Between, your human body is stored in limbo, not in the World of the Written, but not in the World of the Writers either. No one knows where it goes. Even so, it's safe, and your spirit, or whatever you are now, returns to your body when you re-enter the human world. Any injury you sustain in the World of the Writers—your world—will be reflected here in the Written. So, you can't come to this world to escape pain in the other one."

"Oh," Will said, blinking a few times. "Weird."

Tam relaxed a little bit, his shoulders falling. "I suppose it is a bit odd. With that being said, injuries you sustain here will only affect this body. All the same, keep in mind that if you hurt yourself while here, you'll have that injury every time you enter the World of the Written. The plus side is, even if you're not in the Written, your body will heal. So, if you don't come here for a few weeks, your body will get better on its own, barring anything too serious."

"Good to know," Will muttered. Everything made as much

sense as it could at this point. "Is there anything else I need to know tonight?"

"Not really," Tam replied, eyes bright. "I think you getting here on your own, ending up in the middle of the woods, and fighting Shades by yourself covered everything I wanted to."

"Alright," Will started. "So, what now? Can we spar a little bit?" He jumped into a fighting stance but couldn't suppress the massive yawn that escaped him.

Tam gently lowered Will's fist, face cracking into a smirk. "I don't think you're in any state to spar. I totally forgot that it's almost two in the morning. You need to sleep."

Will wanted to protest despite the fatigue swiftly taking over his body. "I guess our fated match will have to wait." Will winked. "And now that I can get here by myself, you can't avoid me."

Tam chuckled, and Will held out his hand to summon a portal.

"Wait! Will," Tam called out, his voice tense. "One more thing. I know I've said it before, but be careful. From what you've told me about that mysterious woman and your dream, the strange things that are happening seem to be targeting you. You need to be on your guard constantly."

"Oh. That reminds me."

Will rushed into an explanation of the mysterious being standing outside Peter's house. Tam's lips dipped into a scowl.

"The whole point of the Writer's Eye is to give you the power to act as a guardian for the World of the Written and the World of the Writers. As a Writer, you need to be able to protect yourself and others. We can't put off training too long." Tam sighed. "These occurrences. This mysterious figure. Your dream. They all mean something. We need to figure out what."

"What happens if I get in trouble? What if I'm attacked before I'm ready?"

Tam eyed him seriously. "You fight. You fight as hard as you can. Use your brain. Because I'm your Pontifex, if you call out to me, I'll be able to hear you—so long as you want me to." He smiled. "I've got your back."

"I appreciate that," Will replied. He turned to summon a portal once more before he was struck with another question. "I just realized … the *Byrrus* books take place over different centuries. You're from the first book Arthur wrote, but I know he wrote prequels. Do Characters from all different time periods exist in the World of the Written? Like each book has its own? Or is it only one world for the whole series?"

Tam snorted. "Your brain is all over the place, isn't it? Well, ordinarily the most recent work of an author determines which world exists in the Written. Furthermore, the world will be created in the state that the book ended. So, for example: if you have a five-book series, each time the author finishes and publishes an entry, that book's world will exist as it did at the end of the story; however, that state changes each time another book in the series is finished. So, if an author finishes a series, that book's world will exist as it did at the end of it all. In our case, however, Arthur was a Writer, so he couldn't stand the idea of us fading away when he wrote another *Byrrus* book that took place a generation later. Because of that, he decided to use his powers to keep our world alive."

"So, the world just kind of dies off when a new sequel is written? That's morbid."

"Only if the sequel has a significant time skip," Tam countered. "Either way, the World of the Written is the product of humans. We see it as the circle of life. The same way humans see aging and dying. It's natural."

"Fair enough. Goodnight, Tam." Will wasn't sure if he agreed, though he didn't want to press further. He let out another long yawn.

"Get some sleep."

Will created the portal and walked through. When he exited, he was on his front lawn. A terrified yelp came from behind him.

One of his neighbors, an older woman with frizzy hair, was staring at him, open mouthed. Her dog growled at Will.

"Hi. Hope you're having a good evening." His voice was weak.

"Don't jump out at people like that!" she scolded. "You almost gave me a heart attack!"

Will looked down, pretending to be filled with shame. "I'm sorry ma'am." He bowed lower.

Will raised his head to see the woman already walking away, talking to herself in anger. The dog craned its neck back at him, still growling. Will let off a sigh of relief—he could never let that happen again. He needed to concentrate harder when he summoned portals. No distractions.

He ducked back into the shadows and summoned a portal directly to his bedroom, just to see if he could. This time, it worked. His clock indicated three hours had passed. He put on clean pajamas and threw his muddy ones into the laundry hamper. His slippers were a lost cause.

"Bad luck with the portal. It happens to everyone at least once—just be glad it wasn't during the day."

Will yelped before turning around.

"Simon! You scared me."

Simon sat on Will's windowsill, twiddling his thumbs, wearing a gray peacoat and black pants. He looked wide awake despite the time.

"What are you doing here?"

"Just came to say hi. See how your day was. You know, the usual," Simon remarked.

"Why have I never seen you with other Characters? Why do I have to keep you a secret?" Will asked, genuinely curious.

"Maybe I'm not a Character." Simon jumped off the windowsill.

Will jumped up and instinctively summoned his new sword, the weapon appearing in a burst of white light.

Simon put his hands up in mock distress. "You scoundrel!" he cried out. "Turning a man's own weapon against him! The horror!"

"What do you want, Simon? How do I know you aren't here to hurt me? Frankly, I was going to give the sword back. Now I'm not so sure." Will crossed his arms, ignoring Simon's quips. "I really should tell Tam about you. I should let him know there's some ominous figure following me around, giving me weapons and sneaking into my room."

Simon rolled his eyes. "I would hardly call me ominous. I literally saved your life. Plus, Tam wouldn't be able to do anything. Need I remind you, you're the only person in the universe who can see me."

"So, I'm hallucinating. Great."

"You know I'm not a hallucination, Will," Simon stated flatly, rolling his eyes even harder, if that were possible. "Don't be dramatic. That's why I came here." He put one of his hands on his hips and gave an overly-enthusiastic thumbs-up. "I'm more of a spiritual guide to your journey within the World of the Written. I was born when you were and was awakened when you received the Writer's Eye."

"According to Tam, I got my powers when Arthur O'Neill died." Will's eyes narrowed. "Do you know anything about his death?"

Simon's expression darkened. "I wish I did, Will, but I don't. I can only offer you two truths. One: I feel as if I was linked to him in a past life. His name is familiar in my mouth and I feel an unquestionable sense of connection to him. And two: I can't help but feel his death and your new powers are inexplicably linked. Your Eye was awakened when he died. There must be a reason."

"Does that make you another part of Arthur's powers?" Will asked.

Simon shook his head. "My existence has nothing to do with Arthur O'Neill. I'm here because of you. I'm your Familiar."

Will raised his eyebrows.

"Have you never read or watched anything about witches?"

"Not really," Will replied.

"Well, in folklore a Familiar is a sort of supernatural being who aids witches in their magic. In your world, that's crap. There's no such thing as witches. In the World of the Written, however …" His eyes flashed dangerously. "Anything is possible."

"Are you implying I'm somehow a witch?" Will shot, feeling himself becoming warier of this conversation by the moment.

Simon's pupils were on the verge of being completely hidden. "No, but I am to you what a witch's Familiar is to a witch. I'm a part of you, and I'm here to help you in your Writer's journey. In folklore, witches are the only ones who can communicate with their Familiars. Similarly, you are the only Writer who can communicate with me. The main difference," Simon said, waving his finger, "is that not all Writers gain Familiars. You're special, Will. You're powerful."

"How do I know you're not lying? How do I know you're not some Shade or evil Character trying to kill me in my sleep?"

"Two reasons," Simon said, leaning against Will's bedroom wall.

"The first is that the sword you used today is the same one I had on me the day we met. That sword was born from your psyche, the same place I came from. I can't use it against you, and I have no other weapons. Secondly …" Simon held out an outstretched palm firmly.

Will grasped it, figuring he had nothing to lose. Warmth filled his chest. There was a sense of completeness coursing through his body, and he knew Simon wasn't lying. The two were connected.

He stared at Simon blankly, not sure of what else to say. Simon ignored the silence and put his other hand on top of Will's.

"See?" Simon grinned. "Now, Will, I do have a favor to ask of you. Help Tam find out as much about Arthur O'Neill as you possibly can. The more in tune you become with your powers as a Writer, the more I'll remember about who I am. I can feel it. I know I'm here for something; I just can't remember what."

"Do I have to do this without telling Tam about you? If having you here makes me more powerful, why can't he know?"

"If you feel like you need to tell him, you can." Simon's tone was warm. He poked Will in the forehead rather sharply.

"Hey! That hurt! Why did you do that?"

Simon flashed his teeth mischievously. "You'll know soon enough. Only good things."

The Familiar then walked toward the wall and disappeared in a flurry of colors, leaving Will with nothing but confusion and an aching face.

5

The Sword and
the Piano

The next few days passed by much too quickly. Will found himself continuously making excuses to Peter and Iris as to why he couldn't spend time with them. Most of the time he was able to chalk it up to his parents wanting him to relax and focus before the school year started, yet Iris didn't hesitate to call him out.

"I know your parents, Will. You're making them out to be way stricter than they actually are."

"Okay, fine. In all seriousness, I don't feel well," Will lied, trying to appease her. "I can't be sick the first week of school."

Every day Will went to the World of the Written to meet with Tam. They discussed different aspects of the Writer's Eye: how to fight, how to travel between worlds, how to communicate telepathically, and how to interact with different Characters. Will found it fascinating.

"You're able to slow down time to react to your enemies," Tam said one day during a sparring match. He swung his sword in a downward arc, forcing Will to sidestep the blade and counter it with his own. "The stronger the enemy, the more trouble your eyes will have keeping up with it. The better you get with your weapon—in your case a sword—the stronger your eyes will become, and you'll be able to defeat stronger enemies. If you end up fighting whatever killed Arthur, you're going to need your eyes to be as strong as possible."

Tam was an incredible swordsman. Even with the Writer's Eye slowing down the Character's movements, Will was barely able to keep up. Every move Tam made was precise, and everything he did was purposeful. Watching Tam fight with other Characters was like seeing a dancer glide across a stage.

During a break in the training, Will brought up Simon.

"Is he here right now?" Tam turned around, searching for the invisible Familiar.

"No. I've only seen him a couple times." Tam was searching around like a dog chasing its tail. Will chuckled.

"You are a lucky Writer, Will. Familiars are incredibly powerful. They're supposed to give their Writers extreme abilities and allow them to be more in tune with the World of the Written than even Characters are. Arthur certainly never had one."

"Should I be concerned?" Will asked.

"I don't think so. Familiars are rare, but there are recorded cases, and the Writer is always better for it. The real question is, why do *you* have one? I wish I could see him. Talk to him." Tam sighed.

Will felt his frustration. It was the weight of another mystery.

All too quickly summer ended, and the night before his first day of high school Will sat on his bed, counting his school supplies and feeling the anxiety and apprehension that always came before a first day. He talked to Peter and Iris earlier, and they were just as nervous. Peter charismatically blew it off—though no one bought it—while Iris went through all of her usual panics that accompanied this sort of thing. Will didn't make fun of her, but merely snorted when she showed him numerous pairs of blue shoes, asking which one would make the best first impression.

Will laid back on his bed and wondered what Tam was doing. He wanted to go train tonight.

Seriously Will, Tam said in his mind, *you can't slack off. Your other life doesn't stop just because you have the Writer's Eye. You need to think about your future!*

Tam, you don't need to worry about me. I'll be fine, Will replied, lightly brushing him off. *I didn't realize being a Writer meant I had a second dad in my head at all times.*

Good luck tomorrow. You'll do great.

Will's head hit the pillow, his eyes closed, and what felt like only a moment later, his alarm went off. He got dressed and boarded the bus that would take him to his first day of school.

Will exited the bus to a dark sky, the engine nearly drowning out the sounds of cicadas in the distance. Peter shuffled off behind him, wearing his regular get-up. Iris followed, hopping up and down on the balls of her feet, wearing a long dress that screamed, "Freshman, First Day." Her bag was slung over her shoulder and she looked at the school with excitement. Peter just looked bored.

The trio entered the mall area, which was already filled with students. The lights shined onto the cool linoleum floors, with banners advertising the Morrison Cardinals flowing from the rafters.

"Might as well get school spirit jumpstarted as soon as possible," Will observed.

Peter, Iris, and Will stood in the center of the room, looking around awkwardly. Will waved at a few people he recognized, though he was shocked by how many people he had never seen before. Iris waved to almost every person she saw, beaming with familiarity.

One of the people Will recognized was a girl named Madison Colbert, standing nearby with her usual friends. Will's first distinct memory of her was from seventh grade. Back then, she announced to the world—rather dramatically—she was finished with the name Madison and would exclusively go by May from then on. One of the boys in their class made fun of her for it, and in response she punched him in the face. Will remembered thinking it was one of the coolest things he had ever seen, though it almost got her suspended.

Two years later, not much had changed. May was about five-foot six, with long auburn hair that fell halfway down her back. It had a mesmerizing ripple effect when she walked. She always had an air of confidence about her that made it clear she knew where she belonged, and it always served her well. While May was a bit intimidating, she was also ridiculously cool.

They made eye contact, and May gave him a small, polite smile. Will blushed and looked away, embarrassed.

"You were staring at May again, weren't you?" Peter said. His eyes were closed as he leaned against a column, half asleep.

"No," Will grunted, blushing harder.

Iris wagged a finger at him. "We know you like her, Will. Just admit it." She was wearing an irritating and mischievous look.

"I don't even know her," Will grumbled. "How can I like someone I don't even know?"

"I think her blonde friend is prettier anyways," Peter countered.

Like clockwork, the first bell rang out, a bright sound that echoed throughout the hall like an electronic pulse. Will was swept up in the rush of students pushing forward into the hallways. He had English first period, and according to his map, it was at the other end of the school. He said goodbye to his friends and began his journey, alone.

Almost immediately, Will careened into another student, his textbook slipping from his hands. He deftly snatched it out of the air before it hit the ground, displaying dexterity he didn't have before meeting Tam Desmond.

"Whoops ..." Will started.

"Sorry about that," May said in a flustered tone. "Will, right?"

"No worries," Will replied, trying to come off cooler than he actually was. "May, right?"

May smiled. "Do you know where this room is?" she asked, showing Will her schedule. "I feel like an absolute moron, but my friends ditched me, and you're the only person I've seen who I recognize."

Will took the schedule and glanced at it. "It would have made more sense to go with someone you don't know. That way you can never see them again and it's no issue."

She laughed airily.

"We have the same class. I'm actually heading there right now. It's just down that way." Will pointed to a hallway about fifteen feet to their left.

"Awesome! Let's go."

As they walked, the two swapped stories about their summers, and Will made her giggle a few times over the course of their two-minute journey. At the door, May thanked him before going to claim a seat by one of her friends.

Will scanned the room for anyone he recognized. Failing, he grimaced and sat at a pod of desks in the back of the room, praying someone he knew would walk through the door.

His patience wasn't rewarded. Other than May and her friend, Will wasn't familiar with a single person in the room.

"Hey, sorry, are any of those taken?"

A boy with curly blonde hair that stuck out in every direction stood near him. His tan complexion made way for rosy cheeks, and his body seemed relaxed despite it being the first day of school.

"No. Be my guest."

"Thanks," the guy said. "Jaser Solomon. Nice to meet you."

Will shook his hand, trying not to seem too enthusiastic. "Will Morgan. Likewise."

"Are you from around here?" Jaser asked, pulling out his schedule. "My family just moved to town, and I really don't know how to navigate this school. Or talk to people, frankly." He rubbed the back of his head. "Do we have any overlap?" He handed Will the timetable.

Surprised by his forwardness, Will scanned the paper. "Yeah. We have band together during third period." Will looked up. "You play?"

"Yeah, I guess you could say I play clarinet. I'm pretty garbage at it. What do you play?"

"I've played piano ever since I was a little kid, and I started playing the trumpet in fourth grade. I'm hopefully going to be playing both in class, but we'll see, I guess."

The bell rang and Will settled into his seat and took out a notebook and pen. Their teacher introduced herself and jumped into a rant about books and language.

As she spoke, Will let his mind drift to Tam and the World

of the Written. How would knowledge of the Written affect this class? Would authors change the way they wrote if they knew they were creating real worlds? Would they make everyone always live happily ever after, or the opposite? And given that another universe existed, was Will just wasting his time in class? If he had this unique power, shouldn't he be spending every waking moment perfecting it, despite Tam's wishes for him to have a relatively normal life?

After English, Will said goodbye to Jaser and headed to geometry, which was just as boring as he initially expected—Will had never liked math. After an hour and a half of his teacher droning on about the beauty of triangles and SAT math prep, Will trekked to band class at the other end of the school. This semester was definitely going to be a workout.

He rushed into the room just as the bell rang. Other students milled about, unpacking their instruments and testing a couple notes. He made eye contact with Jaser, and the two waved at each other before Will saw what he was really searching for: a gorgeous baby grand piano, its keys uncovered, begging to be pressed.

Will slid onto the bench. He placed his hands on the piano and began to play. He wasn't sure what he was producing, apart from how it reminded him of a mix of "Rhapsody in Blue" and a Chopin piece.

Eventually, he felt a tap on his shoulder. Will found himself face-to-face with another student.

The teenager carried an air of knowing he belonged in the room and appeared to be roughly a year older than Will. He was dark-skinned and had a mildly stocky build, coupled with short black hair that was clear of his eyes as he stared down at Will. The stare wasn't menacing, but it was contemplative.

Will extended his hand. "Hey!" He tried to sound as friendly as possible. "The name is Will Morgan. It's nice to meet you."

The boy put his hand out hesitantly. "Dane. Dane Richardson." He gave Will a once over. "I guess we're both playing the piano, huh?"

"I guess so," Will responded. Dane's words sounded like a challenge.

Will scooted across the bench so Dane had room to sit. Instead of joining him, Dane pulled a stool from nearby and sat down, leaning against the piano haphazardly. Several quiet minutes floated by. Dane occasionally reached out his hand for a high five from a fellow classmate, but other than that, no words were shared. Will looked at him, warding off the defensiveness growing in his body, wanting to get a conversation rolling before the awkwardness became palpable.

"So, do you *just* play piano?"

Dane was playing a game on his cellphone now. "Nah, I play saxophone too, but piano is my primary." He looked up, showing a bit more interest. "What about you?"

"Trumpet," Will admitted. Before he could say anything else, Dane looked back at his phone, and it was painfully clear he had absolutely zero interest in talking. Will sat back on the bench and huffed. He looked around the room, and the majority of the students were shifting around in their seats, aimlessly tapping their feet. The teacher was nowhere to be found, and the students didn't seem to know what to do with themselves.

"I wonder why the teacher hasn't shown up." Dane put his phone away. "No one even knows who it is."

The door opened, and every eye in the crowded room darted toward it to see if it was their mystery band director.

"Hello, students. My name is Miss Raina Morano," said the tall blonde woman as she rushed in. "Sorry I'm late—I underestimated the traffic." She gave the room a reassuring smile, and some students began calling out to her that it was okay, and they hadn't minded waiting.

Will noticed Ms. Morano had an extremely calming effect on the entire room. Students who were being the most obnoxious before she entered were sitting in their chairs, paying attention as if their lives depended on it. Will understood—her voice was intoxicating, carrying a calculated careless air, and it was the first time in his life he could see himself having a crush on a teacher. She was strikingly beautiful. She smiled at the class once again.

"I don't have much of a lesson plan today. Just go ahead and practice on your own, get warmed up, and be ready to start full throttle next class. Okay?"

There was a resounding chorus of "yes ma'am's" from across the room, and everyone began playing on their own.

"Dane and Will, right?" Ms. Morano said, addressing the two. They nodded, and she glanced down at her notes before pointing to the back of the trumpet section. "Only one of you can be at the piano at a time. You can switch off. Dane will go first."

Will frowned and moved away from the bench, waving goodbye to Dane. He took a seat at the back of the trumpet section, thankfully behind Jaser, and took out his instrument. He ran through his scales to warm up, starting with the most basic and slowly getting more complicated. He followed up with some of the pieces he learned over the summer, trying to really get in the groove of the music. Once he was in a rhythm, Will spent the next half hour jamming out to himself, getting in a headspace that was difficult to break out of.

Will didn't notice the silence around the rest of the room until the bell rang. He fizzled out, putting his head down in embarrass-ment. Ms. Morano nodded approvingly, and Will could see Dane at the piano, silently applauding. The rest of the class made their way out for lunch. Will was about to join them when Jaser clapped him on the back.

"Dude," he said, "when you said you played trumpet, I didn't realize you could play like *that!*"

Will blushed. "Yeah," he replied, feeling anxious about this par-ticular conversation. "It's not a big deal. So, where did you and your family move from? We never got to finish our chat in English."

"My dad got a new job in the next town over, so we moved here from Kansas over the summer. Now I'm just trying to fit in," Jaser said. He shrugged. "The people here are nice, and I'm enjoying my-self so far. What about you?"

"I've lived here my entire life. Not much of an interesting story here," Will explained nonchalantly. Tam guffawed in the back of his mind.

Will and Jaser continued to talk until they made it to the caf-eteria, which was bursting with students talking to their friends and buying food that really didn't look as unappetizing as it could have. Will scanned the crowd and couldn't believe his luck when his gaze fell on Peter and Iris sitting across from each other at a window in a corner.

"Hey, if you don't have anywhere to sit, you can come chill with me and my friends. You know, if you want to," Will added hastily.

Jaser grinned. "Sure thing!" There was an extra bounce in Jaser's step as they walked over to the table where Peter and Iris were sitting.

Will introduced Jaser, and Peter and Iris said hello him, amiable as ever. Iris went back to reading her book.

"Don't start, Will. The theater troupe is doing *Dracula* for their fall production. I figured it was a good opportunity to read it."

"It's a good book," Jaser interjected. "A bunch of filmmakers made some pretty poor adaptations of it, though. I'd stick to the novel."

"I feel like there's a certain irony in watching bad movies," Iris said, putting the book down. "You can learn a lot from bad movies—bad books too."

She and Jaser jumped into conversation about the books they'd read, and Peter opened his planner and scanned the pages.

"I'm trying to be more organized this year," he said in response to Will's inquisitive look. "I'm just happy we don't really have any homework yet. It means I can keep being lazy for at least another week or so."

"Speak for yourself." Iris shoved *Dracula* into her bag. "I want to get as far ahead as possible. That way I can be lazy once all of my homework is done."

Jaser's ears perked up, and he asserted himself. "If you guys want, I made an app for my phone that takes a picture of a teacher's board and imports it into a calendar. So you don't need to write it down in a planner."

"You made an app?" Peter whistled.

Jaser blushed. "Well, yeah, kind of. A lot of the code already existed, except I made some additions so that it works for school schedules. Not super hard, honestly."

"I don't think I will code anything in my life," Peter commented. "Please send it over."

Jaser's frame relaxed as if a weight had been taken off his shoulders. He was officially part of the group.

The four spent the rest of the lunch period chatting about the mundane nature of school and when the sterile sound of the bell filled the room, they all wandered to their classes, waving goodbye to each other.

The end of the day came, and Will, Peter, and Iris rode the bus home—Jaser lived in a different direction.

The bus eventually pulled to a stop right in front of Peter's house, and the three friends got off. Peter waved goodbye as he made his way to his porch, and Iris and Will bid farewell as Will began the short walk to his house. The sound of the bus faded into the distance, and Will turned the corner to his home.

He was greeted by a small army of Shades lurking on his front lawn.

6

When Words Fade

"This doesn't make sense." Tam appeared next to Will, sword at the ready. "They shouldn't be here."

Will didn't move, the darkness of the Shades rooting him to the spot like his feet were in concrete. They didn't look particularly strong, but there were a lot of them—Will's exposure to fighting was limited, and he couldn't imagine taking this many out would be easy.

"Why are they in the World of the Writers?" he asked Tam. "I thought they couldn't get here on their own."

As soon as the Shades saw Will, they prepared for battle, moving into a triangular formation and grabbing their weapons.

Tam didn't immediately respond, instead keeping his sword poised in front of him, eyes trained on the Shades. He whirled around, putting his back to Will's.

"What?" Will yelped, sword coming to hand. He glanced around wildly, feeling the tension in Tam's shoulders.

"Maybe you need a reminder of one of our first lessons," he started. "The only way Shades can make their way into the World of the Written is if there's a Writer controlling them. That means there's a Writer near us. And if they're targeting you, it means they know you have Arthur's powers."

"And that means they might know something about Arthur's death." Will tried to keep his voice level. "If we can catch them, we can figure out what happened." He looked at the horde, and his resolve made the mass of shadows look a bit smaller. "Maybe if we take them out, we'll be able to get the person controlling them to face us themselves."

"Will? Who are you talking to?"

Will turned to see Peter and Iris standing about five feet behind him, looking confused. There he was, standing in an absurd position—if one couldn't see he was holding a sword—talking to an invisible man, preparing to fight invisible slimy ghosts brought here by another magical person.

"Tell them you're practicing for a play, or something! You need to get them out of here! If the Shades are in the World of the Writers, they may be able to hurt them!"

Will's heart sank. Even though Peter and Iris couldn't see the Shades, the Shades could absolutely see them, and could hurt them if they wanted. This was no longer just about Will—Peter and Iris were in grave danger, too.

The Character gave him a crazed look. "Just make something up!"

"Uh," Will started, "I'm thinking about auditioning for the play. So I was rehearsing some lines."

"Pretty weird place to rehearse lines, Will." Peter scratched his head. "Couldn't you do it indoors, where it's a bit cooler? And less embarrassing?"

"In front of a mirror always helps," Iris chimed in, and Will grunted, keeping an eye on the Shades.

Tam growled. "They're getting ready to charge. Just tell them to go away. Think of a better story later. We need to fight them *now*."

Will hoisted his sword. "You guys need to run. There isn't time to explain. Trust me!" And with that, Will charged at the Shades, hoping his minimal practice with the Writer's Eye was enough to handle them. As he swung his sword at the first monster, something clicked into place in Will's brain.

Go, a small voice in the back of his head said, one that sounded very much like Simon. Will connected his blade with a Shade, and his movement felt intentional, as if he gained the grace he observed in Tam. Somehow, Simon had boosted his fighting abilities. Will's mind floated back to the last time he spoke with Simon, and how the Familiar tapped his forehead, saying good things were coming— Will guessed this was Simon's gift.

Will dodged most of the Shades' blows and cut down their group by a third within the first minute or so with only a few small injuries to show for it. The Shades were mostly focusing on him, which made it easier for Tam to take them out from behind.

The momentum of the fight eventually changed, and the Shades backed away.

"Maybe they're retreating?" Will said hopefully.

"No. They're not retreating—they would have faded away instantly if that was their plan." Tam looked around. His eyes widened. "Dang it, Will … that's why. Your friends didn't run."

Peter and Iris were rooted to the spot, staring at Will. The Shades shifted their attention and began running at the two Readers, weapons poised to kill.

"No!" Will cried. "Stay away from them!"

It didn't matter—he wasn't fast enough. The Shades had too much ground on him. The one in the lead leapt into the air, sword raised over its head to strike at his friends.

"RUN!" Will screamed desperately one more time.

The Shade threw its sword directly at Iris.

At the last millisecond, Iris raised her hand and parried the blow. It took a moment for Will's eyes to adjust, but in her hand was a dagger, bright blue, glistening like a ghost in the sunlight. A moment later, Will realized it *was* a ghost, or at least partially. The dagger had an ethereal look to it. In her other hand was an old book, which had brought itself to a seemingly random page. Iris was focused directly on the Shade, and after she sliced through it, she looked at a few others approaching her. Her lips moved and the effect was instantaneous. A blast of energy radiated from the book, and a diaphanous wolf took a spot at her feet, growling and swiping at the Shades.

Iris had gained the Writer's Eye.

Another Shade launched itself at Peter, who parried the attack, a staff in his hand. When his staff made contact with the Shade's body, it sparked and burst into flame, searing the Shade until it faded away.

"Who would've thought," Tam started breathlessly, "three people with the *Potential* were all best friends?"

The Shades were outclassed and began to back away.

Peter, sensing their retreat, growled menacingly. He raised the staff over his head and twirled it. He then pointed it in the direction of the Shades, where a column of fire erupted, enveloping a large portion of them. Iris said another word, unclear to Will, that created another ethereal being from her book, this one a large cartoon bomb. It rolled over to the Shades, who looked at it, perplexed.

The bomb exploded, leaving behind a simmering pile of shadow where the last few Shades had stood. Will looked around, making sure they were all gone before letting his sword disappear. Tam wiped his brow.

"Well," Will looked to Peter and Iris, "you guys embraced that pretty easily."

His glee turned to panic when both of them began teetering on their feet. Iris's unconscious form fell into his arms. Tam stood at Peter's side, keeping the groggy teenager from falling down. Will looked around, clearing his throat and forcing a laugh—it was a relief none of his neighbors were out in their yards.

"They used a lot of power very quickly. They will need some time to recover," Tam observed.

Will shifted uncomfortably under the weight of Iris's comatose body.

"We should take them to Byrrus. We have medicine there that can help them get over the exhaustion, and it'll be better to explain what happened as they wake up." Tam sighed, resigned. "And we'll figure out what to do about all of that." He pointed to the lawn where the Shades had been. "I guess you see now why you need to train and practice with your powers."

Tam summoned a portal to Byrrus's medical bay and the two lugged Peter and Iris through, allowing the nurses to take over.

"Basically," Tam started, "another Writer knows you live in that house. I don't think they were trying to hurt you. Those Shades were way too weak."

"So, they were trying to see how I would react?" Will asked, looking out the window at the dots of people below.

"No. I think the natural reaction would be to fight. I think they were trying to test your strength. See how good you are at controlling the Writer's Eye. You should have taken more blows and let me handle them. Make them think you're a lot weaker than you really are," he joked sarcastically.

Tam put a hand to his chin, voice getting quiet. "If this really is related to Arthur's killer, then it means you're in danger. All of you." He looked at the sleeping Peter and Iris.

"Well, what now?" Will asked. "Whoever summoned those Shades knows I can control the Writer's Eye, so they probably see me as a threat."

"We'll post guards from Byrrus outside of your house, and I'll go to some other worlds to see if I can find some enchantments to protect you and your family. I should be able to find something that will stop Shades from getting through."

"Are you going to do that for us too?"

Peter sat up, coughing wildly. He looked like a man who had just come back from the dead. A nurse rushed over to him and put a cup of medicine into his hands. Peter grimaced and drank the contents of the cup. The color rushed back to his cheeks and he let out a deep sigh, clearly feeling better.

"Hi there!" Peter threw a peace sign up at Tam, his smile too wide to be genuine. "Peter Roitman. Nice to meet you. Now, I feel like I've been hit by a truck, and I'm sitting in a hospital room that doesn't look like any hospital near Alexandria, and I have a distinct memory of blasting a bunch of shadow men with a magical staff that shot fireballs. Now, Will." Peter leaned forward. "I love you, my best friend, my brother, but what is going on?"

"Seconded," a very weak voice said, and Will was relieved to see Iris was awake as well. The same nurse rushed over to offer her a cup of medicine. Iris pushed it away in protest.

Peter laughed nervously. "Take it, Iris. I don't know what was in it, but I feel eons better. Soon you'll feel like you were just hit by a truck and not thrown out of an airplane."

Iris scowled and begrudgingly took the glass. As soon as she swallowed, the color returned to her face. She sat back and put the cup down, looking at Will expectantly.

Will looked at Tam, expecting the Character to take over.

They're your friends, Tam spoke into Will's mind.

Will sighed and retold the story of the World of the Written. Peter and Iris were attentive listeners, and when Will got to how he first found himself in the World of the Written, Peter nodded.

"I knew you were off in Boston," he said, finger on his chin as if stroking an imaginary beard. "I guess this kind of proves you're not going crazy."

"Let me get this straight," Iris interrupted, putting her hands up. "You're able to see into this parallel universe where everything written down by people comes to life. You're able to do this because Arthur O'Neill, the author of a young adult book series, was supposedly murdered. Somehow, we're able to see this world as well. Now, the person who killed Arthur is trying to kill you, and since Peter and I have this Writer's Eye, they're going to try to kill us too."

"That about sums it up," Will said, rubbing his hands together, his stomach in knots.

"And," Iris continued, hands quivering in the air, "I'm able to summon a magical book, and Peter is able to use some fancy fire stick."

"It's a staff, thank you very much!" said Peter, almost comically defensive.

Tam snorted, and Will felt the tension lift slightly.

"This isn't funny!" Iris shouted, voice shaking. "Will, do you have any idea how ridiculous all of this is?"

"Of course, he does, Iris." Peter replied. "Just because it's ridiculous doesn't mean it isn't true. We have Will as proof of that." Peter gestured in Will's direction. "Like, yeah, I'm freaking out, but Will is here, right here, which proves we're not losing our minds. There's not much we can do."

Iris looked between Peter and Will, then looked at Tam, as if seeking affirmation. When he shook his head, she sighed and laid back against the headboard of her bed, grasping her temple.

"I mean," she started, "it's cool. A bit scary, but still cool. Alright …" She sat up again, folding her arms in thought. "Where do we start? How do today's events add to what we know about Arthur O'Neill's death?"

"While I appreciate the enthusiasm," Tam started, "today is not the day to dive into the mysteries that surround Arthur. We should really start with the basics. I want this to be about you two understanding your abilities and showing you Byrrus. Do you think you can do that? Act like tourists for a day?"

Peter scrambled out of bed, all signs of exhaustion gone. "I think that sounds like a great idea," he commented, stretching his arms to the sky. "I think a good stroll is the best way to get out of a funk caused by magic overload."

Iris gave an exasperated glance at Peter before standing, joining him. Tam beckoned for them to follow him out of the infirmary, as Will had several weeks ago when he first gained the Writer's Eye.

"I think this is an excellent opportunity to show all of you Byrrus. Will, I don't think you've seen much of it, right?"

"Nope," he responded. "I haven't seen anything besides the infirmary and parts of the grounds where we train. If you consider reading the castle and city's description in a book a dozen times, then yes, I've seen it, but I don't think that's what you're talking about."

Tam's face lit up like a child on Christmas. "I'll give you the grand tour."

They wandered around the grounds, and Will glanced about, trying to familiarize himself. He had read the description of the castle and the surrounding city every time he went through the novel, and every time they passed a site he knew, he pointed it out in an attempt to show he wasn't completely ignorant. Peter and Iris held back occasional laughs, admiring Will in his element, and he was pleased to see the two were both stunned and overwhelmed by the sheer majesty of Byrrus, in the best way possible. They passed through the gates of the castle and into the city, where there were a number of structures Will was familiar with. Libraries. Fountains. Bridges. Parks. Places he knew from their associated paragraphs but never a picture.

Tam vocalized the layout of the city perfectly. "Byrrus Castle is roughly at the center of it all. It's not a residence, per-say, but more of a symbol. It's where all of the ceremonial halls are, the archives of the Byrrus libraries, as well as the offices of high-ranking government officials. We also have a lot of the public services inside, such as the infirmary."

They walked down a cemented street, with buildings on both sides. Many of them looked residential, small houses in the style of cottages one would find in a story book; others looked more official, made of stone and glass.

"This is one of the Byrrus libraries," Tam said. "There are plenty throughout the city. They serve as a social space, as well as a place to learn. Our founder was a big fan of the literary, as well as bonding people through shared knowledge." He chuckled. "He also thought people would socialize over food. As a result, he built a gigantic hall for feasts right outside of the castle itself."

Will, Peter, and Iris drank in as much as they could. From the picturesque buildings, to what looked like a bustling market, to the libraries, it was everything Will could have ever imagined, and more.

Eventually, they came to a stop in front of a large statue, depicting a man burying a sword in the ground.

Tam looked at the statue thoughtfully. "And here's the man who started it all. The city, I mean."

"Sampson the Warrior," Will said immediately. "Arthur O'Neill wrote a prequel about him, right?"

"Right," Tam answered, impressed. "You've read all of the *Byrrus* books I assume?"

"We had only read *The Redstone Keep* when we met Will, but he forced us to read the rest of the series in sixth grade," Peter said. "He was pretty aggressive about it."

Will ignored him and kept walking, happy Peter didn't reveal Will blackmailed him into reading them by threatening to tell Peter's middle school crush Peter liked her. Iris snickered; she remembered the story.

"Sampson the Warrior was actually based on a different Sampson. It's a bit of Written lore." Tam grinned. "Sampson was the name of the first Character to ever be conscious of the two universes. Arthur thought it would be cool to honor him in the books."

"Interesting," Will said, genuinely curious. "Is that Sampson still alive somewhere in the Written?"

"I don't think so," Tam replied. "It's been a millennium since his story was written. He's a person that every Character knows about, but no one has seen in living memory. So, our Sampson the Warrior is the next best thing."

Tam got a sad look on his face, so Will tried to change the subject once again. "Did Arthur ever encounter other Writers? Like, is there a way to tell if someone else is a Writer?"

Tam shook his head. "You don't give off an aura or anything like that. The only real way to know is by physically seeing someone interacting with the Written. That, or have them tell you." Tam smirked. "And the odds of that are slim … I mean, do you really want to go around asking people if they have the Writer's Eye?" He sniggered in response to the look on Will's face that clearly said no.

Tam looked up at the castle as if searching through his memories. "There are millions of different universes that Writers could discover and be a part of. There's no way for any one Writer, or Character frankly, to know of other Writers. Well, I've never heard of it, but you three are proof anything is possible." He eyed Peter and Iris coolly. "The gift of the Writer's Eye is rare. You two were only able to unlock it because something from the World of the Written attacked you. Even Characters can't sense a Writer's presence unless they happen to be their Pontifex."

"Arthur, in all his years, never met another Writer?" Iris asked, raising her eyebrows.

Tam stroked his beard thoughtfully. "Arthur met one other Writer in his lifetime: his brother, Warren." Will's eyes widened as he looked at Tam, and Tam shook his head. "It's a long story, but Warren no longer has his powers or any memory of the World of the Written. It's too much to explain now." Will opened his mouth to protest until Tam's nostrils flared with a look that caused him to silence himself.

"Other than Warren, Arthur didn't hear of any others. As I said, the World of the Written is so vast that any Writers would likely not overlap. That doesn't mean the only people who know of the World of the Written are Writers. There are people who know the Written exists but can't see Characters. That comes from someone not having the *Potential*, but a Writer telling them about it." A shadow crossed Tam's face. "That's why I think Arthur was killed. Someone wanted his ability. Someone who knew of it and couldn't have it."

"You're saying he was killed out of jealousy? It seems a bit pointless, don't you think?" Peter replied.

Will jumped in. "Do you think his murderer wanted to steal his ability? If it's possible to steal it, of course."

Tam shrugged, kicking a rogue pebble with his foot. "I've never heard of something like that happening, though given how I'm a fictional character walking and talking and breathing, it would be foolish to outright reject the idea."

"Do you think what happened today gave us any hints to the identity of Arthur's killer?"

"Only a little bit," Tam replied. "It indicates that someone knows you have the Writer's Eye, which means they also know about Peter and Iris. Whoever orchestrated the attack could literally be anyone from anywhere. They're clearly able to control Shades, so it might have been a Shade who told them about you, whoever 'they' are. They could have seen you while you were in Boston, like that woman you told me about." Tam sighed. "But that could also be completely separate from Arthur's death. There's no evidence that says it was unnatural. It's just my gut telling me something is wrong." He was looking at Will, eyes seeking affirmation with a desperate shimmer. "As far as I know, Writers have never been in real danger before. Most

Characters revere their Writers, and Writers have no reason to fight. This whole thing is really strange."

Will nodded, trying to make him feel better. "Yeah, I suppose. It's not like I have anything that could possibly compare to what you're going through, though I can definitely imagine how it feels. The pain of not knowing. It seems almost worse than if you knew what actually happened."

Tam barely indicated that he heard him, lost in thought. Iris interrupted, trying to keep the conversation rolling. "Do you remember anything about the woman who seemed out of place in Boston? Something that could help us find her?"

Will groaned at the memory. "I spent so long trying to get her out of my head, pretending she didn't exist, that I barely remember anything. I know she had black hair, but I don't even remember what her voice sounded like." He let out a disgruntled moan.

"Well look at this motley crew! If I had to guess, you folks were talking about something rather depressing!"

The group turned to see an older gentleman walking toward them. He was very tall and lanky, reminding Will of a jackrabbit. He wore a red button-up coat and spoke with a very thick English accent.

"Pass Mylar, at your service."

The man gave the Writers a deep and dramatic bow. Will bowed as well, stepping on Peter's foot and urging him to do the same. Iris followed suit.

"I of course have heard all about you, Will. Forgive me for not introducing myself sooner." Pass rose from his bow, though his formal posture remained unchanged. "Now, as for you two ..." His eyes narrowed, staring at Peter and Iris, though not unkindly. "You're not from Byrrus."

"They're friends of Will's, actually," Tam chortled, rubbing the back of his head. "There was a bit of a skirmish in the World of the Writers, and these two ended up getting the Writer's Eye, if you'd believe that."

Peter and Iris introduced themselves and Pass dipped his body once again. "I suppose it's a pleasure to meet you two, despite the circumstances. I would have been suspicious before Arthur's death, seeing how rare Writers are—I think three may be the most we've ever had in Byrrus at once. All the same, given everything that's happened in the past several weeks, I doubt anything could surprise me now." He looked over the Writers once again. "With that being said, if Tam is your Pontifex, then you obviously know who I am."

There was a moment of silence after Pass finished speaking before he stopped and covered his face, embarrassed. His entire demeanor changed, and Will threw a hand over his mouth to stop a gargled cackle from escaping.

"I'm so sorry!" Pass muttered, looking away in shame. "That was arrogant and uncalled for! Ugh." He looked at Tam. "It's so hard to introduce yourself as a community's leader without seeming arrogant."

Tam saluted Pass. "Don't worry about it." He grasped Will's shoulder. "The three of them already know of you, and they know what a fantastic ruler you are."

Pass waved him away. "Don't say it like that. I hate that word: ruler. Obviously, my official title is "king," but the formality of it is irritating. It makes me feel like a bloody dictator. Which I'm not!" Pass huffed, crossing his arms across his chest. "I'm the one who handles the bills, the one who deals with policy and all of the boring garbage that people like Tam can't be bothered with. I'm just doing my job as a good Samaritan! There's nothing sovereign about it!"

Will stopped himself from snickering at Pass's accent; it was excessively strong, yet completely natural, which made it funny. The man was one of the most brilliant people in Byrrus and had the IQ of a genius. As a leader, Pass insisted on interacting with the city's residents on a personal level, dressing as closely to them as he could and sleeping in normal chambers with normal commodities. It was truly unique.

Pass rubbed his hands together thoughtfully. "So, you lot haven't experienced a true Byrrus meal yet, have you?" The question was dramatic, asked with the flair of a showman.

Peter and Iris shook their heads. Will glanced at his cell; six in the evening. He grimaced.

"As much as we'd love to," Will started, flashing his phone's time at his friends, "we should get back. Parents and stuff." He hoped his parents weren't freaking out already. He wanted to stay, except there would be uncomfortable questions if he was gone for much longer.

"No matter!" Pass exclaimed. "There's always next time. And I promise, the next time you're here, we'll have a feast!"

"Can we even eat food that's made in the World of the Written?" Iris asked.

Pass nodded enthusiastically.

"Are you sure we can't stay, Will?" Peter begged, the desire dripping into his words.

"Actually," Tam started, "regarding today's events ... I'm concerned about them going back to the World of the Writers unprotected."

"I know all about it and we've got it all taken care of, Tam. At least for now." Pass stepped aside to reveal an old man, one with more wrinkles on his face than sand in the sea. He wore a set of gray regal yet tattered robes that seemed to brim with magic. Will breathed deep and felt the mystic energy seep into his body. It made him feel both powerful and afraid.

"My name is Merlin." The old man's voice crackled with both age and the force of hundreds of years of mysticism.

"Woah," Peter exhaled tactlessly. "You mean, *the* Merlin? Like King Arthur's Merlin?"

The old man cracked a small smile. "More Merlins have been written about than there are pages in a long book, my child." His voice was quiet, yet carried an authority surprising for a man of his stature. Peter shifted a bit at being called a child, but if he was annoyed, he didn't show it. "The story I come from is an old one, so old I don't even particularly remember what it was about or where it took place."

"How sad," Iris said.

"No, my dear, that's just what happens. As stories grow old and are forgotten, their worlds fade, just like the parchment of the books they are written on turn yellow and feed the earth; our worlds fade and feed the Betwixt. Some worlds, like those of Shakespearean legend, will never fade away. Others will fade in the next hundred years or so. Such is the circle of existence." His words trailed off, his withered face losing its light.

"Merlin is a traveling wizard." Pass patted the old man on the back. "When his world faded away, he was able to escape with some of his people. They settled in Byrrus. Though Merlin usually doesn't use his magic in this world, we figured this was a special case." He beckoned to Merlin, who then stepped forward and moved his hands over Will, Peter, and Iris. A mystifying silver dust shimmered over their bodies, and as it touched Will's skin, he felt an unfamiliar power absorb into him.

"I just cast an enchantment," said Merlin, observing them attentively as if looking for side effects. "It will take hold once you return to your homes. It will make it so Shades are unable to enter. They can stand outside, as they did today, but they cannot come in to harm you or your families. That should keep you safe from those of the World of the Written. While it won't hold off Writers forever, it will buy you time to prepare to fight and for Characters to come to your aid."

"And what if they're Readers?" asked Peter.

"The spell I just cast is nothing more than a shield against the World of the Written. I can't protect you from denizens of your own realm. My magic came from humans, and therefore they are outside of my control."

"It doesn't matter," Iris declared, stepping forward confidently, and looking from Pass to Tam. "Because if a human tries to hurt us, it's going to be another Writer. And that'll be a Writer who can tell us why Arthur O'Neill was killed." She stared Tam in the eyes. "We will find out what happened to Arthur. I promise."

"I think I speak for all of us when I say we appreciate your courage," Pass said. "With that being said, let us help in any way we can. We will station guards on rotation outside of your houses, just in case anything goes awry."

Tam stomped his feet conclusively. "Good." He gave Peter and Iris purposeful looks. "You two will face Shades again. You need to be vigilant with training. You have these powers, and you need to learn how to use them. Come here, with or without Will, to practice. Understood?" The two nodded.

"Great! Glad we've got the self-defense sorted out," Pass quipped. "Now, as Will said earlier, you all need to get home before your parents worry."

"Wait, Tam. What about you?" Will shifted in place. "If some of Byrrus's guards are watching us, won't that put the city in danger? Like, you have some pretty crazy villains, and what about things from other parts of the Written?"

Tam tapped the handle of his sword. "The conflict of our world, at least what was written, is concluded. So apart from the occasional Shade, there's not a lot of action. By trade, everyone knows how to defend themselves. We're a peaceful people despite that."

This was enough for Will. He grinned, shook hands with Pass, and created a portal. He, Peter, Iris, and Tam all walked through, finding themselves at the side of Will's house, away from the view of prying eyes. The sky was only just beginning to swim with colors of twilight, and Tam looked at both Peter and Iris expectantly.

"What did you think?" he asked.

Peter bounced on the balls of his feet. "Absolutely incredible. Sure, it's confusing, but way cooler than I could have imagined. Dude, I can't believe you kept this a secret!"

"I couldn't agree more," Iris said, with a calmer tone than Peter. "However, regardless of how incredible it is, we need to start thinking of a game plan. Something to figure out what happened to Arthur."

Peter nodded. "Let's brainstorm and reconvene tomorrow. I've still got to get my parents to sign all those beginning-of-school forms. School, huh? Almost feels like there's no point. Ha! See you tomorrow, Will."

"See you tomorrow," Will said, smiling appreciatively. "Thanks for believing me, guys."

Iris giggled. "Hard not to. Now, if you'll excuse me, I have to go sleep for twelve hours."

Will waved goodbye to Peter and Iris.

He didn't have to hide anymore. No more lying to his best friends. However, as they left, Will's face fell.

"Are you okay, Will? You look kind of flushed," Tam observed.

"What did Merlin mean when he said his world faded away to feed Betwixt and Between?"

Tam looked at him, surprised, then breathed out deeply, the subject clearly bothering him. Will felt slightly guilty for asking, but his curiosity won out in the end.

"Remember, the World of the Written is based upon the World of the Writers. When you write something here, it comes to life over there." Tam's voice was casual, but there was a solemn undertone that couldn't hide beneath his coy inflection. "Well, that implies the success of the World of the Written is based upon the World of the Writers retaining stories. If a story fades from the collective memory of your society, or has all of its copies destroyed, then that world fades away in the World of the Written."

Will raised his eyebrows, flashes of nuclear bombs and fiery explosions coming to mind. Reading his thoughts, Tam gave a motion of rejection.

"No. It's subtler than that. The world doesn't explode—it literally fades away. Turns to dust. That's the best way to explain it."

"Why can't the Characters escape? You're able to fade in and out of Byrrus whenever you want. Surely they could just vanish into Betwixt and Between," Will insisted.

Tam let out a shallow breath, teetering on his feet for a moment before he opened his mouth. "A world fading away is akin to it dying. The story loses its strength. As a result, Characters lose their abilities and can't escape. The few cases where a Character was able to leave are cases like Merlin's, where a Character has some form of magic that can protect themselves and others."

"Where does the world go?" Will continued. "It can't just, you know, stop. There's so much energy and power there. It can't just go away."

"Will …" Tam began, "you need to go home. You said so yourself. Your parents are getting anxious and there's plenty of time for you to learn about this later."

Tam's hesitation caused Will's stomach to twist into knots. What was the Pontifex hiding from him?

"My parents can wait a few more minutes."

Tam looked at Will for a few seconds before reopening a pathway to Betwixt and Between.

"Are you leaving?" Will asked.

"No," Tam murmured. "I can read your thoughts. I know you're not going to drop this, so I'm showing you what you want to know. I'm taking you to a world that's about to fade. It's better if you see what happens."

Will's stomach fluttered as he found himself in the blank expanse of Betwixt and Between. As they walked through it, Will suppressed a shiver. The expanse felt desolate, yet was still filled with power drawn from the worlds it connected.

He and Tam walked for a few minutes, passing several sets of ornate doors, before they came to one that didn't look like the others.

This door was old and peeling, with loose hinges and a forlorn appearance. The wood on the door, once a dark and royal oak, was now dying and losing color. Will could feel the world was on its deathbed. He reached for the door. He had to help it. Tam held him back.

"There's nothing we can do." His voice was barely a whisper. "It's this world's time."

The door opened as if on cue, the frame shuddering as the wood splintered against an invisible wall. A slow trail of dust filtered out. At first it was the deep green of grass and trees, then the dark aquamarine of oceans, rivers, and lakes braided through it. Occasionally white bursts weaved throughout the twisting dust. The colors swirled around Will and Tam before fading into Betwixt and Between, evaporating into the realm.

"What …" Will began, but Tam put a finger to his lips, continuing to focus on the opening. Will followed suit, despite the pressure growing in his chest. Under their gaze, the dust seemed to increase its speed.

Though Will couldn't see a difference in the color of the dust, it's what he *heard* that made all the difference. Human voices moaned and cried as their souls slipped through the doorway. Will choked up, overwrought with the emotions passing by him.

Tam put a hand over his own chest and closed his eyes, as though he were praying. Will watched as the Characters of the world faded into the air; however, unlike the chill of the trees and clouds, the souls of the Characters were completely gone. They didn't hover around the two like phantoms. Wherever the Characters went, it was not Betwixt and Between.

Eventually, the flow of dust stopped entirely, and the splinters of the door crumbled away. Will was left staring at a blank space.

He turned to Tam, the Character's eyes overrun with tears.

"Characters don't die because of old age; we're immortal, in that way. However, we can fade away. That's what awaits us all."

"And Betwixt and Between?" Will pleaded, still horrified. He looked around, feeling like he was being watched by every soul that just disappeared into the air.

Tam gave him a sad look, then spoke a truth Will already concluded despite his best false hopes.

"Betwixt and Between is made up of the essence of every universe that has ever faded from the World of the Written."

7

Sampson the Warrior

Will walked in his front door, his mind still reeling from what he had seen. Tam described it as something normal—a natural process every Character acknowledged they had a chance of experiencing. He explained Betwixt and Between was not made of the souls of Characters, but merely their worlds; their souls went somewhere unknown. That didn't make the passageway's true nature any less unsettling to Will.

His thoughts were interrupted by the sound of his parents cooking dinner. Will took his shoes off and began sneaking upstairs, hoping to avoid human interaction.

"Will," his father yelled, "come to the kitchen."

Will obliged.

"Where were you?" Emery insisted. "Why didn't you call us back?"

"I was in town with Peter and didn't hear my phone," Will said. "We were just walking around talking about our first day back. Which, by the way, was just swell."

Emery tried to keep a dark expression for a few moments before his seriousness broke. He scratched his head and gave Will another stern look. "You better not use your friends as an excuse to let your grades slip. And next time, call if you are going to be late. That's why we gave you a cell. Now sit down and eat."

Will begrudgingly followed his father's orders and sat at the kitchen table. It was a relaxed affair: macaroni and cheese with roast beef sandwiches. His parents asked him about the first day of school, though there wasn't much to discuss. Will put on his best acting performance, trying to keep his emotions in check. His parents picked up on negativity like hawks sensing a wounded mouse.

As soon as he was able, Will excused himself from the dinner table. He couldn't even imagine talking to his parents about Betwixt and Between, let alone the fact he just witnessed a mass annihilation. Thankfully, his acting skills were on point—his parents bid him goodnight, and Will kept a full-toothed grin until his bedroom door closed.

That night, Will's dream started with school, girls, and an outlandish scenario in which Dane Richardson played a piano concert wearing a shark onesie. Eventually, the dream changed. Will was back in Byrrus, in a windowless room lit only by torches. Everything in the room was made of heavy stone and the walls were covered in tapestries and paintings. There was the occasional statue or suit of armor, with a few shields and swords immortalized on plaques. It had to be the Hall of Heroes—a cathedral where all of the past heroes of Byrrus were honored.

A giant tapestry of Sampson the Warrior was hung on a prominent wall. The tapestry actually existed in Byrrus; Will had read about it many times. It stood as a testament to the founder of the city and residents viewed it as a type of religious relic.

Will took his time marveling at the intricacies of the portrait, the fine golden threads interspersed with the once-vibrant shades of a rainbow of colors. At one point there was a rustle to his right. Will turned and standing next to him was an older man wearing a deep forest green habit, something Will imagined a medieval monk would don. Though his face showed wrinkles, the man stood straight, and Will could tell he was in fairly good shape, with the athletic build of a grizzled warrior. The man stared at the tapestry of Sampson, a curiosity in his eyes Will took to be reminiscence.

"Sampson?" he asked, not sure why the thought crossed his mind.

"Do you think there's such a thing as evil, Will?"

"I'm sorry?" Will voiced. He was unsure if the man had actually spoken.

"What makes something evil?" the man asked, eyes unmoving.

"I'm not sure," Will stammered, taken aback. "Something immoral?"

The man was quiet for a few moments. "Interesting answer," he observed. "Not quite correct, but not quite wrong either. There are things going on here that have never happened in the Written before. Bigger than you. Bigger than Tam." His eyes remained focused on the tapestry. "Arthur O'Neill understood it; however, he didn't have time to stop it. Now that responsibility has fallen to you." The man took a step back and put his hand to his head.

Will moved forward. "Sir? Are you okay?"

"You think you're weak. You think because you received your gift from Arthur O'Neill, you don't deserve the ability to see into the World of the Written."

Will paused, mouth hanging open. How did Sampson know that?

"Don't believe those foolish thoughts that diminish who you are," Sampson groaned, grimacing in pain. "You may have gotten part of your gift from Arthur, but that just makes you more powerful. You are the only Writer who has the power to finish what Arthur started. Stop them! Beware of she who lies! She isn't who she says she is!"

"I don't understand! Stop who? The people who killed Arthur? Who is she? Did she kill him?"

Sampson's face got a tired, blank look, and Will could tell he was fading fast.

"There are many realms within the World of the Written. Two of them are more important to you than the rest. The first is Byrrus. The second is one not so different from your own world. When you hear the voice calling for help, help him."

"What voice?" Will cried out desperately.

Sampson let out a heavy, shaky breath. "I can't tell you, Will. My view of the future is in blurry outlines and shadows. I barely have the strength to hold my appearance, and even that is waning." Sampson clutched his chest again, his face in agony. "I don't know when the voice will call out. It could be in a few days. It could be in a few years. Nonetheless, when it calls, you must help, and you'll be that much closer to saving the world in which you live."

"What do you mean?" Will insisted, trying to reach out to him despite his inability to move. "What's going on? And how did Arthur discover it?"

Sampson's image flickered like a dying candle. "Help comes from unexpected places, Will. The *Potential* exists in many people. Don't be afraid to trust. Just remember, sometimes you don't have a choice but to trust people … even though every person you trust earns the thing you want to keep out of the hands of your enemies."

"What is that?" Will probed. To his surprise, Sampson answered.

"I just told you Will. Trust. The power to destroy you."

Will swallowed hard. "If you want to help me, stop talking in riddles! Please!" He grasped Sampson's shoulder.

The warrior radiated power into Will like heat from a furnace. "One last thing. There will come a time when you feel abandoned and like you have to die to protect your friends. You don't. The thing that makes you more powerful than other Writers is that I am always with you."

The man flickered out.

"SAMPSON!" Will screamed.

Footsteps crashed up the stairs and his father threw the door open, eyes wild and mouth agape in panic.

"Will! Are you alright?" He rushed to the side of Will's bed and helped him sit up, and Will covered his face with his hands, flexing his shoulders to stop himself from quivering.

"I'm fine," he lied. "Just a bad dream. Sorry. Go back to sleep." Will glanced at the soldier standing behind his father. "Really, I'm okay."

Will fixed the warrior with an appreciative gaze, and he saluted before leaving the room.

"If you need anything, I'm right downstairs." Emery gave Will a quick hug. "And Will, who is Sampson?"

Will was too scared to come up with something convincing, and everything Sampson said was melding together into a jumbled mess.

"No idea. Is that what I was shouting when I woke up? Bizarre. I promise, Dad, I'm okay. Go back to bed." He had to get his father out of the room before he forgot something important.

Emery gave him a doubtful look before shutting the door gently.

The instant he was gone, Will jumped to his desk, grabbing a pen and paper.

"Help the voice," Will muttered to himself, writing it down. "The power to destroy me," he added to the list, his words twisting together in panicked scrawl. "Two important realms?" Will paused, not sure if that was what Sampson actually said. After a few more moments of racking his brain, he couldn't think of anything else.

Tam? He thought, reaching out to his Pontifex. A voice crackled to life in the back of Will's head.

Will? It's so late. Are you okay?

Will briefly explained his dream, hoping Tam could shed some light on what it meant. When he finished, there was no response.

Tam? Are you there?

Yeah. I'm here. I'm not sure what it means. Sampson, in the stories at least, came to denizens of Byrrus in dreams if he ever needed to pass on information. I've never heard of it actually happening in the World of the Written, let alone the World of the Writers.

Maybe it's because I have Arthur's powers? Will suggested.

Maybe, Tam muttered, *but then why didn't Sampson ever go to Arthur? Warn him he was going to be killed?*

Will had no response. *As to what Sampson said,* he thought, trying to move away from Arthur, regardless of the importance, *I have no clue what it meant. Do you have any insights? He mentioned some woman who lies, which I can only assume is the woman I met in Boston, so I guess that confirms our theory she was involved in Arthur's death?*

Well, even if you're right, it doesn't necessarily help us. We were already assuming that. We're no closer to figuring out who she is. If she is even a she. If they were powerful enough to kill Arthur, they might be able to shape-shift. *Or split in two. If you take into account every evil thing that lives in the Written, anything is possible.*

You're right, Will groaned, his head beginning to hurt. *So, I guess proceed with caution and scour police reports or something to see if we come up with any leads.*

That sums it up, for now.

Tam, Sampson also said my world is in danger. What do you think he meant?

It's too soon to tell, the Character commented. His voice went silent for a moment, hesitating. *As far as I'm aware, no major political figures in your world have the Writer's Eye. That much I'd know. Plus, I can't think of any Shade or Character who has enough power to affect the Writer's world to the level Sampson is suggesting.*

Will sighed. *Any idea what Sampson meant by that voice calling for help? And what he meant by him always being with me?*

No, Tam replied firmly. *And from what it sounded like, it won't matter for some time.*

Will yawned.

I don't think either of us are going to have any revelations about this subject at three in the morning, I think you should get some sleep.

Will attempted to argue, but his heart wasn't in it. He yawned again, grumbling. *Night Tam.*

The Character chuckled before his voice clicked off, and Will was left with a sense of awkwardness, as if he had just hung up a telephone in his mind. He headed back to bed and slept, his dreams filled with images of women in black and dead authors throwing books.

The next day started as a normal school day where Will actively did not pay attention. In English, he distractedly wrote down what he could remember from his dream with Sampson, scrawling the words out in different orders to see if there was some hidden poetic meaning he was missing. Jaser kicked him multiple times, reminding him they were in class. Will shifted back to the textbook, pretending to read through a Kafka passage.

Having decided he couldn't do anything about Arthur O'Neill until later in the day, Will resigned himself to paying attention to his teachers. At the end of biology, Iris and Will met up with Peter and dragged him behind the school, where the three of them faded into the World of the Written. Will tried to ignore the feeling of being watched by all the forgotten Characters as they ventured through Betwixt and Between.

They emerged into the bright afternoon light of Byrrus, where Tam sat on the ground, legs crossed and waiting. He wore a t-shirt, shorts, and sandals, making him look more like a suburban dad than a medieval warrior. He called out to the group upon seeing them.

"I figured it'd be best to talk about this somewhere private. No need to bother the entirety of Byrrus with hypotheses about their creator's murder."

Tam led them to a small building near the castle's entrance. Will was surprised to find the interior looked like a modern-day conference room.

"Interior design does wonders. We even had Merlin cast a spell that gives some of the buildings air conditioning," Tam announced proudly.

They sat at a wooden table near the center of the room, and Iris rummaged around in her backpack and pulled out a thick folder.

"So," she began, "I took the liberty of printing off as many news articles about Arthur O'Neill as I could. All of them focus on either right after his death, or a few weeks before." She grimaced. "The ones before his death were a bit sparse. The guy didn't seem to love media attention."

"Most authors just don't have that powerful of a media presence," Will murmured. "Tell me how many writers you know who have true celebrity status."

Iris wasn't deterred. "I figured we could go through these articles, and some obituaries I printed off, to see if we find anything. Witnesses who might know what happened. Names Tam recognizes. Family members. Something."

"Nice work Iris," Tam said.

Iris divided the papers among the four friends.

Unfortunately, after an hour of reading endless pages of material, Will found nothing of interest. He looked up from his stack, hoping the others were more successful; unfortunately, they were all wearing his same disgruntled and frustrated look.

"I found an article from a creepy fan site that says he bought oranges a week before his death," Peter said, trying to sound positive. "Maybe his murderer was at the supermarket?"

"It wasn't a supermarket," Tam muttered, sighing. "Arthur bought all of his fruit from a bodega near his apartment. The owner's name is George. They were friends."

A gloom passed over the room, and Peter looked at Iris, rubbing the back of his neck.

"Thanks for the work, Iris, but are you sure you found everything?"

"I thought so, but I can keep looking," she said. "There has to be something I missed."

Tam shook his head. "Don't bother. It was worth trying, but we were just fooling ourselves. If he really was killed by magical forces, then there aren't going to be helpful hints in obituaries written by Readers."

Will closed his eyes and leaned back, his mind searching for answers.

"I need to take a walk," Peter announced, stretching and groaning. "I'm not doing any sort of productive thinking while being stuck inside."

"I'll join you," Iris said. "I kind of want to explore, anyways. Get a better feel for the city. Is that okay, Tam?"

"Byrrus is your oyster. Enjoy," Tam said, giving an enthusiastic motion to the door.

"Great! We'll meet back up with you in an hour."

"We'll be here," Will called out absentmindedly, still staring at the papers on the table, deep in thought. He picked up a news article, scanning it before crumpling it up and throwing it to the side of the room. He glanced at Tam, who shrugged.

"Maybe they have the right idea," Will suggested.

They stood and walked to a nearby pond. Will spied a few pebbles and attempted to skip stones.

Eventually, the two heard footsteps approaching them from behind before the now-familiar voice of Pass Mylar filled the air with an encouraging cheerfulness.

"You chaps look a bit bummed out." Pass sat next to Will.

"Just confused, Pass. We just spent an hour going through news reports and obituaries that could've given a hint to what happened to Arthur, and came up completely empty," Tam said. "We have Characters and Writers looking for information, and no one can find anything."

"Sampson the Warrior also pretty much confirmed there's some woman who's trying to kill me," Will mused, staring at the water. "In a dream," he added, as if the add-on would make the sentence any more logical.

"Sampson appeared to you? In a dream? Interesting." Pass put his hand to his chin, eyes trained on Will expectantly.

Will proceeded to tell Pass about the dream and what Sampson told him.

Pass placed a hand on his shoulder, and Will was strangely reminded of his own father. "Lad, this is all part of the journey. I know it may seem scary, but if Sampson the Warrior came to you in a dream, then that means there's something special about you."

"What does that mean?" Will asked. "You'd think that if the ghost of some powerful Character came to me in a dream, he would offer some words of advice or tips on how to move forward, not cryptic riddles."

"Sampson works in mysterious ways." Pass's eyes hadn't moved from Will's face. "It's like a prophecy. If he came to you in a dream, he gave you as much information as he was able to. He doesn't do that lightly." Pass sighed. "In the *Byrrus* stories, Sampson would come to people in their times of need. He only did that for those who were truly powerful or important. That means his spirit, whatever that may be, trusts you. Besides, aren't all characters like him supposed to be cryptic? Don't they all say things that don't make sense until they do?"

"What I do find odd," Tam commented, "is that Sampson the Warrior was speaking about the devastation of the World of the Writers *and* the World of the Written. Powerful as he may be, I can't imagine his power has that much scope."

"You always say you think Arthur was murdered for his Writer's Eye. If Arthur was powerful enough to be murdered because of it, then it's possible his most powerful Character could have the power to predict the end of the whole world," Pass observed.

"Not the most powerful," Will said, thinking hard. "Oldest age-wise, absolutely. Most powerful…" He trailed off, and Tam squinted his eyes thoughtfully.

"It's possible that Sampson's age has allowed his spirit to gain more power and foresight. I'm sure there are other Characters in the World of the Written who are the same way—they just haven't appeared to you because you don't have connections to them."

Will grumbled. "This is fun. Got to love predictions about the end of the world."

"I think in these troublesome times, we can't do much except hope and keep a positive attitude." Pass placed his hands on his hips. "With that being said, why don't we have a feast? To celebrate Will, Peter, and Iris? Byrrus has never had three Writers in its midst at once."

"Do you have enough time?" Will asked. "I don't want the cooks to go through too much trouble."

Tam and Pass looked at each other in unison and grinned like children.

Pass brushed Will's complaint off. "Lad, Byrrus's cooks live for feasts. The last thing we want to hear is you feeling guilty about us cooking. Now you just sit here for an hour, and when dinner rolls around, you'll have the best meal you've ever had!"

Pass scampered off, looking more like a jackrabbit than ever before. Tam laughed to himself, and his look of contentment made Will feel better.

"You'd think he would be less excited after the countless feasts he's thrown," Tam disclosed. "Just wait until you have the food! Any description you could have read in the book is nothing to the real thing."

Will's phone buzzed in his pocket. "It's my dad." Hesitant, Will answered the call and put the device up to his ear.

"Hello?"

"Hey Will," his father said. "I just got home. Where are you?"

Will's brain froze, not sure of what to do. Throwing his gaze about, his eyes landed on the pond. "I went to the park with Peter and Iris."

His father was silent for a moment before responding, agitation spiking in his tone. "All right, sounds good. Tell me next time so I don't worry. When are you going to be back?"

"Um," he began, "probably around 7:30. We're going to go to dinner in town afterwards."

"Alright ... see you then."

Will ended the call.

"How does this even work?" Will asked Tam, holding up his phone. "I'm not even on Earth, am I?"

Tam chuckled. "In relation to Earth, I have no idea where we are. Technology from the World of the Writers has always worked in both places. Think about backwards compatibility. Humans made the Written, so your technology works here. The reverse is only true if it's something that belongs to a Writer, like your sword."

"That's really good to know," Will commented. He lied back on the grass, feeling the late summer heat fall onto his body. He and Tam spent the next hour talking about the two worlds, Byrrus, and Will's own experiences in Alexandria, and Will was glad to see Tam looked happier, though there was still pain in his eyes and mind.

They were interrupted by the bell in the clock tower letting off a loud chime, signaling dinner was about to be served. Tam and Will walked into the long, wide dining hall, and what met Will's eyes caused his mouth to water.

Long mahogany tables lined the building, each one large enough to fit at least ten people. The room itself could have fit at least a thousand Byrrus residents—more if they squeezed in. The ceilings were high, stretching up several stories, sound echoing through the building up to the roof. The tables were littered with every kind of food imaginable, from salads and steaks to bread lathered in every type of topping one could dream up. Will's stomach grumbled, and Peter and Iris walked up behind him, their expressions the same as his.

"This is freaking incredible," Peter stated.

Will and Iris nodded silently. The three friends sat at the nearest table and piled food onto their plates, stuffing it into their mouths at a breakneck pace. Tam sat with them, taking small bites of a steak, chewing thoughtfully. Pass slid onto the bench next to Will, clapping the teen's shoulder with a hearty sigh.

"So, what do you think?"

"Ish amashing," Will choked out, mouth overstuffed. He swallowed then repeated himself. "It's amazing. Better than anything I've ever had in my world."

Peter agreed with dramatized motions, not bothering to swallow his food. Even Iris had to slow down, putting a hand over her mouth as she realized how much bread she had attempted to eat at once.

"Very good. Very good. Now, if you'll excuse me," Pass said.

Will watched the ruler of Byrrus talk and joke with all the Characters he saw. He even addressed all of them by name. "He really is a good leader," Will said.

"The best there ever was. There are so few rulers who would actually take the time to talk to their people individually. It's why Byrrus is such an effectively run city," Tam maintained.

A small boy approached their table.

"Um, excuse me. You're a Writer, right? Do you have to go to school?" he asked Will.

"Yes," Peter jumped in, sounding frustrated. "Even in the Writer's world, we still have to learn."

The boy immediately frowned. "Darn. I was hoping if I went back with you, I would get out of going." The boy sulked back to his table.

Will silently grimaced at the fact he had school tomorrow. He was glad he had finished all of his homework at lunch.

"So, you're Will, huh?"

He turned to find a woman standing behind him, hair done up in a ponytail, wearing a leather hunting jacket and boots. She had silver earrings that were shaped like daggers, matching an aggressive hunting knife looped through her belt. Her presence made his arm hair stand on end, and Will couldn't tell if he was caught off guard because she was beautiful, or because she was intimidating. In all honesty, it was probably both. Will was struggling to come up with a response when he was saved by Tam.

"Hey, Amelia."

"You're Amelia Brown! You were one of the other protagonists of *The Redstone Keep*!" The name struck a chord with Will.

She blinked at him, not unkindly, yet analyzing him nonetheless. "I feel like you have something else you want to ask."

Will blushed, frustrated his face was clearly so revealing. "Um, yeah. Can you actually see the future?"

In *The Redstone Keep*, Amelia had a gift where she was able to see the future in quick glimpses. The flash of a sword here, or the silhouette of a person there. The origin of her ability was a mystery until it was later discovered her great grandmother had been a seer.

"I can, though it's less useful than you would think." Amelia gave a bemused smile and scratched her temple. "And I wouldn't call myself much of a protagonist. I helped Tam not get himself killed fighting Daegan. I'm nothing more than a support character—at least in the story Arthur wrote."

"Please. You're much more than that," Tam interjected.

"I'm fully aware, Tam Desmond," she stated, chuckling at him in a mocking yet loving way. "Arthur wrote me that way in the story, but you know I could take you down at any time."

Her words sparked a look in Tam's eyes, an anomalous combination of irritation and excitement, like he wanted nothing more than to spar with her. Instead he just sputtered a bit, struggling to come up with a comeback.

"Nice to meet you, Will," Amelia said politely. She then walked away, though not before smirking at Tam's reaction. The Pontifex watched her retreating figure.

Will wanted to make fun of Tam when his thoughts were interrupted by another tap on his shoulder. He turned and ended up face-to-face with a boy about his age, if not a bit older. He was burly, a little shorter than Will, with messy yet stylish hair. He looked pretty cheerful and reached out his hand. "Matteo Gavin," he said.

Will shook his hand. He recognized Matteo's name as the primary strategist in *The Redstone Keep* who, alongside Tam, helped create all of the plans that eventually took Daegan down.

"Nice to meet you," Will replied.

Matteo nodded curtly, though his facial expression was warm. "I just wanted to say hey. I've always thought the idea of the World of the Writers was fascinating, except I've never met another Writer besides Arthur, and he, well, *created* me."

Will could appreciate the curiosity. "Yeah. It's kind of crazy for me too. A few weeks ago I found out my favorite book series is real."

"I'm sure we'll talk more as you learn more about Byrrus," he stated, shoulders relaxed. "I do a lot of combat strategy work for Pass," Matteo leaned in and whispered, "and if you're trying to do anything even remotely sneaky, I'm your man."

"I'll be sure to let you know," Will replied, grateful for the offer.

Matteo winked and walked away.

"What was that about?" Peter asked.

"Just normal introductions," Will responded. He wasn't particularly bothered by it. Matteo seemed like a nice guy, and his offer to help was reassuring.

The rest of the night passed in a sea of joy and carefree ease, and when Will's phone alarm went off at 7:30, he couldn't help but feel agitation shoot through his body.

"Time to go," he muttered to Peter and Iris.

"Yeah, I have to finish my bio homework," Iris moaned, eyeing a dish of custard hungrily. Peter grumbled something about math. Will thought of school the next day—he chose to ignore both it, and his father.

"You two head out without me, I'll see you tomorrow," he said.

The two agreed nonchalantly, waving goodbye to everyone and creating their own portals. Will shook hands with Pass and walked outside, Tam following him. The moon was up, casting a misty glow on the pond. Will snickered at Tam.

"What?" he demanded, and Will turned around to face him.

"That woman, Amelia. You like her!"

Tam's face blushed a beet red. "No, I don't! That's ridiculous! She's just a friend, nothing more."

"Yeah, and that's why you kept looking at her the way you did." Will grinned. He certainly wasn't the suavest when it came to crushes, and judging Tam's reaction to Amelia, Tam wasn't particularly talented either.

"I mean, I wanted you two to end up together at the end of *The Redstone Keep*," he mused. "I don't know why you didn't. I figured it was one of those things where it was implied, you know?"

"Well it certainly wasn't," Tam stated haughtily, crossing his arms. "We were not meant to end up together, nor do either of us want to."

"Is that so?" Will gave him a look, trying to read his mind.

"Don't try to read my mind, Will! You know you can't force me to let you in."

"Sorry," Will said, though he wasn't sorry at all. "So … what Sampson said about me being more powerful than other Writers … did Arthur have any other powers? You know, like invisibility, or control over wind?"

Tam grimaced. "No. He was extremely talented with words, though that was just on written paper. As a Writer I never noticed anything. Then again," Tam sighed, "Arthur never had any real reason to use his power to its full extent."

The conversation was interrupted by Will's phone. It was an angry text message from his father demanding to know his location.

Will waved. "I'll see you tomorrow." He looked back and saw Tam was shaking his head.

"What's wrong?" Will asked, and Tam dipped his shoulders, though only a fraction of an inch.

"It's nothing," he said. "It's just that Arthur's funeral is tomorrow. His family held off until all of the investigation stuff was over. I'm going to go. It's in Boston."

"Alright then. Let me know if you want to talk or anything."

Will wasn't sure what else to say, so he summoned the portal and walked through.

"I don't like her!" Tam shouted.

Will let off an overly enthusiastic howl of amusement. "I don't believe you!" he called back, and when he exited the portal, he was in the shadows near the front door of his house. He walked in, hoping he looked and sounded inconspicuous.

"You're late."

Will grimaced. "Sorry. I was … uh …" his mind searched around desperately, and he heard himself say, "Just taking a bit of a walk. I wanted to think."

Ruth walked in, wiping her hands on a towel. "Anything wrong?" she asked.

"Nope! Everything is great, Mom! More than great!"

Her face was downcast, and she took a step forward, only a foot away from Will. He braced himself for the inevitable question.

"Are you okay, Will? Are you sure there's nothing going on?"

"Yes," Will insisted, trying to time his words so they weren't too quick. "Everything is great, I promise."

Will stared his mother and father in the eyes, not blinking or smiling. Though they were seemingly dissatisfied with his response, both were unwilling to pursue it further.

"Don't make us ground you, Will," Emery warned. "We

don't want to. All the same, we will. You're not going to become a degenerate."

Will gulped and nodded. Was there anything else he could really do in this situation? His parents walked away, and though Will was nervous about the lies, he acknowledged telling the truth in this situation could put them in danger—that, or they would freak out and have him tested for a brain tumor.

He went upstairs to get ready for school the next day. He opened his closet and found the suit his mom bought for him at the beginning of the year.

"Looks like I'm going back to Boston," he muttered to himself, sitting down to get as far ahead on homework as he possibly could.

8

The Funeral

The next morning, Will plopped down in English, saying hello to Jaser. May walked in with her friends and smiled at him.

"How's it going, Will?" she asked as she passed.

"Good!" he stammered to her retreating figure. *Was she being sarcastic? It seemed like she was being genuine. Maybe she was just being nice for the sake of being nice?*

"Girls are so freaking weird," Jaser muttered, as though reading Will's mind.

During class, Will did a bit of digging and found out Arthur's funeral was at 5:00 p.m. at a church a little outside of Boston. The website had a small label stating the funeral was closed to everyone but family and close friends. Will had no idea how he was going to get in, considering he didn't fall into either of those categories, but he sensed it was worth the risk. Tam and the other denizens of Byrrus would likely be too distraught to do any sort of investigating; Will wouldn't be. Even though Arthur was Will's favorite author and all, he didn't know him the way the Characters did. And what if the killer was at the funeral? He had to go.

Will feigned interest in class until he got to band. He was on piano today and the music they were playing was fairly easy, and he was able to let his fingers move on their own, his mind elsewhere.

One of the pieces was a mournful, slow ballad that sounded like it belonged in a movie during a scene where the main character died. Ms. Morano explained it was a piece written by the composer in honor of a friend's daughter who had passed away unexpectedly. The piece's tone matched the occasion for which it was written, and when Will played it, he tried to pull out as much emotion as possible.

For the band's first concert in November, there were two songs with piano solos. Dane and Will had a brief discussion that ended with Will getting the mournful piece, which was what he wanted in the first place. Something about its slow and sad melancholic tune made it more entertaining than the alternative, which was fast-pace and high-strung. So far, Will hadn't been able to get the pace he wanted to flow through his fingers. Every time he played, it felt too hard or too unmalleable. Today he had an idea of how to make it work.

While playing, Will took a moment to try and speak to Tam. He couldn't read the Pontifex's thoughts, and it was clear Tam didn't have the channel of communication open. This was understandable; no one wanted unfettered access to their mind, especially on a day like today. However, even though Will couldn't hear Tam's thoughts, he could feel Tam's emotions: longing. Grief.

Will used Tam's sadness to his advantage. As the band approached his solo, he found his mental persona nudging the block aside, just enough to allow some of Tam's feelings to leak through. The band reached Will's solo, and he gave it one good push, knocking the barrier open just a tiny bit more.

The pain was overwhelming.

Will coughed, and his chest heaved. He had never experienced pain like this; it was as if every part of his body was breaking, and

Will could feel his mind screaming, wanting to reach a hand into his chest and wrench his heart out, knowing the pain of crushing his feelings away would be only a fraction of the torture this life brought him.

And that was only a whisper of Tam's agony.

Gulping, Will kept the door cracked and continued playing, forcing himself to embrace Tam Desmond's torture in order to turn it into something beautiful. His hands brushed over the piano's keys in a way that felt *right*. They pressed the keys, the weight falling with the exact strength Will desired, and he allowed the melody to flow over his entire body, letting itself into the room. The pain of playing was almost excruciating, and Will now knew this was exactly what the composer intended—to bring the pain of losing someone to life. To be felt through sound. Conversely, he wanted it to be an outlet, a relief. It was a moment of comradery in misery between both the player and the listener.

Will's solo slowly came to an end, along with the rest of the piece, and he let the last few notes ring out over the silence. Ms. Morano had cut the band off by the time Will let the notes end, but he didn't care. Those notes were for Tam. Those notes were for Arthur.

"Thank you," Tam whispered, sitting next to Will. Will hadn't heard him appear, but he felt Tam grip his shoulder tightly before disappearing again. Will closed the door within his mind, and the feelings of sadness faded until they were a scar that had several weeks to heal.

"That's ... something else."

"I respect the commitment."

Will's ears perked up. At first, his heart swelled with pride. It then came crashing down when other comments reached him.

"Dude, he *cried*. Are you joking?"

"That's just ... *so* much."

"How embarrassing."

Will put his hands to his face, and realized his cheeks were indeed wet with tears. Using his shirt, he desperately wiped at his face. Will looked up uncomfortably. Ms. Morano was staring at him, her face a mixture of confusion and concern.

"Sorry," he started, his voice tight, "could I be excused for a moment?"

Will stood and walked out of the room, not waiting for a response. Once he made it to the hallway he slid to the floor, put his face in his hands and took a few steady breaths.

"You okay, Will?"

May sat against the opposite wall ten feet away from him. Her eyes were red and puffy, and Will laughed awkwardly.

"I should be asking you the same question. I'm all right. Just got a bit emotional at a song we played. Kind of embarrassing."

May shrugged weakly. "We were reading *King Lear* by Shakespeare and we got to the end where Cordelia is hung. It was awful. I couldn't really keep it in."

"That's a much better reason to cry than a piano solo." Will wiped his eyes again.

May chuckled, hiccupping. "The crying wasn't really from the play. Someone I really cared about died recently, and his funeral is today, so I think the sadness of the scene got away from me."

"I'm in a ... sort of similar situation, believe it or not," Will said. "My favorite author died a few weeks ago, and his funeral is today. He had a lot of influence on me, so it just kind of hit me. Stupid, I know."

"Arthur O'Neill?" May replied, looking at him strangely. Will nodded, and she gave a light snort, both shocked and pleased. "No way. Small world. Who would've thought our high school would have two people crying about the same author on the same day at the same time?"

They looked at each other for a minute before they began to laugh, some of the tension disappearing. "I didn't take you for a medieval fantasy fan," Will said, and she giggled.

"I'm a storyteller. A theater person. I have to be able to appreciate the genre." Her eyes looked less sad now. "Well, cool. Most people haven't read Arthur O'Neill's books. It's neat to meet someone who cares so much about him."

There was a moment of silence, one where Will wasn't really sure how to respond. May opened her mouth to say something when the door to the band room opened. To Will's surprise, Ms. Morano walked into the hallway.

May glanced at Ms. Morano. "I should get back to class. I'll see you tomorrow, Will. Chin up." She retreated to the back door of the theater.

Will stood and faced Ms. Morano, prepared to apologize.

"Before you say anything," she started, "I wanted to tell you that was some of the finest piano playing I've ever heard in my life. You made *me* want to cry."

"Definitely one of my more embarrassing moments," Will muttered.

Ms. Morano gave him a frustrated look, very unlike her usual persona. "Never apologize for letting emotion take control of your music. Yes, you cried. Was it embarrassing? It shouldn't have been. Because your crying led to some of the most explicit musical talent I've ever seen."

"That means a lot." He opened his mouth twice more but fumbled his words. "Er … um. I … Thank you."

"Do you need another minute or so?" she asked.

Will shook his head. "I'm good."

"Well then, let's go back in," she replied. "High schoolers have short attention spans. No one will remember by tomorrow."

Will nodded and reached for the door, but Ms. Morano stopped him one more time. Her eyes had a sympathetic shine.

"One more thing. I overheard part of your conversation—forgive me for eavesdropping. I've never read any of his books, but my father was a big fan. Arthur O'Neill was a great author. Being sad about his death just means you cared about his work. He'd be honored you remember him so fondly—that's all any artist wants." She sighed. This was more for her than him. "Death isn't always fair. Knowing that, the only thing you can do is live in a way that makes the deceased's life mean something."

Will found this line rather odd and somewhat pointed given Arthur's relationship with him, but Ms. Morano was gazing at the theater, completely lost in thought.

Once she was back at the podium, Will made his way to the trumpet section, the band having moved on to another song. Will glanced at Jaser, who was giving him a thumbs-up, and returned it with a small smile. No one else in the room was paying Will any mind. Except Dane—he was eyeing Will with both suspicion and awe. Will tilted his head politely, and Dane returned the gesture before facing Ms. Morano, ready to continue. Will put his trumpet to his lips and began play, ignoring the emotional exhaustion that had overcome him.

After school, Will biked home in silence, not really wanting to share the day's events with Peter and Iris. While the two were talking enthusiastically about the World of the Written, Will was quiet, focusing on the road and, oddly enough, the fact that May Colbert was a fan of Arthur O'Neill.

"So, Arthur O'Neill's funeral is today."

Iris's words shocked Will out of his stupor as they neared his street.

"Yeah," he replied. "Someone did their research."

She adjusted the pace of her biking, now level with Will. "I feel like it would be irresponsible of me not to. This guy is so important to us now. We should know as much about him as possible."

"Yeah. I wish we could go." Peter bit his lip, distracted.

For a moment, Will considered telling them about his plan before rapidly changing his mind. *He* shouldn't have been going. It was extremely rude and invasive and it would be worse to bring friends. The only excuse he had was the possibility of a clue as to who killed Arthur. He wanted to help Tam.

They biked the rest of the way in silence, and eventually split off to their houses, waving goodbye for the day. Will put his bike away and ran upstairs to his room. Thankfully, no one was home. He rushed through his homework, and when the clock hit four, he lowered his pencil and closed his textbooks. He donned dress pants, a black button up, and a black tie, brushed his hair back a little bit, and concentrated. If he could travel to Byrrus, he figured he could use Betwixt and Between to travel between different parts of the World of the Writers. At least it was worth a try.

Earlier in the day he had done some research on the church where the funeral was going to be held. Keeping the image of the church in his mind, Will entered a portal. At the other end of the hallway was a large wrought iron door. It looked like the door of a church, coincidentally enough, and had large stained-glass panels woven into the metal that made up the entrance. Will pushed it open and walked in.

Will's eyes took longer to adjust due to the darkness that met him. Aged and broken pews were stacked around the basement, bibles littered the tables, and there were a few large crosses that had likely been mounted on the walls of the church at some point.

Above his head, Will could hear voices, dampened by the ceiling, walls, and the shuffling of feet. He found the stairs that took him to ground level and proceeded to crash his favorite author's funeral.

Will emerged to see a hushed congregation, all dressed in black. No one paid attention to him, and he was able to freely observe the group, which was brightly lit by late-afternoon sun filtering through stained-glass windows that enveloped the church. Most of the attendees were older, but there were a few scattered teenagers, presumably someone's grandkids, standing around awkwardly.

Will walked to the back of the room and stood with his hands folded in front of him, unsure of what to do.

"Well, I'm certainly impressed." Tam walked toward Will, dressed in a dark suit. Freshly shaven, hair combed back, his eyes seemed tired, like he hadn't slept in several days.

Thanks, Will thought, not wanting to look like he was talking to himself. *Nice suit. Very different from your usual getup.*

Tam's lips curved upwards. "I spent close to forty years in near-constant contact with a Writer. A lot of things from your world rubbed off on me. Books, movies, phrases ... and sometimes clothing."

Tam was momentarily distracted by a woman walking through him; Will sidestepped hurriedly to avoid making eye contact with her.

"There are advantages to being invisible to Readers," Tam observed. "But really, good job. The fact you figured out how to travel across a continent using Betwixt and Between is something Arthur took years to figure out."

I guess, Will responded to him.

"All that aside, why are you here?"

Will didn't answer immediately, and stalled by looking across the guests. There was a woman wearing a pantsuit, typing into her phone—a reporter? An agent? An older gentleman wiped a pair of eyeglasses on the front of his suit, looking misty-eyed. A friend of Arthur's? Perhaps a fellow writer? Arthur never married and had rarely dated—a tidbit Will had been reminded of while doing research with Peter and Iris, so he didn't bother looking for a spouse or significant other.

I wanted to see if there was something I could do. For you. For Arthur. And I wanted to pay my respects to the man who gave me this gift, you know? Maybe do some digging to see if there's anything I can find out.

Tam smirked. "And what are you going to do to investigate? I know you have enough tact to avoid asking attendees of a funeral if they murdered the deceased."

I guess I don't know. Maybe if I recognize someone. That woman from Boston, perhaps. Or something that sparks a memory or a vision from Sampson. I figured it would just be good to expose myself to the possibility.

Tam grunted and picked up a glass of champagne from the table next to him. He sipped it gingerly.

"Tam! What are you doing? Someone will see you!" Will whispered more loudly than he intended, causing a few heads to turn. He blushed. A woman walked behind them, clearly a Reader, and passed through the table.

Oh. I didn't realize you could bring stuff in from the World of the Written.

"Refreshments, yes. Just not Shades." Tam winked.

The two passed a few minutes in comfortable silence before Will looked up, catching the eye of a man standing a few feet away. His jet-black hair was slicked back in a very pretentious way and looked too made up when compared to his gray goatee. He was strikingly attractive, and it was clear he had aged well. The man was intimidating and coming toward Will.

"Do I know you?" the stranger barked.

Will gulped. "I don't think so, sir. I'm a representative from the Boston Student's Association. Arthur O'Neill was such a respected literary figure it was requested I be here." Will didn't even know if the Boston Student's Association was a real thing. Any quick Internet search on this man's smartphone would destroy his entire story, and sure enough, the man pulled up a webpage on his phone, then snarled.

"Like hell you are. If you're going to lie, you might as well lie using an organization that actually exists. You're not welcome here. Get out."

"What's this? Who are you, young man?" The woman wearing the pantsuit walked over. She glared at the man, and though he stood his ground, Will could tell the two weren't particularly fond of each other.

"Being Arthur's agent doesn't give you any particular clout here, Laura," the man in the suit said.

Will gulped for the umpteenth time and decided to be honest.

"My name is Will Morgan. I know I wasn't invited to this, ma'am, and I'm sorry, but Arthur was a huge inspiration to me. I just wanted to pay my respects. I wasn't sure how else I could." There was silence for a moment. "And I'm sorry for your loss," he added, hoping he didn't sound too tactless.

"Will," Laura the agent started, "it means a lot to know someone values Arthur's work that much. He would have been thrilled to know you're here. Feel welcome to stay, if you want." She turned to the man next to her. "Warren, be polite. Please. This is tiring for all of us. I'd rather not make a scene."

Warren bared his teeth, his resemblance to a rabid wolf uncanny. "My mistake, Laura. I didn't realize your wishes were more important than mine. I just didn't want random teenagers interrupting the *private* ceremony dedicated to my *dead brother*."

Warren brushed past Will, pushing him into Tam. Will stumbled, and for a moment he thought Warren's eyes ran over the Character. His gaze pushed past the both of them and he walked out of the room. Will felt guilty.

"I'm so sorry about that. I can go …" Will began.

"Don't go. It's not you," Laura replied. "Warren is taking Arthur's death really hard, obviously. And he sometimes forgets I've known both of them for decades. I was the agent who picked up the first *Byrrus* book." She sighed. "He's Arthur's younger brother, and though they had their fair share of fights, Warren always looked up to Arthur. They gave each other a competitive edge. And now that Warren no longer has that, he's lost within himself. But you don't need to hear all that." Her eyes were warm. "Thank you for coming, Will. I know I said it before, but I'm sure Arthur would've taken comfort in knowing he inspired people."

"The pleasure is mine."

She gave him a sad smile and walked away, and Will sighed in relief, his heart rate slowing down. He patted his forehead with his shirtsleeve before glancing over at Tam; however, the Character was giving the door to the room a reminiscent look, Warren clearly on his mind. A memory stirred within Will.

Tam, you said Arthur's brother was also a Writer. Was that him? Do you know him?

"We've met," he responded. "As I said, it's a bit of a complicated history. He knew the World of the Written existed, and he could, at least for a time, use the Writer's Eye. It got a little bit messy, and Arthur eventually took measures to erase his memory."

What? Erase his memory? How did he do it?

"I don't know," Tam responded. "I wasn't there for it. All I know is there was tension, and one day Arthur told me he managed to eliminate Warren's powers and his memory. No one got hurt, and there was nothing I could do, so I just trusted that Arthur made the best decision." Tam's expression took a dark dip, challenging Will. "You probably think that was foolish. Regardless, at the end of the day I'm loyal to Arthur. He wouldn't have done anything that wasn't for the greater good. That much I know for certain."

Do you think, Will replied, *it's possible he killed Arthur? Maybe his memory returned, and he got angry, or something?* He immediately winced at how tactless his thoughts sounded.

"No," Tam said plainly. "Regardless of how he appears, he isn't a bad person. He has his bouts of anger, though so do most people. I'd like to think that even if his memory *did* relapse, he wouldn't kill his brother. They were too close for that."

So what happened? What do you mean it got messy?

Tam shrugged again. "Arthur didn't like to talk about it so I don't know the whole story. From what I could tell, Warren was angry Arthur was more powerful than he was. As you can probably guess from that interaction, Warren likes to be in charge. He felt as though Arthur was restricting his power. He couldn't accept Arthur just had a greater grasp on the World of the Written than he did, so Warren got jealous. They argued and it turned physical. Arthur didn't want to hurt his brother. The only thing he could do was take away his memories and make Warren forget everything, which he did." Tam sighed, face getting downcast. "That's at least what Arthur said, and I would've been able to tell if he was lying."

Sounds like a very normal brotherly fight to me, Will thought, snorting to himself. Tam chuckled, though it was clearly more out of politeness than anything. They passed the rest of the wait in silence, and when the service began, both of them sat in a pew toward the back of the church.

People told stories about Arthur, about his life and work, and about how much he changed the world. It was nice, except Will felt like something was missing; no one really touched on what Arthur O'Neill actually did.

His life had been about so much more than writing. His life had been about taking ink on a page and turning it into adventure, about changing lives. Arthur O'Neill wasn't just a writer—he was a world builder. There was a society that revered him as a god. An entire kingdom of ink and paper. And nobody in this room knew he had been murdered—well, not most people, anyway. Arthur O'Neill could have continued writing about Byrrus, maybe have written a sequel to Tam's adventure. Maybe Tam and Amelia could have ended up together. But no—someone took it from him. Taken it from all of the Characters who loved him.

The preacher spoke briefly, and Tam sobbed, the sound muffled by his hands in his face. Will looked at the people around him. Every corner of free space, from the sides of the aisles all the way to the entrance, was filled with Characters. All of them had the same stoic look Tam now wore, the tears falling down their faces.

That's when it truly hit Will.

Their lives had been created by Arthur O'Neill. He created their universe, and in doing so, brought all of these people into being, giving them lives, hopes, dreams. The reason they were able to love, were able to mourn, were able to live, was Arthur O'Neill.

Will's initial judgement of the author being a god to them was patently false; Arthur hadn't just been a god. He had been *everything.*

Tam stood. In a smooth baritone voice, he began singing, the entirety of Byrrus joining him.

"Light races across the dusk,
Failing to beat night's fall.
But don't fret, friend, and just trust;
Please listen and hear our call.
All feelings repaid, all follies dismissed,
And to your life meaning is given;
Your purpose did indeed exist,
And toward good your goals were driven.
Goodbye my friend, into the unknown you go,
With hesitation yet joy in your heart.
Though your smile is missed, your love desired,
It is here that your journey will start."

Their voices ceased in sync with the preacher's prayer, the final note of Byrrus's song clinging to the air. Tam sat, one final tear leaking out of his eye, and looked at Will, a sad yet peaceful emotion on his face. He grasped Will's shoulder, voice shaky and quiet.

"I wasn't sure how I felt about you being here, but I decided I'm happy. Thank you for coming."

"Come, friends. Let us go see our friend safely buried," Pass intoned as he walked by Tam and Will.

Will nodded politely at Pass as Tam joined the other Characters. They left through the main door. Will didn't follow. He didn't deserve to participate in this part. Regardless of how unpoetically it had been put, Warren had been right—Will was just a teenager who hadn't known Arthur, despite any connections they might have now. Will walked to a coffee shop across the street from the church and ordered a soda that sat untouched.

He leaned against a window and watched a long procession of people make their way to a cemetery on a hill. It was a very picturesque scene, one from a storybook, which Will found fitting. Even the sky looked like it wanted to cry with the mourners as they passed by the open grave. Will watched as people threw handfuls of dirt into the open plot; the preacher said a few words and the group dispersed. A few folks, Warren included, lingered for about fifteen minutes, then walked away with slumped shoulders, dabbing at their eyes.

After the last of the funeral attendees left, the Characters from Byrrus circled the grave. Pass said something and they left through a portal. The hill empty, Will left the coffee shop, making his way to the graveyard.

He pushed past a wrought iron kissing gate and walked among the gravestones. It was easy to tell which was Arthur's; the hole had yet to be filled in, and instead of a gravestone there was a shiny placard, a temporary representation of the marble that would be there in a few months. In expressive cursive, it read:

> *"Though I walk through the valley*
> *of the shadow of death,*
> *I will fear no evil:*
> *for thou art with me."*

Upon reading the quote, the corners of Will's mouth twitched. It was a verse from the Bible, yet he also recognized it from somewhere else: *Sampson the Warrior*, the book in the *Byrrus* series that described the life of, well, Sampson the Warrior. The line was said to Sampson at the end of the novel, after the love of his life was killed by a tyrant named Abaddon. The line encouraged Sampson to continue on and use his pain as a tool. That advice led him to create Byrrus, a safe haven for those in need of one.

Now that he stood in front of the grave, Will wasn't sure what to do. He had never been particularly religious. Nevertheless, he sat on the ground and said a small prayer, hoping it encompassed some sort of thanks for Arthur and what he had done for the world and the people of Byrrus. He summoned his blade to his hands and buried it in the ground next to the grave. Next, from his bag, he drew the first copy of *The Redstone Keep* he had ever been given. Will laid it down next to the open plot. The book fit in next to the flowers and wreathes.

"I don't know how I got this ability," he said to the gaping hole. "I don't know if you chose me. I don't know if the World of the Written chose me. I don't even know if I was chosen or if this is some big mistake." He paused. "I know my gift is … different. I know my Writer's Eye used to belong to you. Plus, there's the weird guy named Simon who keeps showing up. Tam doesn't know who he is. He can't see him or sense his presence, but I know he's important. I just need guidance. I need answers."

The moment passed and Will felt silly. Standing, he ripped his sword from the ground and let it fade into the Written. He needed to get home. If his parents found out he went to Boston, there would be way too many questions.

As if on cue his phone began vibrating. He looked down at the number and didn't recognize it. At first, he was relieved—it meant his dad wasn't calling to yell at him for being late again.

"Hello?" Will's voice pitched up, and he gulped.

"Uh, hi. Is this Will?" A female voice crackled to life on the other end.

"Yeah," he replied. "Who is this, if I may ask?"

"Oh, yeah, sorry—it's Madison Colbert. May."

Will froze. The definition of ridiculousness was him talking to May Colbert while standing in a Boston graveyard. He cleared his throat, standing up straighter despite himself.

"Oh, hey! What's up?"

"I know this is going to sound really weird," she started, "but do you want to get dinner tonight? I just really want to talk to someone about Arthur O'Neill, and my parents don't really get it, and most of my friends would lose their minds making fun of me if I brought this to them, so … yeah."

Was this some sign from the other side?

"Do you like pizza? There's that new place that opened up downtown … Jersey Stove," Will suggested. "I've been meaning to try it."

"Sure. Does eight work for you?" she replied. Will was somewhat pleased to hear there was a hint of excitement in her voice.

"Absolutely. I'll see you then," Will stated.

"Awesome, see you!"

Will ended the call, confused, yet encouraged he had somehow become good enough friends with May that she wanted to grab dinner with him. He also relished in the fact that Peter would be beyond jealous, though he'd never admit it.

With one final look at Arthur's casket, Will ducked into an alley, summoned a portal to Betwixt and Between, and made it to his room when his mom's car pulled into the driveway. A few minutes later there was a knock on his door.

"Will?" His mom opened the door and walked in. "Why are you so dressed up?"

"I had a presentation about Victorian Literature in English today. I figured I'd get bonus points for dressing the part." The lies were coming more smoothly now.

"I didn't realize you took your suit with you to school." She raised her eyebrows.

Will kept his face straight.

"I put it in my bag and changed when I got to school so I wouldn't damage it on my bike ride over. Is that okay?"

"You didn't change before coming home? Oh well, no matter. Maybe I'll go ahead and buy you a bag for your suit. It'll keep it nicer. Do you know what you want for dinner?"

"Sorry, Mom. I kind of made plans. Is it okay if I grab dinner with a friend downtown?"

Ruth's eyes softened. "Of course you can. Peter and Iris?"

"No. A new friend."

"Who is it?" she asked, always curious.

Will turned away from his mother, kicking his foot against the carpet of his bedroom floor. "Just a girl from school. My friend May. I haven't mentioned her before. And before you get any ideas, she's *just* a friend!"

His mom's eyes lit up in a mischievous way. "Well, I hope you have fun." She winked at Will as she left the room.

A little while—and a change of clothes—later, Will headed to the pizza parlor. It was a crisp night in late September, and Will savored the fall air. He biked past the bookshop and eventually reached Jersey Stove. Like every other restaurant in the area, it was packed with teenagers and young adults enjoying an inexpensive meal.

He locked his bike to a lamp post and jogged up the steps to May, who was sitting at a table. She was dressed in faded jeans and a baggy sweater. Will was glad he changed out of his suit.

"Hey," he said, throwing his hand into the air as he approached the table. "I'm glad you chose a table outside. It feels good out here."

"Yeah," she whispered. "It's nice."

The server approached their table. Will asked May what she wanted and she shrugged in a non-committal fashion. Will ordered a large pizza for the both of them, hoping that May couldn't see how quickly he was bouncing his knees under the table.

May seemed extremely distracted. He went to open his mouth to make small talk, but she cut him off, shaking her head.

"You don't have to do the whole small-talk-to-make-me-feel-comfortable thing," she started. "I know this is weird. I just … I feel like I'm losing my mind, and you're the only person who I feel like could empathize in some way."

Will's stomach fluttered, feeling more confused by the minute. "Go on," he replied. His chest tightened, and he began tapping his fingers against his left leg.

She took a deep breath. "Recently, I've been having these really weird dreams. And not like, 'oh they're obviously not real dreams,' but real, vivid, I-can't-tell-I'm-actually-asleep dreams." She bit her lip. "Have you ever had anything like that?"

Will thought back to the dream where he watched Arthur O'Neill die. "More or less, yeah."

May looked relieved. "Okay, so you know what I'm talking about. Well, in these dreams—and this where it's going to sound crazy, mind you—I see … um …" She blushed.

"It's okay," Will said. "Go ahead."

She took another deep breath before continuing. "I see characters from *The Redstone Keep*. You know, the book by Arthur O'Neill."

Although Will's brain was on fire, he kept a straight face. "Not the craziest thing I've ever heard. What are the characters doing in the dream?" There. Casual tone, check.

A look of relief spread across her face. "Well, it's not what they're doing in the dream that's weird. It's what else is happening around them. The dream starts with them just being normal, or what I assume to be normal. They're smiling, cheerful, happy, but then a really dark cold comes over the castle, and in the distance, there's a rumbling. I zoom through the trees and end up in front of a church."

Will tilted his head, his confusion genuine. There was no church on the outskirts of Byrrus. Just woodland. And nothing like May was describing ever happened in the books.

"And that's always weird to me ..."

The server, with impeccable timing, delivered their food.

"And that's what's weird to me," May picked up as soon as the server left, "because there's no scary church in the books. Anyway, a woman stands in front of the church and at one point she puts her arms up, and the entire church breaks apart, and I wake up. The only thing I can feel when I wake up is just, terror.

"I've woken up screaming once or twice." She covered her face, embarrassed. "My parents are starting to think I'm going nuts. And it's just so creepy and scary, and I don't know ..." She put her hands down and clutched her knees. "It's the same exact dream, every time. I figured maybe you had gone through something similar. Or it has something to do with Arthur O'Neill's death. I don't know, this was stupid, I'm sorry ..."

She stood like she was going to leave, and Will instinctively grabbed her hand. She looked over at him and he dropped it, blushing.

"It's not weird," Will insisted, trying to keep any confusion or panic out of his expression. "I haven't had dreams like that, but I don't know, it's not out of the ordinary. Do you think it means something?"

May didn't answer, but instead was running her hands through her hair, deep in thought.

"Do you remember what the woman looks like?" Will asked. The woman was the same person he ran into in Boston. She had to be.

May scowled at the ground. "No. Every night it's the same. I can't see anything about her except her black hair."

Will heard himself grunt in response, completely lost in thought. He was no stranger to vivid dreams, and it was clear to him May had the *Potential*. Even so, why was she having this dream specifically? Were they visions of the future? Of the millions of stories in the World of the Written, why was she having a dream about Byrrus? And where was this church?

Will looked up, pressing the tips of his fingers together. "That's absolutely wild," he commented, not sure of what else to say. "Maybe the dreams will expand? And they'll show more as time goes on?"

"Yeah. Maybe." May didn't sound convinced. She sighed. "I'm just glad to hear I'm not crazy. I really appreciate that." She looked at him for a moment as if she were going to say something else, but then stopped. "I should probably get going. You've been really sweet about this, and it's late. Thank you."

Will gave a small smile. He made an offer to pay for her food, but she shook her head insistently. After splitting the check, May waved goodbye, and Will leaned back in his chair, perplexed.

"Bro, were you on a date with May Colbert?"

Jaser walked through the crowd and sat across the table from Will, looking both impressed and confused. Will put up his hands, feeling a little violated.

"No, nothing like that," he stuttered. "We just … ran into each other and decided to catch up a bit and talk."

It was clear from both Will's hesitation and the look on Jaser's face that Jaser didn't believe him.

"It's a shame," Jaser bemoaned. "She's way out of your league."

Will blushed profusely, hating the fact he was embarrassed.

"What are you doing here anyways? You live too far away to bike or walk." Will desperately wanted to change the subject.

"I'm taking a class at the local college. I meet my parents here so they can drive me home. Nothing too exciting." Jaser put a hand to his chin contemplatively, then snapped his fingers. "I mean, I guess the class itself is kind of exciting." He grinned. "I want to learn to be a hacker, and that's not exactly a skill high schools appreciate. Surprisingly enough, colleges do. My parents aren't thrilled about me taking it, but they thought it might be a way for me to feel more comfortable with the move." Jaser helped himself to a slice of Will's now-cold pizza.

"Why do you want to be a computer hacker?"

Jaser shrugged. "It's cool, I guess. I like computers. I built my own last year. I figured this was the next step."

"You built your own computer? That's awesome."

Jaser grinned. "Yeah. It's not that hard. Anyways, I have to run. I just saw you, and I figured I'd say hi. See you in class tomorrow!"

Jaser took another slice and winked at Will once more before getting into a red minivan that had just pulled up.

That night when he got home, Will called Peter and Iris and told them about May's dream. While they were just as confused as he was, they didn't seem as concerned.

"It could just be a coincidence," Peter said. "I mean, is it bizarre? Yeah. Can we do anything about it unless May happens to get the Writer's Eye? No. So it'd be best to just stash the information until she gives us more to work with. Maybe the dreams will give her more information, eventually."

Will begrudgingly agreed, though his sleep that night was restless. The woman who he was sure played a part in Arthur's death was appearing to a random girl in dreams.

That couldn't be good.

9
The Woman with Raven Hair

Time moved forward and the world reached mid-October. For Will that meant midterms. Tam came back, having recovered from the funeral, and was as cheerful as ever. He also agreed with Iris and Peter's assessments of May's dreams.

"I don't know what church it is," he said one night, sitting at Will's desk. "Regardless, involving her more than necessary will just put her in danger. Besides, you need to focus on your exams instead of the Written right now."

Will pressed Tam about this occasionally, because there always seemed to be some sort of uncertainty in his voice, a quivering that almost betrayed a lie. Will even called him out on it at one point.

"Will, I assure you I'm not lying. There have been millions of demonic churches throughout history. May could be dreaming of any one of them. Search my brain. Tell me I'm lying." When Will looked into Tam's thoughts at his invitation, he realized Tam was telling the truth—he had no idea what May's dreams were about.

Tam reminded Will of his dad in a lot of ways. During the lead up to exams, whenever Will would try to go to Byrrus to train, Tam yelled at him and sent him scampering back to the World of the Writers and his desk to study.

"Come on, Will," he said one day, after escorting Will to his room. "You're a student. Your life comes first. We're working on things on our end too. If we see something unusual, we'll let you know. Right now, you need an education."

"Tam, I know you want me to study, but my grades are fine, and I want to help catch Arthur's murderer. It seems like that should be more important than me getting an A in biology."

"Look, Will," Tam groaned, "you'll be no use to the World of the Written if your parents start micromanaging you because your grades dive down a cliff. Remember, I'm doing legwork on my end too. You should be allowed to live your double life without having to do everything for me. I'm competent, you know."

He raised his eyebrows, as if inviting Will to push back, so Will did.

"I didn't realize you were investigating the murder without me. What have you done?"

"Poking around Arthur's apartment. Walking around Boston. Questioning Characters in other worlds. That sort of thing," Tam said. "I assure you Byrrus isn't sitting quietly while you take an English test. We have much more free time."

Will blushed. After a few stutters failed to turn into a retort, Will put his sword down and picked up his trumpet.

Tam smirked, satisfied, and closed his eyes and crossed his legs, waving his hands like a conductor. Will did his best to ignore him.

It was the middle of the night, and Will's dream featured him playing the saxophone, serenading a woman who looked suspiciously like Ms. Morano.

Someone shook his leg, and Will's suave musicianship was interrupted. Groggy, he opened his eyes, and was surprised to see Simon, looking alert and happy.

"Jeez, you sleep like a freaking koala." He leaned farther onto Will's bed. "I've been shaking you for, like, two minutes."

Will sighed. If Simon was paying him a visit after more than a month of silence, he must have had something important to say.

"So," Will started, "long time no see. How's it going?"

"Fine. Bouncing around the back of your brain can get exhausting, so I decided to pop in and pay you a visit. I hope that's all right."

"Absolutely," Will grumbled, not even bothering to hide the exhaustion in his voice.

"I know you're tired, fool. I won't be long. I just wanted to check in and tell you some stuff I've been thinking about. And some stuff I've noticed."

"What do you mean?"

"I mean being your Familiar, I see things you and some Characters don't. I'm able to notice things you might not be privy to."

"Seriously, Simon. You have to tell me this in the middle of the night? I have school tomorrow."

Simon giggled childishly, putting his hand to his head. "Sorry, sorry, I know you want to go back to bed, you wimp. But," he whispered, putting his finger up in a commanding manner, "there's something suspicious about your school. There's a force there that isn't entirely of the World of the Writers. It's not of the Written either. I've never felt anything like it before."

Whatever Will was expecting, this certainly wasn't it. "What?" he asked, suddenly awake. "You mean there's some evil demonic force hiding in Morrison High School?"

"Maybe," Simon muttered. "I can't really tell. Just, be careful." He groaned. "I know it's not a lot of information, but I feel like the more steps you take toward figuring out what happened to Arthur O'Neill, the more I remember about myself."

"And have you remembered anything?" Will wondered.

"I remember I'm old," Simon began. "Very old. And occasionally, when I think super hard, I can see the outlines of things. Unfortunately, they're mostly shapes, like squares, and occasionally people." His expression faltered, yet quickly snapped back to a grin. "That means I'm getting there!"

Will tried to fake a happy face as his brain picked up speed. "Thanks for warning me. Let me know if you remember anything else." He paused. "Talk to you later, I guess?"

Simon flashed a toothy, noncommittal smile before fading away, leaving Will with nothing but an empty bedroom and his own thoughts.

The day of his band midterm, Will slid into his chair behind Jaser. Today, Will might move up in the trumpet section, if he played well enough. Although he took out his trumpet and began to warm up, he put it back as soon as the first few notes left the horn. No amount of practicing was going to make the piece cleaner. Will looked at the other trumpet players, all of them looking confident, and he sighed. He hadn't been chosen to sit higher in the trumpet section because

Ms. Morano thought it better for him to focus on the piano for the first half of the semester. He was tired of sitting at the back.

"Hey." Dane pulled Will from his reverie.

"Oh," Will commented in surprise. "Hey."

"Not going to lie," Dane began, "I'm pretty psyched to see you blow the smug looks off everyone's faces. They're still making fun of you for that whole crying thing, and it really ticks me off."

Will blushed. "Wait, they're doing it behind my back? That's annoying."

Dane grimaced. "I thought you knew. Some people thought it made you seem like a wimp, but that's just because none of them are good enough to realize real music comes from emotion." He patted Will on the back. "You can kick my butt at the piano. You can kick the butts of everyone in this section at trumpet. They'll be the ones crying after you're sitting first chair."

"I wouldn't say that's completely true," Will admitted, smiling to himself. Will had played with Dane a couple of times when Ms. Morano was running late for class, and Dane was just as good as Will, if not better.

"Richardson! Sit down!" Ms. Morano called.

"Crap. Good luck, dude." He hit Will's shoulder as he walked away.

Will let out a small sigh of relief—another solid interaction with Dane for the books. While the first month with him had been pretty rough, Will had come to find he was a pretty good guy.

He tapped Jaser on the shoulder. "So, you nervous?"

"Um, yeah! I didn't realize we'd have to be playing in front of the entire class! I feel like I'm going to have a panic attack."

"What did you think was going to happen?" Will asked in disbelief.

"I don't know! A recording in a quiet room! A private test in her office while the rest of the class had study hall! A guy can dream, right?"

Will's thoughts were cut short by Ms. Morano, who stepped onto the podium and began drawing names from a hat to see who would be playing first. As people played, Will zoned out, listening to the dull sound of music echo across the room. Some of the performances were average; some were pretty good; some were just awful.

"Jaser Solomon. You're up."

Jaser put his mouth to his clarinet. Despite the shaky start, the solo was mostly passable. He finished, and the class rewarded him with a single clap: the customary applause for the group.

Ms. Morano nodded, and drew another name.

"Alright, Will, you're up next, on trumpet."

Will took a deep breath in, put his trumpet to his lips, and blew air into the horn. Because the piece he chose wasn't hard technically, Will needed to make sure every moment of the song counted, and every note drew some sort of feeling. As his horn rang, he closed his eyes, letting himself get lost in the notes. The waves of music flowed up and down throughout his body, and though it was a short song, he could feel his soul passing through his instrument into the watching crowd. The final notes rang out with vibrato across the linoleum floors, the fresh sound of his trumpet lingering for a few moments after he removed the mouthpiece from his lips.

The class was silent, and Will heard two things. The first was Jaser, turning around to face him, thumbs up. "That's how you do it.

Freaking awesome." The other was Dane, across the room, giving a loud whoop and clapping his hands together more than once.

With the band exam out of the way, Will was able to coast through the rest of the week with ease. Biology hadn't gone as well as he hoped, but life moved on. A few days later in English, May walked in, visibly stressed, clutching the script for *Dracula*.

"Hey." Will stared at her, gaze soft. "You good?"

"Yeah," she muttered, not putting down her script. "I'm just nervous. Tonight is opening night. I need to make sure I'm on my A-game."

"Kind of fitting they put opening weekend on the weekend of Halloween, right?" Will joked.

"I'd say so," May responded, her voice excited. "Are you coming?"

"Of course. As long as you come to my band concert next week," Will teased.

"For sure! I would love to hear you play. And I could really use the support tonight. It's going to sound pretentious, but I need to steal the show!" She put down the script. "Sure, they'll love Dracula, but I'm just this random freshman! I'm playing Lucy. Have you read *Dracula*?"

Will shook his head.

"Well, I'm the pretty face who's the first to die. It's an important role, but I'm dead, like, halfway through. I need to milk this part for all it's worth. I'm the only freshman who made it into the cast, so I need to establish myself with the department *and* the audience. It's the only way to keep getting on stage!"

"You're going to kill it," Will assured, giving her what he hoped was an encouraging thumbs up.

"Fingers crossed."

"May! Are you *so* excited for tonight? We're all coming." A group of girls came over to the table, one pushing Will to the side. May grimaced at him apologetically.

"Break a leg, May!" He slinked back to his desk, sliding in next to Jaser.

"First dinner by yourselves, and now you're going to her desk to talk to her," he commented suggestively. "You two are moving awfully fast."

"Shut it," Will grumbled apathetically. "Speaking of moving fast, do you want to go see the play with me, Peter, and Iris? We're going tonight."

"Let me just check my busy, jam-packed schedule." He pretended to flip through a notebook. "Hmmm ... aside from pretending to practice clarinet and staring at my ceiling, I've got nothing planned. I'm in!"

The two agreed to meet in the theater before the show started.

As the day went on, Will got his grades back and was pleased to see he had done well enough. Sure, his parents probably wouldn't be thrilled, but he was satisfied given how he kept getting woken up in the middle of the night by nightmares and invisible Familiars.

Peter, to his own mock surprise (though no one else's) aced all of his exams.

"I don't see the big deal about it," he told Will later. "I didn't even study for them. Geometry is literally the easiest class I've ever taken."

Will walked into band that day worried, not because of the letter grade he was going to get back, but rather because of where he'd be placed amongst the trumpets. The chair placements would go into effect after the upcoming concert, and most of the sections fell pretty much where Will expected them to, and Jaser was relieved when he received his test score: a B, written in thin, feminine scrawl.

"I thought I did so much worse!" he whispered to Will, and Will patted him on the back.

"Of course not! I told you, dude, you were fine!"

When Ms. Morano got to the trumpets, her facial expression didn't betray anything; however, her eyes twinkled as she looked at Will and pointed to the very front-end of the section, signifying he did better than everyone else on the test. Will kept his face straight as he moved his stuff to the front, nodding at Ms. Morano thankfully. Inside, he was bursting with joy.

The day eventually ended, and with the fear of midterms behind them, Peter, Iris, and Will all got ready to go to the play. Iris's parents dropped them off in front of the theater doors, and they walked inside to find Jaser saving seats for them.

"Figured these would be the best seats in the house." Jaser tapped his fist against his chest. "I've done some work in the theater with sound, and anywhere else the microphones can get kind of screwy."

"So not a fan of the nose bleeds, huh?" Peter asked, leaning back in his chair. "I've always found those to be the best seats, because you can pass out without anybody noticing, in case the show gets really boring."

"I think that means you just have poor taste in art," Iris mused.

Jaser and Will cackled while Peter blushed beet red.

Quickly, the lights in the house dimmed and the play began, telling the story of a Dutch professor who got tangled in the business of the ever so dangerous Count Dracula. Though Will had never read the book, he was familiar with the story, and when May, as Lucy, Dracula's first victim, came on stage, Will was blown away by her talent. May was known throughout the school as being a drama kid, and most people who had seen her in plays said she was gifted. This was the first time Will was seeing her in action, and he was awe struck. She played the role, albeit small, beautifully, and when she died, Will wasn't just watching May die on stage; he was truly watching Lucy die.

There were versions of Dracula's story where the vampire didn't die. To think Dracula could be alive, somewhere in the World of the Written, and could easily do this to any person in his world … The hairs on Will's arms raised. He shook away the thoughts.

Then again, that world was also protected. While Byrrus had Tam, Dracula's world had Van Helsing. The real Van Helsing was protecting his little corner of the Written, and Will could rest easy knowing that even though the real Lucy had probably met the same fate she met on stage, other Characters didn't have to.

In this version, Van Helsing was the one to kill the Count, and when he stabbed Dracula, the special effects were brilliant; a bunch of smoke went up and lights flashed, and afterwards a pile of ash was all that was left of the vampire. After the stage went black, the lights came back on accompanied by some cheesy music, to which the entire cast walked out in their own respective groups.

When May walked out about halfway through, Will stood and cheered. Dracula and Van Helsing got the loudest cheers of all, naturally, and when the house lights came up, family and friends in the crowd rushed to greet the cast members.

After about five minutes, May appeared. Will smiled politely and gave a small wave. However, instead of going to her friends at the other end of the hall, May made her way to Will. She threw her arms around him in a friendly hug.

"Thank you for coming!" she beamed.

"Wouldn't have missed it," Will chuckled abashedly, awkwardly putting his arms around her before quickly removing them. "I don't think you all have met."

Will introduced May to everyone, and they all greeted her amiably.

"May, you were great!" Iris said. "The tech was so cool, and it all just worked out so well!"

May breathed out appreciatively, looking a bit shaken. "I know! I didn't expect it to go as well as it did, but the show was amazing, especially for an opening performance!" She turned back to everyone, face flushed and bright. "Seriously, thank you so much for coming. It means a ton."

May went to say something else but was swept up by a group of her usual friends. One blonde girl gave Will an angry death-glare, and he flashed his biggest, cheesiest, toothiest grin. May grimaced apologetically before walking away with them. Will turned back to the group.

"Well that was fun," he said. "Shall we head out? Jaser? Are you good, man?"

Jaser nodded furiously. "Yeah, absolutely. Just appreciating the tech of the show is all." He swept his arms out wide. "The way they pulled off Dracula's death at the end ... the smoke and how the actor just disappeared! I wonder if there's a trapdoor on this stage. There probably is. If so, it's really freaking neat!"

"There is," Iris confirmed. "I did a theater summer camp here once, so I know about the stage. That's why there was so much smoke and why the sound effects were so loud; they wanted to make sure you couldn't see or hear Van Helsing pulling open the trapdoor or Dracula jumping through a hole in the stage."

"Well it certainly worked," Will remarked.

The joy and excitement running through the auditorium made Will more excited than ever to perform in the band concert, and when he got home, he sat down at his piano.

Tam peered at Will's sheet music. "Okay. I know you say I like Amelia, which is patently false, but you can't say I like her and deny that you like May."

Completely different cases, Will replied, speaking to him through his mind as to not make his parents think he was a crazy person. *I barely know May. There is a book that canonically suggests you're in love with Amelia. Have you ever done a Google search and read what people think of your romance?*

"I can't say I've ever been inclined to do so," Tam grumbled.

The night of the concert, Will warmed up as the various band members trickled into the room. Jaser plopped down into an empty seat.

"How are you feeling?" he asked. "Think you're going to cry tonight? Your parents and everyone else in the audience would eat it up."

Will shoved him lightly, glad to have a friend he could joke around with. "Maybe. I think that would probably give me major points with the adults, but not so much the other students in the audience."

"Yeah, not sure how May would take your crying."

Their banter was interrupted by the arrival of Ms. Morano, who motioned for all of the students to take their seats. She looked rather flustered, much more than usual. Her outfit was extremely professional: a long black dress to match the boy's tuxes and the girl's dresses and skirts. She wore a silver star-shaped necklace. A memory nudged at Will. He brushed it away. He had other things to worry about tonight.

"This is a big night." Her eyes sparkled with excitement. "We get to perform. And we get to feature some great musicians." She winked at Will. She proceeded to help the band warm up with various exercises.

"Good. I think we're ready."

They all stood, the majority of the students bumping into each other before they clumsily got in the right order. It was concert time.

The band walked onto the stage to polite applause. Will searched the audience. Along with the smiling faces of his parents, Will saw Peter, Iris, and May. Will grinned and sat at the piano.

The band tensed, eyes focused on Ms. Morano. She looked at Will, his fingers poised over the piano ready to strike. She dipped her head to the percussionists in the back, and with a full swoop upwards, she launched them into their first song.

They all picked up immediately, swiftly playing and allowing the crescendos and decrescendos of the melody to flow throughout the auditorium. Will stopped paying attention anything beyond his fingers on the keys and Ms. Morano's direction. Everything else was irrelevant. At one point he almost closed his eyes to just let the song flow out of him.

The final song of the concert was the one with Will's extended solo, the one the other band members had begun to affectionately call the "sob song." Once they got to Will's solo, although his eyes were dry, the melody wasn't. Tam stood behind him, letting Will take in some of the Character's power and emotions. The song flowed from his fingers, the final note ringing throughout the auditorium. It sat still in the air for a few moments, like a dew drop perfectly balanced on a spider web, before it dropped into thunderous applause. The entire audience stood, clapping, and though Will suspected most of the applause was out of parental obligation, he couldn't help but beam with pride.

All too quickly the curtain fell, and the musicians filtered their way back into the band room to put away their instruments.

Dane patted Will's back as the two walked in together. "Nice playing out there. I can't tell if you're better on the piano or on the trumpet."

"Thanks man." Will blushed. "You did awesome, too."

Dane grinned before walking away. Someone then grabbed Will's shoulders and pulled him into an awkward hug.

"I didn't pass out!" Jaser cried, hands waving above his head before placing them on his hips in superhero fashion. "I honestly thought I was going to have a panic attack up there, but I totally pulled it off!"

Will snorted before throwing his arm across his face, coughing as loudly as he could. "You were great. Anyone who says differently is a dirty liar."

Jaser looked at him appreciatively before leaving the room.

Will took another glance around, expecting to see Tam, or at least a silent signal he was impressed, but the Pontifex was nowhere to be found. Will tried to contact him mentally and received no response. He didn't pay much mind to this—Tam was probably just distracted, or giving him time with friends. Will chose to leave the channel of communication open just in case Tam needed him; he had done it so often it was as easy as opening his bedroom window.

Will finished packing up his instrument, put his music away, and hoisted his trumpet case into the air.

"Hey, Will, would you be willing to stay behind for a moment?" Miss Morano stood expectantly, her hands clutching various pages of music.

"Of course. The concert went really well, I think!" Will exclaimed. "Everyone seemed to like it. I've never gotten a standing ovation before."

Will walked a little bit closer, and the two made eye contact, Ms. Morano's bright lips curving ominously. Will's brain began to get fuzzy.

Why am I putting my trumpet down? Will's thoughts were getting hazier. *There's no reason for me to do that. My parents are waiting.* He felt as if he were walking through Betwixt and Between; his sight in the corners of his eyes faded until he had a curious sensation of tunnel vision, where the only things in the world were him and Ms. Morano. Eventually, he was face to face with her, his arms hanging limply at his side. He hadn't been this relaxed in months. *Why was I nervous before? Is there something wrong?*

"You're a very talented musician, William Morgan." Her voice took on a velvety tone. Will had never heard that timbre from her words before. "You've just got a certain talent when it comes to making music sound emotional."

Will glanced from her face to the chain around her neck. The dull metal stood out against her skin, not as a normal star as he initially thought, but one that was turned on its head. As Will looked at it, the necklace lifted from her throat, pushing its way toward him. Will's vision got hazier, and he wondered if Tam could tell him why the necklace was making him feel this way.

The necklace! He remembered—he had seen it before.

Will watched as Raina Morano's face melted away. Where there was the rosy complexion of a tan woman in her thirties, there was now the pale, sharp looking face of a younger woman, one who couldn't be older than twenty-five. The rosy hue was gone from her features, and her blonde hair melted away into a dark, raven-black color.

The woman from Boston.

Raina grabbed him by the neck with one hand, lifting him off the ground with way more strength than any human should have had. Will struggled and kicked but found the harder he moved, the harder she squeezed. Her necklace fell back to her throat, and Will's strength returned slightly, though not enough to break free.

"Color me impressed. I really thought I'd be able to do this without you figuring out who I was. What gave it away?" She glared at Will. "Ah, the necklace. You must have recognized it from our little encounter in Boston."

"Yeah," he coughed. He threw out his leg once again, and this time he managed to connect with Raina's body. She grunted and dropped Will, and he rolled back and summoned his sword, ignoring the pain in his neck.

"I guess I should have made the necklace change shape too. Stupid mistake. Won't happen again."

"Who are you?" Will glanced at the door.

"No one is coming to save you, Will." Raina ran her hands through her hair. "I have a way with humans. Some would call it mind control. Right now, all of your fellow students, and your parents, are making their way to the front of the school. They are going to leave and forget you exist."

Will searched for a way out. There had to be a way out!

"That is, unless, you decide to cooperate." She huffed, her face taking on an unsettling look of innocence. "I don't like doing this, you know. I don't want to kill you, or your friends for that matter. Unfortunately, I can't let you keep running around unlocking people's *Potential*."

"What do you mean? How do you know about that?"

"I know everything, Will. I didn't fake being a band director just for fun. I know that your two friends have the gift. I was the one who sent the Shades to your house that day. Peter Roitman and Iris McAllister had the bad luck of getting the Writer's Eye. Now they're just another set of obstacles standing in my way."

"Who are you?" Will demanded. "You can't be a Character. Everyone can see you. You teach a class at a high school. Still, no one could see you in Boston." Will stood up straighter. "What do you want with me?"

Raina snapped her fingers. "I forgot you didn't know. Then again, isn't it obvious? You have Arthur O'Neill's power. It attached itself to you before he died. I need it." She extended her hand. "I can take it without killing you. You'll lose your Writer's Eye, but you and your friends will live. Make no mistake, I will end you if you don't cooperate. It's up to you."

"You want Arthur's power? For what?" Will gripped his sword tighter.

Raina's eyes darkened. Her bright red lips pursed together in frustration. "There are things you don't understand about the Written, Will. Things you don't want to know. Trust me."

"You just threatened to kill me and my friends. How can I trust you?"

"Think about it, Will. The Writer's Eye is scary. It's a major burden to carry. Sure, there are some fun things about it, but there are so many nasty things you haven't seen yet. Wouldn't it be much easier to just go back to your life the way it was before?" Her tone was almost kind, as if she truly thought Will would agree and give up.

He snarled in disbelief. "You're out of your mind. I won't betray Tam." He raised his sword, prepared to fight.

Raina ran one of her hands through her hair, disappointed. The emotion almost seemed genuine.

In a flash of red and black light, a scythe appeared. The long handle was made of a sleek black wood, the blade curved and embossed with stars. It was hauntingly beautiful, and even though Will was in grave danger, he couldn't help but appreciate the weapon.

He gulped. *Tam! Where are you?*

Nothing happened, and he backed up until he hit a bookcase.

The scythe whirred threateningly through the air as she walked toward him. "My magic works on Characters too. Currently, Tam and the rest of your Character friends are back in the World of the Written, politely waiting." The hint of kindness was gone from her voice. "And don't even try contacting him— part of my magic is I can cut off communication between Writers and their Pontifexes."

"Is that why Tam wasn't there to help Arthur the night he died?" There was a beat of silence before Will's voice roared. "It was you! You killed him!"

Raina shrugged. "I suppose you could say I did."

Will needed to get out of there. Tam needed to know who was

behind Arthur's murder. He ran at Raina, the Writer's Eye slowing everything around him.

Raina smirked and thrust the butt of her scythe, catching him in the chest. Will flew across the room and slammed into a set of chairs. He cried out as he breathed. He tried to stand and promptly fell back to the floor. His ankle was definitely sprained; maybe broken.

"That's not going to work here." Raina sounded bored. "I'm stronger than you. Even with the Writer's Eye, you can't keep up with my movements. You can't beat me."

She swung the scythe again, the tip of the blade breathing across Will's face, slicing his cheek.

"Don't fight, Will. I know this probably sounds rich coming from the person about to kill you, but I don't want it to hurt. If you stop fighting me, I will make it quick."

"You're funny," he spat, baring his teeth and ignoring the blood curving its way down his face.

"You should have just ignored Tam and minded your own business," she said, the tip of the scythe slamming into the ground, two inches from his hand. "I can't leave loose ends. I'm sorry."

Will tried again to stand, cursing as he fell, the weight too much for his foot. Definitely broken.

"Goodbye, Will."

As Raina raised her scythe, the door opened.

"Will ... what the ..."

The terrified face of May Colbert swam in his peripheral vision. He had no time to think before May grabbed a music stand and took advantage of Raina's temporary confusion, swinging it like a baseball bat right into the side of her head. It connected, and Raina staggered.

May took a step back. She looked hypnotized, her eyes glowing with the power of the Writer's Eye. She raised her glowing hands and thrust them forward, shooting what looked like ice in Raina's direction.

Eyes flashing with panic, Raina turned her attention to May, knocking the blasts of ice out of the way with her scythe. Will took his chance. Hoisting his sword into the air, he flung it as hard as he could, aiming for Raina's chest. His wrist twitched at the last possible second, shooting a pain through his arm, but Will's aim was true enough; the sword hit Raina's bicep, cutting it deeply. Will was unnerved although unsurprised to see human blood, not the shadow of Shades, seep from her arm.

Will, what's going on?

Tam's voice exploded in his head. Somehow her spell had broken.

Tam appeared next to Will in a flurry of colors, launching himself at Raina. His sword clanged against her scythe in a storm of sparks, and the force of his blow threw Raina back, slamming her into a wall.

Tam didn't seem to be constrained by the limits of gravity or natural human movement. Even with the Writer's Eye, Will could barely keep up with the Character as he weaved in and out of Raina's attacks. At one point he thought he saw Tam grab Raina's scythe, flip over it, and use it as a balance beam to kick her in the face. The fight was a blur again until there was a brief pause when Tam landed about five feet away from her, barely having broken a sweat.

Tam's attack was interrupted by an ethereal lion running into the fray, knocking into walls as it charged at Raina, fangs bared. She slammed her scythe into it, launching the lion across the room. The beast stood, its roar filling everyone's ears.

Raina scowled at Tam. "You should have stayed out of this. This will not end well for you, same as Arthur."

She snapped her fingers and swept away into the air. As soon as she was gone, Will collapsed, the weight of his injuries fully creeping into his body as his adrenaline faded to nothing.

"Will!" Iris ran to Will's side.

Peter was breathless, chest heaving. "It was insane. It was like we were sleepwalking. I felt super hazy and lightheaded, like I needed to just stand outside and wait for something."

"Then it was like someone turned a light on," Iris continued, almost equally out of breath. "And I knew something was wrong, and I had to get here to help you, and … are you alright?"

"Yeah," Will muttered, groaning. He lifted himself up with his good arm. "I wouldn't be if it weren't for May." He looked at her. "Thanks for saving my life."

May's face was pale. "Well, when someone is standing over your friend, you know, with a scythe, it's second nature to try and step in."

"Wait, she saw the scythe?" Tam asked, looking at Peter and Iris, eyes narrowed.

"Well, yeah, duh, of course I saw the scythe! It was like seven feet long!" She gave Tam a distrustful look. "Also, who are you? And did I imagine it, or did you just appear out of thin air? And what was that lion thing all about? And who was that woman?"

"You can see me?"

May, despite visibly shaking, jabbed Tam in the chest, her fingers clearly making contact with his body. Tam looked at her quizzically, his eyes widening.

"You were lying to me when we talked about my dream, weren't you, Will?" May muttered, staring at Will fearfully.

"You're the girl who was having dreams about the church and Byrrus." Tam gave her a once over, his eyes fixated in serious contemplation. "You may just have a gift, May. Tam Desmond." He reached out his hand.

Recognizing the name, May gripped his hand, trying to keep the fear from her face. "Tam Desmond. Like *Byrrus*? No way."

"How did you know I was here? Ms. Morano ... sorry, Raina, said she cast a spell on the entire school that made them leave and forget I ever existed," Will asked looking at her, more perplexed than anything else.

May sighed a guilty sigh. "Truth be told, I left before everyone else. I had a spooky sense of déjà vu that told me I shouldn't be there. Because of the dreams I've been having, I got nervous, and then when I was walking away from the building, I had another vision of ..." she glanced down, looking scared. "... you, in trouble. So, for some reason I ran here, and there you were. And I saw her with the scythe, and my body just sort of took over."

May sat abruptly, finally processing what happened. "And the ice that came from my hands ... is that something I can do? Summon ice?" She stared at her fingertips. "What's going on, Will? This has to be another dream, right?"

Everyone in the room looked at Will expectantly, and he looked pleadingly to Tam.

The Character's mouth curved into a frustrated frown, and he addressed the group. "It might be better if we show you." Tam summoned a portal to Byrrus. "I take it you've read *The Redstone Keep* by Arthur O'Neill, right?"

"Yes, many times."

"Well, get ready. You're about to do a lot more than read about it. Peter, Iris, help Will up, will you? There's a healer in Byrrus who should be able to patch him up. They'll help you feel better too, May."

Will's friends hoisted him into the air, and Will gave May an apologetic look.

"Listen," he said, "thank you for saving my life. Nonetheless, that woman was Raina Morano. She was trying to kill me. And she would have killed you." Will looked at the spot where some of Raina's blood still glistened on the floor. "If you want to understand what happened tonight, then come with us."

"If I go home, my parents will be wondering why I look like I've just run a marathon. Lead the way."

Will just hoped the healer could fix bones so he didn't have to explain to his parents how he broke his ankle and wrist while playing piano.

10
Powers and Pentagrams

Will was sitting in the Byrrus hospital ward when his father called him.

"Will! I'm so sorry." The distress was audible in Emery's voice. "I don't know what happened. Your mother and I … somehow, we ended up back home after the concert, I don't know how! We're so dumb! We're coming back to get you."

"It's okay!" Will said, his voice as bright and cheery as possible. "I actually went out to get ice cream with my friend Jaser. His mom is going to drop me off after."

"Okay, good. Again, I'm so sorry. Anyways, you were fantastic out there. Really spectacular solo. Congratulations."

"Thanks Dad," Will said, the memory of the last song lifting the corners of his mouth despite the recent events. "I just did my best."

Final pleasantries were shared, and the call ended. Will's friends made similar calls to their parents. While they waited for Merlin, Tam explained the World of the Written to May. "And essentially, the dark feelings writers write about come to life in the World of the Written as Shades," he concluded.

May ran her hands through her hair. "So, Raina is a Writer then?"

Tam faltered, then sighed. "I don't know. Her ability to disappear was very Character-like. Her fighting style too. She's no novice." Tam growled. "Plus, the magic she used was extremely powerful, and I don't know if that's something a Writer could do. But people from your world could *see* her … she can't just be a Character. She's something new."

They were interrupted by Merlin's entrance. He looked tired. "Hello again, Will."

"Hey, Merlin. Nice to see you again."

"I've never been the most adept at healing magic," he muttered. "Be that as it may, I can try. If not, we'll come up with another plan." Merlin sighed.

"Actually," Iris interrupted, "do you mind if I try? This book," she began, summoning the leather-bound tome to her hands, "it has a bunch of spells written in a language I don't really understand, but as I've practiced with it, I can read more of the pages. I think some of them are healing-related."

"Where did you get that?" Merlin asked.

"It's part of my Writer's Eye, I guess. The first page has the name written on it: the Gilmarye. Have you seen it before?"

Will strained his eyes to look at the book, now open to the title page, and saw that it was completely covered with symbols. He couldn't make heads or tails of it. Merlin shook his head.

"No. But its magic is powerful—I can feel it from over here. You have a special gift, my dear." Merlin beckoned to Iris, and she approached Will.

"You sure you know what you're doing?" Will asked, raising his eyebrows, ignoring the flutters in his stomach. "Not that I don't trust you, but I have to explain whatever you do to my parents."

"I think so," she replied, flipping to a page in the book.

"Merlin, what do you think?" Will asked.

"May I?" Merlin asked Iris.

Iris handed the book to Merlin. As he took it from her hands, it disappeared in a flash of light and reappeared in Iris's arms, distraught at being separated from its master.

She tried again with the same result. "I don't think you can hold it."

"Uncanny," Merlin muttered.

He stood at Iris's side, studying the page. After some time, he broke the silence.

"This is very promising. I think we should try. If it's not the right spell, it shouldn't do anything bad. Is that okay, Will?"

"I think so."

"Don't you trust me?" Iris joked.

"Okay, let's do it."

Eyebrows furrowed, Iris stood next to Will and began, *"Ad poshakat ossium, ruadare claudtiment."*

She waved her right hand over Will's body, and the Gilmarye glowed a bright blue that reflected in her palm. As she moved her hand, Will could feel his bones shift back into place and see his cuts disappear. After about five minutes, Will was able to stand and stretch, his encounter with Raina wiped from his body.

"Wow," Will said. "That's really useful."

Merlin straightened up, eyes eager. "Extremely powerful. I'm impressed. Do you think it would work on Characters?"

"Yeah," Iris replied. "I can use it to summon creatures to fight for me, create weapons, and now, apparently, heal someone. The only downside is I can only do one thing at a time—so I can't fight while healing, or vice-versa. There's a lot this thing can do and I want to test it more." She took a seat, shaking slightly. Will made a move toward her, stopping when she held up a hand. "It's okay. I'm just ...

really tired all of a sudden. I don't think that's something I can do too many times in one day."

"So, I want to know more about why I can shoot ice from my hands." May was out of bed and flexing her fingers, sending shards of snow popping out of them haphazardly.

"Each Writer's power comes to them in different forms," Tam said. "For Will, it's a sword. For Iris, it's the Gilmarye. For Peter, it's a staff that allows him to control fire. Yours is clearly control of ice; maybe even water." He smiled. "Quite useful, if you think about it. You don't even need an object to control your power; you can pull moisture from the world around you."

"And it's clearly not her only power," a voice from behind them said.

Amelia, wearing long pants and boots with a leather jacket across her shoulders, stood in the doorway. Will thought she looked like a steampunk superhero.

"May," Tam started, "this is ..."

"Amelia Brown." May's voice was quiet, barely a whisper. "You knew I was here because you get visions too."

Amelia nodded.

"You understand them. You understand me."

Amelia extended her hand and May grasped it. At once, there was an almost visceral current that passed between them, and Will looked on in awe as May's gaze became focused. Her furrowed brow and bright eyes suggested she understood the World of the Written better than any of them, her *Potential* being fully unlocked.

"It must be because of May's gift of being able to see the future— her dreams," Tam whispered. "That gives them a special connection.

That was an ability exclusive to one person in this universe, until now."

"And you've never seen anything like this before?" Will asked.

"Never," Tam replied, and they fell into silence as they watched Amelia and May talk in hushed tones.

"Let's leave them alone for a little bit so they can talk and figure everything out," Tam whispered. Will, Iris, and Peter dutifully followed him out, shutting the door quietly.

Of everything that had happened that night, May was the most overwhelmed by Amelia's appearance. When she first read *The Redstone Keep*, May had been infatuated with Amelia. While most readers were obsessed with Tam, she had been drawn to Amelia's fierce independence, her skill and wit, and her insistence on standing up for what was right. Unlike most of the *Byrrus* fan base, May had been happy Amelia and Tam didn't end up together. Having them be together at the end would have cemented the already too-common perception that Amelia had been merely an accessory to Tam's journey.

Seeing her in real life, it was clear that Arthur O'Neill had written her from a man's perspective of feminine beauty; however, he had still done her the service of giving her strength and dominance. This was made clear by the dangerous looking knife on her belt, and the way her strong hand grasped May's.

"Are you okay?" Amelia asked after a few moments of silence.

"No," May stated firmly. Amelia raised an eyebrow at May's honesty and leaned in. May's knee-jerk reaction had been to lie, but

Amelia's touch felt like that of a sister, someone she could trust whole-heartedly. "I mean, I knew that my dreams meant something. I knew that something bad was coming. But this is just so … intense." She gestured to the walls of the infirmary. "I mean, come on. I'm in a world where book characters come to life, with a bunch of people who are nice enough, but I don't know them at all. It was probably easier for Peter and Iris to believe it … they're good friends with Will, as far as I know. But me?" She looked down at her hands, which began leaking small shards of ice. She clenched her fists. "Yeah, they're nice enough. Except I don't know them. Why me? What made me special?"

"There's never a rhyme or reason to what makes people special." Amelia's gaze held steady with May's. "My ability to see the future didn't come from any significant backstory. Sure, I had an ances-tor who was a seer, but what does that mean, really? Why did my great grandmother have visions of the future? I don't know." Amelia shrugged. "The answer didn't matter. Because of my gift, I was cho-sen to help save Byrrus. I wasn't anything before I told Tam and Pass about my abilities. I had no reason to be saving my city other than total randomness and chance. But I did, because I knew I had to. And I think you feel the same way."

May didn't quiver under Amelia's gaze, though she did feel the weight of the statement.

"Of course I feel that way. Now that I know what's out there, now that I know my nightmares mean something, I can't just ig-nore them. But …" May's voice faltered. "I'm scared. Terrified, ac-tually. I don't know what to do. Sure, I have these ice powers, and I know mastering those will come with time. But how do I master my dreams? My visions?"

"It took me years to even remotely control my dreams." For

the first time, Amelia's voice carried the weight of disappointment. "Even now, I don't know if it's actually control, or just luck. That's the blessing and the curse of clairvoyance. We have the power to save our friends and loved ones, learn valuable information, and change the course of battle. Sadly, we're at the whim of our own magic." She ran a hand through her hair as if trying to reach into her brain. "When it's important, the dreams of that church will become clearer. There's nothing you can do other than channel that energy."

"I don't want to channel it." May's voice cracked, the words barely audible. "I'm tired of being scared. I'm tired of waking up crying because of nightmares." She looked down at her hands, which were absentmindedly patting against her legs. Knowing Raina Morano was the woman in front of the church didn't make the dreams any less scary. The force that always came right before May woke up was the thing that caused the fear, panic, and anxiety.

Amelia gave a small smile and touched May's shoulder. The familiarity shot through her like a breath of fresh air and gave her more confidence.

"I know it's scary," Amelia replied. "I still get scared sometimes. That said, you need to understand they're not nightmares. They're gifts." Amelia didn't move her hand. "There's going to come a time when your dreams show you more than Raina Morano and some scary church. You're going to dream worse things. Embrace that fear. Use it as inspiration. Seize onto it and use your gift for good."

May nodded. It made sense, after all. She hadn't asked for this gift. She hadn't asked for the Writer's Eye. Before tonight, she had never considered Will Morgan anything more than an acquaintance. However, this wasn't going to go away. She wasn't going to be able to ignore the dreams anymore. And as a result, she could choose to be afraid of what they showed her and cower, as she had outside the theater when Arthur O'Neill died, or she could fight. She could stand tall, do as Amelia had done in *The Redstone Keep*, and embrace what now made her special.

"Okay," May concluded, her voice carrying a new power. She sat up straight. "I guess that settles it. Whatever Raina is doing, we'll stop her. I know it."

"So, Will, care to explain what happened tonight?" Iris asked.

Will, Peter, Iris, and Tam were walking away from the infirmary. Distancing themselves from the door and eventually finding their way outside, Will told the night's events as they walked. He was surprised by how strong his memory was of every moment: the concert, Raina's form changing, and how she suddenly became aggressive and attacked him.

"I guess when Tam came to the concert, she cast a spell that stopped him from thinking she could be anything more than a normal teacher, huh? If not before," Peter inquired.

"It was before," Will realized. "There was a day Tam came to class and helped me play. The day of Arthur's funeral. She must have seen him then."

Tam dipped his head thoughtfully, and Will sighed. It was a dangerous power.

"Mind control like Raina's has its limits. The biggest rule is you can only control the minds of people who don't know you have the ability. When Raina revealed herself to Will, and to the rest of us, she forfeited the ability to control us." Tam's eyes were narrowed.

"Secondly, mind control gets weaker the wider radius you cast. In this instance, because she was trying to control so many people at once, one good hit from Will broke the spell. Because of tonight, she can't use her biggest strength on any of us."

"How do you know all of that?" Will asked.

Tam tapped his head. "I read about it while looking for information on who could have killed Arthur. I just didn't think it worth mentioning since it's not an ability Writers are supposed to have—just Characters, and even that is rare, or restricted to specific stories."

"Wait," Peter interjected. "What you're saying is she can't control any of us now that we know who she is? That's awesome! We can totally take her out."

"There is one thing, though," Will mentioned, biting his thumb. "She was wearing this weird silver necklace. The necklace was almost pulling itself from her neck to try and get to me. And I felt weaker the closer the necklace got." He paused. "It looked like an upside-down star."

"An upside-down star?" Iris squinted at him, and Will felt a rush of embarrassment. Nonetheless, he nodded, and she leaned down in the dirt and traced a shape with her finger. "Like this?"

"Yes! How did you know?"

"Will, you dope," Iris blurted out. "That's not a star. That's a pentagram. Like, the literal sign of the devil."

There was silence amongst them for a few moments. Will snorted in amusement, then tilted his head like a confused dog. "Wait, like, *the* devil. The devil devil. Satan. Enemy of the Christian God. Ultimate evil. Hell. That devil?"

Iris nodded.

Will laughed, his insides squirming. "Nice! We're fighting Satan! I love it!"

Peter put his hand on Will's shoulder. "Not necessarily. The pentagram is a symbol that's been used by hundreds of religions and groups for centuries. Pythagoras used it while developing the Pythagorean theorem." Will looked at him blankly. "Come on, you guys. Pythagorean theorem? Remember? Triangles. Geometry."

"Well, why was Raina wearing it?" Will asked, ignoring Peter. "And why did it react to me like that? She said something about trying to take my power. I felt myself getting weaker when the necklace was near me. Do you think it was absorbing my abilities?" Tam put a hand to his chin, tentatively believing Will. He continued. "What do I have that other Writers don't?"

"I'm not sure. Have you been feeling capable of summoning an incarnate of Hell recently?" Peter asked, pupils flashing.

Will and Iris snickered, and some of the tension broke. Tam, however, was staring at the sky, where a few stars twinkled.

"Are you okay, Tam?"

The Pontifex was quiet, not taking his eyes off the expanse above them. "Yeah. It's just … we have our answer. We know who killed Arthur."

There was a solemn understanding in Tam's voice, and it made sense to Will. Tam, for months, had been seeking the identity of the person who had murdered the equivalent of both his god and his father. Now that the person was known, the way forward was clearer than ever before.

"We'll figure out why. And we'll make sure Raina can never hurt anyone ever again." Will stepped forward and firmly placed his hand on the Character's shoulder.

Tam nodded, though he didn't take his gaze away from the night. Eventually, the group returned to the infirmary where they found May, who looked tired yet less overwhelmed than she had when they first arrived.

The teenagers returned home with some answers, and definitely more questions.

The next day in English, May grabbed Will by the arm and pulled him into the hallway. She dragged him to a corner usually reserved for couples making out before class.

"So," she started, ignoring the startled looks and snickers from onlookers, "after we went home last night, Amelia came to my room. She filled me in about what you told Tam about Raina's necklace. Think about it. The devil is a sign of religion. Where are religions usually based?"

Will's eyes widened. "Churches. Like your dreams."

May nodded furiously.

"Would you be able to take us there, to the location in Byrrus?"

May nodded again. "It'll be dangerous, obviously. Remember—I saw Raina in my vision. That being said, I don't think she's going to be there for a while. The vision feels like an ending, and not like something Raina is just waiting for. If we can find that church before she does, maybe we can stop whatever she's doing, and figure out what's up with that necklace. Maybe that will give us a clue as to why she killed Arthur and why she wants your powers."

"Nice work, May," Will responded. "When do we start? Should we wait until the stuff at school has blown over? The band room was destroyed, and Raina left quite a bit of blood all over the floor, and for all we know, she's going to be pronounced missing or something like that."

May flexed her fingers thoughtfully. "I think we're okay. If we were going to get questioned, we would have already been called into the principal's office. Or arrested."

"You know, fun stuff," he commented, and he was rewarded with a small chuckle from May.

The bell rang and they rushed back to the classroom to the giggles of their classmates. Jaser raised his eyebrows in an I-told-you-so manner, and Will waved him off. He sent a quick text message to their group chat, telling everyone to be ready to go to Byrrus after school. He decided not to tell Tam. This wasn't something he'd ever approve of, and part of Will was itching to figure it out on his own.

When third period rolled around, Will debated skipping, filled with the reasonable fear he was going to be grabbed by a dozen FBI agents and interrogated about Raina Morano's disappearance. However, when Will walked in, there was nothing immediately out of the ordinary. Everyone sat in their seats politely, instruments in their cases. No blood or mayhem anywhere. Jaser waved Will over.

"Apparently Ms. Morano is sick. We're just getting the day off." Will glanced at the wiry-looking substitute, who didn't look like a threat, physically or mentally, and he breathed a sigh of relief. He texted the group an update.

No Raina in band today, room looks totally normal—no blood, no mess, Will typed. *We have a substitute. Apparently, she's "sick." People still think she exists, so that's good, I suppose.*

Peter texted back immediately. *Who called in sick for her though? Why didn't she just alter people's minds?*

Plotting, responded May. *She's trying to figure out what her strategy should be. Leaving the slate clean is probably easier than manipulating an entire school system into thinking she never existed.*

Will deleted the messages—they had all agreed to delete regularly to protect the information—and put his phone back into his backpack, away from prying eyes. Just because Raina wasn't there didn't mean they were safe. Will put his head in his hands.

Jaser turned around and winked. "It'll be all right, bud! She'll feel better, and you'll still get your piano solos."

At the end of the school day, the four Writers gathered behind the building and walked into Byrrus. The group appeared on the outside of town, at the edge of the woods. They looked at May expectantly.

"I don't know exactly where we're going," she began. "I know that in my dream, I start at the gate and then go straight in that direction." She pointed south-west. "I think it's only about two miles. I'd suggest we use Betwixt and Between to get there, only I think it's safer if we walk." She scowled. "That way we don't walk into a trap."

The group agreed and trekked in the direction May pointed.

"Keep your weapons out," Will cautioned, summoning his blade to his hand. He had no way of sensing Shades, and he wouldn't be able to protect his friends if they were to get jumped by a group of them.

The four continued like this for some time, journeying through the woods, making sure they didn't stray too far from walking south-west. Will kept his ears peeled for any sort of malicious sounds. For the first twenty minutes or so, there was nothing, and they continued walking, only speaking when necessary.

"Are we going the right way?" Will asked.

"In my dream, there was a cut in the line of trees right after a river. And look." She jerked her head, gesturing ahead of them.

In the distance, Will could see a few splashes of water through the greenery.

"Be careful, everyone," Will whispered.

As they crept through the forest, Will heard voices. Signaling to the group to stop, he snuck forward on his own.

"Do you think they're going to make us wait until the cathedral just appears? How often does that even happen?"

The voice was muffled and gravely, as if the vocal cords of whoever was talking were covered in sharp rocks. Every word sounded painful, like it was drawing blood from the speaker.

"I've never seen it. I don't think the witch has seen it either. Somehow she knows it's here, so we're stuck patrolling until that thing just rises out of the ground."

"Could be hundreds of years, but of course, who cares about that? As long as she's got someone doing her dirty work." A sword scraped across a stone. "At least the group in front of the brat's house knew they'd be seeing action. I don't think any of them expected to be wiped out, though."

"She did," another voice said. "That's why she sent weaklings. They were disposable. She obviously wanted to test the boy's power. That and see the infamous Tam Desmond at work for the first time."

Will watched the Shades through the branches of a bush. These

Shades were more human than others he had seen. He could distinctly make out the shape of a nose, mouth, and eyes. Remembering what Tam said about the varying levels of strength Shades could have, Will crept away and went back to his friends.

"Okay," Will whispered, "there's a group of four Shades." Will told them what he overheard. "The only problem is they're different from the ones we've seen before. They might be stronger than what we're used to. Should we call Tam?"

Peter rolled his eyes as obviously as possible. "For a guy who's had the Writer's Eye longer than any of us, you worry a lot." Will got a cross look on his face, and Peter laughed. "Look, Will, if Raina is as strong as we think she is, she can easily summon way more powerful Shades to take us down. It'll be better if we fight them now when we *don't* have to worry about other enemies. The more enemies we fight, the stronger we'll get."

They continued to talk in hushed tones. Losing the element of surprise could be disastrous. However, while May was lecturing Peter on his brashness, Will heard some scuffling and turned to see one of the Shades standing behind him, sword in its hand.

"It's them!" it hissed.

Will swung his sword, catching the Shade off guard. It parried and whistled for its comrades to join the fight.

The Shade swung its blade at Will, but Peter parried it with his staff, the wood erupting into flames. The Shade yelped and jumped back as the sparks flew from Peter's weapon.

"Be careful, Peter!" Iris shouted as she summoned two wolves. "You're going to burn the entire forest down!" The wolves howled and charged at a Shade, jumping at it as Iris held out her hands in focus. It was clear that all of her energy was going into controlling the creatures she had brought to the fight—any more than two or three would be too much.

"You be careful!" Peter shouted back at her, shooting a ball of flame at one of the monsters. "You don't know how many summoned creatures is too much for you!"

The Shades, though having more power and skill than the ones Will previously fought, didn't have any extra speed. As long as he was able to watch the Shade's longer-ranged sword, it couldn't touch him. As Will ducked he saw it had a smaller knife attached to its belt. He thrust his sword into the Shade's chest without even thinking, and it disappeared.

"Watch out! They've got knives on their belts!" he shouted to his friends.

"Way ahead of you!" May called in response while she dodged a knife strike, kicking the blade from the Shade's grasp. Will watched as May blocked a sword strike with her hand, ice forming over her palm as she caught the blade, the ice capturing the Shade's entire arm. She then summoned a knife of ice to her other hand, and swiftly ran it through the monster. It burst into a cloud of dark smoke.

With that, all of the fights ended. Peter was waving his staff around, looking happier than he had in weeks.

"That was awesome!" he exclaimed, though he was out of breath. "I can control where my flames go. And I'm getting better at controlling what they burn." His eyes lit up. "Look!"

He pointed his staff to the ground and caused a small flame to erupt on a pile of dead leaves. The flame didn't spread even though it was surrounded by potential tinder. He grinned maniacally as the fire flickered until May shot a bullet of ice, extinguishing it. Peter grunted, and May bowed dramatically.

"That's because all of your skills have improved. Speed, strength, endurance … the Writer's Eye gives you capabilities you'd never have in the real world. The only problem is your enemies have them too."

Tam walked toward them, whistling and twirling his sword as if it were a toy. Amelia followed closely behind. Will's face went white.

"Yeah, but you can also push yourself to exert more power than you're ready for," Amelia cut in, looking directly at Iris who was breathing heavily. "You shouldn't be running around looking for enemies." She eyed Will suspiciously.

"Is everyone ok?" Tam asked the group.

They all nodded.

"May, what's wrong?"

May stuttered for a moment before she got her words out. "It just felt … kind of weird. I mean, the Shades were definitely evil. Monsters, if I can say that. But …" she looked down, embarrassed. "They still spoke like people. In their own abnormal way, they had faces like people. And when I hit them, even though the ice looked like it was hitting an immaterial thing, I felt like I was attacking a person."

Tam scratched his head thoughtfully. "That's not uncommon, and I'm glad you have some compassion. However, compassion isn't going to stop your enemies from trying to hurt you. Think of it this way." He threw his sword into the ground. "If a man pointed a gun at your head, you would want to fight him, right? You wouldn't hesitate."

"Right," May said. "And I know where you're going, but …"

"Just hear me out."

She looked at Tam reproachfully yet nonetheless allowed him to continue.

"These Shades aren't human, regardless of how they look. And Raina? She may look human—she might even *be* human. It doesn't matter. She's evil. She and her Shades won't hesitate to kill you. They *want* to. If you feel compassion for your enemy, you'll die. Most Shades don't have feelings. They certainly don't have souls." He sighed. "Character, Writer, Reader, whoever—if killing is the best way to survive, then you do it. Don't hesitate. I know it sounds cruel, but in reality, very few things are more important than your own survival."

May stayed silent, though Will could tell she didn't fully agree. Will didn't know if he did either. Sure, he did his best to take Tam's words to heart, but he was left with his doubts. When he fought Raina, Will never stopped to think about what he would do if he was *really* able to kill her. If he had a clear open shot, and he knew he wouldn't miss or be deflected, would he be able to land the blow? Would he be able to stab a person who shared all of the qualities that made him human? Will shook away the thought.

"So, should we finally see what we came here for?" Peter looked at the clearing.

"What do you mean?" Tam asked.

Will shot off an explanation. Tam bowed his head at May.

"Well, May, you should lead the way."

May closed her eyes and took a calm breath before moving forward. Amelia took her side as they walked through the open tree line into a wide field. They approached the expanse and were disappointed—though not surprised—to find nothing except grass and flowers.

May didn't seem shaken. "This is it," she declared. "The place where the building appears." She pointed to the tree line on the other side of the circular field. "Look at how much space there is.

Look at how the trees line the border—this space has a purpose. Are you really telling me nothing big has happened here?"

The two Characters shook their heads. "Especially not what you're talking about," Amelia said. "A giant building that appears out of nowhere? We've had warlords, pirates, thieves, but no magical churches."

Tam frowned as he glanced around the empty field. "Maybe we should spread out and look for something? An indentation, a symbol, anything."

The group fanned out but was unable to find anything significant.

"We should probably get going. It won't take long for Raina to find out her sentries have been eliminated," Will said.

"Shoot!" Iris was looking at her cell in panic. "It's 6:30!"

Yet another day where Will was out and his parents had no idea where he was.

"We have to go! Now!" she moaned, rubbing her head and while staring daggers at the Writers. "My mom is going to kill me! Then she's going to kill all of you, because she knows I'm with you!" Iris gave Will an accusatory look and opened a portal. "Bye, Tam! Amelia!"

"Is it really that late?" May said, and she rushed after Iris. Peter shrugged and waved goodbye to Tam, Amelia, and Will, and followed the other Writers.

Will resisted the urge to rush home immediately, knowing his parents' anger wouldn't dissipate if he were home at 6:35 versus 6:40.

"How did you know where to find us? I was purposefully blocking our telepathy," he asked as Tam and Amelia began walking back to Byrrus.

"Will, c'mon," Tam chortled. "You should have more faith in the

Byrrus guards. A group was patrolling when they heard the fighting and alerted us immediately." He pointed at the ground. "Plus, you weren't exactly covering up your tracks."

"You know how to track? Can you teach me?" Will inquired, his interest piqued.

Tam fixed Will with an aggressively fatherly look. "You need to get back. It's been a busy day for you, clearly, and your parents are sure to be worried."

"You're not my dad, Tam."

Amelia shot Will a look that was clearly telling him not to argue. Will huffed and bit the inside of his cheek before saluting them and leaving the Written.

As their backs retreated, Will stepped back into the woods and studied the path, trying to figure out how they were able to find him.

"That's pretty rebellious, don't you think? Sneaking and poking around behind Tam's back?"

Will's sword appeared in his palm.

Matteo stood on the side of the path, a knife in his belt and a sack of dead turkeys on his back.

"Matteo! Geez, dude. You scared me." Will caught his breath, glad he didn't have to fight again. "That's pleasant," he joked, motioning to the turkeys.

Matteo shrugged. "Food doesn't come out of thin air. We send occasional hunting parties out, although I usually do a lot of the day-to-day stuff since I'm the best hunter in Byrrus. Well, second-best." He scowled. "Amelia has me beat."

"Really now?" Will said, intrigued. "Are you any good at tracking?"

Matteo placed his hands on his hips importantly. "I heard your conversation with Tam. You want me to tell you how he was able to find you?"

"You can do that?" Will grinned pleadingly.

Matteo pointed to the ground, where the dirt had been disturbed.

"It's not just that the dirt has been disturbed." Matteo followed Will's gaze. "It's that it's been disturbed in a pattern. If you look behind it, you can see the disturbances happen at specific intervals. And when you're not on a path, you leave a trail in the plants." He walked into the trees and pointed to a branch, which looked off balance.

"This looks a little bit off-kilter. Now, that can happen from any number of things, from animals to the wind." Matteo whipped out his knife and swung it through the branch, taking it down in one aggressive swoop. He caught the dismembered wood and used it as a pointer, gesturing to the ground. "But if you look under it, you can see there's an indent in the grass."

Will pursed his lips, impressed with the simplicity. "Seems pretty basic," he observed, and Matteo smirked.

"Everything seems basic once you know the answer. Just remember this about tracking: it's all about noticing the little details."

Will whistled, impressed. "Thanks, Matteo."

"Don't mention it! If you ever need extra help with your investigation, feel free to reach out. I'm rather good at mystery stuff."

"Noted. Guess I better get back. I have homework to do. Thanks again." Will then walked through a portal to the protected side of his house. He found exiting Betwixt and Between to someplace discreet—and outside—was the best move when going home. This way, if his parents were already inside, Will could enter the house normally, so they didn't wonder how he managed to magically get upstairs. Will nodded to the Byrrus guard stationed at the front door and walked into the living room.

"Hey bud," Emery greeted, with a reserved look. "How was your day?"

Ruth looked angry.

"Hi there. It was good. I was with Peter and Iris. We were doing homework after school. Normal stuff." He fidgeted, bouncing lightly on the balls of his feet.

"We got this in the mail today." Ruth pulled out a brown envelope and put it down on the table. It took Will a moment to register it wasn't a court-ordered arrest warrant, but his report card. In this situation, he'd almost prefer the warrant.

"Ah," Will said. "I see the problem."

"Will, these aren't good grades."

"They're fine!" he lied. Though he would never say it out loud, his parents had every right to be concerned. He earned all As in middle school. The drop off of straight As to a couple Cs was a bit stark.

"What's going on?" Ruth asked. "This really isn't like you. Are your friends distracting you? Are you drinking? Please tell us."

Will's faced went dark red. "I'm not drinking!" he spluttered. "And my friends are fine. I think Peter got straight As, like always. It's … uh …" He trailed off, looking for a convincing lie. "The transition has just been hard. The classes are tougher. Plus, I've been focusing a lot on music."

"You can't let this happen again, Will." Emery's voice was low and calculating. "We want you to get into a good college. That trip you went on at the beginning of the year was supposed to inspire that."

Will nodded, allowing a look of defeat to take over his face. "Okay. You're right. I'll do better. I promise. I'm sorry."

His parents didn't say anything more and Will retreated upstairs. His mother and father were reasonable people, and they'd want to give Will the chance to improve on his own. They wouldn't do anything drastic.

Not yet, at least.

11
Sensorship

While waiting for Raina—who was still out due to illness—to make her next move, the group kept working. They helped May get used to Byrrus and the World of the Written; they trained a lot; most importantly, they came up with the perfect excuse to not be home after school when they went to Byrrus.

"An unofficial book club," Iris announced one day at lunch. "It's perfect. It's related to the World of the Written, *and* it's something school-related. Our parents would be out of their minds to not approve."

"I'm sure my parents will be happy I'm doing something educational. They think my grades dropped because I'm out drinking with you all," Will grumbled.

It was settled—any time they needed an excuse to stay after school, they were at the Morrison High Book Club.

One day in band class, the principal greeted them, looking much twitchier than usual.

"So, kids, I know that this is going to be a shock ..." She took a deep breath in. "Your band teacher, Ms. Raina Morano, passed away last weekend."

"Death, huh? That's kind of dramatic." Tam appeared behind

Will. "I guess it eliminates any loose ends." Around them, students were clapping their hands to their mouths in shock. Several cried.

Will kept his face straight, staring at the principal.

"We've got grief counselors in the front office if needed, and they'll be stationed here at the school for the next month or so." She sighed. "There will be a special announcement at the end of the day, but we wanted to talk to you first, since you were her students. Try not to … gossip." The principal said the last word as if she knew it were in false hope.

"Will there be a funeral? I'm sure many of us would like to go, ma'am," one mousy-looking flute player asked. Her heavy mascara ran down her cheeks.

"Unfortunately, the majority of Ms. Morano's family lives in Utah. That's where the funeral will be held," the principal concluded.

Good choice, Will thought to Tam. *Believable but far enough away that no one will go to the funeral out of obligation or guilt.*

"What happened?" another girl asked.

"We're not entirely sure. Rest assured, the police are looking into it. We'll have a new band director for you guys soon enough. For now, just hang tight. We've found another substitute, but as far as music goes, take this period over the next few weeks as a study hall." The principal looked around, and seeing there were no further questions, gave a sigh of relief.

A nervous-looking man who had been standing behind her shook the principal's hand—definitely the new substitute.

"Hello, students. I am …"

As soon as the principal walked out of the room the class erupted, not even bothering to contain their volume.

Jaser sat next to Will with a horrified look on his face. "Geez, dude. What do you think happened? Murder? Suicide? She was so cheery all the time. Maybe that was covering up how depressed she was."

Even if Raina just manipulated the minds of those in charge to think she was dead and from Utah, that wouldn't explain how she ended up in Alexandria in the first place. Unless she was manipulating people's minds every time they tried to give her a paycheck or file her taxes, she had to have some sort of record on file with the school, Will thought.

And a record on file at the school … Tam responded.

"Would tell us exactly who she was!" Will shouted.

"You alright, buddy?"

"I'm fine. I have to go. I'll be right back."

Will grabbed his bag and left the room, followed by Tam. He didn't return. He and Tam paced in the hallway until the lunch bell rang. As students streamed into the halls, he pulled Peter, Iris, and May to the side, away from the crowd. They sat down outside.

Will explained everything from band class.

"So, we need to figure out a way to get Raina Morano's employment file from the school. And if we do that, we'll have her personal information." Iris bit her thumb.

"Or at least the information she used for employment," Peter muttered. "If there's anything real in that file, anything at all, we can use it. If we can track where she's been living, then maybe we can find out who she's connected to."

"Which could give us more information about why she killed Arthur, and if there's anyone else involved," May added.

"Okay, that's all well and good, but Peter brought up a good point. How do we know any of the information is real?" Iris stared at Will.

"We don't," Will replied, having already thought through this. "It shouldn't affect our decision. At the end of the day, if the information is fake, it's fake. If not, then we have something we didn't have before." He gazed at the group with what he hoped was a convincing stare. "Maybe, hopefully, she didn't think of changing her information. She was very careful to only reveal who she really was when she thought I would either give up my powers or die. I doubt she expected us to investigate her, let alone try to get her personal information from the school."

The group was silent, and Will took this silence for agreement, no matter how begrudging it might have been.

"How do we do it?" Tam asked. "I guess I can go into the school's back office and see if I can find it, though I'm not sure how much use that will be unless it's lying open on a desk."

May snapped her fingers. "I've got an idea. I'm going to put my acting chops to good use."

"Let me come," Will interjected.

"Listen, Will, no offense, but you're too impulsive. It's also simpler if one person does it. Plus," she scoffed, "I'm prettier and more innocent-looking. They'd never suspect anything nefarious from a poor freshman girl."

Without waiting for a response, May ran off to the main office.

Ten minutes later, she came back huffing.

"I take it that didn't work?" Will asked.

May groaned. "It's not that it didn't work. It actually worked perfectly." She put her hands in front of her chest in a begging motion. "They told us in band Ms. Morano passed away … and I know the funeral is in Utah, but she really helped me get through some awful stuff earlier this year." May's eyes teared up, and she wiped the liquid away, looking extremely convincing. "Can I please see her file? Just so I can figure out who her family is, so I can thank them? Or try to attend the funeral?" She rolled her eyes and dropped the act. "The woman in the front office was super nice! She actually went into the back to find it. That it's for good news. She came back a few minutes later and said it wasn't there!" She breathed out, face getting red as she looked at the sky. "Looks like Raina covered her tracks better than we thought."

"I guess she thought more about this than we gave her credit for. What about an electronic file?" Peter mumbled with his head in his hands.

"I tried that," May replied. "Apparently there's some law that makes the school treat electronic files and physical files differently. And at that point, the lady was freaking out about the paper file being gone, so she wasn't really paying attention to me."

"Good try anyways, May," Will said, though his voice was airy and lacked bravado.

"Do you think we could hack into the school's mainframe and steal the file?" Peter jumped in again. "We'd probably need to break into the office at night. That shouldn't be too difficult."

"You don't need to break into the school to hack the mainframe. If you have the right equipment, you can do it remotely." Jaser sat next to Peter. Peter yelped in surprise and fell over, and Jaser raised an eyebrow. "What's going on? Missed you at lunch."

"How much did you hear?" Will asked, trying to keep his voice level.

Jaser shrugged. "I heard you talking about hacking the school. You guys look terrified," he added. "I'm not going to rat you out. I've talked to Will about hacking before. It's a fun subject."

"Haha … yeah," Peter muttered, sitting up and rubbing his hands together aimlessly. "Exactly."

"Don't tell me you guys were actually debating hacking into the school's mainframe."

The words lingered in the silence that followed.

"Seriously? I can't believe you're talking about hacking and didn't think to invite me!" Jaser chortled. "This is my thing! I'm literally taking a class at the university on computer hacking." He pointed his thumb back at the school. "I've already done it once or twice for fun. The security is really basic. If you're just looking at information, and not changing anything, you can get in and out without leaving a trace. Just takes a few clicks."

The group stared at him blankly for a few moments. "Wait," Will began, "you can't be serious. You've already hacked the school? Jaser, that's probably a felony or something!"

"And?" His eyes narrowed as if Will had said something stupid. "I wouldn't do it if I thought I would get caught. Plus, I'm not doing anything dangerous or bad, like changing my grades. I'm just looking at interesting stuff. Like how much teachers get paid or where they live. Things like that."

Amelia appeared next to Tam, who filled her in.

"I don't like this," Tam said to the Writers. "You could be arrested. No. There has to be a better way."

Amelia grimaced. "And you could put him in danger! You've gotten lucky so far. What if Jaser doesn't have the *Potential* and just gets hurt? Or worse? What if Raina uses him against you?"

Matteo appeared next to Amelia, squinting at Jaser.

"He seems trustworthy. Plus, he and Will are already friends. He has no reason to betray them." There was a glint of respect in his eyes.

"Where did you come from? And why are you eavesdropping?" Amelia barked condescendingly.

"I have every reason to be as invested in this mess as you." Annoyance crept into Matteo's voice. "Arthur also created me, my dear Amelia. You and Tam don't have exclusive claim to being involved with Will just because you're mad Arthur never concluded your love story."

Amelia looked like she was about to slap Matteo, and May stifled a snort that left her coughing into her arm. Tam ignored everyone except for Will.

"No one is going to tell you what to do here, Will. I trust your judgement. Just ..." He sighed. "Don't feel pressured to do anything one way or another."

"Stop talking, everyone!"

"No one was talking, Will. You okay? What are you guys staring at?" Jaser was looking at Will and the others with trepidation.

Trust him.

The reassuring voice of Simon filled Will's ears. *We need his help,* the Familiar whispered, though he was nowhere to be seen.

"Can you help us then? Since it's so easy," Will asked.

He looked to the group, hoping some affirmation would get rid of the nausea taking root in his stomach. Amelia groaned, eyeing Matteo with malice. Everyone else seemed to agree with Will.

"What do you keep looking at? Are you alright?" Jaser began tapping his foot against the pavement. "Of course I can help you. What exactly do you want me to do?"

Will breathed a sigh of relief, only a little bit of the tension in his chest being released. "We need you to hack and retrieve the employment file for Raina Morano. Her birthday. Home address.

Emergency contacts. As much information on her as you're able to get."

Whatever answer Jaser had been expecting, this certainly wasn't it. He stared at his friends blankly. "Haha! Good one." His laugh faltered when no one else joined in.

"Wait, you're not joking." His eyes went wide. "Why the hell do you need the personal information of a dead woman?"

"It's too complicated to explain. Just, please," May begged. "We're not doing anything illegal with the information. We just think there's something weird about her death."

"Then go to the police," Jaser stated. "And why do you guys care? None of you were in band with me and Will."

"You already said you go into files to see where teachers live. This is way less invasive since she's dead!" Iris was staring daggers at Jaser.

"It makes it way less kosher too!" Jaser cried loudly.

"Keep it down, Jaser. You don't have to help us, you know," Peter said. "Just remember that you *are* the one who volunteered."

"Okay, fine. It's not hard to do. But jeez … I'm going to have a lot of questions afterwards." He clapped his hands together. "When do you want to do it?"

"As soon as possible. When are you free?" Will hoped his voice conveyed the urgency.

"Let's do it this afternoon," Jaser concluded, "after school. I can skip my hacking class and get some real-world experience. Meet me in the library. It's worked for me before." He grinned at their confused looks. "This school is a dead-zone for technology signals. While that means it's harder to get internet, it also makes it harder for them to trace signals back to individual computers."

"I don't know. Maybe there's a better way?" Iris asked.

"I've done this before. I know I can pull it off, but if you don't want to, just tell me and we can pretend this never happened."

"If this is our best option, I think we should go for it. We need to find her before she makes her next move," Tam said.

"Let's do it," Will affirmed.

"Well that settles it! See you all in the library at three." Jaser stood to leave. "I'll let you guys continue discussing whatever secret stuff you were talking about." He waved and walked to a group of band students in the distance.

Peter sighed.

"What's with the long faces? Jaser isn't Raina in disguise," Matteo vocalized, eyes rolling.

"Will, we have things to take care of in Byrrus. Can you do this without us?" Tam asked.

"I don't want any part of it anyway," Amelia spat reproachfully, habitually tugging at the knife on her belt.

Will saluted the Characters. "It's okay. We've got this. I'll let you know if something comes up."

As the principal promised, there was a heartfelt message during the afternoon announcements about Ms. Morano's death. The principal detailed available mental health resources, which was nice, except most of the students were more confused than anything else—very few students knew who she was. There was very little mourning, from what Will could tell. Most students just packed up their stuff to head home.

At three, the group found the library empty.

"So what do we do?" May asked, putting her bag down in a booth.

Jaser opened his laptop and stretched his fingers. "You do nothing," he muttered, distracted. "You don't even need to keep watch. Just be here to observe the modern marvel that is technology."

Will watched over Jaser's shoulder as he opened an application and began typing. From what Will could tell, it was entirely code, and none of it made sense. As Jaser typed, words Will recognized flash across the screen. "Name," "Students," "Grades," and "College Information" were just a few of the labels that popped up before Jaser scrolled over to a label that said, "Teachers."

He began muttering to himself. "Unless they removed her file already, this is where it should be." He clicked the tab, typed in a few more lines of code, and eventually the name "Raina Morano" appeared on his screen.

"Excellent," he muttered. A moment later, though, his face fell.

"What's wrong?" Iris asked.

"Nothing," Jaser said. "Well, nothing that pertains to us. This just says the previous band director decided he was going to move to Europe three days before Ms. Morano was hired. Kind of odd, don't you think?" He looked at Will.

Will widened his eyes in mock-surprise. Inside, his rage was coming to the surface. How many lives was this woman going to uproot?

Jaser typed in a few more commands and a file popped into view as a PDF. He pressed a few more buttons on his keyboard and the hacking software closed, fading off his screen like it had never been there. He then removed a flash drive from the computer.

"I'll print this and give you guys copies," he said, flipping the piece of plastic between his fingers. "I'm printing it from a PDF and not the hack itself, so it can't be traced." He waved the flash drive around. "No need to thank me."

Peter and Jaser high-fived.

"Um, guys," May interrupted, her voice getting noticeably higher. "Not to worry you, but why are there four policemen walking into a high school library?"

Jaser's eyes rapidly darted between his friends and the entrance. "What the hell? I know for a fact it's not traced. The program would tell me if it was." He gulped. "These guys don't know we hacked the system. There's no way. It wouldn't tell them that fast."

Contrary to Jaser's thought process, there they were. The four men approached the group. One pulled out a wallet, showing them a badge.

"Officer Clary, Alexandria PD. We traced a signal here that suggests someone was hacking into the school's computer mainframe. You kids know anything about that?" The officer's voice was rough and ominous, making it very clear that his question was just a formality.

"No, we don't," May asserted, taking a textbook out of her bag and waving it at Officer Clary. "We came here to study for a quiz and were just getting ready to head home."

One of the officers looked at Jaser's laptop, still in his hand. He pointed at it. "I'm going to need to confiscate that, kid," he barked, casting a shadow over Jaser as he bared down on him.

Jaser clutched it to his chest in a bear hug.

Will looked the officer directly in the eye. "Forgive me," he said, "don't you need a warrant for this type of stuff? And why are four school police officers investigating this, and not the FBI?"

"Computer hacking is a serious crime," another policeman said.

"Suppose we had hacked the school," Iris said slowly, her hand going behind her back. The Gilmarye appeared in her clutched fingers. "It would've taken way longer for you guys to sense the signal, track it, and corner us here. Plus, as Will said, I don't think cyber terrorism falls under the jurisdiction of the police. So, why are you using that as an excuse?"

Officer Clary flipped his badge away and whipped out a gun. Jaser screamed, and Will summoned his sword to his hands. The policeman raised the gun higher.

"Drop the sword, Morgan!" he shouted.

That's when all hell broke loose.

"*Clipuroje!*" Iris shouted, the Gilmarye glowing blue.

A large bubble appeared, shimmering as it floated. The officers open fired, their bullets ricocheting off the shield. Peter summoned his staff.

May grabbed Peter's hand, pushing the weapon down. "Don't hurt them! They're human."

"How do you know?" Iris asked, attempting to keep the wall intact. The police were still shooting on the other side. One started talking into a walkie-talkie, and Will's face blanched.

"Jaser can see them, so they're clearly not Shades. That means Tam and Amelia can't help," May growled. "They're being controlled by Raina. There's no way the police would trace a high school hack signal that quickly. Plus, that guy knew Will's name, and he reacted to Will's sword."

"We have to take them out without hurting them. Excellent," Will muttered.

"What do you mean, *Jaser can see them*? Of course I can see them!" Jaser exclaimed, looking wildly between Iris and May. "And Iris, get down! What are you doing?"

Iris was sweating, the effort of keeping the shield up too taxing. Will shifted his gaze to May, who nodded.

"Iris, on three, you let go of the shield. May is going to create a blockade of ice, and from there we can figure out what to do, okay?"

"Sounds good," Iris grunted.

May readied herself. "One, two, three!"

They all jumped back, and as the shield dropped, May summoned ice. It cascaded from the ceiling, blocking the police officers from view. They stopped shooting.

Will turned to Jaser.

"Hey, Jaser. You okay?"

"What … is going on with them? What is that shadowy stuff around them?"

Jaser couldn't see the ice that had been summoned; however, there had been nothing coming off of the four officers. Whatever Jaser was seeing was something only he could. His pupils were bright, and Will could sense a new power radiating from his friend.

"What are you talking about, Jaser?" Will asked.

Jaser didn't respond. Instead, his face got a crazed urgent look, and he threw Will down, desperately looking at the others.

"Duck!"

The group didn't hesitate. Right where Will's body had been a moment before, a bullet sliced through the air, cracking the ice in a dozen places and causing the wall to crash down around them. May cried out and put her hands up, the shards turning to snow as they fell.

One of the men took a step forward, but Peter waved his staff, causing a column of fire to erupt in front of the advancing officer.

The man snarled, his face contorted into a look more akin to a Shade than a human.

"You have five seconds to walk over here, without your weapon, William Morgan," a different officer said. "We don't want to hurt you, but we will. Five seconds before we open fire and kill your friends. We'll be taking you to Raina regardless. Five …"

"What do we do?" Peter moaned. "My fire won't stop bullets."

Iris leafed through the Gilmarye. May looked worn out.

Don't go. You can figure this out, Simon whispered.

Jaser moved first, walking straight toward the officers.

"Jaser, what are you doing?" Will shouted. "Peter, put the fire out." Peter obliged, though his eyes followed Jaser, terrified.

"Leave my friends alone," Jaser commanded, his voice steadier than Will's would have been. One of the policemen smirked and held the muzzle of his gun level with Jaser's head.

"You should not have meddled," he said, teeth bared in an antagonistic smirk.

The gun went off, and May shrieked. A window shattered and Jaser, who stood a few inches to the right, stared straight ahead, right as rain. The men looked confused.

"You lucky little punk," a different officer said. He aimed his weapon at Jaser and fired two quick shots.

Will used his Writer's eye to slow time. In the moments it took the policeman to fire, Jaser was already out of harm's way, advancing toward the men.

In a spark of lightning, a halberd came to Jaser's hands. Will watched in awe as his friend fought with incredible precision. Jaser knocked the pistols from the policemen's hands with the sharpened axe and used the staff of the weapon to hit them.

What Will found even more wild was that Jaser seemed to be predicting every single movement his enemies made. There was not a single instance when an officer's hands made contact with Jaser's body. Then it was over. The police officers were all on the ground, unconscious, but alive.

Jaser stared at his friends, the halberd resting at his side. His face grew calm, the surge of power fading from his eyes. He rubbed his face as if waking from a dream and looked around at the wreckage of the library. He began to panic.

"Seriously," he looked at his four friends, eyes widening in fear, "what's going on?"

"It's okay, Jaser. What do you remember?" Will asked.

"We need to figure out what to do with them before anything else," May said, biting her bottom lip as she stared at the unconscious men.

"I got it!" Iris shouted. "I found a spell that should just do a complete reset of magic on them! Raina's mind control will disappear, and they'll wake up with nothing but a bit of memory loss, and some nasty headaches." She kneeled, the Gilmarye on the floor as she waved her hands over the police, focused. *"Shumaj depel."*

A bright white light flashed over the men and they began to stir. Iris took a deep breath in, not letting her exhaustion get to her, before casting one more spell. Though it wasn't perfect, the room was mostly back to what it had been before. There was a massive puddle on the ground from the ice, and a well-trained eye would see a few silk-thin cracks in the window, though nothing would indicate the damage came from anything more than a few rowdy kids causing trouble.

The Writers emerged outside, where some students milled

about. They clearly didn't notice any of the noise coming from the conflict upstairs.

Will looked at Jaser, hoping his voice sounded calm. "Okay. I know this seems absolutely nuts. Just hear us out."

"What happened up there, Will?" Jaser's eyes lit up with a combination of both fear and exhilaration. "That was crazy person stuff. Magic stuff. I hack the school for information about a dead teacher, and all of a sudden, cops try to kill me. Then I knock them unconscious with some spear axe thingy!"

"You also seemed to be able to predict their movements and gunshots. And you had crazy reflexes," Peter commented.

Jaser's nostrils flared. "Please explain!"

"I'm glad to see you didn't pass out from exhaustion. In fact, you seem quite energetic," Tam said, appearing and walking up to Jaser. Jaser yelped in shock, and the onlookers who weren't staring before were certainly staring now.

"Uh, Jaser," Iris whispered, glancing around them. "We should probably go somewhere else to talk about this. Somewhere more private."

The group sat in the grass away from the other students who were hanging out after school. Tam took a moment to introduce himself and explained what happened. Will explained what happened with Raina and how she tried to kill him the night of the band concert.

"The one good thing is," Iris said, "this is just another thing Raina can't use to hurt us."

"What do you mean?" Will asked.

"Well, we know how to dispel magic from the humans she tries to manipulate." She put a finger up. "Plus, Merlin gave us protection against Shades when we're in our homes, so we can't be assassinated in the middle of the night. He'll give you the same protections I'm sure," she added to Jaser.

"Well that doesn't stop Readers from hurting us when we're out and about. If Merlin's magic doesn't protect us, and our attacker isn't under a spell, then we're sitting ducks," Will commented.

May shook her head. "No, you dolt. Then we fight. We can't come up with a solution for every possibility. That's why we train."

"Train?"

"Yeah. We spend a lot of time fighting to sharpen our skills. It can be fun."

"Cool. Sounds great. First of all," Jaser started, straining to keep his voice steady, "given our obvious distraction, I didn't print the file. Here." He handed a flash drive to Will. "Just take this. Print it out as soon as you can. Second of all," he took a deep breath in, "you realize this is some of the most mental stuff I've ever heard? Right?"

They all nodded, and Jaser crossed his arms.

"I mean, I'd be stupid to deny any of this," he continued. "Unless I'm on some wild hallucinogen, people outside of our group can't see you, Tam, and I clearly can summon some axe from fantasy land."

"Halberd," Tam interrupted, voice bright and cheery. "That's what you call it when there's a long pole with the axe blade on the top."

"Right," Jaser muttered.

"Were you able to predict your enemy's movements? From what you're describing, it sounds as if you knew exactly what they were going to do."

"Yeah. It wasn't just the movements though. I could almost tell something was up with those guys. They had black shadows seeping off them." Jaser scanned the group, looking for a reaction. "Did none of you see that?"

Tam placed a hand on his chin. "Interesting. Jaser, you have a gift called Sensorship. I have a version of it, though it's much lighter and less useful. You can essentially sense energies within the World of the Written: good, evil, etcetera. You can also predict what enemies are going to do, which helps you in combat, and general tracking and avoiding danger."

Jaser stuttered a few times, trying to get words out, but eventually just sighed heavily and dipped his head.

Tam gave a small smile. "I know it's a lot to take in. Don't worry if it's a little bit confusing. You'll get there."

"I mean, given I've already been in a fight, I feel like I understand most of what's going on, in theory at least," Jaser offered, chuckling despite the light tremors shaking his body. "The only thing missing is seeing the World of the Written." He looked at Tam, leaning forward. "When can I go?"

Tam winked at Jaser. After everyone texted their parents with the excuse of a meeting for book club, Tam summoned a portal to Betwixt and Between, and they walked through it to Byrrus. The rest of the Writers had been sick on their first trip to Byrrus. Jaser was different. He was surprisingly unaffected by the fact he just knocked four adults unconscious, and peppered the group with questions.

When they entered Byrrus, the city and castle were awash in November colors, the trees that still held leaves reflecting vibrant hues of yellow and red, and Jaser whipped his head until he almost fell over, trying to see everything at once.

"This is more than I could have ever dreamed of."

The reverence in Jaser's voice reminded Will just how cool the

Writer's Eye really was. He felt a greater need to do everything he could to protect it.

Jaser assumed this afternoon was one his friends had gone through already. They walked around Byrrus, introduced him to Pass, then sat him down in a massive hall that was apparently exclusively used for feasts.

It was the most overwhelming yet best day of Jaser's life.

During dinner a boy Jaser didn't recognize slid into the seat next to him, bumping into his shoulder. He was fairly muscular, roughly Jaser's height, and had hair that, despite its rumpled appearance, looked extremely soft, as if it were made from down. Jaser had a weird urge to touch it, which he swallowed along with his food.

"That's a lot of food there," the boy smirked. Jaser blushed and covered his mouth, reaching his hand out to shake the stranger's.

"I'm Matteo. Matteo Gavin. I'm a friend of Will's."

Will gestured from the other side of the table.

"Jaser Solomon," Jaser coughed out, choking on the massive amount of food he had just tried to consume. "Wait, Matteo! Of course! I know you. You're the greatest hunter in all of Byrrus. Everyone knows who you are."

Jaser felt more embarrassed than he had all day and was extraordinarily conscious of how new he was to this world. He didn't know why.

"That's very kind." Matteo's face turned a slight shade redder. "Who cares? Hunting isn't that interesting. You, however? I heard you dodged a bunch of bullets without blinking an eye. That's a bit more exciting than trapping birds."

"Yeah, I suppose I did. I don't really understand the gift yet, though." Jaser swallowed another bite, shocked the news had traveled so quickly. "Anyways, you act like hunting is easy. You should take me sometime. I feel like it would help me get more experience with my Sensorship, or whatever it's called."

"Sounds like a plan. I'd love to see it in action. Tam's the only person I've ever seen with that power, and from the sounds of it, yours is much stronger." Matteo then turned away, engaging Will in conversation and leaving Jaser to question himself. Was he really that powerful?

After a while, Jaser stopped staring around and slid closer to Will. "I know it took me almost dying to get here," he started, "but this is spectacular. Thank you, Will. Truly." As he stood, Jaser tripped and grabbed the side of a table, the exhaustion showing on his face.

"I guess I'm a bit tired. Don't worry. I'll be fine!" A shaky laugh escaped him.

"Oh no you don't," Matteo interjected as he grabbed Jaser's shoulder to keep him standing. "You're clearly beat. Using your powers as much as you did would take a toll on anyone, especially a newbie. You need to go home and rest."

"I'll take him home," Will said. Jaser looked at his friend gratefully, and Will nodded. Will and Jaser waved goodbye to the Characters and other Writers before walking into Betwixt and Between.

Will dropped Jaser off in an alleyway near his house, and the two made their way to Jaser's front door before Will saluted him.

"You feel okay?" Will asked, and Jaser grinned.

"Yeah, I feel great. A bit tired, but nothing a good sleep won't fix. You have the flash drive, right?" Despite all of the evening's excitement, Jaser hadn't forgotten about the original reason he had gone to the library.

Will held up the small USB drive. "I'm going to go home and read into it right now. I'll have the full report ready for you tomorrow."

Will then glanced around, looking for observers before summoning a portal and stepping through. The golden archway disappeared in a flash, and Jaser was left with nothing but the empty street, the chilly air, and the knowledge that his life had been forever changed.

12

The Handwritten Story

The next day, everyone—minus May—met at their usual lunch table. They passed the time by making small talk, all understandably nervous. Jaser looked around the cafeteria, eyes narrow and unblinking.

"What are you trying to do, Jaser? Predict everyone's movements?" Peter asked.

"Yeah." A sly grin played on his rosy face. "It's really bizarre, actually. I can almost *see* what people are going to do. Oh no." Jaser winced as the boy he was staring at tripped on a spilled carton of milk and landed on his back with a hard thud. "It's only momentary, mind you. I can't predict the future like May and Amelia." He shrugged and went back to his sandwich.

After a few minutes, May slid into one of the empty seats, looking flustered.

"Sorry for the delay." She cracked open a can of diet soda. "Some of my other friends got mad I haven't sat with them for the past few weeks, so I told them I had to work on a project with some other people. They're still upset, but I bought some time. They can be kind of annoying."

Will glanced to his left and made eye contact with a set of girls staring daggers at the group. He winked in their direction and turned back to May, pulling some papers from a folder in his backpack.

"Tam and I looked at Raina's file last night," he said. "It was a lot of basic information like we predicted. Age, phone number, social security number, stuff like that." He raised a finger, wagging it. "What's important is there's an address attached to the file. It's not much, but it's a start."

"And you don't think she's going to be there waiting for us? Or have traps waiting?" Jaser whispered. "She knew we were going to try and get her file. Do you think she's just going to let us waltz into her house?"

Will gulped, the obviousness of Jaser's fear hitting him. "To be honest, I didn't even think about the possibility of traps. How likely do you think that is?"

"Probably pretty likely, considering she sent cops to arrest us," Peter said.

"I have an idea." Iris summoned the Gilmarye to her hands.

"Iris, what are you doing? Someone will notice," Jaser hissed, pupils shooting in every direction.

"It's fine, Jaser. No one else can see it."

"Oh, yeah. Forgot." Jaser blushed. "It takes some getting used to, I guess."

"We've all been there. Anyway, I was wondering if there was a way we could have been safer about getting Raina's file. You know, checking to make sure she hadn't set any enchantments on the school, or set anything to explode if we used our Writer's Eyes." She tapped the book. "I found a spell. Good news: the school is now magic-free. Any traps she had set were either sprung already, or she removed them. However, I could still use it on her house to see if there's anything malicious waiting for us."

"You're brilliant, Iris," May chimed in.

"And you're certain it'll work?" Jaser asked.

"Positive. It'll warn us of any traps she might have set, magical or otherwise."

Peter breathed a sigh of relief. "Alrighty! That settles it."

"She probably took everything valuable with her," Will groaned. "Still, it's worth a shot."

A few days later, the Writers, joined by Tam and Amelia, waited in one of Byrrus Castle's meeting rooms. Iris sat cross-legged on a large table, leafing through the Gilmarye.

"It's simple," she began. "We teleport to the backyard of the house, I cast my spell, and I immediately know if it's safe. If it is, then we can either teleport in or walk in the front door."

"Okay," Tam responded. "You know your magic better than I do. I still think it's reckless." He gave a small scowl. "Amelia and I will come along, just in case."

Will was about to mock him when there was a hurried knock on the door.

"Come in," Tam called.

Matteo, red in the cheeks and unusually disheveled, walked into the room.

"Hey stranger," Jaser said, voice bright and welcoming. "What brings you here?"

"Nothing much. I ran into Pass while I was walking through the grounds. He mentioned that you guys were going to investigate Raina's place." Matteo stood up straighter and made a desperate attempt to fix his hair. "I'd like to come with you. I've got experience in espionage, after all, and it would be good to have someone with my background there, you know, to make sure you don't miss anything obvious."

"'Espionage.' I like the sound of that. It's cool," Jaser said.

"It's not all it's cracked up to be, though I guess the title is pretty cool," Matteo replied, winking. However, his confident manner faded when he looked at Tam. Will followed his gaze and found that the Pontifex was fixing Matteo with an uncharacteristically cold look.

"We'd love to have you join us." Jaser was looking at Matteo with welcome, not having noticed Tam.

The other Writers agreed wholeheartedly, and Will stood tall, clapping his hands together.

"All right. No time like the present."

Will summoned a portal to Betwixt and Between, funneling the Writers in.

"We'll just be a minute, Will. You guys go ahead. We want to make sure we have everything prepped," Amelia said.

Will turned back, forcing himself to stay calm. He stepped into the portal and closed it; however, instead of following his friends, he opened another portal, this one leading him to the outside of the room they had been meeting in. Will put his ear to the door.

Matteo eyed Tam and Amelia, furrowing his brow before taking a step back. His sudden appearance might have been jarring, or even unwanted, but was there really harm in offering his assistance? Pass had told him where the group was meeting and why. It was only natural he'd want to help.

"You seem to be extraordinarily interested in what the Writers are doing, Gavin," Tam said, though there was a growl distinguishable behind his calm tone. "You haven't had any interest in the affairs of the World of the Writers before now. Not with Arthur, and not when it was just Will with the Writer's Eye. So, tell me," his gaze narrowed, "why is your interest piqued when Raina Morano is hidden from view?"

This shocked Matteo. That was why Amelia and Tam were suspicious? They thought he was working with Raina? Instead of instilling fear, the question brought a boiling anger to the pit of his stomach that rose through his throat.

"I don't see what your problem is, *Desmond*," Matteo snarled in response, hoping he was putting enough vitriol behind his words. "Is that really what this is about? You think I'm spying for *Raina?* You're out of your damn mind. I'm Arthur's child, just as much as you or Amelia. I should have a right ..."

"Watch your tone around your elders, you little upstart. Don't you dare pretend for a moment you know anything about Arthur O'Neill. How many times did you meet him? Twice? Three times?" Amelia's words dripped with aggression, and Matteo put his hand on the knife at his belt, feeling uneasy at the look in her eyes.

"I still have loyalty!" he shouted in response.

Tam took a step forward, and Matteo hoped Tam hadn't seen the light quiver shoot through his frame; he forgot how much taller Tam was than him.

"You're a spy," the Pontifex said. "You take a lot of pride in that. You're very good at it. So, let's be real, Matteo. You and I don't have a relationship. We're not friends. Hell, I haven't really ever spoken to you outside the context of a war. And as Amelia said, you never knew

Arthur. You can mourn him, but you don't have much motivation to try and apprehend his killer. Now that the killer's identity is known, you're trying to get involved? No. There's more to it."

Tam whipped his sword out of its scabbard. In return, Matteo pulled the knife from his belt, gripping it in a defensive position.

Tam pointed his weapon at Matteo. "As far as I see it, you're spying for Raina. I'm going to give you until the count of three to tell me what your actual intention is. If you don't, I will go to Pass right now and have you expelled from your little spy duties. I might even get you thrown in prison. I don't care if it's drastic; I will not let you hurt Will or his friends. Do you understand me? Now, one …"

"I don't have evil intentions!" Matteo shouted. He didn't want to be forced into telling the truth. Not now. It was too embarrassing.

"Two!" Tam yelled. Matteo's face went beet red.

"Fine," he moaned, frustrated. "You want the truth? Fine! Jaser is cute, okay? As soon as he got involved with Will's computer hacking crap, I figured he would unlock the *Potential*. Happy?"

The awkwardness in the air was palpable. Matteo stood straight, resisting the urge to cover his face in embarrassment.

"I mean, okay. But you don't even know Jaser is … well …"

"Gay, Tam." Matteo rolled his eyes, his embarrassment giving way to irritation. "The word is gay. It's not a slur. And I know." Matteo sighed. "Who cares? We're around the same age, we have a lot in common, and I like being around him. That's why I keep trying to step in on your investigation. I'm not a Shade or working for Raina or anything like that. Just because the two of you are afraid to pursue the person you love doesn't mean the rest of us have to follow suit. So just back off, okay?"

Amelia spluttered. "You don't even know the guy! You've met him, like what, twice? Three times?"

"That doesn't mean I can't find him attractive! You traditionalist dinosaurs! That's why I want to *get to know him*!"

Tam grunted, which Matteo took to be some form of blessing. "Well, now that that's out of the way, can we go?" Matteo demanded. "*We* have a murder to solve." And with that, he turned to summon a portal, hoping that Tam and Amelia felt at least a little bit guilty.

Will pulled away from the door, heart thumping. He was glad he didn't need to burst in to protect Matteo—or Tam and Amelia. A crush though? How would that even work? Matteo was a Character. Jaser was a Writer. Could anything romantic happen between them? What was more, Will always just assumed Jaser was straight from the comments he made about girls.

Putting the thoughts out of mind for the time being, Will walked out of the portal to the back of Raina Morano's house, joining the rest of the group. It was nothing unusual; a one-story building in a suburban neighborhood, right outside of Winston-Salem. Tam, Amelia, and Matteo materialized a few moments after Will did, acting as if nothing happened.

"Can we go inside?" Will asked Iris.

"One moment please." She flexed her fingers around the Gilmarye and closed her eyes. "*Ostende sihri. Gostende periculi.*"

A soft wind seemed to flow off the pages of the book, rippling across the grass of Raina's lawn and around the house, scanning it. After a few moments Iris opened her eyes, looking at the building with relief.

"No traps to be found, human or magical. I think it's better if we enter like normal people, though. I'm pretty sure I did the spell right but better safe than sorry. There's a lockbox next to the door."

"Did the spell show you the lockbox?" Will asked, impressed.

"My magical eyes did." Iris smirked as she walked over to the back door and picked up a clearly visible stout box with a mechanical lock pad on the front. She winked and tossed it to Will.

Will stared at it, dumb faced, considering grabbing a rock to break it open. Jaser held out his hand.

"I'm not just good at hacking computers," he said, a hint of pride in his voice. He took the lockbox and held it up to his ear, rotating the dials slowly and with purpose. Eventually, the box clicked open, revealing a silver house key.

"Impressive." Matteo grinned. Jaser unlocked the door.

"We'll keep watch." Tam motioned to himself and Amelia. Will nodded and walked through the doorway, taking it one step at a time as he peeled his eyes for any sign of danger.

Even though the blinds were open, the house had a very dark, old feel. The walls inside were covered in aged wood that Will would have expected to see in his grandparents' home. All the furniture appeared to be vintage, except cheap vintage, like the owner wanted to appear sophisticated but failed. The whole place smelled like it had been shut up for months with a water leak in the basement.

The rooms were in complete disarray. The furniture was flipped over, with one bookshelf having crashed to the ground. Chairs were scattered and cut open, one or two had missing legs, and there was debris strewn across the carpeting from a few broken knick-knacks.

"Someone was in a hurry ..." Jaser muttered. He picked up a dismembered chair leg and twirled it around in his hand, as if hoping it would reveal something. "She must have been really freaked out after your fight, Will. It looks like she was just running around and grabbing things. Doesn't seem like she cared too much about leaving a mess behind." He nudged the remains of a lamp with his foot.

"Once you guys knew her identity, she probably wanted to escape from here as quickly as possible. I can see her coming in here, running around and trying to grab the things that were important. See here." Matteo pointed to the hollowed-out chair leg Jaser held. "Something was hidden in here. And this," he continued, motioning to a broken picture frame dangling on the wall, "is because she forgot she had turned over the chair and tripped over it, knocking into the picture. Look, there's a little blood on the glass."

"Spoken like a true strategist," Jaser chuckled, lightly thumping Matteo on the arm.

The group fanned out, looking at the items Raina had left scattered throughout the house. There were blank expanses of wall, desks that were empty of everything, drawers in her bedroom that were completely barren.

"Hey, guys? I think I found something. Something really weird," May called.

Will met his friends in a small den. A few shelves were filled with dust-covered antiques.

"How is there so much dust?" Will wondered. "It's like no one has been here in years."

Several empty picture frames filled the rest of the space. Will wondered who Raina could have been taking pictures with.

May stood in the corner next to a lamp. At her feet was an upturned waste basket, trash scattered on the floor. She held up a crumpled photo.

"I must be going blind or something—or I haven't seen his face in a while—but this picture … it's Raina, with Arthur O'Neill. Without her disguise."

The picture was at least fifteen years old, slightly faded with age. Raina was a child, no older than ten, although Arthur looked relatively the same. He was a little thinner, his hair less gray than it had been in his recent photos.

Matteo glanced over Will's shoulder. "Would you look at that. The plot thickens." He put his hand to his chin. "What's even stranger to me is it was in the trash. That means one of three things. One: she didn't want us to find that picture. Two, she didn't want to see it herself. Or three, she just didn't care about it."

Will took another glance around the room, and his eyes landed on a set of bookshelves. They were lined with a number of worn-out books—Raina was an avid reader. The second thing he noticed was the copies of the *Byrrus* books. All of them featured older versions of the cover art and were dog-eared beyond belief. They were old enough to be originals. On top of the *Byrrus* novels were neat stacks of paper, piled together with care, though still loose of any bindings. Will took the papers in his hands, blowing the dust off, making sure to not ruffle the loose-leaf.

"More dust. It's so weird," he coughed.

He scanned the papers carefully. After a moment, his quivering voice broke the silence. "Guys. This is a handwritten copy of *The Redstone Keep*. Like, the book."

"Bull," Peter shot back, taking the stack from Will.

"There are more handwritten versions," Peter said with his mouth wide open. "How can that be?"

"Look for letters!" Jaser exclaimed. "Anything else hand-written.

Something that would offer an explanation. Maybe even something from Arthur himself."

A window shattered somewhere in the house, followed by a small explosion.

"You guys need to get out of here! Now!" Tam stepped in from a portal.

The group ran into the portal just as the house burst into flames. They exited across the street.

Two men wearing sunglasses and suits stared at the group for a moment before walking away. Peter summoned his staff, but Jaser put a hand on his shoulder.

"They're not going to fight us," he muttered, sounding confident albeit disheartened. "They were only here to set the house on fire."

"I don't understand how that's possible …" Iris tilted her head to the side and gazed at them. "I know the spell worked. I would have felt it if we triggered some sort of magical sensor."

"Maybe it was just coincidence," May suggested.

"Or they've been watching the house from a distance," Matteo groaned. "We were only there for fifteen minutes. Maybe they saw us walk in, and then set up their Molotov cocktails, or whatever they used. Doesn't seem too complicated."

Sirens wailed in the distance.

Will sighed. "We should get out of here. We don't want to be the only people here when the police and fire trucks arrive."

Tam opened a portal to Byrrus, and once through, the group laid out the papers they saved from the fire.

"And you're sure you never saw Raina before all of this started?" Will asked Tam for the hundredth time.

"Unless my memory is being warped, I had never seen her

before that fight in the band room," he muttered. "I'd say she was just a big fan, except they look too friendly in that picture. And the handwritten manuscripts? They're something else entirely. I never even knew Arthur had written the books out like that."

"Maybe they were just placed there to trick us?" Matteo suggested, leaning back and scratching his head. "There were people staking out the house. Yeah, Raina took a bunch of her stuff, but why leave things that directly tie her to Arthur O'Neill, someone she killed?" He sighed. "We know she's not on our side given how many times she's tried to hurt you guys. So frankly, I say we ignore everything we found today. If we focus on it, we could end up walking into a trap."

"Or wasting a bunch of time while she prepares," Jaser agreed. "Raina isn't an idiot and wouldn't have just forgotten about those things. She wants us to think there's some connection to Arthur O'Neill to throw us off track. She could've easily used magic to create the picture and the manuscripts or stolen them from Arthur's apartment when she killed him. There are so many possibilities. We need to stay focused on the goal: figuring out why Raina wanted Arthur's powers and what she's trying to do with them."

"In the event she just messed up," Will pressed, "we do have these now." He put the manuscripts on the table.

"I guess it's the only thing that survived," Tam muttered. "Let's take anything we find in there with a grain of salt. Get reading."

They sat for another hour or so, delving into the manuscripts, tossing ideas around and brainstorming.

Tam put his pages down once it was clear they weren't making progress. "Well, I was hoping we could celebrate Will's birthday a bit early with some good news, but I guess we're not going to have the breakthrough I was hoping for."

Will blushed. "No, it's fine, really. We don't have to do anything for it." He hadn't given any thought to his birthday, which was the next week. He hadn't done anything special in years. Between Raina and the constant feeling of needing to figure out why Arthur was killed, he felt guilty even acknowledging something so silly to the denizens of Byrrus.

Tam sighed. "Can we at least go have a lot of food and use it as an excuse to celebrate? I need a pick-me-up."

"I mean," Peter mused, failing to lighten the mood, "if anything, we can all say we've had a Molotov cocktail thrown at us. That could be a good conversation starter at parties in ten to twenty years."

What followed was probably the most depressing birthday dinner Will had ever had. Though Pass threw his all into it and tried to make the meal a special occasion, the only ones who got into it were the citizens of Byrrus who didn't know what was going on. Will tried to be merry and go along with a raucous "happy birthday," even though it was hard to keep up the pretense—he was frustrated.

Will eventually made the excuse of needing to go home to watch a movie with his parents. Though he looked disappointed, it was clear Pass believed the fib, and Will waved goodbye to his friends.

A few minutes later he arrived at his doorstep, halfheartedly waving to his parents and offering a quiet greeting as he entered the house to go upstairs.

"Are you alright, Will?" Ruth asked. "You look exhausted."

"I'm okay," Will replied, putting a little bit of pep in his voice. "Just a long day."

Will could tell his mother wanted to talk. She would want to discuss plans for his birthday, or classes, and that wasn't something Will could manage right now.

When he got to his room, he pulled out the picture of Raina and Arthur and one of the manuscripts he took from Raina's house: the original copy of *The Redstone Keep*. Though they were unable to find anything going through the book as a group, he couldn't help trying again. He combed through the pages.

There was no "To my dearest long-lost daughter," or "I know your plan, you wench." Just notes like "make this character more believable" or "this paragraph needs to be fixed." Will groaned. Eyes blurry, he slipped the manuscript into the desk along with the photo. *Just in case,* he thought to himself.

The next week floated by, and Will's real birthday came and went. His parents tried to make it an exciting affair, despite Will's moody attitude. They celebrated with a nicer dinner than usual— grilled steaks—and Will did his best to let the disappointment of investigating Raina's house fade away. They would figure it out eventually. That, or Raina would make her next move.

Will usually had pretty uneventful Christmases, getting one or two nice, reasonably-sized presents and enjoying a day of food and relaxation with his parents. This year was different. When he walked downstairs Christmas morning, he found his mom and dad already up, facing the stairwell in a suspicious manner.

"Um," he muttered, "you guys are up early this ye—"

"It's really early, Will," Ruth interjected. "Shouldn't you still be in bed?"

Will scoffed. "It's Christmas morning. What did you expect me to do? Sleep?"

Emery laughed. "Fair point. I guess we've been caught." Before Ruth could stop him, Emery stepped out of the way.

Will's mouth opened wide, and he blinked several times to confirm he wasn't making up what he saw.

It was a grand piano: a real one.

It had a smooth black lacquer finish across it, and the top looked as if it had been freshly polished. The gloss of the piano's cover reflected the lights of the Christmas tree, shining back at Will like twinkling stars, and he could see an entire song and dance just hidden on the surface of the instrument itself. He ran his fingers across the piano, feeling the formless texture of the lid, and breathed out a sigh of contentment. Will tackled his parents in a huge hug.

"You like it?" Emery asked

"It's incredible!" Will exclaimed gleefully, looking at his parents with dumbstruck thankfulness. "But ..." his face faltered. "How on earth did you pay for it? Grand pianos like this are thousands of dollars. You didn't actually drop that much for a Christmas gift, did you?"

Ruth beamed. "Of course not! We got it for really cheap, actually. A wholesaler was selling thousands of them, and we had it checked out by a professional. It's high quality, and it's brand new. Getting it in the house was the hardest part. The movers took care of that, thankfully."

"How did you hide it? It's huge!"

"You've been a bit preoccupied for the last couple days," his mom said.

"Oh. Yeah. Sorry," Will mumbled.

"Hey, son. We love you. Merry Christmas," Emery finished. "Go. Play us something."

The keys were heavy and weighted, as if they were made of marble or ivory, and Will was all too aware of the power emerging from the instrument's body when he pressed down. As his fingers sped up and notes began pouring out of the piano, Will became lost in the tones that echoed around his head on the still air.

This is what Will was doing when his parents finally retired after a filling Christmas dinner.

Will had been playing for about thirty minutes, appreciating the clarity of the sound, when Tam appeared in front of him, leaning against the piano. He was waving his hands, trying to conduct Will, although the (likely made-up) time signature Tam was using was a mystery to him. Will tried to play in time with what Tam was doing. Eventually the Character messed up, and Will stopped, letting the sound fade away.

"I'm not a director, you know." He crossed his arms over his chest. "Don't associate me with musical skill."

"I wasn't," Will snickered, closing the cover of the piano on top of the keys and leaning his elbows on top of it. "How come you aren't in Byrrus right now? Shouldn't you be celebrating?"

"The funny thing about Christmas in Byrrus is everyone is so stuffed and intoxicated by midnight they pass out," Tam mused.

Will whipped to his right, eyes finding the clock situated over his wall and cackled out of what he realized was exhaustion. It was about one in the morning, and somehow Will's parents had managed to sleep with the loud music notes floating through the house.

"I need to go to bed," he said, standing up in a tired haze.

"I wanted to give you a gift," Tam said, thrusting a box in Will's direction. He took it, feeling guilty; he hadn't gotten Tam anything, and Tam read it on his face. "You didn't need to," he promised. "Think of this as a gift from mentor to student."

"Now you're just embarrassing me," Will muttered before he took the gift and ripped it open, the crinkling of wrapping paper filling the room just as the piano music had been. However, when Will finally got the packaging off, he was merely able to tilt his head and stare. The only thing in the box was a stack of handwritten papers, about a hundred sheets thick, written in a scrawl Will could decipher by squinting. He could already tell it was another *Byrrus* manuscript; however, the pages were newer than the ones he found in Raina's house.

Tam grinned widely, tapping the papers. "This, my friend, is a handwritten rough draft of Arthur O'Neill's final *Byrrus* book. One that never got published." He got an air of sadness on his face, but he wiped it away. "Arthur gave it to me a few weeks before he died, asking for me to read it over. Naturally, I said it wasn't a good idea because I was a Character. Still, he insisted. I figured you'd like it."

Will flipped through the manuscript lightly and looked at it with a sort of reverence. He carefully went through the pages, taking in the smell that accompanied them, and looked at the writing, the warmth in his body making him feel like he had come into possession of words written by God himself.

"This is probably the best gift I've ever gotten, Tam." Will gave the Pontifex a huge, grateful smile. For a moment, he wasn't sure whether to hug him or give him a high five. Tam took the initiative and placed his hand on Will's shoulder, giving it an affectionate, strong squeeze.

"So, the piano … did you have anything to do with it?"

Tam shrugged nonchalantly. "I may or may not have discovered a warehouse sale, and I may or may not have told Peter to tell your parents. It was too good of an opportunity. Plus, I figured it would be a nice material gift to go along with that old stack of papers."

Will threw caution to the wind and hugged Tam. He figured the Character deserved it. Tam's body tensed up, but he then patted Will on the shoulder, somewhat awkwardly, yet not devoid of affection.

They separated and sat for a moment in silence before Tam clapped his hands together in a dramatic motion.

"I need to go back to Byrrus," he declared, beginning to walk away in his usual swirly fashion. "Let me know what you think of the book!" He paused. "It doesn't have a title, so I suppose you can make one up as you go along. It adds to the fun."

Will grinned. "Thanks, Tam. Merry Christmas!"

He smiled in response and disappeared, leaving the usual whoosh of air that took his place. Will made his way upstairs after switching off all of the lights and threw himself onto his bed, falling into a comatose state from which he didn't want to wake.

A few days later Will sat on his bed, manuscript in his lap, ignoring the looming prospect of school. He decided reading the book exclusively in his room was the safest bet. If his parents were to see him reading a hand-written stack of pages, they'd want to see it, and that would lead to a whole bunch of potentially awkward questions.

Despite the haphazard appearance of the manuscript, Will was unwilling to put it down. It was a very simple, standard *Byrrus* tale: two friends on a quest to cure the people of Byrrus from a mysterious illness that had taken ahold of the castle. Even though he knew the pattern of the stories by now, he was still captivated.

A loud yell interrupted his reading and he ran to open the window. Peter and Iris, the former jumping up and down, waved up at Will.

"COME OUTSIDE!" Peter shouted like a mad man. "JUST DO IT!" He had a maniacal grin on his face, and as Will scrunched his eyes, he figured out why—fluttering around Peter and Iris were wild flurries of snow, so fast and thick they were nearly obscuring his two friends' faces.

Will ran down the stairs and out his door to Peter's excited exclamations.

"It's snow!" Peter cried, running around Will's yard, flapping his arms like a bird. "Snow in North Carolina! It's truly the year of miracles!"

The last time Alexandria had gotten a major snow was about eight years ago when a wild storm killed the power for a week. Will had been holed up in his elementary school for an entire day until the teachers could figure out how to get all of the students home. He sighed longingly at the memory. Iris giggled like a little kid, joining Peter and running through the flurries, whooping with joy. Will followed suit, launching himself into the air and trying to catch flakes with his mouth.

He eventually found his mind long enough to go inside and get a sweatshirt, returning to find Peter madly scraping light layers of flakes into one consistent snowball. As soon as he created a small ball of the stuff, he pulled his arm back like a baseball pitcher and hurled it at Will, trying to catch him off his guard. Will was too quick, and he snatched the pellet out of the air like an outfielder. Peter gave him a worried glance and gulped, right before Will threw it at him. It hit Peter square in the chest, and he fell back into the now sodden grass. Iris snorted uncontrollably and joined him, letting the flakes fall on top of her. Will collapsed as well.

It was a glorious moment to just be William Morgan,

fifteen-year-old high school freshman, playing in the yard with his friends.

Alexandria wasn't prepared for snow, and the storm that purveyed through the next several days proved just that. When it stopped, there was a foot of white powder on the ground and snowball fights happened every day.

Will found he was much more agile during these events than he had been in previous years. He was able to run longer and felt significantly more fit than he did before he gained the Writer's Eye. His friends all noticed the same thing. May and Jaser, who long considered themselves the least athletic of the group, found they were able to keep up with even the most agile runners, and they made sure to take full advantage of it.

"It's probably the Written," Tam said one day when they were lying out in the snow. "Even though your Reader bodies aren't technically exercising, your minds are more used to being athletic. I can't say Arthur was as spry as you all, so I don't have first-hand experience with this phenomenon. It makes sense though."

Will didn't have the heart to tell Tam it didn't. Regardless, the group decided to take full advantage of the break from school to train more in the World of the Written. Not only did they practice with their normal weapons and powers, but Tam also took to training them in hand-to-hand combat.

"If you ever have to fight someone without your weapon, it's important you're prepared," he'd say as he threw uppercuts at Will, who was able to block or dodge them most of the time.

They also had opportunity to learn more from Amelia, who hadn't had the role of instructor yet. Her most interesting lesson was one on throwing knives.

"I didn't know you knew how to do that," Tam said to her, eyebrows raised. Amelia laughed, a sound too light to be coming from a woman who hit three bull's eyes in a row.

"Call it a hidden talent." She then hit a fourth bull's eye without looking, and Tam rubbed the back of his neck, a bright sheen of sweat breaking out on his forehead.

Every day over break they trained and would then head home. Will felt more relaxed than he had in months; everything seemed almost *normal*, and that was something he never thought he'd feel again.

Sure, there were mysteries that needed to be solved, but why worry when he had someone like Tam to back him up?

13

The Cathedral

Will was dreaming. He was floating above the clouds with his arms outstretched, the horizon extending for miles and miles. He moved with the wind, his body weighing no more than a feather.

After a little while, his mind began to wander, questioning why he had been brought to the sky. As if on cue, he sank closer to the ground, greeted by the familiar sight of Byrrus Castle. It was a welcome change. He felt at home in Byrrus. He felt comfortable.

The moon was unblocked by clouds, letting a soft silver glow flake its way to the grounds. There were torches lit, though there was no other sign of humanity. The only other light came from lamps lit in various windows of the castle.

There was a movement to his right. Tam was walking along the wall of the city, which loomed over him ominously like a wave preparing to crash down. He was on patrol, twirling his sword and kicking it against the heel of his boot every few steps. Will tried to call out to him only to find his voice didn't work; he couldn't even raise his arms to wave. Then Tam pointed his sword into the darkness.

"Hey!" he called. "Who's there? Hello?"

Will floated closer to Tam until he was on the ground behind him; Will still couldn't move, and when he tried to call to Tam again or cast his thoughts out to him, the Pontifex was unresponsive. Tam stared into the darkness for a few more moments, and as soon as he began to walk away, a figure stepped out onto the path. A familiar scythe came to their hand.

"Tam Desmond," Raina said, chest heaving, eyes excited and bright. "Long time no see."

"What do you want?" Tam growled, sword raised. "You might be too strong for Will, but you're nothing for me. Why did you kill Arthur?" He paused, his weapon raised higher. "And better question, how did you know him? And how did you get your Writer's Eye?"

Raina kicked the dirt. "That's a lot of questions. Clearly your little brain is too focused on what you think to be true and not what's in front of you." She swung her scythe through the air, the blade whistling, before burying the tip in the ground in front of her.

"What do you want with Will?"

"He has Arthur O'Neill's power," she stated with no emotion in her voice. "Arthur's power is the secret to unlocking the most powerful force in the World of the Written. That's why I took care of him, if you must know. He didn't have to go. He chose that—he was unwilling to give the power up."

"Why do you need Arthur's power? You're a Writer—use your own!"

"As I said, Arthur's power is a key. A key that makes whoever possesses it the strongest Writer to ever live. I'm shocked you never realized it."

It was clear Tam had no idea what Raina was talking about. Will certainly didn't. Arrogance dripped from her gaze like poisoned honey.

"It doesn't matter. I think what's really important is why I've come to see you." She kicked a stone on the ground, causing the dirt around it to flare up. "I can't believe you haven't really taken May's dreams seriously. The church? Jeez, Tam." Raina's eyes bore an emotion close to sincerity. "The person who killed Arthur needs a mysterious strong power, and that power is tied to a church. I know you're thick, but surely even you can get there."

Tam continued to stare at her blankly for a few moments, at a loss. Eventually, his eyes widened, pupils shaking furiously as anxiety took over his entire frame.

"That's not possible. It's a story made up by Characters, Raina. You are holding out hope on something that's not real. It can't be." Tam's voice was trembling with a panic Will had never heard before—hearing that tone from Tam made Will's heart drop to the pit of his stomach.

"We aren't real either! None of this is. It's all a story, Tam!" She took a deep breath. "Isn't it funny how we find things in the places we least expect?" She took another breath, this one more controlled. "You didn't expect something this powerful to appear in your tiny little universe, but where else would it go? Of course it went to the world created by the only person who has—had—the power to control the beast that lives there. It's real, Tam. The whole thing. You are just blind to it."

Tam gripped his sword so tightly his knuckles turned white. "You're just an arrogant child. If you are right, he is no Shade. You can't control him. None of us can."

She laughed coolly. "You're just unwilling to see the truth. The power Arthur passed on to Will is the key to controlling him." She smirked. "You could have more power than God. Why don't you want that?"

"Because I'm no fool!" Tam shouted, teeth gritted together. "You will not use Will for this."

Raina ripped her scythe from the earth. "I don't recommend you fight me. That cathedral is here now. I've spent years studying Shades, and I know how to harness its power without hurting myself." She jingled the pentagram necklace, which was giving off a soft, poisonous purple glow. "It's particularly useful against Characters."

Tam launched himself at her. Raina calmly raised her hand and snapped her fingers. The necklace glowed more harshly, and as Tam soared through the air, his eyes got foggy and he faltered. His sword fell from his grip as he crashed into the ground, unconscious. Raina moved her hand over him, and he disappeared. Will tried to scream but was unable to make a sound.

"I'm impressed you're able to see Tam when he's in danger, especially when you don't mean to. That's certainly something Arthur could never do." She faced Will.

"Now, Will, what will you do?"

"I'll kill you!" he managed to shout, eyes white with anger as he tried to move from his position.

Raina laughed coldly. "I'm sure your friend May has had a vision of what's to come. Have her take you there. I'll be waiting with Tam."

Will tried to shout again in response, but he spiraled out of control, falling through space until he suddenly stopped, facing a large door, one that looked like it belonged to a church. Simon stood in front of it, looking older and more powerful. He stared Will in the eyes, expression bright and knowing.

"I remember."

Will flew up from his bed immediately and looked at his clock; it was Saturday, eight in the morning. None of his friends were likely to be up, yet he threw on his clothes and ran outside, the crisp February air flickering across his skin. Will tried to contact Tam using his mind, and there was no response—Will's pulse quickened. He began running to Peter's house before throwing caution to the wind, opening a portal in broad daylight. The distance was much shorter through Betwixt and Between.

He heard Peter's snoring before he entered his friend's room.

"Peter, get up!" Will jumped out of the portal and on top of his blankets, shaking Peter's body vigorously. Peter tried to swing at him with slow, sluggish punches through the mess of sheets. Will moved to the side and Peter jumped out of bed.

"What the ..." A bit of drool came from his mouth. He looked at Will and did a double take. "Geez, Will, what's going on, man? Why are you in my room?"

"I had a dream last night," Will replied, trying to stop his feet from moving—he failed.

"Good for you," Peter grumbled, rubbing his face. Knowing him, he didn't get to bed until a few hours ago, and was probably running on about four hours of sleep. Regardless, Will told Peter about his dream, and when he finished his story, Peter looked worried.

"It was just that. A dream. Right? Tam's tough, Will. Your mind is playing tricks on you. He beat Raina easily during the fight in the band room, remember?"

"I don't know," Will replied. "Whatever it was, it happened a few hours ago, and Tam could be dead right now for all we know. Plus, she had some new power that let her subdue him. It's related to that pentagram necklace."

"Can Characters even die?"

Will nodded, remembering Tam's lessons and becoming

increasingly agitated. "We have to go. Raina has Tam at that weird church from May's dreams." He looked out the window. "I'm going to go get Iris. You get dressed and meet me in front of your house in five minutes. The three of us can get everyone else."

True to his word, Will showed up at Peter's house five minutes later with Iris in tow, having filled her in. When Peter came out to the driveway, Will gave the two a rough outline of what he hoped was a decent plan.

"I'm going to go to Byrrus and see if Tam has really disappeared," Will started. "He's not responding to me when I try to contact him mentally, but maybe he's asleep, or distracted, or something. That way, if he wasn't actually kidnapped, we aren't overreacting for no reason. While I'm gone, the two of you need to find May and Jaser and get them back to Peter's house. That way we don't waste any time. I'll be back in thirty minutes max. You guys try and do the same."

Peter and Iris signaled an understanding before ducking behind Peter's house to summon portals. Will made his way to Byrrus and found it just as it always was. The city's people were milling about, preparing for the day's various activities.

Some folks waved to Will and he gave them a halfhearted response, feeling his heart move into his throat with every person he encountered who wasn't Pass. Will found him speaking with a carpenter, who was lugging a giant stack of wooden planks behind him.

"Pass!" Will shouted, sprinting up to the king. "Have you seen Tam today?"

"Will! Good to see you! Tam? Why?" Pass scratched his head and looked up at the castle, his eyes screwing up in concentration. "No, can't say I have. I know he had patrol last night, and I'm sure he came back after the morning patrol went on duty. Did you check his room?"

"Not yet."

"Well, let's go find him, shall we?"

Pass and Will walked to the castle and Will filled him in on his dream. Pass listened intently, and when they finally reached the residential part of the castle, Pass led Will to Tam's room. Sure enough, Tam's bed was still made, his weapons and combat gear gone. Tam was nowhere in sight.

Pass looked angry. "All right, I don't want you getting any ideas of heroism. You stay out of this. I'm going to go get a squad ready and we're going to track Tam."

"No! You can't!" Will's voice caught in his throat. "You've never fought Raina! She literally waved her hands and Tam passed out. She made him disappear. She's something more than just a Writer. She's fast. I can barely slow her down to a run with the Writer's Eye. I know the warriors in Byrrus are strong," Will said to Pass's offended look, "but if Raina was able to knock Tam unconscious that easily, she would take out your entire city without much effort." He grimaced. "She can't do that to us, at least she couldn't in the World of the Writers. We're the only ones who can do this."

"Look, Will, I don't care how strong you and your friends are. This is a matter of security. And don't you forget I'm the king of this world. I trust you, though you can't expect me to do nothing. I raised that man from the time he was a child to the time he defeated Daegan. He's nothing short of my son, and if you expect me to sit back and let my son be kidnapped and tortured, you've got another thing coming."

Will rose to his full height. "Pass, I understand, believe me. That doesn't mean you're equipped to handle this. You didn't see what she did. And besides, I know what she wants. Please, protect your people and let us do what we were created to do."

Pass stared at him with flaming aggression before sighing and turning away. "I'll give you four hours; it'll take me that long to mobilize a squad. Just remember: when that time is up, we're coming." He walked down the stairs without another word, leaving Will to his thoughts.

Will had forgotten Tam was an orphan; when he was just a baby he was left at the castle's steps, and Pass took him in and raised him. The reason the two were so close was Pass was essentially Tam's father. Will might not have been as close to Tam as Pass was, but Tam was still his friend. And Raina was his problem.

Will made his way back to the human world to find his friends sitting in Peter's driveway, all wearing jackets to combat the cold North Carolina air. May paced back and forth, unfocused and restless.

"You had a dream too, didn't you?" Will asked, lowering his voice and moving closer. May bit her lip, and Will's chest squirmed.

"There's no use waiting around. Let's go. Whatever that building is, it's appeared. I don't know why, or how, but that field isn't empty." May started tapping her foot before beginning to pace again.

"What if it's a trap?" Jaser asked, fear plain on his face.

May grimaced, her long hair floating around her face. "It's not. And even if it is, we have two options: leave Tam with her, or walk in and try to get our friend back." She looked at the group. "Does anyone have any better ideas?"

"We should transport ourselves halfway to the field and walk the rest of the way, just in case there's a trap waiting for us," Iris suggested.

Will breathed a sigh of relief at the group's resolution and opened a path that inevitably led to Byrrus. They came out in a small clearing, and Will looked at the pathway in front of him; he recognized the foliage from their first adventure through these woods. May walked past him and began pushing through the trees, knowing exactly where she was going.

They had been traveling for about five minutes when the hairs on the back of Will's neck stood up. As he summoned his sword, a large knife lodged itself in a tree, just missing his head. He broke out in a sweat; Amelia was trailing them, red in the face, looking ready to kill. Pass lied to him. He supposed he shouldn't have been surprised.

"You could have killed me!" Will screamed at her.

"I know exactly what I'm doing, Will. I see that look of anger," Amelia spat, her voice suppressing rage. "I'm on my own. Don't worry, your little plan isn't compromised—I can see the future, remember? Now—how idiotic can you be? You know how dangerous Raina is! Do you really think the five of you can take her?"

"You know how dangerous she is too, and yet here you are!" he shouted in response, teeth clenched. "Besides, this is a fight between me and her. I'm sure you saw that in your vision. I'm the person she's after. Not you or Tam."

"So you're willing to put your Writer friends in danger then? Just not me, a lowly Character?" Her eyes flared, and Will's face went white under her intense stare. "Since you clearly haven't read *The Redstone Keep* in a while, let me remind you: I have saved Tam's life more times than years you've been alive. You're a child, Will."

"I—"

"Regardless of who you are, and regardless of what Raina can do," Amelia started, no longer trying to mask the fury in her words, "Tam is my friend. More than a friend. I don't care that he's Byrrus's

Pontifex. He could be a janitor and I would still be here, with or without you. Rest assured, I care much more about Tam Desmond's life than you do, regardless of how important you may feel."

Amelia's eyes were filled with a resolve and confidence Will himself didn't feel. He quivered under her gaze; he couldn't control Amelia. This was a woman who knew more about the world he was currently traversing than he could ever hope to. Will tried to stutter out an apology, but Amelia put her hand up.

"It's fine. Just trust me, Will. Trust the Characters in the same way you trust the Writers. We're all powerful in different ways."

Will nodded. "Let's hurry."

They continued to push forward, May in the lead.

"Be careful guys. It's going to be different," May said.

They walked into the field, and the differences were immediately noticeable. The grass had turned into a marshland, without any of the buzzing of life that would usually accompany it. The trees on the rim of the field were dead and hollowed out, and the air was cold and wet in a way that cut through their skin. The vegetation wasn't dead because of the winter chill—there was something more sinister at play.

The most striking difference was the structure in the middle of it all. What May described as a church was actually a cathedral, much larger than what Will expected. The top was masked by a fog swirling about a hundred feet above their heads. Stone gargoyles stared down at the group from ramparts that wrapped their way around dark, stained glass windows. A distinct pressure pressed against Will's body, constricting him like a snake.

"Do any of you feel that?" Will asked, straining to get his words out against the force.

"Feel what?" Iris whispered.

Peter shivered and pulled his jacket on more tightly. "That place doesn't exactly look pleasant. Do you really think that's where she took Tam?"

"Yes," May and Will said in unison.

Will could *feel* Tam's presence, like he was sending out a signal to let them know where he was. Will walked forward, and the rest of the group followed, their weapons and powers summoned.

Amelia strode forward. "I don't think anything is going to attack us out here. We're way too out in the open. If anything, we're going to be in real danger once we enter the building."

"I agree," Jaser muttered. "I can sense Tam's energy from within the building. Raina's as well. There's nothing else that should be an immediate threat." He pursed his lips. "There *is* some other force here, something bad. I can't make out what it is specifically. I'm sorry," he added, grimacing in Will's direction.

Will felt legitimate terror for his friends, and his heart pounded with guilt. They were only here because of him. Because he had some stupid power that gave them all the Writer's Eye. At the same time, he was glad he wasn't alone. "Are you guys ready? You can turn back now if you want. I'll forgive you."

"I didn't get up before noon just to go home, Will," Peter commented, his joking tone not successfully masking his fear. "I think that goes for all of us. Now quit stalling and open that door."

Will braced his hands against the cathedral's iron-wrought entrance, pushing it forward with a loud creak that sent shivers down his spine. After much effort, the door swung open and crashed against the inside of the building with a resounding thud. The mysterious force that Will had felt earlier was much more powerful now.

"She knows we're here for sure now. No one could miss that." Will took a step, entering the cathedral.

As soon as the group was inside, the doors shut behind them. Will rapidly turned around to find they were locked, without any sort of handle to help them escape. Torches lit the windowless entrance, revealing the bareness surrounding them. Two staircases spiraled on opposite ends of the room, one down and one up. Against the far wall was a table littered with books and stacks of papers.

"Any insight, Jaser?" Will asked. His friend closed his eyes for what seemed like only half a second before they shot open, gazing at the staircase burrowing into the earth.

"Down the stairs on the left. That's where Tam is," Jaser asserted.

"Why does every story have scary stuff in basements?" Peter bemoaned.

The group walked down the staircase, torches lighting their way. At the bottom Will motioned to the door that greeted them. Tam was on the other side, but so was *it*. Will felt it too, and they were going to end up facing it, whatever *it* was.

He pushed open the door. Tam was bound to a chair, a solitary lamp hanging over his head, swinging back and forth, just like every scary movie or book ever written. The shadows cast around the room were ominous and danced in the strange light. Will always thought it was cliché when writers would use that motif but seeing it in real life proved to be frightening.

Amelia was unfazed. She sprinted to Tam and unbound and removed the gag that had been forced into his mouth.

"Tam, are you okay?" She tenderly put her hand on his chin and caressed the side of his face, expression softer than any Will had ever seen her wear.

Tam looked up at her, blinking slowly, the exhaustion in his eyes apparent.

"What are you doing here? You have to run! Get out while you still can!"

Will ignored Tam while Amelia sliced through the chains binding him to the chair. She helped him stand up as he leaned against her. "We're not leaving you. I don't care if it's a trap."

"Cute."

Will turned around, unsurprised, to find Raina sitting on top of a bannister, eyeing him coolly. She didn't have any visible weapons.

"Amelia, I can knock you out instantaneously. Don't move," she stated. "And Writers … we all know I'm faster and stronger than any of you. So those of you whose weapons have range, I suggest you don't make any sudden movements if you value your lives."

Jaser dropped his halberd, allowing the axe head to clang against the ground. Peter lowered his staff, and May kept her hands up for only a moment before frowning and putting them down, the frost seeping from her fingertips onto the floor.

"You too, girl."

Iris's Gilmarye disappeared.

"What's going on here?" Will demanded. "Why bring him here? Why bring *us* here?"

"I suppose I can explain a little bit." Raina pretended to yawn. "Based on how things have gone so far, none of you are leaving here alive."

"Start talking," Will commanded, his voice holding an air of confidence he wasn't feeling.

Raina saw through his façade and leered at him. "Well, I'm sure you've already noticed what this building is. May has dreamed of it for months. Care to take a stab at it?"

"It's a cathedral. Or a church. Tell me something that isn't obvious," Will spat.

"It's not obvious," May whispered, the building's presence finally giving her clarity. "It's not obvious because it's not a church. It's a tomb."

The word floated over Will's body like a burst of cold air. The force that had been pressing down on him got stronger. Will stared at the wall behind Tam, realizing it wasn't a wall at all; it was a giant stone panel. The ominous force was coming from behind it. Will backed up and bumped into Peter.

Raina smiled, her lips curling in a subtle, unpleasant way. "Very good, May."

"What is it?" Will asked Raina, no longer trying to mask the fear in his voice.

"I don't know his name." A brief look of panic flitted across her face. "It's a very old story and the beast's true name has been lost in time. For our purposes, he can be known as Darkness. Adversity. Evil. He is part of every story and makes up every antagonist. He is ever present in the World of the Written. He is opposition."

"Why does it matter?" Will whispered. "You said this is a tomb, right? That means he's dead." He gulped, the obvious hitting him full force: dead things didn't give off this type of energy.

Tam growled, regaining strength and standing tall, no longer balancing against Amelia. "Because he's not actually dead; just imprisoned. She wants to free him. She wants to do the most foolish thing anyone could do in the World of the Written, and free the most evil force in the universe."

"Close," she snapped, balling her fists. "I will free him. Then I will control him. I want to undo the wrongs in the World of the Written. And that's where you come in, Will. Arthur O'Neill's power was the key to controlling this monster. That power now resides in you."

"Wait, why would you do this?" Will shuddered, chest pounding like a hollow drum. "If this thing is so evil, why do you think Arthur's powers can control it?"

"Because, I just know," she said. "There's an energy radiating off you, Will, just as it did Arthur. It's different with you, ever so slightly, but they're on the same wavelength. You are the key to controlling him." She flashed her teeth. "When you die, this will absorb your powers." She held her necklace. "Then they'll belong to me. That's why I had you come here." She motioned to Tam. "I knew you would come rescue him. And this is the only place in the universe I can guarantee the power will come to me, and not go somewhere else. That was my mistake the first time." She glared at Tam. "I will not make it again."

Raina dropped from the rafters and landed like a dancer.

"Now, Will, I'm going to give you one more chance. Let me take your powers. You will all live. No one has to get hurt."

For a moment, Will thought of his own fear, and about the fear his friends must have been feeling. He wondered if it really could be that simple—give up the Writer's Eye and keep them out of danger. He hadn't taken Raina's offer seriously the first time, and he didn't think he was going to now. However, hearing the shallow breathing of his companions made him think twice.

"Don't listen to her Will," May shouted. Will was broken out of his stupor, taken aback by the force in her voice. May's tone stayed steady, her eyes piercing into Raina. "We can't let her take your powers. You feel that force. We all feel it." She looked at the other Writers. "We can't let her release whatever evil is buried here."

"I'm going to do what I have to," Raina insisted, glaring at the Writers. "I want to prevent bloodshed. None of you will help me? None of you will just hold Will still? Not even to save your own lives?"

Will tensed, but there was no need. Eliminating his doubts even further, Peter stepped in front of Will, raised his staff, and put his arm out, blocking him from Raina like a bodyguard would.

"We'd die before betraying him. Do you think any of us would just turn our backs on our friend? Especially now we know what's at stake? I don't know about the rest of you, but I have no intention of meeting whatever is buried here." Everyone else in the group nodded furiously. "Bring it on, Raina."

For a moment, before the panic of the decision settled in, Will was immensely grateful for his friends, and a rush of affection swelled his heart like a balloon. It felt like they could do anything. It didn't matter what was buried in the tomb. It didn't matter what magic Raina possessed. They could stand up to her.

Raina broke this mystique with a shake of her head.

"Okay. At least I tried. I won't be bringing anything on. He will." She turned her back to Peter, walking toward the stone panel. Before anyone could move, she knocked on the wall, the sound echoing throughout the room like a gong. "Ashes to ashes and dust to dust. Die in darkness, William Morgan."

At first nothing happened, but ever so slowly, a small trail of black smoke leaked from the cracks in the stone, and as the impenetrable shadows filled the room, the pressure became overwhelming. Will collapsed.

It was Arthur all over again.

Tam was lost in a vision of slow motion as he watched Will's eyes roll into the back of his head. The Character caught him as he fell to the ground

"No! Will! Stop! Wake up!"

Tam shook the Writer, but to no avail. Whatever Raina had done, Will was unresponsive. Tam put his finger to Will's neck; his pulse was still there, though it was slowing.

"What did you do?" Tam growled, wincing as he stood up. "What did you do to them?"

"I sent them to the world of the beast," she said. She played with the pentagram necklace that hung around her neck. "This brings me no joy. It didn't have to be all of them. Be that as it may, as long as Will has Arthur's powers, I can't rest. This was the only way. I'm sorry." She looked to the giant stone tablet. "Once Will dies, Arthur's powers will be released. The beast won't be able to contain them, and they'll come to me. Then I can finish what I started."

"And what is that?" Tam growled. Raina clenched her fists.

"I won't tell you that. Tam, though I have no reason to explain myself to you, just know that this is for the greater good. *Your* greater good."

There was remorse in her words. Rather than confusing Tam, it infuriated him. "The greater good?" Tam's voice was almost at a screech. "You killed Arthur. You killed Will. How dare you try and pretend like you care? How dare you try and pretend that you're anything other than an evil witch hell-bent on destroying the world?" Tam stood up straight, and though he was still weak, he grasped his sword, pointing it at Raina. "I'll kill you right now."

"Will and his friends were unfortunate casualties in a fight that goes way past your purview." The remorse was gone, her pitch significantly lower and darker than before. "Don't meddle in things you don't understand."

"You lost the right to keep me out of this mess when you killed Arthur!" Tam bellowed. "The most incredible, kind, loving man the world has ever known, gone for your own evil and selfish gain!"

Faster than Tam could keep up with, Raina jumped and slammed him into a wall, and he slid to the ground, body and heart too weak to get up. Amelia went to counter, but Raina slid around her, repeating the motion and throwing the Character to the other side of the room. Though Amelia bounded up as soon as she hit the wall, she didn't move closer. The Character stared at Raina, poised on the balls of her feet and ready to make a move at a moment's notice.

"Arthur O'Neill was a spineless coward, and he deserved to die. That is one thing I'll never regret." Raina shut her eyes. "You'll never understand, Tam Desmond. Although I wish you could."

And with that she sprinted up the stairs. For a moment, it looked as if Amelia was going to follow her; instead, she slid to the ground next to Tam, resting her hand on his shoulder.

"Are you okay?" she whispered.

Tam stared blankly at Will's lifeless body, his waxy form looking too much like that of Arthur's the day he discovered him in his apartment, gone, dead from some dark magic. The scene swam in front of his vision, and he grasped into the air, afraid he was going to pass out, until he realized that his vision was only blurry from tears.

"No," he whispered. "I'm not."

The darkness consumed everything. Pushing him down, making it hard to breathe.

"Will!"

Someone was shouting his name, but why? Who?

It no longer mattered as the black infinity invaded his soul.

This was death.

Will didn't know what else it could be. He floated in a black space, and though he reached out his hands and moved his body, there was nowhere to gain purchase. In fact, there was nothing around him whatsoever. The darkness seemed to stretch for miles and miles—or maybe just inches from his body, he couldn't tell. He could clearly see his feet and hands as if the sun were shining on them.

"Hello?"

Nothing.

"Tam?"

Not even an echo.

"Anyone?"

Will tried summoning his sword to his hand but nothing happened. Time stopped yet ran ahead. He had no idea how long he floated.

"Grab my hand! C'mon, a little closer!"

Will twisted around and saw Peter and May clawing through the air at each other, though not making much progress. What were they doing here? Was he supposed to do something? A small memory tugged at his mind. He had to get to them. Will tried swimming through the darkness and found he could control his direction. With each pulsation of his legs he was a little bit closer to the two of his friends. When he finally reached them, he grabbed their arms and all the memories returned. The fog in his brain disappeared, and he snapped back to reality.

"I thought we were screwed," Peter whispered. "Are you okay, Will?"

"Yeah," he muttered. "I think so. What about you two?"

"Where are we?" May asked, shivering.

"I have no idea. I can't contact Tam. I can't summon my sword either. We're pretty much on our own at the moment," Will said. "Have you seen or heard anything from Jaser or Iris?"

May frowned. "No. If we had, we would have stayed with them."

Silence passed over them, luckily being broken by the desperate shouting of Jaser.

"Will! Peter! May! Are you all right?"

Jaser began paddling over to them, accompanied by Iris. Both of them looked unscathed, though the panic in Jaser's eyes was still present, his eyes widened with fear. Iris looked fine, though she was more subdued than usual. Will grabbed them and pulled them in, connecting the entire group.

"It could be worse," Will muttered. "At least we're together."

"We still have no idea where we are. Or how we got here," Peter implored. "We all passed out when Raina released that smoke, right?"

They all nodded in response, and Peter put a hand to his face, contemplating hard.

"Okay. Now, I'm no expert on magic, but that would lead us to believe we didn't physically transport here. Only our minds did. Our physical bodies are still in the cathedral with Raina, Tam, and Amelia. Not that that's necessarily a good thing," he said to himself, trailing off.

Iris jumped in. "Which means, since we have total control of our minds, we can escape. We just need to stay positive and figure it out."

Silence fell over them once again, and they were left to float in the darkness that trapped them, having no idea where to go or what to do. Will occasionally made a swipe at the air as if to summon his sword, but nothing happened, and he would huff in despair. Tam could be *dead*, for all they knew, and there they were, stuck in some netherworld.

At one point, Peter gripped Will's shoulder a little too tightly. "Hey Will, I don't mean to cause alarm, but you should probably look down."

Will's heart rate picked up, and he followed Peter's advice. Iris shrieked, and Will could feel Jaser begin to shake.

What before had been a blank expanse of darkness was now an ocean of Shades—colossal monsters scratching their way through the black soup that enveloped them. Even though the beasts were at least fifty feet below the Writers, their mere presence was enough to incite panic.

"What is this?" Iris whimpered, staring at the Shades. "Where are we?"

"That's simple. You're as close to Hell as any mortal has ever come."

Will whipped around and came face-to-face with Simon, who was covered in a surreal ray of light. His legs were crossed, and he floated in the air as if biding his time, twiddling his thumbs like there was nothing better to do.

Something shifted and Simon and Will were caught in a time rift. All of his friends and the Shades were frozen. The two were alone in their conversation.

"I see you're frustrated. I came to tell you something. I finally remembered more about who I am, and where I came from." He grinned, and there truly was a new-found knowledge in his eyes. "I can help you."

"How? You're not even a real person. You're a part of me, right?" cried Will, voice pitching uncomfortably.

Simon sighed. "There's no time. I can only keep us like this for maybe another minute. So, Will, I need to ask you something." He stared at Will hard, dead in the eyes. "If I help you, I'm going to be unlocking the true power that lies within you. Not just Arthur's power—*your* power. The monster that lies in this tomb is going to see you as a threat, and Raina will be even more afraid of you than she already is. Any semblance of a normal life you've retained up until now will be completely gone. You have to be ready to take on the responsibility and see this adventure through to the end."

"What power are you talking about?" Will hissed, feeling more stressed as he felt time speed up around him.

"The power to save your friends," Simon said. "We're out of time. Make your choice."

"Give me the power, obviously!" Will shouted, and as he did, he felt time around him begin moving again, the clutch of May's arm around him growing tighter. In front of him, Simon gave a small smile.

"You got it, Will."

Simon snapped his fingers, and the sound cracked throughout the endless blackness around them as it would in an echo chamber. Will's friends tensed, looking through the empty space to find the source of the noise.

Will turned back to Simon, but the Familiar had turned to a fine golden dust, trickling away into the darkness. Will's heart was met with a deep sense of loss, as if he just watched a part of himself die. Had he just watched Simon die?

Will's thoughts were interrupted by Jaser, who began to hyper-ventilate. "We need to do something!"

You know what to do, whispered a voice in Will's head. The voice wasn't his own conscience, and it wasn't Simon's voice. It was a voice he vaguely recognized, though from where he wasn't sure, sound-ing almost like the breath of a long-lost brother. The strangest thing though was as Will contemplated the voice, he realized he *did* know what to do.

"Leave it to me," he declared. His friends looked at him, both expectant and confused. Will closed his eyes and blocked them out. Focusing all of his energy into his hand, he imagined an escape. He pointed to the sky, channeling as much power as he possibly could. As he focused, his hand and head began to vibrate, almost over-whelming Will with strength he could barely control.

"Release!" he screamed, and as the words left his mouth, a burst of energy left his hand, arching its way into the sky before exploding into a flurry of colors, ripping the darkness. Shards of light showed cracks where they could escape.

"Go! Guys, swim up!" Peter shouted. "Will, you're a freaking miracle!"

They all swam as fast as they could.

"How did you do that?" May asked, their bodies getting closer to the tear in the sky.

"I have no idea," he said. "It just popped into my head."

May tugged his arm. "It doesn't matter! We're almost out!"

Will gazed toward the exit. Peter made it to the rip and was clutching the edge of it—whatever *it* was—like the wall of a swim-ming pool, holding his hand toward Jaser. Will felt relief flood his body; they were safe. They were going to get out.

They will. What about you?

Will's face blanched as he felt a hot breath on his ear. His own breath became shallow. A cold dead breeze swept around his body.

You cannot do anything. You belong to me. You will always come back to me.

"He's here," Will whispered, his body trembling. Around him, his friends quivered, as if hit by a chill. Below them, the sea of Shades faded away, leaving behind nothing more than an empty pit. Will understood—the Shades were merely the monster's calling card.

"Go faster! Will, May!" Peter cried, terror in his eyes.

Will made eye contact with May, and her eyes widened, realizing what Will was about to do a moment too late. Will pushed her as hard as he could. The lack of gravity made it easy, and she soared toward the rest of the group, despite her desperate attempts to get back to Will.

Tears streamed from his eyes, and he didn't bother wiping them away. He had never felt this much fear.

He was going to die. The worst part was he was going to die without knowing if he was able to save his friends.

Below him, the monster wrapped invisible tentacles around Will's legs, pulling Will toward the bottomless trench below his feet.

"Will! I'm not letting you die!" Peter screamed.

"Go! It's here!" Will choked back the panic in his voice, trying to be as confident as he could. "I can't hold the portal open for much longer! You need to get out of here! You have to stop Raina!"

The monster's energy drifted upward, attempting to grab his friends. Will had one shot to save them.

"Close," he whispered, closing his eyes and channeling as much power as he could into his hand. He imagined the light of the portal absorbing the people above him. It wouldn't help Will—the darkness holding him hostage was more powerful than anything he could conjure up on his own. His only hope was to fight and pray whatever gifts Simon left him were enough.

Will watched as Peter was swept back, his friend crying out and making desperate movements toward him, to no avail. All four of his companions were sucked into the light.

As he predicted, Will's power wasn't enough to save himself. Though a warm wind lifted him up, he was held in place by some invisible power, keeping him from reaching the exit. The light faded, and Will found himself once again with nothing reaching his ears except his own shallow breaths, and the movements of whatever force surrounded him.

"Please, don't leave me," he whispered as tears fell down his face into the nothingness below.

Around Will, the air picked up, the presence of the darkness taking up an aggressive friction against his skin, making his body convulse as the feeling of evil, slimy and hard, crawled around him.

You are alone, the voice growled, though behind the gravely undertones of the words, there was a layer of seduction. *I can sense it in you. His power. And more than that. You are special. Unfortunately, you're not special enough.*

"I will not let you kill me!" Will screamed, and he somehow summoned his sword to his hands, slashing at the surrounding darkness; it hit nothing. Where there was pressure on his arms before was now merely an empty, expired air. Whispers and cackles echoed through the space.

You have energy, but I am more, the monster whispered. The words crawled across Will's ears like bugs drawn to his body as the only source of light. *You cannot win. I am the universe. You cannot destroy the universe—you can merely exist until the universe decides you must disappear.*

The more Will fought, the more the cold pressure forced itself down on him. His body hit something solid—a flat plane, coated in water. He looked at the floor, his own face reflected in its glassy surface: pale, terrified, and sickly.

That foolish woman thinks your power can control me. She doesn't understand anything. I am what begins life. I am darkness. Life began in darkness. Then God made light.

Will began to sink into the ground. Fighting was pointless. Trying was useless. Nothing mattered. He was a part of the darkness; he had never been anything more than a useless human. His powers were nothing. He was only a small cell in a world that would eventually die.

You close your eyes at night because darkness is where you find rest. Solace. The embrace of death gives you darkness. You crave me—lust after me. That is why you cannot escape me. Give me what you have.

Give me your power. Help me escape this wretched tomb. Let me cover the world in the end. Death lights in hellfire and subsides in the shadow from whence it came.

"It's yours," Will whispered, his voice not his own. As his head began to sink into the darkness, he let out a final tear, thinking of his friends above.

"I'm so sorry."

Above Will, a flash of light broke the black expanse: Simon. He looked different—older. More powerful. He roared into nether, voice reverberating power. Simon then disappeared in a golden twinkle; however, the light remained. Instead of fading with him, the light circled around the nether at lightning-fast speed like a hell-bent shuriken before it curved its way toward Will's chest, shooting through his heart.

Will felt like someone opened a floodgate within his body, releasing every emotion he had ever felt into the world.

"I told you—I am always with you!"

The darkness broke once again.

"I will never bow down to you, beast! No matter how many times we fight!" Sampson the Warrior cried as he sliced through the air, the force that had been holding Will recoiling. Sampson? Will's head reeled—Simon was Sampson? What was going on?

Sampson the Warrior from the *Byrrus* books didn't have this much power. How was he able to break through the evil surrounding Will?

Sampson! the monster sneered. *Be gone from my realm! You don't belong here!*

"We meet again, my old friend. You will not take William Morgan!" Sampson's robes danced behind him as he gripped his sword, light shining across it like metal made of the sun itself. "Your time has not come!" Sampson turned to Will. "You are more than you could possibly imagine, Will. Never fear the darkness. We all come from darkness. The light is always there, waiting for you—be afraid of losing the will to find it."

Raising his sword, a blade of bright gold, he slashed into space, revealing a portal of light through which Will could see his friends, and Tam. "Fight another day."

Will woke up with a jolt and nearly slammed his head into Tam, who was hovering over him, tears streaming down his face.

"Will … I thought …" Tam choked through his sobs. "I thought you were dead."

"Will?" Peter's voice was a whimper. Will looked at his friends. They were all there. All alive. Most crying. Amelia, dry eyed, looked more distraught than Will had ever seen her.

"You were dead. Your body was gray, and it looked like it was almost *decaying*. You were gone. And now …" May whispered.

"I'm here." Will sat up. "I was saved by Sampson." He explained what happened.

"Well I'll be." Tam's eyes widened. "That's a story I've never heard before."

Will surveyed the group. "Are you guys okay?" They looked understandably shaken.

Peter stood, muttering to himself and dusting off his pants. "We're fine. When we came to, Raina was gone."

"Tam and I tried to fight her, but we really were no match. She ran," Amelia snarled.

"I think we should get out of this basement." The cold of the monster crept back over Will. "We really, really should go."

"Can either of you sense where she went?" May asked Tam and Jaser. "Your Sensorship powers should allow you to sense enemies' movements or whatever. If we can still catch her, we should, especially if she's weakened."

"The darkness is conflicting with my senses. I've always been pretty average at Sensorship, so it's more easily affected by stuff like this. I probably can't Sense anything within a mile of this place." Tam rubbed his temple, wincing.

"I can." Jaser gazed up at the ceiling. "She hasn't left. She's on the roof."

"She wouldn't have gone. She brought me here to end this, and she's not going to waste more time. Every day I'm alive is a day she can't resurrect that … thing." Will walked up the stairs, followed by the rest. Tam put his hand up.

"I don't care what you think, Will. We're leaving this place altogether. You're not strong enough to beat Raina, not here. You just came back from the dead after a struggle with … I can't even describe. This place is evil. That thing is evil. You need to get away from here as quickly as possible."

"I think Tam is right, Will. We shouldn't stay here. Raina will show up again another day, after you've had time to rest. You can take her out then, especially if you somehow have Sampson's powers on your side," Jaser added.

Will bit back his reply; if his friends were scared, then he had no right to keep them here. As they reached the entrance hall, the ground trembled beneath them.

Will looked back and was greeted by hordes of Shades pouring from the stairs. Tam shouted something indiscernible, and the rest of the group ran toward the front door. The Pontifex had his sword out and began clashing with the Shades as they pushed him back. He was holding his own, though regardless of the acrobatics he performed, he kept his eye on the door, making his way to the exit.

Will forced himself to follow his friends out, knowing that though the number of enemies was high, Tam would be okay.

That was until he saw the other staircase across the entrance hall.

Will understood now—these Shades weren't coming from the tomb downstairs. They were coming after them because of Raina. Raina knew he didn't die.

She wanted Will to fight her alone. She still needed his powers.

Choosing not to say anything as his friends sprinted out of the building, Will ran toward the staircase, refusing to look back. It may have been selfish, but the best choice for him now was to fight Raina. He was stronger because of Sampson. He knew, somehow, it to be true.

Will climbed the stairs toward the roof. He was alone. At the top, he found a large circular antechamber with a single door at the other end.

Are you okay? Will asked Tam, hoping the Pontifex wouldn't be angry.

You're more like Arthur than I thought, Tam replied. *You're reckless, but you're smart. And you know, in the end, what's best for the people you care about.* Tam paused. *We're okay. Go figure out why Raina needs Arthur's powers.*

With Tam's blessing, Will sighed and walked forward. The tiled floors of the room echoed as Will marched, and he was guided toward the door with the hope that what lay on the other side wasn't the end of his life.

14

Thou Art with Me

Will stepped out onto a wide roof spanning fifty feet in each direction. He looked out to the horizon, no end in sight. In front of him, Raina leaned against one of the ramparts, staring out across the open sky. Will didn't speak, but Raina answered his questions right on cue.

"I've worked for years to understand and manipulate the power of Shades. Most parts of the Written are under the dominion of Characters; however, there are a few, like this building, that are under the control of darkness. It possesses powers that the rest of the Written does not."

Her gaze shifted to over the ledge, staring down. Will followed suit and found the environment below was constantly shifting. At one moment there were rolling green hills, then puffy white clouds, and then a raging ocean. Raina's face was screwed up in concentration, searching for a message in the changing sky.

"I'm surprised you're still alive," she sighed. "The monster that resides in this tomb is more powerful than anything you could imagine." She looked at Will, eyes filled with a soft, almost warm curiosity. "I was hoping you would die. Now, however, I'm not so sure that would have been the best outcome."

Will felt a guttural anger rise in his throat. "Why bring me here then? If he's so dangerous that you need my power to control him, why not just kill me in the outside world? You could easily ambush me in a hallway at school. Or attack me while I'm walking home."

"We talked about this earlier." Raina sounded bored. "I figured by locking you in the tomb, he would kill you. It would've saved me the trouble of fighting you myself. In his current state, he's too weak to hold onto Arthur's power. They need someone capable of wielding them. That's why they found you. If you had died, they would have escaped the tomb, and they would have been drawn to this." She tapped her necklace. "Arthur's power would slip into the necklace, and then I would be able to begin the process of controlling the beast."

"You can't control him." Will stared daggers at her, the anger bubbling in his stomach beginning to boil over. "If you had ever encountered that ... that *thing*, you would know he's too powerful." Will shivered, the feel of its body still a ghost on his skin. "If I wasn't able to control him, why do you think you'll be able to?"

"Because I'm stronger than you," Raina said. She stepped away from the edge of the tower. "I have spent the last decade of my life learning about the Written. Observing it. Taking in and absorbing knowledge on every power and ability of Shades, Writers, and Characters. This is my mission." She gave Will a long, hard look. "Will, you're more powerful than Arthur. You have a spiritual energy in you I've never seen before. It's almost intoxicating."

"Even with Arthur's powers and whatever special energy I possess, I couldn't control him. I didn't even stand a chance."

"That's because there's another piece to the puzzle. Arthur's powers aren't what will control the monster. Arthur's powers are merely a key. Got that?" She looked at Will in almost desperation, as if she wanted him to remember the information. "The key, not the whole."

"What do you mean?" Will spat. "I thought his powers were the thing that could control the monster?"

"You never tell the enemy all of your secrets," she said curtly. "Even so, seeing as you could be an asset to me, the least I can do is tell you some of the truth." She snapped her fingers. Two chairs appeared, about ten feet apart. She sat in one and motioned for Will to take the other.

"Maybe once I tell you everything, Will, we will no longer be enemies. Maybe then you will help me." She sounded genuine. Still, Will didn't trust a word she said.

"Fat chance."

"Sit, Will, and let me talk to you. It's not mind control. I'm just going to tell you a story. Don't you want to know why I want to release him?" she asked, staring at him hard. "I know he's evil. I'm not the idiot here, even though you seem to think I am. I want to tell you everything I can. And if, at the end, you still don't want to help me, then we can fight. But only if that's what you truly want."

Will sat, holding his weapon in his hands. His eyes were trained on Raina, his senses ready for the slightest change or provocation.

"Let's start with where we are," Raina began, looking around the rooftop. "This tomb shouldn't even exist. It comes from a story older and darker than the Bible. We shouldn't be able to access it. Shades have tried for a millennium. Writers with darker souls than us have tried to seize its power. They've never even gotten through the front door."

"But you've been trying to get in," Will interjected, "and you succeeded. Why is that?"

"It's all related to what I'm about to tell you," Raina commented.

"But first things first: you need to understand my motivation." Will did his best to match her gaze. "I can see your soul, William Morgan. I know you understand what Betwixt and Between is."

His face went white, and he gulped.

She dipped her head solemnly. "There's no shame in that reaction. The Characters of the World of the Written have accepted it too. The first time I saw a world disappear, I vomited. I was disgusted by it, just like you were." She snarled. "Characters just see it as an unavoidable truth, because their existences rely on us. Humans. Writers. It's terrible."

"So, are you just a Writer, then? Same as me?" Will asked.

"Yes, and no," Raina muttered, looking in the distance. "I'm not just a Writer. I'm more than that."

"What do you mean? You're not a Character. You're clearly from my world."

Raina shifted her gaze back to Will, her eyes almost wet with mourning.

"A long time ago, when I was just a child, much younger than you, I was introduced to the World of the Written by the Pontifex of another world, different from Byrrus. She was a beautiful woman—Cornelia. You wouldn't know her story." Raina's eyes got darker. "I came to find out she was my Familiar."

Will's face showed recognition at the word, and she smiled.

"You and I may be the only two people in existence who know what that word really means." A hint of genuine sympathy hovered in her tone. "Familiars are beings who are so deeply intertwined with their Writers they are almost one—they share more than just blood. They share parts of their souls." She took a deep breath. "But there was one big difference between your Familiar and mine."

Raina's gaze shifted once again, lost in thought. "A Writer is born with their Familiar—you were no different. Writers meet their Familiars once their *Potential* is unlocked. The biggest difference between us is that my *Potential* was unlocked from the moment I was born. Cornelia wasn't just my Familiar—she was also my mother. Though I am from the World of the Writers, I am also a Character."

"Your mother was a Character?" Will's head began to hurt from processing the information. "Then that means …"

"My father was a Writer, yes," she concluded. "He met her in a world not her own, and they fell in love. But her story was fading away, and she went back to help her mother and father, my grandparents, escape. While she was in her story, it all ended." Her words were quiet, her eyes unfocused as she stared off into the sky. "My mother died because the existence of her world relied on the pathetic attention-spans of humans. I plan on fixing that. I need to fix that."

"That's the circle of life!" Will shouted, not being able to wrap his head around what she was saying. "You can't change it! How does unleashing something horrible and evil save people?"

"Because I'm going to destroy Betwixt and Between," she said plainly. "When I do that, the World of the Written and the World of the Writers will have nothing connecting them, and Characters will be independent of the influence of humans. New stories won't come to life, but humans won't be able to kill off entire worlds due to sheer ignorance. Think about it."

She waved her hand, as if encouraging Will to envision Betwixt and Between. "If the worlds are no longer connected, Writers won't have power over Characters. The memories of people will no longer be able to dictate when Characters die. They will live normal lives, just like us. I wasn't able to save my mother. That doesn't mean I can't save the rest of the Written from the same fate."

"If he destroys Betwixt and Between, how do you know he just won't *destroy* the Written too? You can't control that monster," Will insisted. "You haven't seen him. You won't be able to stop him. I was in that tomb. I felt it. The moment we were alone, he crushed me. I couldn't even move."

"Let me finish, Will. You couldn't fight him because a Writer's powers alone are not enough to stand up to the beast," she said. "You and I are powerful. However, there's nothing more powerful than words and, therefore, nothing deadlier than a Character. A Character helped you escape, right?" She raised her eyebrows.

Will prepared to lie.

"Don't lie to me, Will. My years of studying didn't just teach me about Shades. They taught me about light, too. I can feel the energy in this place." Raina breathed in, chest inflating with a power Will couldn't feel. "I felt the power shift. Sampson the Warrior came to your aid."

"Yes, I was helped," Will confirmed through clenched teeth, "but, *again*, that thing almost killed me. I can't control him."

"He didn't kill you, you stupid little fool," Raina barked.

Will shifted back in his seat, the aggression in her voice catching him off guard.

"You were in the belly of the beast, a creature more powerful and more unforgiving than God, and not only did you survive, but you also were able to help your friends escape." She shook her head. "You have strengths and energies within you that you don't even know how to consciously tap into. You saved measly human beings from the epitome of darkness."

"What does that have to do with Arthur's powers though? Sure, if what you're saying is true, then it's *my* power you should be after. So why are you so focused on Arthur?"

"For now, I will tell you this. There's a place in the World of the Written, one Arthur wrote himself. I'm not going to tell you where it is, but in that place, there is a box. And in that box is the power that can defeat the monster." She sighed. "You have a tiny piece of it within you, in the form of your Familiar. However, the rest of it is guarded somewhere only Arthur can access. His powers are the way to get past the guards he put up."

Will nodded. Everything started to make sense. Simon was a part of Sampson's memories; that's why Simon felt like he was forgetting something. He was forgetting his *entire life.* Simon was the half of Sampson Will had been born with, at least according to Raina. And the rest of Sampson's powers, the ones that could control and defeat whatever was in the tomb, were hidden somewhere.

"You seem like you understand," Raina said. "That's good. You have a grasp on what's at stake here, and you understand the potential you have. You can save the worlds, Will. All of them." She closed her eyes.

"The reason I'm so powerful is when my mother's world faded away, the rest of her became a part of me. I thought I was the only Writer to ever live who had that kind of power, until I met you." She eyed him with hunger. "I didn't think it was possible. After all, neither of your parents are Characters. You're as human as they come. Still … for better or for worse, you are the only human being in the universe who has the power to fight and control the monster that resides here. After all," she pointed at Will's chest, "your Familiar is more powerful than darkness."

Will kept his gaze straight, truly curious. "Okay. Say that's true.

Say I really have the potential to control the monster, and all I need to do is follow you to whatever mysterious box you're talking about. Sampson the Warrior wasn't that powerful. I suppose I should say he *isn't* that powerful. Yeah, he founded Byrrus, but that's a castle in *one* story in *one* part of the World of the Written." Will shuddered, flashing back to inside of the tomb, the enormous expanse of darkness spanning farther than the darkest corners of a single universe. "The monster that resides here is more powerful than Byrrus. Sampson is no more powerful than your mother was."

Raina looked at Will blankly for a moment before roaring with laughter. "You truly are naïve." She wiped a genuine tear from her face. "You have much to learn. I guess that's better for me in the long run."

Will kept his eyes focused on hers, waiting for her to continue, yet Raina merely smiled, the air of fake kindness returning, leaking from her mouth like poison.

"You'll figure it out, I suppose. For now, what you need to understand is this: you do have the power. I promise." Her gaze was becoming more serious. "As you saw, there isn't much keeping him in at this point. He will eventually break free from this prison; I need to be able to control him when he does. If I'm not, then none of the worlds are safe." She reached toward him. "Join me, and I will take you to the rest of Sampson's powers. You can help me save the Written."

This woman was absolutely out of her mind. Will knew— Sampson knew—that the beast couldn't be controlled. Raina had no idea what she was talking about.

"Take my hand, Will," she continued, her eyes sparkling, ignoring his hesitation. "You have the power to fix Betwixt and Between. I knew you were going to be powerful from the moment I saw you in Boston." The curve of her lips was teetering on seductive. "That's why I sent you that copy of *The Redstone Keep*."

The shock gave way to confirmation. Of course Raina sent him the book—it was the safest way to trigger the *Potential*.

"That was your mistake," Will replied. "I still won't help you. And even if I did, you're putting a lot of faith in me. If I can't control it, then we all die. You haven't felt that monster's power. None of us are strong enough, even with Sampson's gifts."

Raina looked sad. She closed her eyes and breathed out. "I will ask you one more time, Will. You'd be a powerful ally. You're better off alive than dead, and we can help you become even more powerful than you already are. I do not want to kill you. I will if I have to."

"Wait a minute, 'we?' I thought you were working alone."

Raina's hold on her scythe tensed, and she gritted her teeth, looking as if she was about to curse herself. "Forgive me for that—a slip of the tongue. That said, I unfortunately just made the decision for both of us. If you aren't going to help me, then I can't let you live. I'm sorry."

Raina raised her scythe into the air, and it looked like there was no longer any opportunity for negotiation. Will clutched the handle of his sword. He couldn't die here. He had to warn the others Rania wasn't working alone. More so than that, he couldn't let her release whatever was in the tomb.

Raina jumped at Will and swung her scythe with the intent to kill, and sparks flew as their blades collided, pushing each other back. The Writer's Eye combined with his new powers helped slow Raina down, but Will was overly cautious.

Raina managed to counter every blow Will threw. He needed to get closer so her scythe wouldn't be effective. As Will ducked the blade he ran into her, throwing his sword against the scythe's handle as he moved in, thrusting his foot out and catching her in the chest. At the same time, Raina grabbed Will's foot and flipped him onto his stomach. She went to bring the scythe down, and Will slid out of the way, jumping back, sword up. His chest was heaving, and he was more out of breath than he should have been. Raina, on the other hand, didn't seem to be having any problems. There were no signs of breathlessness, no indication that she had exerted effort.

"You can't beat me, Will. You're strong, but I'm stronger."

In a display of power, she ran directly at Will, carefully sliding his blade along her ribs. She balled her fist and punched Will in the stomach with the power of a speeding car. Will fell back and skidded to a stop at the edge of the roof.

"I'll give you one more chance." She looked down at him, voice almost pleading. "As I said, I don't want to kill you, but I will."

"I will not help you destroy this world. That's what you'll end up doing!" Will growled.

What do I do, Tam? He called out desperately.

No reply.

Will stared up at her and thought back to Matteo's lesson in tracking. *It's all about noticing the little details,* he had said. He slowed Raina's movements and paid attention. Her scythe arm was taut.

Her weapon swung down, and Will rolled to the side, thrusting his sword up. Raina caught the sword with her bare hand, blood leaking from the cut. She held the blade firmly in her grip, and Will was unable to move it. She kicked Will in the stomach, and he let go of the sword. Raina flipped Will's weapon around and put the blade to his chest.

"Good try. Maybe in death you will find I was right."

As she pulled her hand back, Will called to the only person in the universe who could save him now.

"Sampson! If you truly are a part of me, then help me! Please!"

I can give you what I have.

Will wasn't filled with the immense energy he expected. There wasn't an overwhelming flood of power that poured out of him. Instead, Will's brain opened, filling him with what he could only describe as creativity. Sampson hadn't given him raw power—Sampson had given him knowledge. He had shown Will things he could do with the Writer's Eye he didn't know were possible.

His first task was to escape Raina's blade. Closing his eyes, Will focused on the world around him, and the thing that was overlapping with every stone atop this tower:

Betwixt and Between.

Will sank into the ground, fading into the nothingness of Betwixt and Between. Raina let out a rage-filled shriek. Even though he was floating in the nether, he could still hear her and see the outline of Raina's body. There was only one place she could be. Will prepared the next step of his plan.

Will focused on the space right above Raina and jumped back into the World of the Written. She turned just as he appeared, and Will punched her as hard as he could. She flew back.

As Raina regained her balance, Will ran around her, reaching his hand through the Written, into the Betwixt, and back into the Written. When his hand disappeared, he could see it emerge in the armory of Byrrus Castle. Raina growled, raising her scythe. When Will pulled his hand from the nether, he clutched three throwing knives, which he threw at Raina, using all of the skills imparted on him by Amelia. She dodged them all.

Raina's eyes widened, now on the defensive. This time, Will disappeared completely back into Betwixt and Between, grabbing three more knives from the armory before he reappeared above her. He threw the weapons down like deadly rain.

Although the first two missed, the final one scraped across Raina's cheek. Blood traced its way through the air, and she cried out in anger as she threw her scythe in Will's direction. As he jumped out of the way, the blade tugged at his arm, leaving a sizeable gash, before Will fully disappeared.

When he reappeared, he launched himself at Raina, simultaneously summoning his sword, and though she deflected Will's blow with her scythe, the blast of energy threw her ten feet back. She ran to escape, but with another jump, Will beat her to the edge of the tower, grabbing her and pinning her to the ground. His chest began to heave, energy draining from his body as if a spigot had been left on. He couldn't keep up the portal jumping for much longer.

"Who are you working for?" he shouted.

"I will die before I tell you that. Kill me and get it over with."

He recalled Tam's advice. *If you feel compassion for your enemy, you'll die.*

Will raised his sword to deal the final blow.

He reminded himself killing Raina was the best thing to do; then he remembered May's hesitation to agree. Here he was met with the realization the person below his blade was a human. Despite her misguided ideas, she was a human being through and through. Could he really kill her?

As his blade went through her body, he knew it wasn't a fatal injury. There was no look of fear in Raina's eyes, nor was there any change in the detestation that drilled into him. Raina was hurt and wouldn't be able to keep fighting. Nevertheless, Will had not killed her. She screamed and kicked Will away. Raina ripped the sword from just below her rib cage and collapsed.

"I will find another way, Will Morgan," she screeched, clutching the open wound. "And when I do, you will be on the losing side." With those final words, she faded into the air.

Exhaustion washed over Will, and he fell to the ground, his body feeling more tired than ever before.

He didn't have time to recover. The tower shook underneath him, as if it were trying to pitch him from the roof. He scrambled up, summoned his blade, and slammed it into a crack in the stone below, using it to remain steady. He closed his eyes and held on as the building continued to pitch and roll. When the shaking stopped, Will opened his eyes to find he was in the marsh outside of the cathedral. The building had disappeared.

"Will! You're alive," Peter cried out, eyes wide with relief.

Will laughed weakly and fell to the ground. Tam caught him and helped him up.

"What happened up there?" Iris asked, eyes wide.

Will told the story of the fight, including the powers he gained from Sampson, and how Raina was working with a group of people. He left out all of the information he learned about Raina's plan to destroy Betwixt and Between. It had been an overwhelming day— they could discuss it later.

"Whoever they are, they've done a great job of staying hidden," Tam murmured. "If she hadn't let that slip, we would have never known."

The group was silent for a few moments, absorbing the information.

"Those powers are wild though, Will," Jaser commented, eyeing him with reverence. "Do you think that's just a functionality of the Writer's Eye people don't think about?"

Testing it, Jaser flexed his hand away from and toward his body, attempting to reach it through Betwixt and Between. Nothing changed. Will followed suit. As expected, his arm faded away, pulling out a book from the Byrrus library. Everyone watched him in awe until Will began to feel himself black out. As he careened over, Tam caught him and helped him back up, Will's head reeling.

"I've heard of Writers learning to do what you just did. It takes a tremendous amount of energy. How many times did you fade into Betwixt and Between without using a portal?"

"At least four," Will replied, voice hesitating just a little bit. Tam's eyes widened.

Peter scratched his head, impressed. "Do you think that's because Sampson the Warrior is just that powerful? And his being a part of Will gives him a bit of extra strength?"

"I do have a question about that, actually," Will started, looking at Tam. He sat on the ground, forcing himself to fight off the exhaustion-based delirium. "Why is Sampson so powerful? Why was he able to give me these abilities? He was just a normal Character, right?" He sighed, embarrassed. "I asked Raina, but she just laughed like I told a joke, and told me I still have a lot to learn."

"He was the same man you saw in your dream?" Tam asked.

"Yes."

"Then it's still the same Sampson," Tam mused. "He's a legendary figure in the world of Byrrus. He probably was able to use magic we didn't know about. Don't use that power too often. It drains you of your energy, and if it's used too frequently it could kill you. Alright, Will?"

Will gulped, and Tam seemed to take that as an acknowledgement.

"What about the tomb?" May asked, staring at the empty field. "I figured it wouldn't disappear once it showed up, yet here we are."

"This one would," Amelia replied, looking at the spot with concentration. "There are stories about this place, except they're supposed to just be stories. Legends. Written folklore. When May told me about her dreams, I didn't even think the two could be connected—that's how unbelievable it would've been. But according to the stories, it's evil and has to constantly move, or else it destroys whatever it's around. Look."

Amelia pointed to the grass where the building had been standing, the ground brown and dead, looking as unstable as a sinkhole. Will rubbed his injured arm, worried they had been affected by it. He hoped their insides weren't being destroyed like the grass.

He turned to the group to get his mind off of it. "What about your fight? Did you just take out the Shades yourselves?"

They nodded, Jaser jumping into an explanation. "They were pretty weak, even though there were a lot of them. A few blasts here and there, a few monsters summoned by Iris, and they were toast. Wasn't too tough."

The thunder of hooves and shouts interrupted Jaser. The group turned to see a stampede of horses, led by Pass. The horses made their way to the group and stopped short. Pass jumped down and ran to Tam, grabbing him by the arms.

"Tam, are you okay?" he demanded, shaking him.

Tam looked hilariously embarrassed. "I'm fine, Pass. Really."

"Thank god! You're all okay." Matteo grabbed Will's shoulders in a brotherly way before hugging Jaser, who returned the hug, surprised.

"Watch your form, Matteo," an aggressive looking general said. "Don't let emotions get the better of you."

"Sorry sir." Matteo rubbed the back of his head. "I'm just relieved everyone is alright."

"We all feel that way. And the rest of you?" Pass looked at Will, pointedly.

"Yeah, Pass! Everyone's okay!" Peter said. "A bit shaken up, though all alive. And Will fought Raina and survived."

"By yourself?" Pass's eyebrows raised even higher. "That was very foolish Will. I'm glad you're alive. Did you finish the job?"

Will winced. "Unfortunately, no. I, uh, had a lapse of judgement."

"What he means, Pass," Tam interrupted, putting his hand on Will's shoulder, "is our friend Will was too kind to kill another human." Tam looked at Will, squeezing his shoulder harder. "Don't hesitate next time." He forced an encouraging smile. "Now, all of you," he continued, looking at the group, "you all need to go back home. Get some rest. Will, you're injured, so please come back with us so we can get you healed. I don't think Iris is in a position to do so."

Iris grimaced apologetically, trying to hide how heavily she was breathing. Will put his hands up protectively.

"No, Tam," he muttered. "Can I just do it next time I come to the Written? My Writer's body is fine. I just want to sleep."

Tam frowned but nodded approvingly.

For the first time since the invention of teenagers, there was not a single look of rebellion on anyone's face, Will's included. The only thing on his mind was he desperately needed his bed. He went to summon a portal until Peter grabbed his arm, shaking his head. Will conceded and Peter summoned one, waving to the Characters. They all branched off within Betwixt and Between, making their ways to doors that led to their respective homes, Peter helping Will make it to the doorway.

"Can you make it the rest of the way?" he asked.

"Yeah. Thanks for everything today, Peter," Will replied.

Today, they had gone to the darkest part of the universe, though no one wanted to say it out loud. They were alive. Something had changed within each and every one of them, filling them with strong senses of both drive and hopelessness. How could they possibly rest easy knowing what was inside of that cathedral?

Upon emerging into his backyard, the air crisp and hard, Jaser concluded he couldn't face his parents—he wasn't in the state of mind to do so. He had put on a tough face for his friends, but the truth of the matter was he had been scared from the moment he had entered the World of the Written that day. The anxiety was choking him from the inside out, and he couldn't shake it. Desperate for solitude, he returned to the woods on the outskirts of Byrrus, finding a sunny area, trees aplenty.

He walked up to the biggest one, a tall, strong oak, and eyed it deftly before he gripped the handle of his axe as tightly as he could. He swung it at the tree, taking a branch off in one sweep of his arms. Despite the successful blow, his arms shook with rage—it didn't feel right. He didn't feel fast enough. Raina wasn't dead and would come after them again. The monster in the cathedral would come after them. They were no better off than they had been the day before. And here he was, unable to properly chop down a tree. How would he protect the people he cared about if he couldn't even get the rhythm of his strikes right?

His vision went white as he slashed at the tree, the blade swinging through it as if the wood was made of butter. Occasionally there would be a flash of sparks, and Jaser *wished* it would burst into flames, consume him, burn his desperate self to a crisp.

"Did that tree look at you in a funny way? Or do you just feel like a lumberjack today?"

Jaser turned to see Matteo leaning against another tree, a toothpick in his mouth. Jaser huffed and threw his halberd into the ground blade first.

"How long have you been here?" he asked.

Matteo shrugged and walked closer. "Long enough to see you're tense. Why are you out here all alone? Tam said you should go home."

"I didn't want to be home. And I didn't tell anyone I was coming back," Jaser said.

"Would it help if we sparred a little?" Matteo asked.

"Nah. Although if you'd like to just sit and keep me company, I'd appreciate that more."

Matteo nodded, perplexed, but followed Jaser's request and sat down next to him. The two boys existed in silence for a few minutes, with nothing other than the soft sound of wind and forest birds chirping to bridge the gap between them.

"You don't age, right?" Jaser looked at Matteo, eyes curious. "So, you're like a 40-year-old man on the inside?"

Matteo began cracking up.

"That's a reasonable question," Jaser grumbled, embarrassed.

"I know, I know," Matteo replied, wiping a tear from his eye. "It's totally reasonable. The answer is just kind of weird. Time flows differently for Characters." He picked at the grass while he spoke. "Sure, my mind has been around for what feels like forty years to you, but for me, it just feels like one very long year. Since I was written as a sixteen-year-old, I stay that way, brain and all."

"And that doesn't bother you?" Jaser asked.

Matteo scratched his head. "No, not really. I suppose I've never thought much about it." He relaxed in the grass. "It is what it is. Being a Character means I'm consigned to the life my author set for me. Even the children—the way Arthur wrote us is the way we stay until our world eventually fades away. And that's okay."

"Why though?" Jaser asked. His blood simmered. "That isn't fair to you. Or any of the other Characters. You should be able to age, and grow old, and live a life like humans do. You should be able to have … I don't know, what's the word? Anatomy? Authority?"

"Autonomy," Matteo said gently. "And we do." Matteo sat up and put a hand to Jaser's shoulder. Jaser tensed but didn't move. "It might be a different life from what you know. However, we do have lives. Actual lives. We feel the emotions you feel. We mourn. We fight. We love." Matteo sighed and moved his hand from Jaser's shoulder back to the ground. "It's just that where you have death and aging, we don't. We watch the world outside of ours turn, but we live within our own bubble."

"I won't pretend to understand," Jaser murmured, staring at his feet. "I suppose that's just it. I can't understand. After all, I'll age. You won't. That's just how it is."

Matteo smiled again, this time more softly, though Jaser could sense a shadow of doubt behind the boy's curved lips. He wondered why his heart ached so much.

Will was in bed, analyzing his fight with Raina when he was met with a sharp pain in his chest.

"Agh!" he cried out, bracing his arm against his mattress before sitting up. His skin was tender to the touch. He pulled up his shirt to reveal a large number of red marks, welts, and bruises, right in the places where he had been hit by Raina. He looked at his arm and saw it was still bleeding, the injury from Raina's scythe still present. He felt himself on the verge of a panic attack, and he stood, steadying himself against his bedposts.

Will tried to stay as calm as possible, though his throat still shook. "Tam? Something is going on."

Tam appeared next to Will and gave him a once-over. Seeing the cut on his arm and the welts on his chest, Tam's eyes widened. "Those can't be from your fight with Raina."

"I'm not supposed to be hurt for real in the World of the Written, right?" Will asked, looking at Tam in fear.

The Pontifex shook his head. "I … no. Arthur never was."

"I think the rules have changed," Will said.

"That's impossible. Your mind is separated from your body in Betwixt and Between. What happens to you in the Written shouldn't affect your body in this world."

"Well, there's only one way to find out," Will asserted. He gulped once again and, using what was left of his energy, opened a passageway to Betwixt and Between. He opened the door to Byrrus and stepped out into the winter air of the castle. He summoned his sword and winced as he made a small cut on his arm, near the other injury. It was small enough to where it would heal naturally, yet big enough to where Will would see it in the Writer's world. He headed back to Tam, who was shaking his head in disbelief.

"You didn't do what I think you did, right?"

"I did," Will stated, as emotionless as possible. When he held up his arm, Will was rewarded with a fresh injury. He shivered; this wasn't okay. He could be hurt in the World of the Written. And if he could be hurt, he could be killed.

"That doesn't make any sense!" Tam exclaimed, staring at Will in blatant confusion. "You shouldn't be able to get hurt! You shouldn't …" he looked down, looking as if he was about to punch something. "I don't understand. How can I fight something I don't understand?" He looked up. "This has something to do with that tomb. Your body in this world has never been hurt from the World of the Written before."

The panic in Tam's voice was unlike anything Will had ever heard from the Character. It was a sobering moment: Will's always calm and reasonable teacher, shaken and confused like a child.

For a moment, Will blocked Tam out, trying to keep his panic at bay so he could focus. He thought back to his fight with Raina, and everything she said. About her goals. About how the creature in the tomb would help her achieve them. He then thought about how easy it was for Raina to send them to the creature's realm. Her words floated back to him.

As you saw, there isn't much keeping him in at this point. He will eventually break free from this prison; I need to be able to control him when he does. If I'm not, then none of the worlds are safe.

"Raina wants to use the monster's power to make the worlds

exist separately. To get rid of Betwixt and Between entirely," Will stated. "That would mean Writers would be equal to Characters, and we wouldn't have any power over them. There's no evidence that would happen. Regardless, she's basing her entire plan on that assumption. What if," Will muttered, turning his head to Tam, "it's already happening?"

"His power is leaking out of the tomb already." Tam spoke quickly, voice getting louder with every word. "Raina wants to seize it because she thinks she can use it to force the separation. After all, she knows it's already working its magic on the boundary between the two universes. Except they're not separating—they're merging." He rubbed his temple. "That's just a side-effect though. The moment that monster breaks free, unless he's being controlled …"

"It'll collapse the entire universe as we know it," Will said, as plainly as he would tell Tam the weather.

Tam stared at Will blankly, and Will leaned back into his bed, the stress and the exhaustion of the day hitting him in one fell swoop. "I guess my not killing Raina didn't matter, in the end. Because we're all going to die anyway."

15

Arthur's Box

Will's friends, though deeply unsettled by the news their real bodies could be hurt in the Written, were understandably more concerned about the tomb's seal breaking.

Will told everyone about Raina's plan and what she told him about Sampson. This also involved Will explaining what happened to worlds when they were forgotten. They knew this, of course, in the general sense, but hearing it in detail from Raina's point of view was unsettling for everyone. What was surprising was not everyone thought that Raina was out of her mind.

"I'm glad you didn't join her, Will," Iris said. "Still, it's understandable, right? Especially if her mother died because her world was destroyed. I get why she's doing what she's doing." Iris looked to Tam for some sort of affirmation.

Tam didn't seem moved at all. "It's a Character's fate, Iris. We're all born knowing it, and we all accept it." He gestured to the sky. "Eventually, your human body will die. You go somewhere new. It's accepted when you are born. While our death is different, it's still death. Right now, I'm more interested in this mysterious box in this place Arthur created. Why didn't he tell me about it?" He eyed Will as if expecting him to know the answer. "And Raina gave no indication as to where it would be located?"

Will shook his head.

Peter jumped in. "I guess the upside is we have a new goal. Find the rest of Sampson's powers before Raina does. And once we do that," he grinned, looking at Will, "maybe Sampson can give us some more direction."

They didn't know where to start. They were once again at the whim of something they couldn't control. As a result, Will and his friends fell into the melancholy of everyday life with a new agenda: determine who Raina was working with, find Sampson's powers, figure out what the tomb actually was, and survive high school.

The real world didn't stop and let you cope with events that happened in your alternate universe when you led a double life.

March came and went. May was caught up in the excitement of the school's spring musical, and she even managed to drag Iris into it. For fear of missing out, though he never would have admitted it, Jaser involved himself in the tech for the show, putting his engineering brain to good use.

"I want to make it just as good as *Dracula*'s was! Plus, it lets me do something I'm good at. I suck at clarinet," he said with relish when Will asked him. May snagged the lead role, even as a freshman, and a lot of people gossiped about how that could happen.

Tennis season started for Peter—his favorite part of going to school. The guy was incredibly gifted, and Will was sure his extra athleticism from the Writer's Eye wasn't hurting him.

Jaser and Will were finally introduced to their new band director—the substitutes were getting tiresome. Jeremy Russell:

an absolutely normal-looking man in his mid-forties. One of the most ordinary, run-of-the-mill people Will had ever seen. When he talked to the class, he was just as unassuming as one would expect a stereotypical high school band director to be.

Will had never been more relieved in his life. Finally—all of his teachers were normal human beings.

Will carried that mentality with him to the beginning of April. While preparing his trumpet for rehearsal, Mr. Russell approached him, a stern look on his face.

"What's up, Mr. Russell?" Will asked, stomach churning unpleasantly. For a moment, he had the mental image of Russell spouting fangs and ripping out his throat. Force of habit, he guessed.

"We have enough trumpets, so I found a second part for the piano for our first piece," the band director replied. "It's difficult. I want you and Dane to play together. Think you can handle that?"

Will looked up in surprise and proceeded to put his trumpet back in its case. He tried to hide his excitement as he ran over to the piano bench, sliding onto it and slamming into Dane's side. Dane looked up and grinned.

"So we're doing a duet, huh?"

"Looks like it!" Will replied, sensing the playful joking in Dane's voice. He grinned again and slid over a bit to give Will more room.

Russell hadn't been joking; it *was* a hard piece. Some of the runs were so crazy Will found himself crossing Dane's arm, having to hit notes that were on his part of the piano. They struggled through it, and at the end Dane gave Will a high five, looking thoroughly worn out.

"Well dang," he said, hands on his knees. "He wasn't kidding. That thing was hard. We sound pretty good together, don't you think?"

"Agreed," Will responded. "So, have you ever done something like this?"

"Can't say I have," he chuckled. "Do you like piano or trumpet more?"

Their conversation continued like this for the next thirty minutes, talking in low voices underneath Russell's conducting. When class was dismissed, Will waved goodbye to Dane and walked to lunch.

Will sent Jaser a text letting him know he was skipping history class and dodged into the bathroom, where he opened a portal to Betwixt and Between. Instead of going to Byrrus, however, he thought about the outskirts of Boston, Massachusetts, where he exited into the early spring sunshine.

Will often sat near Arthur's grave to think when he was confused. At this point it had become habitual. Will kept hoping Arthur's ghost would appear and tell him what to do. He clung to that hope as he climbed the hill and sat in front of the tombstone, talking to the air.

"Hey, Mr. O'Neill, it's me again. Tam's doing well. He's afraid of coming to your grave with me, though I don't know if he comes and visits on his own. I'm sure he does. We're trying really hard to figure out how to stop that monster from escaping, but we're kind of at a dead end. I need to find that box. If you could give me some sort of sign it would be really helpful. So ... um ... thanks?"

Will thought he believed in an afterlife, but something about talking to a headstone was unnerving. If Arthur O'Neill's spirit was actually present on earth, he wouldn't be floating over his grave. He would be watching over his family and friends.

Footsteps in the freshly mowed grass interrupted Will's soliloquy. Feeling a little uncomfortable, Will stood to leave and crashed into someone.

Will fell to the ground and almost cracked his skull on a headstone. He stood and began apologizing profusely until his eyes gazed upon the man from Arthur O'Neill's funeral: Warren.

"I'm sorry, Mr. O'Neill," Will stuttered.

The man reached his hand out to help Will up. He looked much kinder than he had at Arthur's funeral, and Will took the hand, standing.

"Sorry about that. My name is Warren—Warren O'Neill. Do I know you?" He began analyzing Will, trying to recall his face, and got an embarrassed look on his own.

"You're the boy I met at Arthur's funeral. I'm really sorry about that." He looked horrified. "I was awful to you. You must think I'm the world's most horrible person."

Will was taken aback. "Not at all. Your reaction was … um … reasonable. I'll just go. Sorry to get in your way."

"It's okay. Why were you visiting my brother's grave?"

"I just wanted to pay my respects is all. I was a big fan," Will shrugged. "Anyways, I'll let you go, Mr. O'Neill. It was nice talking you."

Warren bowed his head and turned to his brother's grave, chatting amiably to it as Will had been. Walking away, Will checked the time. He was about to create a portal when his eyes grazed over a building a few hundred feet away. It was the entrance to a coffee shop, one that definitely had no connection the Written. Will was captivated by the sign that hung over the entrance. It was a gold plate, hanging on a long chain. It was an odd display, and as Will looked at it, he couldn't help but feel it reminded him of something.

Think, Will, Sampson whispered in the back of Will's consciousness.

Will's memory opened, and he remembered a plate just like this sign, one he had only seen in one place before: in his dreams where he spoke to Sampson, inside the Hall of Heroes in Byrrus.

What if Arthur O'Neill chose to put Sampson the Warrior's hiding place in the most obvious location? The part of the World of the Written dedicated to honoring him?

Will ducked into an alley next to a department store and opened a portal. He had never been to the Hall of Heroes outside of his dreams, so it took him a bit to find the large iron door. The door was difficult to open, its hinges relatively unused, which made sense— in the books at least, the door wasn't opened unless the leaders of Byrrus were seeking advice from warriors passed.

Well, Will thought to himself, *if this isn't a situation where I need advice, then I don't know what is.*

Like in his dream, the room was made of stone, with tapestries littering the walls, depicting powerful men and women and genderless figures, and great battles that raged in the past. The artistry was incredible and must have taken years to complete. Will was overwhelmed by the room's history.

Once Will finished basking in the reverence of the hall, he began the task of finding what he came here for: a golden plate that looked similar to the one hanging from the coffee shop, one right next to the tapestry of Sampson the Warrior.

It wasn't hard to find the tapestry. It was at the very center of the room, honoring Byrrus's founder. Despite how fascinating it was,

Will didn't look at the tapestry. He was more concerned with what was next to it.

On the plate was inscribed a simple-looking symbol, consisting of a sword hanging from a chain. Will looked behind him, making sure the door was closed, before pushing and prodding at the plate. Nothing happened, no matter how hard he slammed himself into it. He cursed and summoned his sword, tempted to stab it; after all, it could be a keyhole. Or it could have been covering up a hole in the wall.

When Will's sword came to his hand, a burst of light appeared at the tip, illuminating both the room and the plate he was facing. The wall sank back with a loud crash, making way to a long set of stairs sloping downward into darkness. Will reminded himself he was currently a few stories above ground, so hopefully this passage wouldn't descend into a basement. Figuring there was nothing to lose, he went down.

When he hit the bottom, Will found the darkness made way for a bright light, filling the space like a beacon for weary travelers. He followed it and emerged into a large, circular room.

The first thing that caught Will's eye was the window. It was a large rectangular pane of glass, at least twenty feet long and ten feet high. Outside of the window was a beautiful, picturesque scene, made up of trees swaying in a breeze and a crystalline waterfall off in the distance. When all was said and done, the thing that really shocked Will was the distant strip of pavement he concluded was a highway.

"This place is in the World of the Writers," he murmured to himself, afraid of rupturing the moment. As he expanded his senses, however, Will understood the world outside the window wasn't real;

it was a mirage created by magic, and if the window were to be broken, he would only see the grounds of Byrrus Castle.

Will turned his attention away from the window and looked around the rest of the room. It reminded him of an old library, with thousands of tomes lining wooden shelves across the walls. There were open books littered across the space, with a long desk facing the window. Curious, Will walked over to see handwritten notes strewn across the desk, no apparent rhyme or reason to their organization. Will's breath caught in his throat.

This was Arthur O'Neill's private study.

Will sat at the desk and flipped through the papers. There was handwritten research on the history of Byrrus, the outlines of characters O'Neill created, and settings he invented. Will sifted through the paper and found Tam's character, written out in neat handwriting, accompanied by a rough sketch.

"His favorite drink is fresh spring water. Classy," Will muttered to himself. Will continued to flip through the papers until a red, leather-bound book caught his eye. The book radiated a strange power, as if it held information more important than the thickest encyclopedia. Will opened it, wondering if this was the box Raina spoke of.

What he found were diary entries, the earlier pages looking incredibly old, with the later pages looking fresh. Will began reading.

Dear Warren,
I don't know why I'm addressing this book as Warren. I suppose
it's something of a formality that stops me from calling it Diary.
That or maybe it's because I want to tell my brother so many
things, some of them I know he wouldn't believe. Maybe one day

I'll give him this book, in order for him to understand everything that's happened over the years.

I had an epiphany today over my morning coffee, the idea for a story. Now, I've never really considered becoming an author for anything more than a hobby. That was until this story came to me. It's different. It's a magical story about a castle in a far-off land, and the people of the castle trying to protect themselves. Sure, it's simple. But the magic comes not from the plot, but from the characters. I'm going to start writing it soon.
All the best,
Arthur

He turned to the next page and continued to read, eyes blinking rapidly with hunger.

Dear Warren,
The most incredible thing happened today: I was visited by Tam! Now, today was the day The Redstone Keep *was finally published. I was standing outside a bookstore in downtown when all of a sudden, I saw a child walk out of the building with his mother and open the book. As soon as he did that, a man who introduced himself as Tam Desmond appeared, rambling on about some world called "The World of the Written." At first, I didn't believe him, but then he took me to this place, and Warren, you wouldn't believe it! It's absolutely incredible. To think everything people have ever written has come to life in this world, and I'm able to see it and explore it! It's like a dream come true!*

No, I'm not crazy, Warren. It's real.

All the entries continued like this, and Will was able to track Arthur's introduction to the World of the Written. He read about his first encounter with Shades, his adventures with Tam, and his continuation of the books and everything that happened to him. It was like the diary of someone who wanted to keep consistent notes but kept forgetting. The entries were sporadic, spanning forty years, and felt like they didn't give the whole story of Arthur's life; merely a brief outline. Will flipped to the last entry, and began reading, wary of what awaited him.

Dear Warren,
Sometimes I regret taking your memories. I have no one to turn to except for this strange world I've found myself in, and even Tam doesn't know what's going on.

I can't shake the feeling someone has been watching me, and while it doesn't feel malicious, it certainly doesn't feel benevolent. I'm beginning to feel afraid there is more to this gift than Tam and I know, and I'm about to find out the downside. I can't go to Tam or the other Characters; involving them would just put them in danger, and that's something I can't do. Going forward, I just have to continue living as if nothing is wrong and keep my guard up.

For now, I'll watch the summer turn to fall and the people around me grow up. It's odd to think it's been more than forty years since I published the first Byrrus novel. I suppose time really does take its toll.

Either way, I've enjoyed the life I've created for myself. If this presence persists, I can't involve you. If I have to involve people, I'd rather it be those I can protect within the World of

*the Written … not those such as yourself who I am powerless
to defend.*

Take care, brother. As always,
Arthur

Will shut the diary. It made sense. Raina had clearly been following Arthur and could have used her magic to alter his ability to sense her. The diary didn't give any clues about who else could be helping Raina, but it did give context to how Arthur died.

He heard a light rustle, like a breeze rippling across the back of his shoulders. He turned around so fast he cracked his neck, wondering if someone followed him. He was met with a still empty room. Will stopped what he was doing and put the notebook down, listening intently.

William.

Will froze. It was barely a sound, little more than a puff of air, but it was very clearly saying his name. Will's breath caught in his throat—the box Raina mentioned was here. The rest of Sampson's powers were here.

"Hello?" Will asked, muscles tensing, but the whispering stopped. He turned back to Arthur's desk and found Simon.

"Hey, Will," he said. His voice was missing its usual drip of playful sarcasm, making way for a tone of professionalism and caution. His hair, usually messy, was combed back, and he wore a button-up shirt and sports coat.

"You clean up well," Will joked. "I thought I saw the last of you in the tomb. I figured you were gone for good."

Simon chuckled. "Nah. It was just too much for me to keep

projecting myself to talk to you, with all of that dark magic floating around us."

"Makes sense," Will replied, feeling more casual, bordering on awkward, about the interaction than he felt like he should. "So, I guess this is a good time to confirm—are you really Sampson the Warrior? Is he my Familiar?"

Simon took a deep breath in, hesitation apparent. "As I'm sure you can imagine, that's a complicated question. Yes, Sampson the Warrior is your Familiar. As am I. That doesn't mean I am he. I'm more of a memory. I'm a projection of what Sampson used to be. I guess you could say I'm only a tiny piece of Sampson."

Will stared at Simon with a blank face. The Familiar laughed. "I can tell you're not totally following."

"I actually am, for the most part," Will said. "You're the part of Sampson that I was born with. The rest of him is in this room."

"I'm impressed," he commented. "For a broad overview, that was fairly on the nose. But." He paused. "There are parts of the story you're missing."

"And I take it you'll fill in the gaps?"

Simon held out his hand. "I think the easiest thing would be to show you."

Will only had to look at Simon's hand for a moment before he grasped it; instantly, he was staring at a man he recognized as Arthur O'Neill. Arthur looked to be about the same age as he was in the obituaries, meaning this couldn't have been more than a year or two before his death. He was in a dark room, face lit only by torch light, the glow spreading out to reveal a vast cavern. As Arthur walked toward the center, Will realized the shiny walls were made of wet stone, and there was a low whistle shooting its way through the cavern, as if there was a crack somewhere far above them.

Will could also tell they were in the World of the Written; Arthur had an unfamiliar sword gripped in his dominant hand, and there was an air of magic about him Will had only felt in that universe. What he found odd was Tam was nowhere to be found. Whatever Arthur was doing, he was doing it alone—without Tam's knowledge.

Will continued to follow him for a few minutes, taking turns within the cavern that had become tunnels, as Arthur muttered to himself, concentrating.

"I feel it," Arthur whispered. "He's close … he's close."

Arthur's muttering was rewarded in the next minute when they exited the tunnels and found themselves in a large amphitheater. The darkness of the underground made it nearly impossible to see anything. Arthur fixed this by dropping his torch and muttering a few words into his palm, where a ball of light came into being. Will raised his eyebrows—Arthur O'Neill had some magic to him, unbeknownst to Tam.

He pitched the orb into the sky like a baseball, and it expanded and hung there like a small sun, illuminating the space.

At the center of the room was a stone casket, its age having eliminated any designs from its smooth surface. Will felt nothing upon looking at the casket, but Arthur's face flared up with child-like joy, his legs moving like an Olympic runner's as he sprinted up to the stone dais on which the casket sat.

"Sampson," Arthur uttered in reverence, and as the words left his mouth, the room erupted into a heatwave of light, a force of incredible power filling every crevice.

However, as soon as it started, it was finished. Will found he was back in Arthur's study. It was still a memory. The room was much brighter and shinier, and Arthur's forehead was covered in sweat, the man's chest heaving with exhaustion.

"I made this room so only I'm able to enter it," he said to no one in particular. "You'll be safe here." It made sense when he pulled out an old and weathered book, its pages yellow from age and nearly falling from the spine like feathers. He threw the book into the air, and it erupted into a ball of golden dust, which filtered away to reveal Sampson, the same one who helped Will in the tomb.

"I've told you, Arthur. You can't beat her," Sampson barked, the fierceness of his voice the absolute opposite of Simon's careless demeanor. "That woman has a Familiar on her side. You aren't strong enough."

"I'm a Writer!" Arthur growled, his voice dripping hot anger. "She's only half of one. I don't need a Familiar!"

"Your arrogance is going to kill us all," Sampson hissed, bringing his face inches from Arthur's. "If she kills you, she will take your powers, get into this room, and take my powers as well. You need to find the Writer who has the other half of me."

"A Writer who might not even exist," Arthur spat disdainfully, blowing Sampson off. "I'm not going to waste my time with that. I'm going to take this witch out on my own."

The scene shifted again in a wind of multicolored blurs, and Will was staring down at Arthur, looking older and more tired, like a man who knew he'd messed up. He was heaving, his entire body covered in sweat, and Will realized they were in the World of the Writers, locked in a room Will presumed to be in Arthur's apartment.

Arthur was holding a sword, looking at a picture of himself, Tam, and Warren, face drooped in mourning. He seemed to make some sort of conclusion internally, as if acknowledging his own death. He then put his hand to his chest and closed his eyes, focusing. As he pulled his hand away from his chest, there was a trail of gold dust following his fingertips. It dawned on Will he was watching the moments before Arthur O'Neill's death—the same moments he witnessed long ago on his way to Boston. The only difference was this time, he understood what was happening.

Will watched Arthur send his powers out the window, and as they disappeared, he whispered, "Tell him I'm sorry. Be careful. It's coming." As soon as he spoke, his door was blasted to bits, and the vision faded away.

Will returned to the study, finally understanding. Simon gave him a small acknowledging smile, seeing the look of comprehension on Will's face.

"Arthur O'Neill found Sampson's powers in an attempt to control more of the Written; however, what he discovered was only half the story. When Sampson faded away, he knew his powers were too powerful to be kept in one place. Because of that, he split them in two. The first half was placed with him, in his tomb. The other half dispersed itself into the world, waiting for the Writer who was meant to hold Sampson as a Familiar. I'm that Familiar." Simon pointed his thumbs to himself, a look of pride on his face.

"Wait," Will interrupted, shaking his head. "I don't get it. You're talking about Sampson the Warrior as if he's this limitlessly powerful being. Like he's been around for thousands of years. *Sampson the Warrior* by Arthur O'Neill was published in the nineties."

Simon stared at Will for a moment, disbelief plaguing his face, before he howled with a jovial incredulity.

"Will," he coughed out between guffaws, "don't tell me you've gone this whole time thinking your Familiar is *Sampson the Warrior*. That irrelevant protagonist? So irrelevant Arthur O'Neill didn't even let him come to existence in the World of the Written?"

Will was taken aback. "Um. Yeah. Kind of."

Simon got his laughter under control and stood up straight. "I'm not Sampson the Warrior. I'm Sampson, the first Character."

Simon gripped Will's shoulder. A burst of energy flowed into him. Sampson's strength, as old as time itself, erupted into his brain, a power that went back to the first days of written language. Of course Sampson hadn't faded away like other Characters—his power was near limitless. He was the origin of the universe. The world was clear for a moment, and Will understood everything and nothing, all at once.

"Arthur's powers made their way to you because you're the only person in existence who was powerful enough to take them in. Call it chance, or call it luck, but you're the most powerful Writer to ever live. And you're the only one who can stop the monster and save the world."

The room fell silent, and despite the hilarious absurdity of the statement Simon just made, Will felt a simultaneous enlightenment and terror.

"Raina knows," Will whispered. "That's why she thought it was funny when I made comments about Sampson not being powerful. She knows I'm the only one who can control that creature."

"I know," Simon said. "And that's okay. That's why I'm glad you're here." He took a step forward. "In this room, in Arthur's desk, is the book with my other half. I can finally be whole again. And together, Will," Simon reached out his hand, "we can stop Raina. We can make sure the worlds stay whole and separate. Only you and I can do that."

His words inspired confidence in Will. If Sampson, the first Character, truly was his Familiar, then Will was the only person who had a chance of stopping that tomb from breaking open and destroying everything. The terror he felt in that tomb and the fear he had for his friends and not being able to protect them—that was something he never wanted to feel again.

"Let's do it, Simon," he said. "Or, I guess, Sampson."

The Familiar's face shone. "I want you to know I'm separate from the Sampson in that box. The glimpses of Sampson you saw during your fight with Raina and in that dark world were only flashes of him I was able to conjure. But I promise you," Simon's chest swelled, looking Will in the eyes, "I will do my absolute best to protect you and guide you and help you save the world."

"Sounds like a plan to me, partner," Will replied, grinning. He gripped Simon's hand, and the boy in front of him stared into his eyes intently before disappearing.

Will turned and opened one of the drawers in Arthur's desk. He found the book he saw in his vision. As he lifted it up and stared at it, Will felt the warmth trying to escape. As Arthur did in his vision, Will tossed the book into the air.

The book began to shimmer in the sunbeams filtering in through the windows, looking right at home among the rays of light. As the book floated and rotated in midair, it faded into golden dust, the specks glittering like fireflies as the substance shifted around the room, surrounding Will as if it were being pushed along by an undetectable breeze. Will reached out his hand and touched the dust, and it began to snake its way up his arm, sinking into his skin. Will's body began to shake, and he was overwhelmed with power.

It was like an electric charge filled his every pore, coursing through his veins as it made its way into his eyes, sparks dancing across his vision. The energy boiled in his stomach like magma, making its way to his feet and fingertips, preparing to erupt.

And it was done. Will was left in an empty room, alone with the thoughts and musings of a dead man, with no one in sight other than his reflection in the windows. However, inside, something felt more complete—stronger, even. Though it was a subtle difference, Will knew Sampson was now whole.

When Will got home, he called his friends, gathering them—and Tam—in his living room. When they arrived, he did his best to explain the discovery. Everything from his first interaction with Simon, all the way to the reveal today. Will also told them about seeing Warren in the graveyard, and how the random sign on the coffee shop made him think of the plate in the Hall of Heroes. Tam stood in the corner, listening, staring at the ground. Though it was a convoluted story, everyone seemed to understand by the end.

Peter was the first one to attempt to unravel it. "You're telling me you have the soul of the first Character ever to exist residing in you, but only half of him was in there? And somehow Arthur discovered the second half, kept it in a magical study only he or someone with his powers could enter, and you just found it and made Sampson whole again?"

"Yep." Will was glad Peter understood the simplicity.

"Will," May whispered, "do you know what this means? We did it. We got there before Raina. You have the power to beat Raina and whatever crazy plan she comes up with."

"Raina obviously understands more about this than any of us." Iris slapped her leg. "There must be something about the tomb that's tied to Sampson's power. There has to be something other than raw strength that allows Sampson to stand up to that monster. Maybe it's the same type of magic that creates the Writer's Eye? I don't know."

"I do," Tam said. "I guess it all goes back to the monster in that tomb. It's an old fairy tale, a story Characters tell their children to get them to go to bed at night. It's not something people actually think is real." He took another deep breath, apprehensively looking at the Writers.

"A long time ago, when Betwixt and Between first came into being, there was a monster who tried to escape the World of the Written and devour the World of the Writers. A Character stopped him. Sampson, the first Character. Sampson stopped the monster and sealed it away with an ancient magic more powerful than anything found in all of the Written and the Writers. That's where the story stops. Simply put, the two are intertwined because Sampson has been this monster's mortal enemy since the dawn of writing itself."

"So much of this makes sense now," May observed. "Raina tracked Arthur because she somehow learned he found Sampson. Then Arthur released his powers so they could find Will. That way, Will could eventually find the study and make Sampson whole." She frowned. "And when Raina found out Arthur didn't have Sampson's powers and released his own, she killed him."

"What's the monster's name?" Jaser asked.

"I don't know. It wasn't in the story." Tam breathed out, looking out the window and rubbing his arm as if overtaken by a chill.

They were all silent once again, absorbing the information.

Jaser sighed. "I want to look at the diary though. That's something tangible we can make sense of right now."

Will handed the book to Jaser, who flipped through a few pages. "This is really cool," he muttered, looking the journal up and down. "Does this have any extra info we don't already know?"

Will took the book back with both hands, shutting the cover. "Not that I saw. I haven't finished it yet, though. I read maybe ten of his first entries and then the last one. I guess we'll see."

They stared at it for a while, as if it would animate and begin talking to them. No matter what they did, the book just stayed immobile on the table, a regular old bundle of paper. After about five minutes of this, Iris picked up the book and held it close to her lips.

"*Historia,*" she whispered.

The diary began glowing, the pages flipping back and forth. Iris traced her fingers through the turning paper, muttering to herself. When the light died down, she handed the book to Will.

"Are you going to tell us what that was?" Will asked, taking the book back hesitantly. Iris grinned and put her hands on her hips.

"A spell to find out the history of an object."

"And you did that?" Peter inquired. "Just now?"

"And ..." Will encouraged.

"Well, as I said, the spell I used is able to tell me the history of an object—what it's done, where it's been. So I used it on the diary, and I figured out it's been around for a little more than forty years." She paused, her facing falling a bit. "That's where it stops being exciting. The diary was never touched by anyone other than Arthur O'Neill. No great mystery there."

The group was silent for a moment until Peter looked at Will, his eyes widened with shock. "Will!" He started bouncing on the balls of his feet. "The manuscripts! From Raina's house! Iris's Gilmarye!"

Will had already bounded off the couch. He sprinted to his room and grabbed *The Redstone Keep* manuscript from his desk, jumping over his banister into the living room, handing the bundle of pages to Iris.

She stared at the manuscript, put her hands on it and, with the Gilmarye opened, whispered, *"Historia."*

The manuscript began glowing white, and the pages ruffled without leaving the table. Iris's eyes were closed, focusing on the information flooding into her brain. After about thirty seconds, her eyes snapped open, and she stared at the group.

"Well, that confirms it," she said. "This manuscript was given to Raina by Arthur O'Neill. More than that," she continued, "it was given to her fifteen years ago, long before Arthur's death."

"So she was a super fan maybe?" Peter asked. Will looked to Tam, who was staring at the manuscript with cautious eyes.

"I have no idea," he admitted, eyes wide and mouth open. "I don't know how she knew Arthur. Arthur was so protective of his journals and drafts—I can't imagine him just giving one up, especially *The Redstone Keep*. I don't know why he gave it her. I can't even begin to imagine … she was only a child then."

The group sat and contemplated for a little bit. Eventually, Will shook his head. "This isn't going anywhere."

They decided to take a recess and reconvene later, hopefully with clearer heads. Will's friends waved goodbye to him and headed home, and Will sat with Tam in his living room, thinking. Tam eventually left as well, the dead end having frustrated him more than anyone.

His parents came home, and Will decided to proactively avoid the conversation of why he wasn't in history class—the school would eventually call.

"Hey Mom, Dad," he said during dinner. "I just wanted to tell you I skipped history class today."

Emery looked up from his soup. "I expect you had a good reason?"

Will nodded. "I wanted to study. Finals are coming up, and I feel kind of behind. I wanted to make sure I got ahead of the material I wasn't comfortable with. I felt fine with history."

His mom seemed please, and his dad raised his eyebrows in his own form of approval. "Just make sure you don't skip too many more times. Even for studying," Ruth commented.

"Won't happen again, Mom."

16

The Locked Door

As the weeks went by, Will and his friends continued to balance studying for their classes with training in Byrrus under the guise of their book club. Will had taken to meditating both in the World of the Written and the World of the Writers in order to make more of a connection with Sampson. No matter how hard he tried, he found he wasn't able to make consistent contact with his Familiar, though he could occasionally get an extra burst of energy. He was getting better at warping through space too.

Will also kept having dreams of the cathedral and of his fight with Raina. More than that, he also had nightmares featuring the beast from the tomb, as if the monster were taunting him.

As they entered May, Will couldn't shake the feeling there was something he missed in the field where the tomb had been. The struggle came to a head one day in first period. Part of Will had the intense burning desire to go investigate. Another part of him was trying to think logically, to avoid killing himself via a demon from another world.

As the day went on, Will continued to wrestle the thought until school was over. He was preparing to leave when his impulse won out. He texted his parents a quick excuse, telling them he was going to an after school tutoring session, then sprinted to the back of the school where he could disappear into Betwixt and Between out of sight; however, when he was finally alone, he heard a quiet coughing noise and turned to find May staring at him, arms crossed.

"Oh. Hey," Will sputtered. "Why are you still here?"

"I could ask you the same thing."

"Uh … I'm going to a, uh, tutoring session. Don't you have homework? Or some sort of rehearsal to get to?"

May poked him in the chest. "Come on. I know you better than that. You're going to the World of the Written, and you're being particularly suspect about it. What are you getting up to?" She gave Will a once over and raised her eyebrows. "Don't tell me you're going to investigate where the tomb was. Will, that's so dumb!"

"I certainly wouldn't call it *dumb*…" Will grumbled, scratching the back of his head. "It's just a hunch is all. I was going to go in and get out, as fast as possible. I figured it would be unnecessary to worry everyone with it."

"And right you are!" she said with a flourish. "Let's go then! Lead the way!"

Will gave her a blank stare and she huffed.

"I'm not letting you go in there by yourself! If you're not going to be responsible and tell Tam what you're doing, at least let me help you out to make sure you don't get yourself killed. I could always just go to Tam, if that's any sort of motivation."

"Please don't," Will chuckled weakly. "Fine. Tag along."

They transported themselves to the grounds where the cathedral had been a few months ago. As predicted, there was nothing there except for a few lone trees and the breath of the wind whistling across the empty, dead grass. May shivered as she moved closer to him, hands up. Wisps of ice appeared, her fists clenched, on edge.

"Do you feel anything?" Will whispered.

"No," May murmured. "That's not really my area of expertise. We should've invited Jaser. It's just a little chilly is all, but not chilly like cold. Chilly like magical."

"Well we *are* in a land where book characters come to life."

She forced a laugh and the two moved closer to the giant impression left by the cathedral. Once Will reached it, he felt through the mud for anything that could be of use. He came up with nothing. He moaned and looked around the field as he shook his head in denial.

"There's nothing here. There's absolutely freaking nothing here. Why is there nothing here?"

May opened her mouth to reply when her eyes darted to her right, and she raised her arm and shot a blast of ice from her palm. Will rolled over onto his side in time to see the blast soar through a figure too far away to make heads or tails of. May grabbed Will by the arm and he summoned his sword, staring the figure down. Fortunately, as the two stared, they realized the being was only a mirage—a sort of ghost.

"That was pretty impulsive," he hissed. May put her hands up.

"Quit pretending like you wouldn't have done the same thing!"

They stayed still, not daring to move. When the figure turned to them, something tugged at Will's heart, like it knew who he was.

"*Sampson...*" it whispered, its voice one of pain and longing. Will's eyes widened, and he walked toward the mirage.

As he approached, he saw the figure was a woman, older looking, with wavy, dark hair. She had a gaunt, sad look on her face, and her eyes were surrounded by crow's feet of both age and worry. Her pupils were gray, outlines blurry, and the closer Will got the more the temperature dropped.

"Help us, Sampson," she whispered, reaching out and clawing at Will. *"Save us."*

"Are you from Byrrus?" Will asked, though the woman didn't react—she clearly didn't hear him.

"She can't be from Byrrus, Will," May said, causing him to jump. "I think she's a memory of some sort. I don't think someone from Byrrus would be like this, so close to the site of that ... thing."

Will reached out to touch the woman, but as soon as his hand made contact with her image, she faded away, color whirling into the air. He jerked his arm back, pain enveloping his fingertips, as if he had come in contact with dry ice. He looked down at his hand where blisters had begun forming. In the woman's wake, Will noticed other people begin to take her place, all of them the same image of sorrow and fragility.

"Help us, Sampson ... "

"Our world is going ... "

"Save us ... "

Soon the entire field was filled with spirits, walking around aimlessly, not paying any mind to the two living, breathing humans in their midst. The sky grew darker, and Will realized somehow, he and May had crossed over to an unknown part of the World of the Written. It didn't even feel like they were in Byrrus anymore.

May tapped his shoulder. "Will, look."

Will gazed where May was pointing and saw the tree line was fading. He spun around to find they were no longer in a field. In fact, the longer they stood, the more Will began to see unsettling details. Doors all around them. A gray sky. A desperate nothingness that felt like it was seeping into his soul.

"I think we've left Byrrus," Will said. "Like the tomb killed this part of the world. It couldn't handle it, so it fell into Betwixt and Between."

May nodded. "I think these might be Characters whose worlds were destroyed. You know, the ones that faded into Betwixt and Between? They've collected in this part of Byrrus."

"Why are they drawn to *us* though?" Will questioned.

"It could be two things. The first is that we're Writers. The second is that they can sense Sampson inside of you." She looked around the field. "There's so much death here ... maybe that's why they're appearing? It's like the Written's graveyard."

A lump formed in Will's throat. He wasn't scared—he was heartbroken. He was drowning in sorrow, the souls around him coming to Will for salvation when it was already too late. A young boy walked by Will and May, clutching a small stuffed animal. He wore dirty rags. A child as lost in death as he was in life. May let out a small sob.

"Help me, Sampson," the boy whimpered. *"Where are my mommy and daddy?"*

Another woman, this one younger than the first, ran through the spirits, a look of panic on her face. Tears streamed down her cheeks as she pushed the spirits aside, floating past Will and May.

"Raina! Leave! You can't be here! You will not die too!"

Will tried to follow her, and May matched his gaze. "She just said Raina, didn't she?" he whispered.

May's eyes widened. The woman faded away, replaced by other figures.

"You don't think this is really them, do you? Are they trapped in some sort of purgatory?"

"I don't know." Will began breathing more heavily. "When Raina told me about her plan, I didn't realize ... *this* was what she was talking about. This is why she wants my powers. She wants to free these people. She wants to stop this from happening."

"Can we go, Will?" May begged. "I hate this. It's awful."

Will was about to agree when something changed in the field. Will didn't initially know why he felt an almost existential presence join him and May. It was subtle at first, but as he opened his mind, a strange sensation passed through his head.

Will.

Will.

"Do you hear that? There's someone calling me," he whispered, straining to distinguish the voice.

"I don't hear anything," May replied.

Will ... help ...

"When you hear the voice calling for help, help him," Will exhaled, his eyes getting wide. He turned to May, grabbing her hands. "I had a dream where Sampson told me someone would call for my help! Don't you see? This is it!"

Will sprinted through the spirits, following the voice, May trailing closely behind. Eventually, they entered Betwixt and Between as they knew it: white everywhere, doors flashing past in Will's peripheral vision as he strained his ears.

Save me.

"Will! Slow down!" May shouted.

"Here!" Will shouted back, skidding to a halt in front of a door that looked like one to a school building. It was out of place amongst the other doors, many of which were tall and regal. "The voice is stronger here."

Will!

Will pulled on the door in excitement only to find it was firmly locked in place. It wouldn't budge no matter what he did. He took out his sword and May grabbed his hand.

"You do remember," she started, catching her breath, "that you can't enter worlds whose stories you haven't read, right?"

Will put his head down, his burst of euphoria being replaced by stabs of frustration. "I forgot about that bit. Darn it!" He slammed his fist into the door.

"It's okay, Will. It's not a big deal. You just need to find that book and read it." May tried to comfort him, wincing as she saw his bruised knuckles.

"No way," Will commented.

Despite May's continuous protest, Will got creative and did everything he could. He tried to fade through the door; he attempted to circumvent it entirely through the World of the Written and Betwixt and Between, creating at least four portals. He even used his sword and hacked at the handle, only for it to be rebounded off in a flash of sparks, his arm vibrating from the impact. He eventually stopped, coughing with exhaustion. May's arms were crossed, eyebrows raised.

"Now, can we please leave? I still have chills from all of those ghosts."

Will blushed, trying not to let the aggravation show on his face. He nodded, and May sighed in relief, opening a portal to the World of the Writers. Will followed her back to the school.

"Well that certainly was … uh … interesting." He rotated his shoulders, the feeling of isolation still lingering.

May agreed shakily. "I guess you could say that. So, the tomb kills everything it touches, obviously," she muttered, "and it also acts as some sort of weird portal to the other side, if that exists. We were able to see Characters who died, but they weren't able to see us."

"At least so we think," Will added. "We don't know if those were the actual Characters, or just mirages representing them."

There was more silence.

"Will," she muttered, "what if Raina is right? What if destroying Betwixt and Between has some merit? What if it actually stops Characters from existing like that? Always stuck in torment."

Will shook his head. "Even if the concept has merit, her proposed execution doesn't. It's too risky. That creature is too powerful. I'm telling you." He shivered despite the warm breeze and sunshine. "Even with Sampson, I could barely hold him off. He can't be controlled. And if Raina has her way, she's going to destroy the entire universe as we know it. We both saw the field. We saw what the tomb did to it."

May frowned and they agreed to take time to reflect on what happened and report to the group when given the chance.

That night Will told Tam about his adventure, and his reaction was exactly as expected. He wasn't thrilled at first, chastising Will for being rash, though only until his curiosity was piqued by the turn of events. He was eventually pleased, however begrudgingly, that one of Sampson's warnings had finally made way for action to be taken.

"I have no idea how you're going to find that book," Tam started, "but if Sampson told you to try and help that Character, then who am I to argue? I guess the question remains: were there any clues as to what or where it could be?"

Will shook his head, having pondered it all day. There was nothing recognizable about the voice, and Will hadn't felt anything special behind the door. Whatever story it was, Will wasn't familiar with it, and that would make it much harder to find.

Tam tried to put on an encouraging face. "Get searching." He then began to quiz Will on world history. Will answered his questions and tried to stay focused despite his mind being elsewhere. He didn't tell Tam about his discussion with May around the viability of Raina's plan. There had to be another way to save the Characters from their fate—one that didn't put the entire universe at risk.

The rest of the month passed in a blur, and Will was impressed with himself. Even though he was doing late-night internet searches for novels that had anything to do with Arthur O'Neill, he was confident about his classes. Will retained what he considered to be an okay GPA and felt good walking into his exams.

During the last band class of the year, Mr. Russell locked himself in his office, doing last-minute grading, and left his students to their own devices. For the most part, the kids lazed around the room, listening to music or playing on their phones. Naturally, Jaser and Will found themselves at a table, laptops out, and lists of books scattered everywhere.

"This is so pointless. The book might not even have anything to do with Arthur O'Neill," Jaser grumbled, typing a search word into the address bar.

"I can't hear you through all of your negativity," Will muttered, furiously staring at his lighted screen. He was so focused he didn't hear someone plop down beside him, leaning into the computer.

"Watchya doing?"

Will nearly jumped in surprise as Dane traced his finger down the list of items that had come up. He was squinting, reading the names under his breath. It was clear he was mentally ticking off items as he went.

"Arthur O'Neill, huh?" he said, faking understanding. "I've never heard of him."

"What? How? He wrote the *Byrrus* books; they're incredible!"

Jaser snorted. "In his defense, not everyone has your taste in reading material, even if they were bestsellers. Your close friends just happen to be very similar to you."

"What are they about?" Dane asked, looking genuinely interested.

Will went into a long speech describing the incredible power and beauty of Tam Desmond, Byrrus Castle, and all of the struggles that occurred within it.

"Arthur O'Neill is so brilliant, and he creates this world that just sucks you in, and before you know it you've gone through the whole series in a week." Will sighed, reminiscing about his first read-through of the books, knowing he looked like a complete idiot. "Dude, you need to read them. Here. I actually have a copy of *The Redstone Keep* with me. Borrow it. Tell me what you think."

"No way, really? Sure you don't need it?" Dane asked, his voice betraying how touched he felt.

Will was elated to lend the book to Dane. The world deserved to know about Arthur O'Neill and his talents, and not just a select rag-tag band of teenagers.

"I've got like three copies at home. Just make sure you read it and give it back to me over the summer, if we see each other." Will rethought his statement. "Actually, keep it. Think of it as a 'Congrats on Surviving Sophomore Year' gift."

Dane's face broke out into a huge grin, and he put his hand out in a fist. Will obliged and bumped it with his own.

"Thanks, dude! I'll get on it right now!" To prove his point, he put some headphones on and walked over to a quieter part of the room to read.

"This would be so much simpler if we could just show everyone that stupid door," Jaser grumbled. "Crowdsource the world. Let someone else do the work for us. Surely someone would recognize it."

Will gave him a pity laugh and Jaser replied with a death glare. "Fine," he caviled, defeated. "Let's keep looking. We've got to find something eventually. Right?" Will didn't speak, instead flashing a supportive, over-enthusiastic smile. Jaser rolled his eyes. "Onward and upward."

After a few minutes, Dane tapped Will on the shoulder, holding a book in his hands. He threw it onto the table in front of Will.

"What is this?" Will asked, holding up the novel.

Dane shot something looking like finger guns at him. "It's a book my parents have had at home forever. I read it when I was a kid, and was going to again, but you've given me another book to think about." Dane winked. "It's really nothing like *The Redstone Keep,* but I figured if we're swapping recommendations, then you should give this one a try."

"Thanks, man!" The two stared at each other for a few seconds in silence before Dane thumbed *The Redstone Keep,* heading back to read. Will smirked. Regardless of where they had been at the beginning of the year, he and Dane were certainly becoming good friends.

Will lifted the book. Something strange flickered, like a cog inside of him began to turn. *The Paradox of Cody Edison* by Richard Finch.

In his mind's eye, Sampson nodded.

"Jaser," Will whispered, excitement bubbling into his guts like lava. "This is it. I don't know how … but this is the book we're look-ing for."

"No way," he breathed, snatching it from Will's hands. He looked it up and down, flipping through the pages, and shrugged. "I don't feel anything special coming from it. Are you sure this is it? It seems way too … I don't know … *normal*."

Will felt more certain about this than he had about anything in the past year. Whatever was inside of this book was going to help them; they just needed to figure out how.

"I'm sure. Buy a copy of this book. Now."

Jaser shrugged and punched an order into an online bookstore. The full text appeared on his laptop's screen. Before either of them had time to dig into it, however, the bell rang, signaling the end of the second to last day of the testing period. In the spirit of keeping his parents happy, Will hoped to finish taking his history exam be-fore investigating the book. While reading over a study guide that night, Will's phone buzzed; Jaser had informed the group of their discovery.

Busy now. Talk tomorrow after my history final. Then we can figure this out.

The next day, Will was attacked in the hallway by his friends, try-ing to wrestle information out of him.

"Why did you have to take your freaking test first?! This is im-portant! Why didn't you tell us about the book?" Peter shouted at him, making a scene.

"If I fail any of my exams, my parents will kill me! I can't inves-tigate this book if I'm in the ground!" Will shouted back, pushing him off. They glanced down the hallway where Tam leaned against a locker, beckoning them. "Now c'mon."

The five of them (six including Tam) headed to Gustafson and Whiteside, entering the store to the familiar clattering of a bell. Carol waved, eyes passing over Tam, and the group began walking through the shelves, looking for names and titles. Eventually Will found three copies of *The Paradox of Cody Edison*, all neatly stacked together. He handed them out to those in the group who needed it, and May started flipping through, wearing a look that would have been at home at a crime scene.

"It's a bit fishy, don't you think? What we need more than anything is this specific book, and your friend Dane just drops it in your lap? Do you even know anything about this Richard Finch?"

"Nope."

Will had researched him the previous night and found nothing. Richard Finch was a one-book wonder, publishing this novel for the world then becoming a recluse, never seen or heard from again.

"Still seems fishy," May said.

"It's not, though! Sampson told me about it ..." Will trailed off, then found his courage. "If we can't trust Sampson, who *can* we trust?"

They purchased the books and walked outside.

"Happy first day of summer! I'll spend it cooped up in my room reading some random novel. Keep that in mind, Will!" Jaser shouted.

Iris giggled in response. "Go to a restaurant and read it! Sit in the sunshine! Lie in a hammock! Really, the possibilities are endless. I'm excited!"

To prove a point, she walked up the steps to an old soda shop and sat underneath an umbrella, cracking the spine of the book and commencing her journey into the world of *The Paradox of Cody Edison*. Jaser blushed, point taken, and followed her lead, sitting next to her and propping his laptop open.

Will smiled at his friends and ducked into a nearby building, disappearing into the World of the Written. He wanted to read the book in Byrrus.

Will emerged into the late evening sunshine, the ponds sparkling, the castle rising over the city like a beacon of hope. No Characters bothered him as he walked up to the castle, taking a spot at the ramparts, where he hung his legs over, unafraid of the drop below. Will opened the book and began reading, the sunshine showering him in its glow, the world finally feeling like it had a purpose.

17

Abaddon

Stress dreams were a real thing. Before Will got the Writer's Eye, none of his sleeping thoughts were memorable. However, once he dreamed Arthur's death, most of his dreams had become vivid and realistic, though he was still able to tell which ones meant something. As a rule of thumb, he needed to pay attention to whether or not the dream contained anything Byrrus-related. Because of this, when Will opened his eyes in the Hall of Heroes, his thoughts immediately became laser-focused.

"Thank you for returning my other half to me, Will," Sampson said.

Will turned to face Sampson, barely daring to breathe. "It was the least I could do. You saved me so many times." The Familiar's image was much clearer than the last time Will had seen him, and his shoulders were straight in a way that accentuated the power he held. He no longer resembled a dying old man but a seasoned warrior.

"I had to, didn't I?" the Familiar said, smiling. "You're my Writer. You and I have been connected since the day you were born. We will need to work together in the coming battles if we are to stop the forces threatening us.

"The world is in great danger, Will, as cliché as it sounds. There is a darkness looming over you and your friends, greater and more terrible than even Tam could possibly imagine. The tomb will break. He will be free. And you're the only one who will be able to make the world right."

"The monster from the tomb," Will affirmed. "Who is he? No one knows his name. Maybe if I know that, I can learn more about him."

Will's heart was thumping a mile a minute. He feared Sampson wouldn't know. What if it had been wiped from his memory? Or worse—what if Sampson had never actually faced the creature before and the story was just a story?

However, the moment Sampson's gaze met Will's, it was clear he was very wrong. Sampson was the only person in existence who truly knew the creature residing in the tomb.

"His name is Abaddon."

In Sampson's eyes Will could see Abaddon, not in physical form but in emotion and action. Scorched battlefields, crying Characters, guns abandoned next to corpses, barrels smoking from fresh shots. The longer Will stared into Sampson's eyes, the colder he felt. His fingertips tingled, and he fell back into the darkness where he first met Abaddon, the beast's tentacles wrapping around his body once again.

And just like that, Will returned to the world of the living, Sampson fixing him with an intense gaze. His hand was on Will's shoulder, rooting him to the spot.

"I'm glad you're here to help," Will whispered, catching his breath.

"I can't always help you, Will," Sampson murmured. "There will be times I can grant you great strength, as I did during your encounter with Abaddon or your fight with Raina. However, just because I am in your heart doesn't mean we can always talk. Our connection isn't constantly open. You know how to use your sword—but to master my power, you will need to learn how to use your mind." He sighed. "My being your Familiar is a blessing and a curse." His eyes left Will's face and scanned the Hall of Heroes. "Nobody can control Abaddon. Not you and not Raina. Regardless of who frees him, Abaddon will return. The seal will break."

"What do I do?" Will asked, holding his breath. "How do I stop them? How do I stop *him*?"

"Stop Raina from releasing him first. We need as much time as we can get to prepare," the Familiar stated firmly. "There is another … I can sense it. In your world, there is one other with the *Potential* who can break Abaddon's seal. Raina will learn of this power and think that means they have the power to control him. They do not." He closed his eyes, concentrating. "Help Cody Edison, and you will find them. Protect them at all costs."

"Is there anything else?" Will asked.

Sampson obliged one final time. "Raina will not try to hurt you again. She knows she cannot defeat you with the power you have. Beware the day of destruction. That's when the true *Potential* in the other will be brought to the surface."

Sampson's image flickered away, and Will awakened, his head reeling from the dream. He immediately grabbed a pen and paper from his nightstand and wrote frantically, though with every new riddle, more panic settled into his chest.

The next day, Will informed his friends of what he learned. "We can't do anything until we figure out what's going on with Cody Edison's world," Peter assured him. "It's our first step, so let's not worry until we have a grasp on that problem. One at a time."

With that, they retreated to the various places they had been reading for the past day. Within a few hours, Will sat in a hammock in his backyard, the sun shining on his face, birds chirping as they flew past him. There was a slight breeze going through the trees, and it was pushing a relaxing feel of coolness across his body. He had *The Paradox of Cody Edison* propped up against his leg, and he was reading it as fast as he could.

Will had always been a fast reader. He was thankful for that, because *The Paradox of Cody Edison* was ... garbage. Will's eyes drifted closed as he read it. He awoke to Tam kicking the hammock. Returning to the book, Will grinded his teeth. Of every book in the world, why did it have to be *this* one?

It was a very basic love story, a slice-of-life novel about a boy named Cody who was trying to get his two best friends, Jack and Rebecca, to end up together. It was fairly boring, wasn't written that well, and the plot was so full of holes and inconsistencies Will felt like punching his hand through the entire thing.

It was so sloppy Will ended up being worried Dane just had really poor taste in books. And worse—what if he had great taste in books, but for some reason gave this to him, and was secretly working for Raina? What if this was all a big trick meant to kill Will?

Tam gave the hammock another kick, nearly tipping it over.

"Dane Richardson is not out to kill you. I'm pretty sure he just doesn't know what a good book is. Keep going. You're almost done."

Will groaned and went back to reading, forcing himself to swallow the last ten pages. As he got to the conclusion, it was as predictable as could be: Rebecca and Jack ended up together. Cody watched them embrace from afar, "heart full of happiness," and Will was left with a vile taste in his mouth he could only associate with watching two juniors get together one day and break up the next all semester, even though they were clearly toxic for each other.

The moment his eyes scanned across the last words of the book, however, Will was reminded of just how important this story was.

Will!

Will glanced around. Who had spoken? As he was about to get out of the hammock and summon a portal to Betwixt and Between, Tam walked over.

"He's emoting through you, trying to get your attention," Tam muttered, staring at the book. "Cody, I mean. Something is off about this story. He's calling for your help."

Will! Help!

As soon as those words were uttered by the mysterious Cody Edison, a bright light flashed before Will. For a moment, Will thought he saw the dark silhouette of Sampson in the brightness, but the figure was gone as quickly as it had come. In its place was a giant door, one that looked exactly like the one he and May found in Betwixt and Between.

"Is this it? Why did it appear to us in the World of the Writers?" Will whispered to Tam, staring at the door in awe.

"I have no idea," Tam responded, sounding just as shocked as Will felt. "Only one way to find out."

Will gulped and nodded, putting his hands to the handles. He could sense Cody Edison on the other side, his energy like a siren blasting through windows to the World of the Writers. "What if this is all a trap? What if we're going to walk through this door to an ambush of Shades?"

"Cody is calling for you." Tam maintained his stare at the door. "This isn't the work of something evil. This is the work of someone who needs you enough to reach out across a universe."

"Alrighty then." Will took a deep breath.

He pulled the door open, swinging it toward him as if it were made of paper. A bright light blocked his view of the world, and he used a hand to shade his eyes from the glare.

"After you," Tam said.

Will looked into the rays, only pausing to think about what could lie on the other side; however, it didn't matter. These steps were the first he needed to take in order to save the world.

Acknowledgements

Wow. What an adventure.

Writing this book was a journey that spanned almost a decade of my life. To have reached a point where it is now readable by the general public is ... joyous. A relief. Terrifying. Honestly, there are way too many words out there to describe how I'm feeling, and writing them all out wouldn't do these emotions justice.

Most times, when people ask me when I began writing *The Betwixt and Between Chronicles,* I tell them it was when I was seventeen. This is somewhat true. My senior year of high school, I began to write what can be described as the first true draft of what eventually became *Kingdom of Ink and Paper.* However, the story goes deeper than that: the initial concept of this book and the World of the Written came as early as June 2011, taking the form of a play. I wrote the first act of it before realizing the plot was much too complex for a fifteen-year-old to bring to stage.

Kingdom of Ink and Paper is the story I've always known I was meant to tell. It has seen me through every major phase of my life thus far, pulsing in the back of my brain like a guiding light. There have been dozens of versions, and the plot has been changed and whittled down countless times to get to where it is now. It's certainly a different book from when I first wrote out the words "Betwixt and Between," but its meaning to me remains all the same.

It would be wrong to take all of the credit for this book. Though the words are mine, this story would never have become what it is without the help of dozens of people who listened to me rant, encouraged me, supported me both emotionally and financially, and validated me in carving this path for myself. I need to take a moment and thank a handful of them.

First of all, to Hannah Coffman, Charlie Smith, and Moriah Sharpe: it was so long ago that you probably don't even remember, but you three were the first ones to read a very different version of this story. You launched Will on his journey when we were his age. Thank you for encouraging me, even then.

To Dan McGough, Daniel Li, and Nick Lockett: the sharpest criticisms usually don't come from those you're closest to, but the three of you over-delivered on feedback that irrevocably changed the path of Will's journey. You three read this book when I was a little older, a little wiser, though still a far cry from the writer I wanted to be. This novel would have been an absolute failure without you.

To Michael Fournier and Kevin Romero: you were the final gatekeepers in the preparation of this novel for publishing. You read a book that, in my head, was done, and you validated me in saying that it *was* good, and it *was* ready. You two were the push I needed to move on to publication, and I hope that this version of the story is better than you could have ever predicted.

To Alex Blumenstock and Bree Ogaldez: my dear friends and my two final test readers. I hope reading this book in print is even better than reading it on your computer screens. I chose you as test readers because I knew your feedback would be honest, critical, and straightforward, and you did not disappoint. You caught errors that would have unraveled Will's story, and helped tie it up as much as possible.

To my spectacular, no-holds-barred editor Chandi Lyn: you coached me in a way that few teachers ever have, and made me a better writer than I could have ever imagined. This story would have never been completed without your hand, and I hope seeing the final version in print makes you proud.

To my incredible copy editor Brandy Vickery: you carried me over the finish line and refined me and the story with a fine-toothed comb, and it's crazy how much you managed to improve me as a writer in a short period of time. I love what we ended up with.

To my parents Jeff and Dale Newman and my sister Meghan: you all have known this story longer than anyone. It's my story: the story of a little kid running through the backyard with a wooden sword, swinging at trees and battling monsters in his head. You watched as this little kid created this fantasy, and listened as he talked about it over the course of ten years. I hope that finally reading it makes all of the watching and listening worth it. Thank you for supporting me and giving me the space and encouragement to pursue what my heart truly desires.

And last but certainly not least, a huge thank you to the following individuals who were willing to support me with little more than a brief outline of a plot, and my voice touting a dream. You're the reason this book is able to exist.

Alex Culbert
Alexander Blumenstock
Ashley Zhou
Cameron Schaer
Cliff Newman
Dean Hazineh
Elliott Rains
Eric Tang
Esteban Chittester
Eva Herman

Grant Mak
Hannah Robinson
Josh Martin
Julian Trajanson
Keith McAdoo
Marcus Reid
Matthew Birk
Michael Fournier
Mitchell Berger
Paul Newman
Raghav Mathur
Rahul Swaminathan
Rene Falzarano
Ryan Wydra
Sari Newman
Scotty Lee
Taylor Euliss
William Brodner

If you're reading these acknowledgements before you read the book, then I hope you enjoy the ride. If these are the last words you read before closing the cover, my only hope is that this novel has left you a little happier than it found you, and a little more eager to read the rest. I'm certainly eager to write it.

Until the next time we enter Betwixt and Between.

With love,
Matthew Newman

Want to stay updated with Will, Tam, and their next adventure?
Visit worldofthewritten.com to connect with Matthew Newman
and be the first to hear information and news.

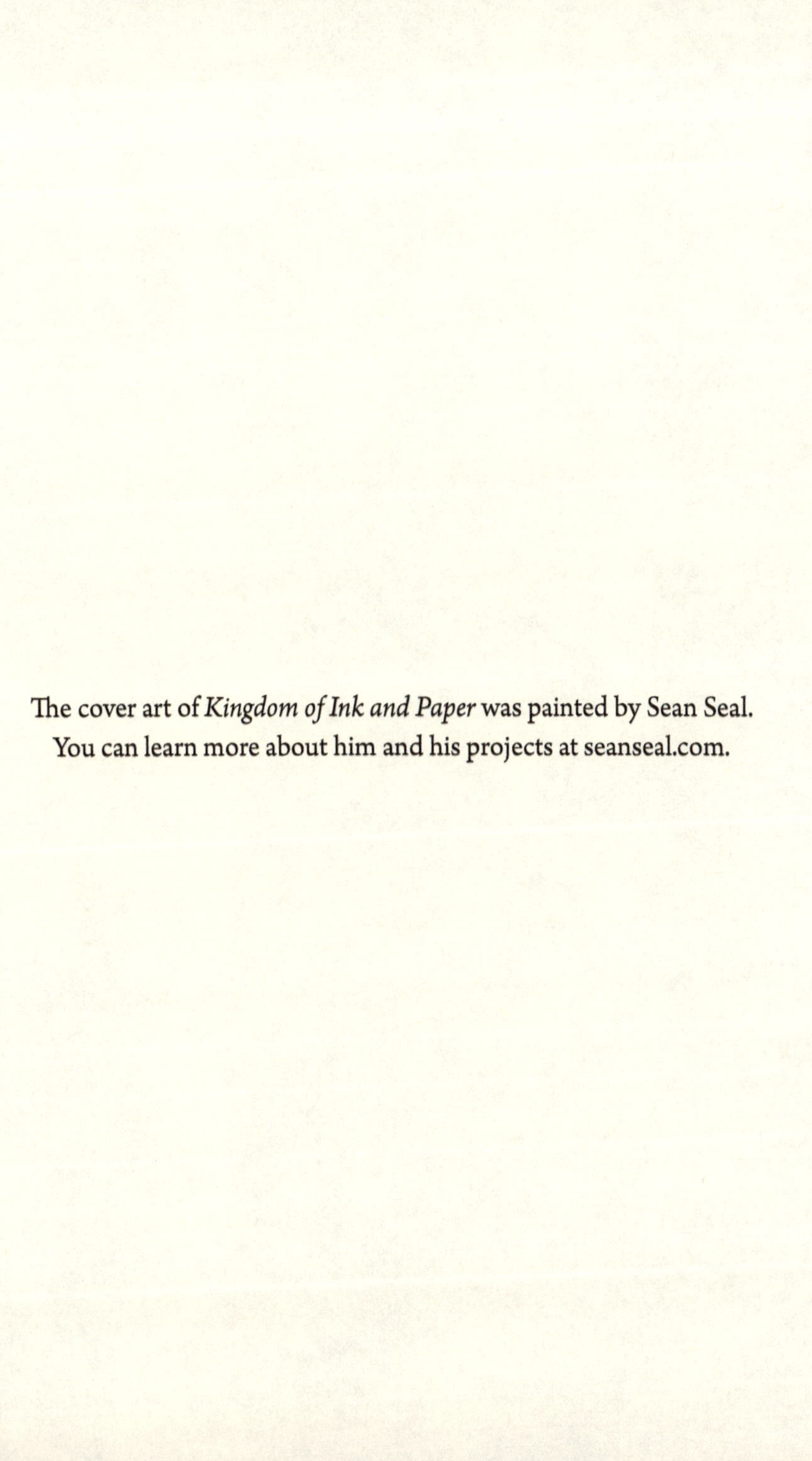

The cover art of *Kingdom of Ink and Paper* was painted by Sean Seal.
You can learn more about him and his projects at seanseal.com.

www.ingramcontent.com/pod-product-compliance
Lightning Source LLC
Chambersburg PA
CBHW031618100726
47898CB00006B/1842